"With a penchant for accura
ible tale of the 1930s and forties while fleshing out her characters. The ending leaves us wiping an empathetic tear yet yearning for more. *Lottie's Gift* leads most assuredly to a sequel and with Jane Tucker's writing voice and ability to craft a story, readers will soon clamor for more."

—RJ THESMAN, author of Life at Cove Creek Series

"Jane M. Tucker has penned an endearing tale of family, faith and forgiveness — a compelling story both tender and tragic. A five-star read."

— ELAINE MARIE COOPER, author of *Road to Deer Run* and *Bethany's Calendar*

"I loved following child prodigy Lottie Braun on her journey from her Iowa farm home to a world-class pianist and all the places in between. A fascinating tale I didn't want to put down."

— SALLY JADLOW, author of *The Late Sooner*

Lottie's Gift

JANE M. TUCKER

CROSSRIVER

BREWSTER, KANSAS USA

To Jon, who said, "Write."

Acknowledgments

I learned to write fiction because of Lottie Braun. She took over my imagination one winter night in 2010, and would not leave. I have many people to thank for helping me share her with you.

Without *Rebecca Thesman*'s six-week course on writing, I would still be unhappily teaching preschool. Rebecca, thank you for being my friend and mentor.

When my husband *Jon* saw how desperate I was to bring Lottie to life, he gave me his blessing and full support. Thank you, dear.

My writing partner, *Shannon Phipps*, read every word I wrote — even the ones I erased. Shannon, we're a great team. Thank you.

Many thanks to my critique group, especially *Sally Jadlow* and *Su-Zan Klassen*. Thank you to everyone who asked, "What happens next?"

For some crazy reason my sister, *Mary Ann Rowe*, believed in this project from the beginning. Thank you for your patient and intelligent advice.

I am grateful for the *Heart of America Christian Writers' Network*, and its yearly conference. They are a wonderful resource for new writers.

I did a lot of informal research through interviews. *Edna Bentzinger*, life-long resident of Southeast Iowa and my husband's grandmother, gave me her first-person account of life during the Great Depression. UMKC Conservatory of Music student *John Kelly* shared the mind of a true musician, and helped me understand the value of emotion in musical performance. My parents, *Sam and Martha Malsbary*, and my parents-in-law, *Lee and Leah Tucker*, did their best to answer my questions about an era they don't really remember.

To *Debra L. Butterfield* and *Tamara Clymer* at CrossRiver Media, thank you for believing in this project. You have been a joy to work with.

Last, and best, I give glory to *God* for the ability to write, and for a story to tell.

Prologue

April 1984

The usher tapped her shoulder. "Message for you, Miss Braun."

Lottie turned from the crowd of backstage admirers and plucked the envelope out of his hand. "Thank you."

She slipped her finger beneath the flap.

Dear Lottie,
You played well tonight. I always did like Chopin. I'll be at Lombardi's until midnight. I hope you'll join me.
Helen

Every five years, the same note. Every five years she fought this wave of fear and longing.

"No answer."

The usher melted into the crowd.

Lottie shoved the note into her pocket. She had a long, sleepless night ahead of her. And her sister would wait at Lombardi's in vain.

She left the concert hall an hour later, followed by an eager young violinist. "You're sure you won't come?" he said. "We're only inviting a few friends. Very intimate."

She smiled. No doubt he'd been assigned to look after her. "I'm going back to my hotel. I have an early flight tomorrow."

His face fell. "Well, in that case, let me call you a cab."

She inclined her head. "Thank you." The attention felt good tonight, though she seldom had trouble hailing a taxi outside Carnegie Hall. Her lofty height and crown of snow-white hair were easy to spot.

A yellow cab slid to a stop at the curb, and the young musician opened the door. "Have a good evening, Miss Braun." He waited politely as Lottie stepped in. Then, closing the door, he ran to catch up with his friends.

"The Plaza Hotel, please." Lottie sat back and breathed a sigh of relief. That young man would have suffered a shock if she'd accepted his invitation. Instead of the fascinating celebrity he expected, he would find only a dried up spinster, longing for her bed.

Helen would be the better dinner guest.

She shook her head at the unwanted thought and leaned forward. "Turn here, driver. Don't go down the next block." Don't go past Lombardi's.

The cabbie looked at her in the rear-view mirror. "Whatever you say, lady."

She read the disbelief in his eyes and looked away. Why should she care what he thought? Everyone knew the great Lottie Braun was crazy. Her eccentric reputation formed a shield around her life. If she chose to stay in Europe for ten years, the classical world blamed her eccentricity. If she refused to live in New York, well, what could they expect? She'd always been odd.

"Here we are, ma'am." The cabbie looked at her expectantly.

"Thank you." She dropped several bills into his hand and walked away before he could make change.

The lobby stood empty at this time of night. Eleven o'clock was too late for families, and too early for the rest of the free world. She rode the elevator alone. Any other day, she'd have taken the stairs to the twelfth floor, but tonight she wanted to reach her room as fast as possible and lock her door against the outside world.

The concert had gone well, aside from one error. She closed her eyes and relived the missed trill in the second movement, a result of wrong fingering. Years of self-discipline kept her from showing any sign of trouble, but she felt chills of embarrassment. She'd missed the notes again in the repeat.

She sighed. Repeated errors were a new development, a product of her aging memory, she supposed. She'd have to find a way to prevent them, perhaps a new method of practice or memorizing. Her assistant might know of something that would help.

Maybe this was the beginning of the end of her public performances, a bleak thought. There was nothing so fulfilling as playing with an orchestra, the wave of music bearing her along on its crest, filling her heart and mind with emotion. It brought out feelings that she didn't allow at any other time. Grief. Joy. Loneliness.

The elevator door glided open. Lottie walked briskly down the hall, let herself into her room, and bolted the door. She pulled off her good pearl necklace and dropped it into its case. Slipping off her shoes, she padded to the sink to wash her hands and caught her reflection in the fluorescent light. Had Helen been shocked at her appearance? Her ivory skin sagged slightly now, and short, prematurely white hair replaced the blonde braids of her childhood. Her eyes were the same bright blue, but Helen wouldn't have seen them from the audience.

She turned from the mirror in disgust. Helen must have seen a picture of her in the last forty years. She couldn't have avoided every magazine article or album cover.

Lottie removed her long black concert dress and reached for the thick terry robe with its Plaza insignia. Tying the belt securely around her thin frame, she looked around in satisfaction. Now she was packed, ready for quick departure, and she didn't have to come back for a long time.

She smiled ruefully. New York always made her want to flee, so she only played here every few years. Her New York fans considered themselves lucky. She wouldn't play Los Angeles at all.

Lottie turned out the lights one by one, and opened the curtains. One of the benefits of staying at the Plaza was the view of Central Park. At this time of night it cut a restful swathe of darkness through the city's perpetual glow. She pressed her forehead to the cool glass to drink in its stillness.

She liked the park, but felt sorry for the children who went there to play. They spent their childhoods on concrete sidewalks, instead of roving over miles of open fields. They shared their playground with thousands of other people, never knowing the joy of a solitary day.

Even the sky overhead was hemmed in by tall buildings. Not so in the country, where earth met heaven on an endless horizon.

Lottie shook herself impatiently. When had she become such a sentimental fool? Without leaving Iowa, she could not have become a concert pianist. She'd done the right thing when she left home.

But she hadn't known she could never go back.

One

November 1936

It's here! It's here!" Lottie flew through the house, her cousin Harvey at her heels.

They found Harvey's mama in the kitchen, kneading a batch of bread. "Calm down, children. You'll wake Mona from her nap." Aunt Cora wiped her hands on her apron.

"Come on, Aunt Cora," Lottie said. "The truck's here and the men are asking for you."

Lottie and Harvey each took a hand and tugged her to the front door, where two burly men waited on the porch. One of them said, "Are you the lady who ordered the piano?"

Aunt Cora's smile was wry. "I'm the one who's stuck with the piano. It amounts to the same thing." She hadn't known she was getting a piano until a few days before, when a telegram came at lunch time. Lottie had been there when she read it aloud to Uncle Otto.

CAN'T KEEP PIANO STOP SENDING IT TO YOU STOP PAPA

Lottie had never seen gentle Aunt Cora look so mad. "The nerve of that man," she'd said, "assuming I'll take his precious baby grand."

Uncle Otto patted her hand. "Look at it this way, Cora. At least your father's not coming with it."

Aunt Cora softened right up, like she always did when Uncle Otto talked to her in that loving way.

The man on the porch shifted his weight. "Are you taking the delivery or not, ma'am?"

"I am." Aunt Cora turned to lead them inside. "Follow me, and shut

13

the door behind you. It's too cold to leave it open."

The second man cleared his throat. "Uh, ma'am? What about the old guy?"

Aunt Cora whipped around so fast Lottie had to skitter out of the way. "What old guy?"

Suddenly they heard singing coming from inside the truck. The cousins took off across the lawn with Aunt Cora right behind. "He wouldn't dare," she muttered as she reached the curb.

One of the moving men shot back the safety arm and opened the back of the truck. Out fell a round-bellied man in a brown plaid suit, tipping backwards off the truck and into the street. He held a cane in one hand and a square silver canteen in the other, and he was singing at the top of his lungs, "Oh, don't you remember Sweet Betsy from Pike, who crossed the wide prairie with her husband Ike?"

Harvey dissolved into fits of giggles, but Lottie was interested. This was the same song Pop sang on Sundays when he shaved for church. She nudged her younger cousin. "Be quiet."

The old man caught sight of Aunt Cora and stopped singing. Flinging his arms wide, he shouted, "What's the matter, Cora? Cat got your tongue? Come give your papa a kiss."

So he'd come with the piano after all. Wouldn't Uncle Otto be surprised?

Aunt Cora didn't look like she wanted to kiss anyone. Glancing at the crowd of neighbors gathering in the street, she said, "What is the meaning of this, Papa? Have all the trains from New York stopped running?"

The strange man grinned. "Trains to the frontier are unreliable, my love, so I hijacked a piano truck."

Aunt Cora primmed her mouth. "You missed the Iowa frontier by a good eighty years, and you know it. Stand up. I'll take you inside."

Aunt Cora's papa struggled to his feet and bowed to the neighbors. "She's a good daughter, folks. She's taking me in."

There was a little bit of laughter as Aunt Cora led the unsteady old man up the front walk, scolding all the way. "You've got a nerve, Papa, moving that piano in this cold weather. You might have damaged it."

At the door he called out, "Don't forget my suitcase, boys."

The moving men looked at each other with a what-now shrug. Lottie wondered what they'd do without Aunt Cora to give directions, but just then Uncle Otto walked up, puffing like he'd run all the way from Westmont National Bank. "Can I be of assistance?"

The men looked relieved. "Where do you want this?"

"Right this way." Uncle Otto led the men into the front room, with Lottie and Harvey right behind. He stopped short when he heard the racket coming from upstairs, but started moving again when he noticed the men were listening too. "Come along, boys," he said, and they did. Most people did as Uncle Otto told them.

The rest of the afternoon, Lottie sat on the staircase landing and watched through the glass doors of the front room as the men put together the big piano. She liked the way it looked, all brown and shiny, and wondered about those pedals at the bottom. Did they make it go, like the pedals in the Ford? She'd love to see that.

When the moving men finished up and left, Uncle Otto went back to the bank, saying, "You kids stay out of the front room until Mama gives you permission."

After a while, the strange old man grew quiet, and Aunt Cora started downstairs. Her legs stopped next to Lottie for a moment and she sighed. "Who could imagine such a beautiful instrument would bring so much unhappiness?"

"Can we try it, Mama?" Harvey asked.

Aunt Cora shrugged. "I don't see why not."

He charged into the front room, but Lottie followed more slowly. She didn't want to treat the piano like a toy. It was too beautiful.

Aunt Cora sat on the bench and settled Harvey on her lap. He pounded away at the keys with flat hands, mashing a bunch of them at once, which made his mama laugh.

Lottie covered her ears against the noise. Harvey was doing it all wrong. She knew because she'd watched Mrs. Swift play the Sunday school piano in the church basement, and she used different fingers at different times. True, that piano looked a lot different, with greenish wood and yellow keys, but she was pretty sure it worked the same way.

After a few minutes of Harvey's noise, they heard a bunch of thumps from overhead. The thumps were so loud that they shook the chandelier above the piano. Aunt Cora looked up at the ceiling and slid Harvey from her lap. "That's it, I'm afraid, Harvey. I need to check on your grandpapa." She left the room quickly, and Harvey ran after her.

Lottie could hardly take her eyes off the black and white piano keys. Humming softly, she slid onto the bench and tried one. "Oh —" She stopped. No, that wasn't right. She tried another. "Oh —"

She nodded, happy with her key. "Oh don't —" It didn't take as long to find the second note. That was good, because she needed to use it a bunch of times in a row. "Oh, don't you remember —" She hunted for the next note.

Pretty soon she had all the notes for the first two lines. She played them through several times, then set to work on the next two lines. When she figured them out, she thought a minute. Didn't Mrs. Swift do something with her other hand, too?

"Cora!"

The bellow from above broke Lottie's concentration. She looked up to find Aunt Cora watching her with a frown. "Where did you learn to do that, child?"

Lottie ducked her head, a little shy. "It's the song Pop sings every Sunday when he shaves."

Aunt Cora looked impatient. "I know the song, Lottie. I want to know where you learned to play it."

She shrugged. "I don't know."

"Cora!"

Aunt Cora glanced toward the stairs. "Don't go away," she said. "I'll be right back."

Lottie nodded. She wasn't going anywhere.

By the time Aunt Cora came back, Lottie had found a note to play with her other hand. It sounded good with the rest of the song, and that made her happy.

Aunt Cora stared at Lottie's hands. "Play it again, from the beginning."

Lottie started over.

"You're in D major," Aunt Cora said in a quiet voice, "and you found C sharp."

Lottie looked up. "What does that mean? D major and C sharp."

"It means —" Aunt Cora broke off with a distracted smile. "I think it means you're ready for piano lessons. Play it for me once more before I start supper."

Lottie started the tune, but stopped right away and looked at the ceiling. "Did you hear that?" she whispered.

Aunt Cora looked mad. "Ignore him," she said with a snap in her voice. "Let him sing if he wants. He won't feel much like it tomorrow."

Lottie started again, and the old man's rumbling voice drowned out the notes.

"Oh, don't you remember sweet Betsy from Pike
Who crossed the big mountains with her husband Ike
Two yoke of oxen, a big yeller dog,
A tall Shanghai rooster and one spotted hog."

"The piano came today," Lottie told Helen as they walked up the lane after school. She'd have mentioned it sooner, but Helen always sat with her friends in the back of the school bus, while Lottie sat up front near the driver. She felt more comfortable there because the rest of the kids went to school together, while she was only allowed to ride as a favor to Pop.

"I know." Helen pulled her hood close against the cold. "The delivery truck drove by when we were outside after lunch."

"Oh." Lottie never got to tell the big news first. "I bet you didn't know Aunt Cora's going to teach me to play it."

Helen tweaked one of Lottie's braids. "Well, then you'll know how to do something I don't, kiddo."

"Yes, but you know how to sing like Mama did, right?"

"Nobody sang like Mama," Helen said, "but I like to try."

Lottie took her sister's hand. Helen always looked sad when they talked about Mama. "Aunt Cora's papa came with the piano. He smelled like rotten fruit. And he sang and laughed and made a bow to all the neighbors."

"Was Aunt Cora glad to see him?"

"No." Lottie remembered her aunt's tight lips when she led the old man inside the house. "She took him to his room and made him stay there."

"Huh." Helen dropped her sister's hand. "I'll race you home."

17

The girls ran toward the white clapboard farm house, Lottie's legs pumping hard to keep up with Helen's easy jog. They reached the front porch door at the same moment and burst into the house, laughing and arguing about who won the race.

○

"I learned to play the piano today," Lottie told Pop at supper.

"Is that so?"

"Yes." Lottie nearly burst with importance. "Aunt Cora is going to start giving me piano lessons on Monday."

He raised an eyebrow. "You'd be better off practicing your snowman-building. They say it's going to be a real snowy winter."

Lottie grinned. "I already know how to build a snowman, right, Helen? Remember the one we made last winter?"

Helen began stacking plates. "Speaking of things I've taught you, it's time to clear the table."

While the girls washed dishes, Pop tuned the radio to WHO's *Barn Dance Frolic,* as he did every Saturday night at eight. This was Lottie's favorite hour of the week, when her family sat together and listened to the show out of Des Moines. She didn't understand the jokes that made Pop and Helen laugh so hard, but she loved the music. Sometimes a new song would take her fancy, and she'd sing it all the time for the next week, until Pop grabbed her up in his arms and said, "Stop it, or my head will explode." Then they laughed together because this was the funniest joke of all.

Sunday morning Lottie saw Aunt Cora's papa again at church. He sat across the aisle in his brown suit, his beard a little shaggy. Aunt Cora sat next to him, a wiggly Mona on her lap. Once in a while Mona nudged her grandpa's arm, and he pulled away. Aunt Cora pulled her arms tighter as if to say, "Mona, behave."

Mrs. Swift started the prelude on the big organ up front, and Lottie scrunched up her face to try to block out all the mistakes. She reached up to cover her ears, but Pop noticed and shook his head. It was rude to cover her ears in church.

Lottie peeked across the aisle. Had Aunt Cora's papa noticed her bad manners? He couldn't have, because his eyes were squeezed shut and he was plugging his ears with his fingers. Lottie felt for him. Mrs. Swift took some getting used to.

Suddenly he opened his eyes and looked straight at Lottie, and she stared back, interested. The organ gave another groan and they both made a face. The man chuckled, and she looked away. There was no laughing in church.

After the service, Aunt Cora's papa stopped in front of Lottie. He leaned heavily on a silver-headed cane and swayed a little as he spoke. "What did you think of the music thish morning, little girl?"

His fierce expression made Lottie feel shy. "It was all right, I guess," she said softly.

Aunt Cora's papa looked disappointed. "Oh. Ish that sho." He turned and stumped down the aisle.

Pop put a hand on Lottie's shoulder as he watched the old man walk away. "That fellow's going to give Cora a run for her money," he said.

"Why does he talk like that?" Lottie whispered.

Pop's eyes flickered to Helen and back. "I couldn't tell you, honey." He took Lottie's hand. "Let's go home to dinner."

Lottie nodded. "My stomach's growling."

But they couldn't leave yet because Aunt Eloise, Mama's sister, was sailing down the aisle with her eye on Pop. "Oh, George, a moment please." She looked at the girls. "Helen, be a dear and take Lottie outside."

Helen glanced at Pop, who gave a little motion with his head. Taking Lottie's hand she said, "Let's go, kiddo."

Aunt Eloise lowered her voice as they walked away, but it carried anyway. "I just met Cora's father, and I think he was drunk. In church! Why, he had the nerve to insult poor Olivia Swift to my face. He said, and I quote, 'he won't come back to church until she's punished for her crimes against the canon of sacred music.' I've never been so insulted! You know I was the one who got the elders to hire her."

Lottie glanced over her shoulder as she reached the sanctuary door. Pop looked like a rabbit in a trap.

"What'd Aunt Eloise want?" Helen asked when he finally reached the car.

Pop made a face. "Nothing important."

Monday morning Lottie jumped off the school bus and ran across the square to Aunt Cora's, her mind on the piano. When she reached the warm kitchen, breakfast had started already.

"Hang up your coat, young lady," Aunt Cora said. "Your oatmeal is getting cold."

Lottie hurried to the back hall and unbuttoned her coat. As she hung it up she heard a booming voice from above. "Where's my breakfast? What's taking so long?"

Aunt Cora rushed past, a loaded tray in her hands. Lottie stared at her. She'd never seen her aunt wait on anybody before.

The kitchen was quiet as Lottie slipped into her chair. Uncle Otto bent over his oatmeal with a grim look on his face. Harvey and Mona didn't say a word.

After breakfast, Aunt Cora set the children up at the kitchen table with some salt dough for making shapes. They had fun for a while, but soon Harvey got bored, and poked his fingers into the girls' work. Lottie pushed him away, but Mona stood on her chair and screamed, "Ma! Harvey ruined my dough."

Aunt Cora ran into the kitchen and took Mona by the arms. "Be quiet this instant, Mona. Remember, Grandpa can't stand the noise." She shook her daughter ever so gently. "Promise you'll be quiet now."

"I promise." Mona started to cry.

For the second time that morning, Lottie stared at her aunt in surprise.

That afternoon on the way up the lane, Helen asked, "Did you have your piano lesson?"

Lottie shook her head. "Aunt Cora didn't have time today, and I didn't want to ask."

Two

 unt Cora's house was topsy-turvy for the next few days. She looked worried all the time, and Lottie and Harvey did their best to stay out of her way. Harvey's grandpa kept to his room, but his voice could be heard all over the house, calling for his daughter.

Thursday morning the old man didn't come downstairs or yell for Aunt Cora. Lottie felt relieved, but to her surprise, Aunt Cora seemed more worried than ever. She made lots of trips upstairs through the day to check on him.

"Is he sick?" Lottie asked when Aunt Cora paused for breath.

"Yes, but you can't catch what he has," Aunt Cora said. "God willing, he'll feel better in a week or so."

Lottie and Harvey played in the attic all morning, since it was too cold to play outside. They came down to lunch to find Uncle Otto feeding Mona a jelly sandwich. "Mother is busy nursing Grandpa," he told them, and handed them each a sandwich. "You must be as quiet as church mice."

Lottie took a bite of her sandwich. "Did you know it's snowing?"

Uncle Otto smiled. "I walked home for lunch in it. We're going to get several inches, by the looks of things."

By the time school let out, the snow lay thick on the ground. The bus couldn't take them home, so Helen and Lottie stayed the night in town. Helen walked to school the next morning, leaving Lottie and her cousins to face another quiet day. They sat on the front stairs, chins in hands, and tried to think of something quiet that they hadn't already done.

"Why the long faces?" Aunt Cora asked, coming downstairs with a tray.

"We don't have anything to do." Harvey didn't bother to lift his head.

"Go outside." Aunt Cora pointed her elbow toward the front door. "You know how to build a snowman, don't you?"

Lottie nodded.

"Well, what are you waiting for?" She blew a stray lock of hair out of her eyes and scooped Mona into her arms. "All but you, pumpkin. You're coming with me."

Lottie and Harvey bundled up against the cold and marched out to the front yard. In no time at all, they rolled three snowballs and stacked one on top of the other, but their snowman looked awfully plain. "At home we'd give it a face and arms and a hat," Lottie said.

Harvey ran toward the house. "I'll go tell Mama."

"No. We aren't supposed to bother her. Let's look in the trash behind the barn." Lottie started around the house with Harvey behind her. When they reached the trash barrel, Lottie stood on tiptoe to peek over the rim.

"What do you see?" Harvey asked.

"There's a shiny thing that would make a fancy hat." She stuck her elbows over the barrel and braced one foot against the metal. "C'mon, Harvey, give me a boost."

Harvey put his arms around her knees and pushed.

"Got it." Lottie slid to the ground and held out her treasure. "It's your grandpa's silver canteen." It looked like someone had taken a hammer to it.

"Neat," Harvey said. "What else is in there?"

Lottie thought a moment. "Boost me back up. I saw some nice looking bottles."

The long-necked glass bottles sported gold labels with fancy black writing. Lottie could only make out the big "7" in the middle of each label. The bottles were the same, so they could give the snowman matching arms.

The two children zipped back around the house to add the finishing touches to their snowman and stood back to look at their work. They agreed this was the best snowman they'd ever seen. Sure, he was small, but with a few acorns for eyes and a mouth, the silver hat, and the bottles for arms, he looked dignified. They pretended he was a policeman and took turns calling on him for help.

After a bit, the cousins got tired and went inside. Aunt Cora met them with cups of hot milk, and they forgot all about their friend the snowman.

As Lottie started for the bus that afternoon, she took one last look at the snowman. My, he was fine. She was so busy admiring him that she didn't see Aunt Eloise pull up to the curb in her Packard. "Yoohoo, Lottie," she called.

Lottie broke into a trot. Aunt Eloise always sounded crabby. "Sorry, Aunt Eloise," she shouted over her shoulder. "I have to catch the bus."

At home that evening, they had a surprise visitor. Uncle Otto asked to speak with Pop alone, so he sent the girls upstairs.

"What's going on?" Helen whispered as she shut the bedroom door. Lottie shrugged. "I don't know."

They listened through the floor to the rise and fall of Uncle Otto's voice, and then the muffled sound of laughter, which seemed to go on for a long time. Lottie made out the words "Eloise," "trouble," and "Cora," and finally, "I'm real sorry."

At last the front door banged shut, and Pop called, "Lottie? I need to talk to you."

Downstairs, Pop pulled Lottie onto his lap. "Aunt Cora's having a real bad time right now. Have you noticed that, honey?"

Lottie nodded slowly. "She isn't happy."

"She feels a little overworked, with her papa being sick and all, so, we're going to have Aunt Emma look after you for a while."

Lottie's eyes filled with tears. "Did I do something wrong?"

"No," Pop said. "Old Mr. Schultz will feel better in a week or two, and then you'll go back to Aunt Cora."

Lottie hung her head. Aunt Emma was nice, but she didn't own a piano. "What about my music lessons?"

"They'll have to wait."

"No," Lottie whispered. She'd already waited a week.

Pop raised her chin. "Lottie, look at me."

She lifted her eyes.

"You want to help Aunt Cora, don't you?"

She sighed. "Yes, Pop."

"Good. Now, go brush your teeth."

She slid off his lap.

"Oh, and Lottie?"

She stopped. "Yes?"

"Next time you build a snowman, ask Aunt Cora for a hat."

"Okay, Pop."

Lottie trudged upstairs and poured her troubles into Helen's sympathetic ear. When she finished, Helen said, "Look at it this way, kiddo. It could be worse."

Lottie frowned. "How?"

Helen chucked her under the chin. "Aunt Eva could be the one to take care of you."

Lottie made a face. Aunt Eva lived in two rooms on the second floor of Uncle Otto's bank, where she worked as a teller. She filled her tiny home with breakable knickknacks and painted china plates that Lottie was sure to break if she bumped into them. "You're right," she said to Helen. "Aunt Eva would be worse."

Lottie spent a dull week with kind Aunt Emma, and returned to Aunt Cora's two weeks before Christmas. By that time, the handsome snowman had melted.

To her surprise, Mr. Schultz ate his meals with the family now, and while he didn't talk much, he minded his manners. He spent most of his time alone in his room, staring out the window or playing solitaire at his desk.

"Aunt Cora, will you teach me to play piano now?" Lottie said at lunch time.

Aunt Cora gave Mona a piece of bread and butter before she answered. "I'll do what I can, dear." She glanced at her father. "Mr. Schultz is really the musician in this family, but I can get you started."

Lottie looked at Mr. Schultz with his neatly trimmed moustache and beetling eyebrows. Was this what a musician looked like? Somehow she couldn't picture him playing fiddle on the Iowa *Barn Dance Frolic*.

After lunch Aunt Cora brought a wooden crate down from the attic. "I never thought I'd use these books again," she said. "I didn't want piano lessons nearly as much as you do, Lottie."

"Was Mrs. Swift your teacher?" Lottie asked. She couldn't imagine learning from the church organist.

"No," Aunt Cora said with a laugh. "I was born in New York City, not Westmont. My piano teacher was a skinny little man named Herr Meiner. He and my papa played in the same orchestra. He wore little round glasses far down on his nose, and a shiny black suit of clothes. Herr Meiner always carried a little stick, called a baton, and whenever I made a mistake he rapped my fingers."

Lottie curled her fingers into her palms. "Did you make a lot of mistakes?"

"I'm afraid so," Aunt Cora said, "but there's no need to look so sad. Later, Papa enrolled me in a special music school in Ohio, and I had lots of fun there. That's how I met your Uncle Otto. I boarded a train from Dayton to New York and he was on it. He was going to a bankers' convention, and I was going home. Isn't that nice?"

Lottie nodded and eyed the stack of music. Plump Aunt Cora and balding Uncle Otto weren't nearly as interesting as the books in that crate.

"Now, this is the first book we need." Aunt Cora pulled a flimsy red book out of the pile. "Sit on the bench, and I'll show you the musical notes."

Lottie got along well in her lessons, partly because she'd learned her letters and numbers already, and partly because she didn't think music was hard. Aunt Cora assigned easy songs and finger exercises and Lottie mastered them quickly. She practiced every chance she got until Aunt Cora chased her out of the front room saying, "Get some exercise, child. You'll wreck your eyesight with all that tiny print."

By the end of her second week, Lottie was pulling other books out of the crate to see if she could play them. One afternoon as she leafed through a thick book with the word "B-a-c-h" on the front, a shadow fell on the music. She looked up into the face of Mr. Schultz, bending to peer over her shoulder. "You can't possibly play that," he said.

Lottie glanced at the page. "I might be able to."

"Show me." The old man stepped back. "I don't believe it."

Lottie placed the music on its rack and sat before it, thinking hard. The page was full of a huge number of notes, but she didn't want to back down. She stared at the music for a long time, but finally said, "You're right. I can't play this yet, but I will some day."

The old man gave a dry cackle. "You'll make a fine musician with that kind of determination." He opened the book to a different page.

"Try this one instead. Do you know the G scale?"

Lottie shook her head. "What's a scale?"

The old man was startled. "What in God's name is Cora teaching you?" he said, and Lottie heard someone gasp.

"Papa!" Aunt Cora stood in the doorway. "Watch your language in this house."

He looked annoyed. "Is this the child I hear at the piano when I'm in my room?"

Aunt Cora nodded.

"And yet you haven't taught her what a scale is."

"I'm getting there, Papa. My time is limited, you know."

He thumped his cane on the floor. "From now on, I will be her teacher."

Aunt Cora narrowed her eyes. "Not without my permission, you won't."

The old man looked surprised. "What's the problem? Sure I was only a humble cellist, but I can teach anyone the basics. What's your name, child?"

"Lottie." She looked him in the eye. "What's yours?"

"Carl Schultz." He stuck out a hand. "There. Now we're acquainted."

Lottie shook hands. "Nice to know you. What's a G scale?"

Aunt Cora placed a firm hand on her father's arm. "I'll let you try this, Papa. But I won't let you bully the child. If I hear one harsh word out of you, you're fired."

The old man raised his eyebrows. "Why, Cora, when have I ever spoken harshly to you?"

Aunt Cora sniffed. "Mark my words, Papa. Mark my words."

On Christmas Day, when Pop and the girls arrived, Aunt Cora's house was filled to the rafters with Hoffmans. Lottie took the pies to the kitchen, where Mama's three sisters and Aunt Cora worked and gossiped.

Lottie barely had time to set down her pie plate before she was grabbed and squeezed by tiny, unmarried Aunt Eva. "Would you look at this little pumpkin?" Aunt Eva cried. "Ooh, I could just eat her up!"

Aunt Emma said, "She's the spitting image of Ethel, God rest her soul," and the ladies fell silent, remembering Lottie's mama.

Aunt Eloise broke the spell. "You're growing like a weed, Lottie. I'll have to bring you some of Diana's hand-me-downs to wear."

"Yes, ma'am," Lottie said. Aunt Eloise's taste ran to bows and lace, which made scratchy places inside Cousin Diana's dresses. Lottie couldn't stand them. She squirmed in Aunt Eva's arms, which tightened around her.

Aunt Emma came to Lottie's rescue. "The rest of the kids are upstairs, dear. Why don't you go find them? Let her go, Eva."

Lottie made for the back stairs. On the way past the gun room, she paused. Pop sat among his brothers-in-law, smoking a pipe from Uncle Otto's collection. Uncle Frank, in his last year at Iowa State, was telling stories. Mr. Schultz sat a little apart, watching the group with no expression on his face.

In the attic, Helen was organizing a concert to show the adults after dessert. Lottie joined the group as Helen read out the list of acts. "Marlene, you're singing 'O Holy Night.'"

"That's right." Marlene tossed her curly hair. "We learned it in the high school choir."

Helen moved on. "And Peter?" She looked at Marlene's brother. "If you juggle this year, you have to use more than one ball."

Peter laughed. "Okay. That was a pretty good joke last year, though."

"No it wasn't." Helen's voice was prim. "Now, Diana, I can hear your tap shoes already, so I know what you're going to do."

Diana fluffed her ruffled pink skirt. "I even wore my costume."

"And you twins." Helen glanced at Diana's ten-year-old brothers. "Card tricks again?"

"They'll be better this year," they said in unison.

"Now that leaves…" Helen looked down her list. "Lottie. What are you going to do, kiddo?"

Lottie lifted her chin. "I'll play piano."

"What are you going to play?" Peter asked, interested.

"Probably 'Mary Had a Little Lamb,' right, Lottie?" This came from Marlene.

"No." Lottie saw the doubt on their faces. "I'm going to play a minuet by Bach."

Helen looked around. "Everyone practice your act. We don't have much time." She stepped over to Lottie. "Are you sure you want to play piano, kiddo? You've only had a month of lessons. You could do 'Ring Around the Rosy', with Mona and Harvey instead."

"No." Lottie straightened her quivering chin. "I'm going to play piano."

"All right then." Helen sat back on her heels. "If you're sure."

The cousins practiced for a while, then started a game of tag until Aunt Emma called, "Wash up, kids. It's dinner time."

Lottie was happy to eat in the kitchen with Diana and the twins because she could leave the table as soon as she finished eating. She felt a little sorry for the older cousins, who had to sit among the grown-ups in the dining room and use their best manners.

She ate her turkey and mashed potatoes, rolls and yams with gusto, leaving the cranberry relish for last. She did not like sour cranberries, but she knew she'd catch it from Pop if she left any food on her plate. She lifted a spoonful of bright red puree to her lips, set it down untouched, swirled it around the plate and started over. Diana and the twins cleared their places and left, and still she sat.

A red-faced Aunt Eloise bustled into the kitchen with an empty dish in her hands, her mouth set in an angry line. Aunt Eva fluttered along behind her. Lottie sank lower in her chair.

"Why on earth would he say such a thing to you?" Aunt Eva twittered. "There's nothing wrong with your face."

Aunt Eloise scooped mashed potatoes out of the pot on the stove. "Isn't it obvious, Eva? The man must be drunk. Where does Cora get off bringing her degenerate father into this family gathering? It just goes to show she's no better than the rest of us, New York or no New York."

Aunt Eva wavered. "Although she has done right by poor Lottie. Why, I hear she even lets her play that big piano."

Aunt Eloise sent her sister a withering glance. "And what good, pray tell, will that ever do a farm girl? She ought to be teaching her to sew and clean house." Grabbing the dish, she sailed into the hall, Aunt Eva following in her wake.

"But Diana takes dance lessons...."

Their voices died away. Lottie sat up in her chair, feeling queasy. She hated angry voices.

After dinner came nap time, officially for Mona and Harvey, unofficially for the uncles, while the aunts washed the dishes and put away the food, and the cousins played hide and seek. Late in the afternoon, they sliced the pies and whipped the cream for dessert.

At last it was time for the concert. Helen and Marlene pushed the grown-ups into the front room while the boys rearranged the furniture to form a stage area. Lottie raised the piano cover and played middle C, followed by a C scale. She moved on to the G scale, the key of her minuet.

"Where'd you learn to do that?" Diana asked. The boys looked on with interest.

She felt too shy to speak. She wished they'd stop staring.

"That's pretty neat," Peter said. "Is that what you're going to play?"

Lottie shook her head. "I've memorized a minuet by Bach."

Diana puffed her lips out. "It's probably not as good as my tap dance, but I guess you'll do all right."

The aunts filed into the room, dragging the uncles behind them. Uncle Frank, who was like a big kid, sat on the floor at the front.

Aunt Cora came last, tugging her father by the hand. He glared at the cousins. "So these children think they can amuse us, eh?"

"Come sit down, Papa," Aunt Cora urged, and led him to the last upholstered chair in the room. She perched beside him on a footstool, and signaled Helen. The concert could begin.

Diana did her best to imitate Shirley Temple with her simple tap routine. She ended with a cute little wave, and gave the stage to a nervous Peter, whose croquet balls refused to stay in the air. After he dropped them for the fourth time, Uncle Frank called for a pitching display instead. Peter took up the red striped ball and threw it straight at his uncle's nose. Frank caught it in one hand, and Peter stormed out of the room to nurse his wounded pride on the stairs.

"O Holy Night" won Marlene a polite round of applause, although Mr. Schultz snored loudly during the last verse.

The twins' card tricks, along with lots of jokes and pratfalls, made everybody laugh. They earned their applause, and Uncle Frank called, "Encore! Encore!" The noise woke the old man, who blinked like an owl at noon.

Helen took the stage with Mona and Harvey, swinging them in a circle while they chanted, "Ring around the rosy, Pocket full of posies, Ashes, ashes, we all fall down."

As the little ones ran to their mama, Helen started the phonograph and called on Uncle Frank, who swung her around the room until the silk flower fell out of her pretty brown hair. Laughing and breathless, she sank to the floor, while Uncle Frank bowed to loud applause.

At last it was Lottie's turn. After a nervous glance at the audience, she sat, legs dangling, and placed her little hands on the keys.

With the first note of the *Minuet in G Major*, the audience disappeared, erased by the elegant melody and simple harmonies of Bach. She kept an even tempo with the left hand and flowed from soft to loud, loud to soft with the right, building each note on the last. The stately old dance sprang to life under her fingertips.

When the last note died, nobody moved.

Nobody clapped. Tears gathered in Lottie's eyes. She must have been awful.

Pop finally broke the silence. "Well, I'll be darned." He sounded dazed. "That was pretty good!"

Everyone started talking at once.

"Why, she's got talent!"

"Her mother was musical, too."

"How did she do that?"

"Well, it's not my kind of music."

"Is that a player piano?"

Thunk. Thunk. Thunk. Mr. Schultz's cane whacked the floor. "Isn't anybody going to clap for the child?" He looked around the room through beady eyes. "I can't expect you people to recognize talent when you see it, but at least you can be polite."

Uncle Fred took the hint. "Bravo, Lottie! Bravo!" He started to clap, and everyone else joined in. Lottie slipped off the piano bench and stood in the glow of her family's approval.

On the way home, Lottie lay under a blanket on the cold back seat of the car. Her chest felt full of happiness as she remembered the admiration in Pop's eyes.

Up front, Pop spoke to Helen. "I've found a place for you to stay next year when you start high school. There's a couple in Collison, the Webers, who are looking for a boarder."

"I can't go away. What about you and Lottie?" Helen said.

"We'll get along all right. She's a smart little girl. Besides, you wouldn't be much help around the house if you had to go all the way into Collison and back every day and do homework every night."

Helen hesitated. "Well, Marta Hansen plans to board in Collison, too. We could ride home together every weekend."

"Good. That's settled."

In the back of the car, a little of Lottie's happiness seeped away.

Three

Nine-year-old Lottie skipped up the lane in the afternoon sunshine, a yellow and white May basket hanging on her arm. She'd made it in art class by weaving strips of construction paper into a box and gluing on a long handle, and she couldn't wait to show it to Helen.

Even though Helen had boarded in Collison for nearly three years, Lottie still missed her. Pop took care of her with quiet affection, but Helen filled the house with energy and new ideas. Friday afternoons when Pop brought Helen home for the weekend, were the highlight of the week.

Lottie hung up her book bag and headed for the kitchen to set the table and sweep the floor. Chores complete, she exchanged her plaid jumper for a pair of overalls and ran outside to play.

The apple tree, covered in blossoms, beckoned her. Lottie climbed from branch to branch inside the canopy of white. She settled on a gently curving limb and looked about in wonder. A bumblebee landed on a flower nearby, reminding her of a recent disagreement between Mr. Schultz and Aunt Cora.

Lottie and Pop listened to a radio show called the *Green Hornet*, and she'd been captivated by its theme song. One afternoon she'd begun working out the notes by ear while she sat at the piano. Aunt Cora stepped into the room and said, "Is that 'Flight of the Bumblebee'?"

"No," Lottie said. "It's the *Green Hornet* theme."

Aunt Cora chuckled. "I see. Well, I know it as 'Flight of the Bumblebee.'"

"I like it."

"I'll see if they sell the sheet music next time I go to Collison."

A week later Aunt Cora brought the music home, and Lottie spent a happy hour learning to play it. She loved the challenge of playing the notes as fast as the orchestra on the radio.

Mr. Schultz didn't care for 'Flight of the Bumblebee'. He had no use for piano adaptations of orchestral music. "There's plenty of great music written for piano without poaching from other instruments," he said, and ordered her to stop wasting her time.

Aunt Cora reacted with outrage. "He needn't think he controls all the music in this house," she said. "You can't be serious all the time, honey. Play it all you want."

Within a week, Lottie had it memorized.

She sat on her tree branch for half an hour, humming soft accompaniment to the yellow and black fellow as he moved from flower to flower, but when Pop's Ford chugged down the lane, she jumped down in a hurry.

She grabbed a knife from the kitchen and cut some apple blossoms for her basket. Her teacher had told the class that May baskets were meant to be hung on a friend's door in secret, as a surprise. But this one would be a centerpiece for the dinner table.

Lottie finished arranging the flowers as Helen breezed through the door. "Mmmm, what smells so good?" she asked, throwing her arms around her little sister.

"It's stew, silly," Lottie said with a grin.

At seventeen, Helen sparkled with health and energy, a sharp contrast to Lottie's bashful manner.

Helen caught sight of the blossom-filled basket. "Is that a May basket?"

Lottie nodded.

"I remember when we made May baskets at school." She picked it up by the handle. "Nice work, kiddo. I couldn't get the handle to stay attached to mine."

Lottie basked in her sister's praise. "You have to let the glue set."

"Ah." Helen smiled at her sister. "Now, what else shall we have for dinner? Is there any rhubarb for sauce?"

Lottie made a face. Rhubarb sauce made her mouth pucker. But seeing the firm set of Helen's chin, she reached for the kitchen knife. "I can cut some, I guess."

When Lottie returned from the rhubarb patch, Helen drew a paper bag full of white sugar out of her book bag. "It's payment from Mrs. Weber for helping her with the spring cleaning this week. I want to bake a cake tomorrow, but we can use some in the rhubarb sauce tonight."

The girls worked until Pop came in from the barn for dinner, but Lottie held back her big news until after they said grace. Raising her head from her folded hands, she said, "You'll never guess what happened, Helen. Mrs. Swift ran off with an accordion salesman."

Helen froze, her fork halfway to her mouth. "Wh-a-a-t?" She looked to Pop for confirmation. "Does she mean our Mrs. Swift, the church organist?"

Pop wiped his mouth and nodded. "Yep. She left town yesterday with some guy named Hiller. Rumor has it he's a traveling salesman."

When he didn't continue, Lottie took up the story. "That's right. He was playing his accordion outside the music store in Collison last week. Mrs. Swift stopped to listen and they fell in love, right there on the sidewalk. At least, that's what Diana said."

"What about church?" Helen asked. "Won't there be any music on Sunday?"

Lottie thought she might burst with pride. "That's the best part. They asked me to take her place." She glanced at Pop. "At least for now. They brought the piano up from the basement — they even had it tuned — and I'll play it on Sunday. But starting next week, Mr. Schultz is going to teach me to play the organ."

"My goodness." Helen eyed her sister with admiration. "That sounds like a lot of work. Will they pay you?"

Lottie nodded. "Aunt Eloise insisted that the board of elders pay me half as much as Mrs. Swift. That's fair, because I'm younger."

Pop looked disgusted.

"Sounds like you'll be busy this summer." Helen kept her eyes on her dinner.

Lottie hastened to reassure her. "Oh, not really. I'll take lessons in the afternoon, just like always. But I'll work on the farm with you the rest of the time."

"Lottie's going to raise vegetables for the county fair," Pop said.

"She's old enough to enter this year."

"And flowers. Don't forget the flowers, Pop." Lottie bounced a little in her chair. "I'll show roses."

Helen glanced sidelong at her sister. "Why, you'll be so busy, I'll bet you wouldn't miss me if I stayed in Collison."

Lottie laughed. It was a good joke. "I guess I wouldn't."

"Well, that's good. Because I am. Staying in Collison, I mean."

Lottie set down her fork and stared at her sister.

Helen hurried on. "You're not the only one with a job for the summer. I'm going to clean houses. Mrs. Weber thought I did a good job, and told some of her friends about me. She said I could clean her house in exchange for room and board."

"You mean you'll only be here on weekends?" Lottie's mouth felt dry.

Helen shook her head. "I've been hired to clerk at Woolworth's on Saturday afternoons. I'll only be home on Sundays."

"But what about Pop and me? How will we get all the work done without you?"

"Same way we do during the school year." Pop's voice was gentle. "I'll exchange labor with Uncle Keith and Uncle Harry, and you can take care of the house. Helen's taught you how. Aunt Emma said she'd have time to help with the canning and such."

Lottie felt cornered. As usual, this family decision was final before she knew about it. Tears threatened, but she held them back. Pop hadn't raised any crybabies. She took a bite of bread and chewed, thinking hard. "I guess that'll work," she said slowly. "Gee, Helen, if both of us have jobs, we'll be rich."

Helen let out a relieved laugh. "We'll do the fair in style this year. I'll buy you hot donuts and everything."

"And we can ride the Ferris wheel." Lottie feigned excitement.

Pop smiled. "Maybe I'll even win my girls a prize in the ring toss."

○

Saturday morning Pop drove Lottie to town in the rain. Instead of chatting to Pop as she usually did, she stared out the window at the drenched landscape, lost in gloomy thoughts. Without Helen, her summer was ruined. There would be no fun, no laughter. Just Lottie and Pop, going about their business. The windshield wipers sang, "Everything's wrong. Nothing is right," over and over.

Mr. Schultz was already at the church. If he noticed her sagging shoulders and glum expression, he didn't comment. As long as her mood didn't affect her playing, Lottie knew he wouldn't care.

A disciplined morning of practice went a long way toward restoring Lottie's equilibrium. Mr. Schultz had chosen music she already knew. Still, he insisted on a thorough rehearsal. He expected a high level of performance, and she loved to meet his standards.

They finished preparing for Sunday with half an hour to spare. "We may as well get started on the organ," the old man said.

Lottie jumped up and headed for the choir loft. She couldn't wait to try out the imposing instrument with its double keyboard and multiple pedals.

"Not so fast, young lady." Mr. Schultz limped forward, leaning on his cane. He indicated the front pew. "Sit down. I will play for you first."

"But I've heard Mrs. Swift play hundreds of times," Lottie protested.

He gave a thin smile. "Precisely. It's time you knew what an organ is supposed to sound like."

What a waste of time. Lottie slumped in her seat. The organ had a keyboard and pedals. How different could it be from the piano?

He ascended the steps to the choir loft, a sheaf of papers under his arm, and seated himself on the bench. He took a moment to fuss over the placement of his music, and she heaved an exaggerated sigh. She was tired of grown-ups who thought they were right.

Mr. Schultz fiddled with the stops and adjusted the bench. He flexed his hands and pushed his spectacles up his nose, then removed them to wipe them on his handkerchief. Finally, when Lottie thought she'd go crazy, he raised his hands.

There was a moment of suspense, followed by an outpouring of the darkest, most urgent music Lottie had ever heard. She sat up, eyes narrowed in concentration. For once her hands were still, not itching to play along. Instead, she was swept up in the majestic tide of sound, the perfect expression of her disappointment. Every phrase poured straight through her soul in a cleansing stream. The longer she listened, the lighter she felt.

The final note died away, taking with it the last of her gloom. She turned her enraptured gaze on Mr. Schultz. "Teach me to play like that."

Sunday morning, when Lottie played for the church service, the staid members of Westmont Community Church applauded after the offertory. Even the ancient Sunday school piano could not mask her talent. Afterward, the grown-ups stood around sipping coffee and tea, and marveling at the wonder child in their midst. Their satisfaction was all the sweeter because Lottie was more talented than that fallen woman, Mrs. Swift.

Aunt Eloise told everyone that she had suggested Lottie for the job. "She's truly a special child," she repeated to all who would listen. "We're very proud."

Which was news to Lottie.

On the way home, Helen gave her a big smile. "You were wonderful! Were you nervous?"

"No. I knew I could do it," Lottie replied. "I'm just glad I could show everyone how a piano should be played. Now they've seen real talent." Mr. Schultz had said that last bit to Aunt Cora when he thought Lottie wasn't listening.

Helen laughed, but Pop caught her eye in the rear-view mirror and shook his head slightly.

After dinner, Pop joined Lottie on the back steps.

"I guess you think you did a real good job this morning, don't you, honey?" Pop fixed his gaze on the horizon.

Lottie looked at him warily. "Yes."

"Well, I do too. I'm proud of you."

"Thanks." She waited for the other shoe to drop.

Pop continued. "There are a lot of kinds of talent in the world. Aunt Cora has a way with children, and Uncle Frank's a good shortstop. And Helen is very good at sewing." He looked down at her. "You follow?"

She smiled up at him. "Sure. You mean my kind of talent isn't the only kind that matters. I know that. Why, the kids at school are better than me at lots of things. Spelling and jumping rope and — and lots of things."

"Good." A slight frown appeared between Pop's eyes. "Honey, everybody's talents, the big ones and the small ones, are gifts from God. The way I see it, since we didn't do anything to deserve our talents, we ought not to take so much credit for them. If God gave you the gift, then the praise for it belongs to God." He paused for emphasis. "Not to Lottie."

Lottie dropped her eyes. "Oh."

Pop put a finger under her chin and pushed until her eyes met his. "Try to remember where the praise should go when you play in church. You're going to get lots of compliments, and I don't want them going to your head."

"Yes sir."

"Now give me a hug and go find Helen. She wants you to help spread manure around the rose bushes."

Four

When school let out, Lottie divided her days between working at home and practicing at church. She got along surprisingly well without Helen.

By July, the congregation was used to its pint-sized organist. Word about Lottie had spread beyond Westmont, and curiosity seekers filled the pews. This suited Reverend Walker just fine, although some of the older members complained about the crowd. There was talk of replacing Lottie with an adult when school started, an idea that Pop endorsed. Lottie crossed her fingers behind her back every time the subject came up.

Pop drove into Collison early every Sunday morning and brought Helen home, and for a few hours it was just like old times. After church Helen helped Lottie with Sunday dinner, and they sat around the table long after the food was gone, telling the news of the week.

Helen's plans had worked out well. She had as many house cleaning jobs as she could handle. She especially enjoyed her Saturday job clerking at Woolworth's. The soda fountain was a meeting place for the high school crowd, and she worked with a few college boys who were taking summer school. At first Helen was careful not to talk too much about any of them, but soon Lottie noticed the name Bill Turner cropped up in every story she told. Bill was funny and helpful and kind, according to Helen, and came up with the cleverest pranks, and he was a star hitter on the college baseball team.

One afternoon after listening to Helen sing Bill's praises, Pop finally spoke up. "I'd like to meet this Bill Turner."

Helen's face turned bright pink. "You would? Why?"

"I'd like to watch him walk on water."

The next Sunday, Pop brought two passengers home for church. Helen emerged from the car, followed by a sandy haired young man with broad shoulders and a friendly smile. Lottie, who had run outside to greet them, pulled up short.

"Hey, kiddo, come meet someone." Helen sounded shy and excited all at once. "This is Bill."

"Hi." Bill looked eager to please.

Lottie didn't trust him. "It's time to go," she said to Helen. "We have to be there early, remember?"

Helen laughed. "How could I forget? My sister's an important person at church these days, Bill."

"Yeah, you've mentioned that." Bill smiled at Lottie. "I can't wait to hear you play."

"Uh-huh." Lottie reached for the back car door.

Helen tapped her arm. "You can sit up front with Pop today, honey."

Helen never offered to sit in the back seat. Lottie glanced over her shoulder. "Why? So you can sit in back with him?" Lottie jerked her head toward Bill.

Pop opened the car door. "Get in front, Lottie."

Lottie sighed. She did not like this situation one bit.

For the first time since she became the organist, Lottie had trouble concentrating. She was too busy thinking up ways to make Bill Turner go away. She stumbled through the prelude, missed the cue for the first hymn, and played the Doxology twice. By the time Reverend Walker started his sermon, she was shaking.

Lottie peeked around the organ, looking for Pop. Several people stared back, some with frowns of deep concern. Others, Aunt Eloise among them, looked irritated. Mr. Schultz teetered on the brink of apoplexy. His eyes bulged and a blue vein stood out on his forehead. Alarmed, Lottie shrank back behind the organ.

She closed her eyes against the threat of tears. This was a disaster. She'd disappointed everyone. It was all Bill Turner's fault. He'd ruined her.

Aunt Cora stepped through the hidden door in the choir loft and put her arm around Lottie. "It's all right, Lottie. You just have stage fright."

Lottie leaned against her. "What am I going to do?"

"We'll get through this together." Aunt Cora's eyes held reassurance.

Lottie slipped her arms around her aunt's plump waist and held on tight.

The rest of the service ran smoothly enough. Aunt Cora's presence gave her the courage to finish, even though she made a few mistakes.

After church, she hung around the choir loft until the sanctuary emptied out, dreading the criticism of her friends and neighbors. By the time she left, the crowd had thinned to a few stragglers. Lottie couldn't find Pop, though the Ford was still parked by the curb.

She heard a shout and turned around. A large group stood at the back of the church lot, watching something she couldn't see. As she made her way toward it, a cheer went up.

She pushed through the crowd and found a makeshift baseball game taking place, with Cousin Peter pitching and Bill Turner at bat. Three Westmont boys stood on base.

"Go, Peter," Lottie muttered.

All the players had removed their Sunday coats and ties and rolled up their shirt sleeves. Helen carried Bill's suit coat over her arm and cheered every time he swung the bat.

"C'mon, Peter," Lottie called. "Get him out!"

Bill swung and missed. Someone yelled, "Strike two!"

Lottie held her breath as Peter wound up. At the crack of the bat, the ball sailed over the hedge that separated the parsonage from the churchyard. Home run. "Aw, shoot," she muttered as the crowd cheered and clapped.

Bill Turner was half-way to home base when Reverend Walker emerged from the hedgerow, the baseball in his hand, and ambled up to the players. "Which one of you boys hit this through my kitchen window?"

Bill stepped forward, looking worried. "I did."

Lottie smiled. It served him right for showing off.

His Adam's apple bobbed. "I'm sorry about your window. I'll pay for it."

Reverend Walker's face split into a big grin. "Never mind the window, boy. Where'd you get that swing? And why aren't you playin' for the Iowa Hawkeyes?"

Lottie sulked all the way home.

During dinner, she chewed her food slowly and thought about how bored she was while Pop asked Bill a lot of questions. He seemed to answer in one long monotonous drone:

"I'm from Chicago blah, blah.... Third year of college blah, blah, blah....play on the baseball team yakety yak....Yes sir, I do think we'll get into the war...Yep, I think the Cubs have a chance this year...."

Helen, who usually dominated the table talk, sat back and listened. She looked like a sap with those soft brown eyes fixed on Bill.

As soon as she could, Lottie excused herself to start the dishes. She took her time over the dishwater, full of self-pity because she had to wash up by herself.

○

"What do you think of Helen's new friend?" Pop asked that evening.

"Oh, he's all right, I guess," Lottie said without meeting his eyes. She'd thought up a long list of Bill's faults, but was suddenly shy of sharing it with Pop.

"I'm glad you feel that way. I think we'll be seeing a lot more of that young man."

Bill came back the next Sunday, and the next, and with each visit Helen seemed a little farther out of Lottie's reach. Lottie refused to be charmed by his efforts to talk to her.

Bill fit right in with the rest of the Hoffman clan. Even the Aunts approved. One afternoon Aunt Emma dropped off some cucumbers from her garden and stayed a while to chat.

"I got such a kick out of Bill last Sunday," she said with a chuckle. "He was giving Peter some tips on batting, you know, and he was so nice about it that I asked him to stay for supper. Well, I served cherry pie for dessert, and forgot to add the sugar. In thirty years of baking, I have never made a pie so tart. But I didn't know that, see, until everybody had already put their forks in their mouths. Peter and Uncle Harry made an awful fuss, but Bill ate every bite and told me it was the best thing he'd tasted in a month." Aunt Emma laughed. "That boy's manners got the best of him there. I couldn't even finish my piece, and cherry pie is my favorite."

A lump formed in Lottie's throat. She found it harder and harder to smile when someone sang Bill's praises.

Aunt Emma looked surprised. "Don't you think that's funny?"

"Yes, ma'am." Lottie mustered a weak smile.

Aunt Emma gave her a hard stare. "You want to tell me what's wrong?"

"N-Nothing." But the tide of tears was stronger than her self-control. "I just hate that Bill Turner. I hate him!"

"Oh, honey." Aunt Emma gathered Lottie to her breast and let her cry. Murmuring words of comfort, she held on tight until Lottie's sobs became hiccoughs. Then she said gently, "Wouldn't you like to tell me about it?"

Lottie blew her nose. "Everybody thinks Bill is so great, but I just don't see it. He's big and dumb, and Helen never comes home without him anymore. I miss her so much, and I think baseball is s-stupid."

Aunt Emma watched Lottie steadily. "I think I see what you mean. Instead of gaining Bill as a friend, you feel like you've lost Helen as a sister."

Lottie was astonished. "Bill isn't my friend. He doesn't even want to be my friend. He just wants Helen all to himself."

"Are you sure about that, honey?" Aunt Emma asked. "Could be you haven't given him much of a chance. It's awful hard to shake hands with a thorn bush."

Lottie's shoulders slumped. She had been kind of prickly.

Aunt Emma put her arm around Lottie and squeezed gently. "Next time you see him, why don't you try acting friendly? I'll bet he'll be friendly right back." She smiled. "If he's not, then you come tell me and we'll figure out what to do about it."

Lottie nodded into her aunt's shoulder. She would try.

That Sunday, Lottie greeted Bill with a friendly "Hi" on her way to the front seat. His look of pleased surprise sent a shiver of guilt down her spine. Maybe she had been part of the problem.

"Uh, Lottie?" he called.

She turned. "Yes?"

"Would you mind if I sat in front today?"

Lottie looked at Helen, who nodded encouragement.

"That'd be fine."

In the back seat, Helen reached for her hand. "I've missed you," she whispered.

Lottie smiled back. "Me too."

Five

Bill and Helen were married the following June. Lottie, feeling much older than ten in her first pair of heels, stood up as a bridesmaid. Lottie and Bill had long since formed a truce based on their love of Helen and their agreement to disagree about baseball.

Helen was radiant in a dress of sky blue, white gloves, and a straw hat with a little veil over her eyes. Bill looked handsome in his best wool suit. Reverend Walker beamed his approval as his favorite young ball player married the prettiest girl in Westmont.

The Aunts held a reception in the church basement, with cake and punch and egg salad sandwiches. The room was packed with guests, but that didn't keep the youngest cousins from tearing around under everyone's feet. They endangered more than one full cup of punch.

Bill's parents sat in a corner looking uncomfortable. According to Helen, they weren't happy about their son marrying a farmer's daughter. They'd expected him to go into the family business after he graduated, and marry a girl from their social circle. Bill's refusal to look at things from their point of view had caused a rift in the family.

Mr. and Mrs. Turner held Helen responsible for the fact that Bill had joined the navy. Though he'd told them he'd rather join the navy than be drafted into the army, his parents believed he'd done it to provide for his wife. Fear of the draft was a silly way to make a career decision. President Roosevelt wasn't going to let the United States get involved in the war against Germany.

After the party, Lottie kicked off her new shoes, which had begun to pinch, and began stacking plates. She felt absurdly happy, giddy almost, so when Harvey yelled, "Hey Lottie, think fast," and threw a gob of frosting, she didn't even holler. She didn't duck, either. The sticky white ball hit her on the chin, and so the frosting fight began.

On the drive home, after a vigorous face-scrubbing from Aunt Cora, Lottie curled up on the seat beside Pop. "You know what?"

Pop glanced at his tired daughter. "What?"

"It's confusing being ten. One minute I'm wearing high heels, the next I'm covered in frosting."

Pop chuckled. "That's about right."

After the wedding, Lottie's days fell into a pattern. She kept house in the morning, practiced in the afternoon, and played for the Sunday service. She deposited half her pay into a savings account at Uncle Otto's bank, and handed the rest over to Pop.

Pop turned her loose on Saturday afternoons, telling her, "No chores and no piano. Do anything else you want."

Pop had found an old Schwinn bicycle at the county dump and fixed it up so she could ride into town by herself. One afternoon she rode to the five-and-dime with two pennies to spend on candy. She wanted licorice drops, but they cost a nickel, so she settled for a bright red cinnamon stick. As she left the store, a commotion at the filling station caught her attention. A big, shiny Packard, steam pouring from its hood, was parked in front of the pump. Next to it stood a well-dressed stranger, waving his arms and talking to Uncle Otto. Lottie walked her bike across the road so she could hear better.

"It's not the first time it's done this," the man said as she approached. "I'm always getting stuck in one backwater or another — I mean no offense," he added.

Uncle Otto nodded graciously.

"Worst decision I ever made, buying a Packard," the man continued. "I always drove Hudsons before this."

"I'm a Ford man myself, and you've convinced me to stay that way."

Uncle Otto stuck out his hand. "Otto Hoffman."

"Matthew Forbes." The man shook Uncle Otto's hand. "I've been in Peoria on business, and I'm headed home to Des Moines. I was hoping to get there tonight."

"I don't think you'll make it." Mike, the town mechanic, ambled toward the two men, wiping his hands on a rag. "I have to go to Collison for the part."

"How far is that?" Mr. Forbes asked.

"'Bout fifteen miles. I'll have to call my brother to take care of the station while I'm gone." Mike stared off into space. "Yup. It'll be tomorrow before I can fix it."

"What am I supposed to do until then?" Mr. Forbes asked.

Mike shrugged. "Dunno."

"There's room at our house," Uncle Otto said. "My wife's already expecting company for dinner. One more won't matter a bit."

Mr. Forbes looked him over critically. Even in his Saturday overalls, Uncle Otto didn't look like a farmer. It wasn't only his lack of a tan or the softness of his hands. He carried himself with a different kind of authority.

"Thanks very much," Mr. Forbes said after a moment. "I'd be in your debt."

Uncle Otto handed a nickel to Lottie. "Ride over and tell your aunt to set another place. We've got a visitor."

Lottie ran for her bike, pausing just long enough to spend the nickel on licorice drops.

Aunt Cora put all the leaves in the dining room table that night. Pop and Lottie were already invited, along with Helen and Bill and Aunt Eva. Mr. Schultz, Mr. Forbes, and the three Hoffman kids rounded out the company.

Aunt Cora plied their guest with fried chicken and lemonade, and asked questions about his family. Under her care Mr. Forbes unbent, and told them about his department store in Des Moines and his young wife Florence, of whom he was very proud.

"She's the finest harpist in the whole state of Iowa," he said. "Talent like hers comes along once in a generation. Why, she's been invited to play with the Greater Des Moines Symphony Orchestra tonight, and I'm missing it because of that blasted car!"

Mr. Schultz raised his head and looked thoughtfully at Mr. Forbes.

"My wife is very civic-minded," the loving husband continued. "Every year she organizes a talent show to benefit the Dorothy Polk Children's Home. The grand prize is $100 and a guest appearance on WHO radio's *Barn Dance Frolic*."

Mr. Forbes had the attention of all the adults at the table, which Lottie noticed when she asked for more chicken. Nobody seemed to hear her, not even Aunt Cora, who was staring at her father in consternation.

Helen said, "Ooh, the *Barn Dance Frolic*? We listen to that every Saturday night. Are you looking for country acts?"

Lottie leaned across the table and snagged a chicken leg off the platter. Nobody noticed.

"Not necessarily." Mr. Forbes took a drink of water. "The show's producer is one of my best customers. He's going to showcase our winner no matter what they do."

Encouraged by Lottie's success, Harvey stood up and grabbed a piece of chicken for himself, prompting his mother to slap his hand. He sent Lottie an injured look.

"What are the rules for this talent show?" Mr. Schultz asked.

"Well sir, with such a big prize on the line, it's pretty serious business. No singing dogs or great-aunties reciting their own poetry. The acts have to audition to get a place on the program so the evening will be worth the price of the ticket."

Mr. Schultz's gaze rested on Lottie. "Is there an age limit?"

"No." The stranger looked puzzled. "They can be as old as they want, I guess."

"What about on the young side?" Uncle Otto asked.

"Oh! Children are a real draw. Florence says if you put a child act in a charity show, you're guaranteed to sell tickets to the child's entire family. Kids are welcome. They just have to have talent."

The Hoffman men digested this information.

After dinner, Pop poked his head around the kitchen door. "Cora? You mind if I borrow Lottie for a few minutes?"

Aunt Cora gave a reluctant nod. "Go ahead, honey," she said to Lottie. "Just don't let 'em bully you."

Most summer evenings, the men gathered on the front porch to catch the breeze, but that night they sat in the front room with the windows open wide. "Play us a tune," Uncle Otto said, so Lottie sat down at the piano.

"What do you want me to play?" she asked, looking around.

Mr. Schultz said, "Begin with *Moonlight Sonata*."

Lottie applied herself to the ebb and flow of the Beethoven classic, making the most of its deceptive simplicity. As the last chord faded, the old man demanded a Mozart sonata full of showy runs and trills. Pop then requested his favorite, "The Battle Hymn of the Republic," Bill wanted Gershwin's "S'Wonderful", and so it went.

By the time Aunt Cora had put Anne to bed and joined the company in the parlor, Mr. Forbes was slumped in his chair, mouth slightly agape, staring at Lottie. His was the look of a man pondering the now-familiar question: How could so much music pour out of such a tiny girl?

Aunt Cora took one disgusted look around the room and said, "Lottie honey, go play outside for a while."

Lottie left the house with a bang of the front screen door, and found several neighbors lounging on the front porch. A few of them applauded softly before drifting off into the night. She sat down on the wide front steps, chin in hands, and strained to hear what was being said through the open windows.

"It's not much, Cora," Mr. Schultz said. "Just a charity talent show with a small audience."

"We're expecting two thousand," Mr. Forbes said.

"What's two thousand people?" Mr. Schultz continued. "Nothing, once she starts playing. When that child plays, the world goes away. You've seen it yourself, Cora. You can call her all day and never get her attention if she's in the middle of practicing."

"I'm not thinking about stage fright. It's the bigness of the thing that frightens me," Aunt Cora said. "Why should we go and make her life extraordinary? Lottie's happy here, in a good little place, doing regular things. If she entered and lost, it'd be hard. But if she entered and won, then what? That's what worries me."

"Well, I can't promise she'd win," Mr. Forbes said, though nobody seemed to hear him.

"With a gift like Lottie's, life is bound to be extraordinary," Uncle Otto said. "Seems to me the child ought to have her chance."

"I think it's exciting! If she needs a chaperone, I'll be free next month." Helen's voice quivered. Bill was scheduled to start boot camp in August.

"That's it!" Mr. Schultz said. "Helen can be Lottie's chaperone. I'll manage the details, and go along as her representative."

Aunt Cora sounded irritated. "You'd like that, wouldn't you? To promote her as some sort of child prodigy. Well, I won't have her exploited just so you can have your shot at fame."

Mr. Forbes raised his voice. "Folks, this is just a charity concert. I hope your little girl will enter, and we'll take good care of her if she does, but it's nothing to get upset about. I love Des Moines, but it ain't New York City."

"If Lottie wants to go, she should go." Pop spoke for the first time that evening. "Sometimes you forget she has a father, Cora. She had a mother, too, God rest her soul. Every time she makes music pour out of that piano, I think of my wife, who sang like a lark. I am not a musical man, but I'm proud of Lottie, and I'd be pleased to let her perform in your show, sir."

Lottie sat in the warm July darkness, slapping mosquitoes and listening with all her might. Uncle Otto thought she had a gift. Aunt Cora seemed to believe she was too talented for her own good. Mr. Schultz wanted her to go to Des Moines and perform in front of two thousand people, and Helen wanted to go with her. Best of all, Pop was proud of her.

She'd have walked through fire just to keep him proud. If he thought she should go, she'd go. Besides, she'd never been farther than Collison. A week in Des Moines sounded as exotic as a cruise down the Nile.

Six

*I*t came! It came!"

Lottie raced up the lane, waving a letter at Pop, who stood on the front porch. "Open it," she panted when she reached the front porch.

Pop slit the envelope open with his pocket knife and pulled out three train tickets, along with a sheet of stationery. "It's from Mrs. Forbes. You're invited to try out for the talent show. You're to bring two guests — that'll be Helen and Schultz — and she wants you to stay with them." He looked at Lottie. "Sounds like she's got it all fixed up."

"Ooh, I can't wait!" Lottie threw her arms around Pop, who swung her off her feet, laughing.

When he set her down, he crouched to her eye level, his expression serious. "Lottie, do you want to be a pianist when you grow up?"

Lottie stared back, feeling the gravity of the moment. She wrinkled her brow. "I'm happiest when I play, Pop. I'd like to try."

"All right, I'm behind you all the way." Pop gave her the letter and started for the barn. "Take that inside. I'll see you at dinner time."

○

Mr. Schultz chose two showy classical pieces for the contest, neither of which Lottie had played before. She put in long hours to learn them, wondering all the while how Mendelssohn might sound on the *Barn Dance Frolic*. Sometimes, to refresh her mind, she switched to "Flight

53

of the Bumblebee," which never failed to irritate her teacher.

"Do you want to win this thing or not?" he'd say. "Get back to work or I'll quit, and then where will you be, eh?"

It was an empty threat, and they both knew it.

The train pulled into downtown Des Moines at 11:30 the night before auditions. Lottie had been asleep for an hour. Helen woke her, guided her off the train and pushed her gently into Mr. Forbes' waiting car, where she drifted off again. She had a fuzzy impression of being greeted by a sweet-smelling blonde lady, and of a soft bed in a breezy sleeping porch.

The next morning Lottie jumped out of bed and put on her best dress, a navy blue seersucker with white rickrack trim. She managed the back zip with difficulty, since the dress was tight through the shoulders.

She followed the smell of bacon and eggs downstairs to the dining room, where Helen sat eating breakfast with their hostess. Mrs. Forbes, a pale, slender woman in a beautifully tailored suit, blended perfectly with the elegant décor. She looked up from a porcelain coffee cup as Lottie entered the room. "Oh, here's our guest of honor," she said in a cultured voice. "Did you sleep well?"

"Yes, ma'am." Lottie noticed her own country accent.

"Have some breakfast, sleepyhead." Helen passed the eggs. She wore a red and white striped cotton dress that had seen better days, but with her abundant brown hair and glowing complexion, she was still a pretty sight.

"We've been discussing the contest," Mrs. Forbes said with a smile. "Auditions start at eight o'clock this morning and will continue all day. Yours is scheduled for 12:15. The judges will meet tonight to choose the finalists, and I will stay to find out if you're chosen. It's a selective process. I can't guarantee anything. I hope you understand that."

"Yes, of course we do," Mr. Schultz answered from the doorway. "Good morning, madam." He bowed over Mrs. Forbes' hand.

His courtly gesture made Lottie want to giggle, but Mrs. Forbes seemed to like it. She invited him to sit down and rang for more bacon. "What music will Charlotte be playing today?"

Lottie dropped her fork. "Who's Char —"

She was drowned out by Mr. Schultz. "Charlotte will play selections from *Songs without Words*, by Felix Mendelssohn." He aimed a warning glance at Lottie.

Mrs. Forbes looked impressed. "I look forward to hearing her play. I will be assisting the judges today, so I get to hear every act." She turned to Lottie. "I'm sure you have a costume. You may leave it with Mrs. Higgins to be pressed."

Lottie, indignant at being called Charlotte, was diverted. A costume? She glanced at her best dress, which she planned to wear throughout the visit. It seemed a little shabby now. She looked across the table for reassurance, only to find her dismay mirrored in Helen's eyes.

"We planned to buy a costume once we reached Des Moines," Mr. Schultz said. "There was nothing suitable in our area, you understand."

Mrs. Forbes nodded. "In that case, have our driver drop you off at Forbes Department Store after Charlotte's audition. I'm sure you can obtain something suitable there."

Helen looked more alarmed than ever. On the way to the audition, she took Mr. Schultz to task. "We don't have money for a costume, and you know it."

He gazed back, unperturbed. "Charge it. You and Lottie can pay for it out of your earnings."

"Charge it?" Helen drew herself up straight. "We've never charged anything in our lives, and we aren't going to start now."

"I have money," Lottie said.

They turned to stare at her.

She held up her purse. "I brought ten dollars out of my church pay. That should be enough to buy a dress, shouldn't it?"

"Lottie, you've saved the day!" Helen gave her a quick hug. Turning to Mr. Schultz she said, "We won't need to charge it."

He looked faintly amused. "So I see."

"Why did Mrs. Forbes call me Charlotte?" Lottie asked. "My name is Lottie."

"Yes, but your full name is Charlotte," Mr. Schultz replied, "so what does it matter?"

Helen shook her head. "Mother named her Lottie. It isn't short for anything. Isn't plain 'Lottie' good enough?"

Mr. Schultz folded his hands across his stomach. "Mrs. Forbes believes your name is Charlotte. It would never do to put our hostess in the wrong, now would it?"

Helen looked doubtful, but Lottie nodded. She didn't want to make trouble.

"Here we are, folks." The driver looked over his shoulder. "You'd better jump out quick. I'm backin' up traffic."

Once inside, Lottie followed Helen into a crowded waiting room. The piano was in use, so Lottie and Helen sat on wooden chairs and looked around. In one corner, a stately woman in a chiffon gown warmed up her voice with trills and arpeggios. Next to her, a mother coached her young son and daughter to "e-NUN-ci-ate" so they could be heard. "Judging from his pantaloons and her long dress," Helen whispered, "they're going to do Shakespeare."

They couldn't hear much of the Shakespeare act because of the dancers across the room. There were eight in all, the men wearing vests and dungarees, the women in short cotton dresses with multiple petticoats. They practiced square dance steps while a ninth man fiddled. Lottie thought this act would fit in best on the *Barn Dance Frolic*, and wondered again how her classical selection would be received.

Act after act was called to audition. For every contestant who left, another arrived to wait their turn. Finally, the door opened and a voice called, "Charlotte Brown?"

Lottie looked around expectantly, trying to guess which contestant would answer.

Helen nudged her. "I think she means you."

Lottie and Helen stood up. "It's Braun," Helen said when she reached the door.

The messenger waved a piece of paper in the air. "Says 'Brown' right here. Which one of you is Charlotte?"

"That's me, I guess," Lottie said.

The woman pointed at Helen. "You'll have to wait in the audience."

When Helen disappeared through the auditorium doors, Lottie felt abandoned. "Come along," the messenger said, and ushered her down a long hallway.

Backstage, a woman in a mustard-colored dress with black piping marked Lottie's name off a list and pointed her to the stage. She walked to the center, squinting against the bright footlights.

A voice came out of the darkened audience. "What's your name, little girl?"

She drew herself up to her full height. "I'm, um, Charlotte Brown."

"And what is your talent?"

"I play the piano."

"I see," the voice said. "It says here you intend to play us some Mendelssohn."

"Yes, ma'am."

"Very well. Proceed."

Lottie sat down at the biggest piano she had ever laid eyes on, adjusted the bench to reach the pedals, positioned her hands and froze.

She could not remember her first note.

"*Songs without Words,*" she told herself firmly.

Her mind remained blank.

"Mendelssohn," she thought desperately.

Still nothing.

Lottie dropped her hands in her lap and looked around a little wildly. She could not see Helen or Mr. Schultz beyond the footlights. She couldn't see the judges, who she assumed were sitting in the front row.

"Little girl?" someone called.

She looked over her shoulder, and caught a glimpse of the yellow and black skirt backstage.

The voice tried again. "Perhaps you should —"

Lottie turned back to the piano, squared her body with the keyboard, and began.

"Flight of the Bumblebee" poured from her fingers, the fastest she'd ever played it. She skipped from note to note just like they did on the *Green Hornet*, finished with a flourish and, acting on instinct, moved directly into "The Battle Hymn of the Republic." When its militant strains ended, she stood up and bowed to the audience.

There was a smattering of applause. A voice said, "That will be all, thank you."

Lottie walked offstage on rubbery legs.

In the lobby, Mr. Schultz refused to speak. He let his furious eyes and quivering mustache do all the talking. Helen put her arm around her shaking sister, and led her to the waiting car.

Lottie slumped against the leather seat, overwhelmed by the seriousness of her mistake. "I'm sorry I played the wrong thing, Mr. Schutz." Her voice quivered.

The old man didn't look at her.

"I promise I'll play the right pieces if they choose me."

Mr. Schultz pinned her with his glare. "If by some miracle they choose you, you will play the same thing you played at the audition. You have no other choice."

Lottie's eyes filled with tears. "I'm sorry."

The driver dropped Lottie and Helen off at Forbes' Department Store. They stood on the sidewalk, gazing up at the limestone façade. As soon as the car drove away with Mr. Schultz inside, Helen reached over and hugged her little sister. "You were brilliant, kiddo. The whole audience was talking about you."

"But Mr. Schultz —"

"Aw, don't let that old wet blanket upset you. He's mad because you did better without taking his advice."

Helen led the way to the children's department, where she asked to see party dresses in Lottie's size.

The sales clerk, a thin, gray-haired woman with a chain on her horn-rimmed glasses, looked the girls over. "I don't think we have anything suitable," she said in a pinched voice. "Perhaps you should try Whelan's on Ninth Street. They have good discount racks in the back."

Helen's cheeks reddened. Standing tall, she copied the woman's sneer. "Mrs. Florence Forbes advised us to shop here at breakfast this morning, but if you insist...." She turned on her heel, tugging Lottie after her.

"Perhaps we do have something after all," the woman said hastily. "Follow me." She took Lottie's measurements and seated them on an upholstered bench while she went in search of dresses.

"We don't belong here," Lottie whispered as soon as she was gone. "Can we afford anything they have?"

Helen's eyes flickered. "I'm not sure." She straightened her shoulders. "But we're not leaving till we know for sure."

The sales clerk returned with five plain everyday dresses.

Helen sniffed. "This won't do at all. My sister is playing in a concert tomorrow, and she needs a fancy dress to wear on stage."

The woman raised her plucked eyebrows. "Party dresses cost a great deal more, I'm afraid."

Helen's voice rose. "Why don't you worry about finding a dress to suit us, and let us worry about the money?"

The clerk bristled. "Well, I never!"

Another sales girl approached. "What seems to be the problem here?" She did a double take as she noticed Lottie. "Say, aren't you the little piano player from the talent show auditions?"

Lottie smiled. "Yes, and you're one of the barn dancers."

"I sure am. My fiancé is our fiddler. Gee, you're really good. When you played, 'Mine Eyes Have Seen the Glory,' I just about stood up and saluted the flag." The clerk turned to her coworker. "D'you mind if I wait on these ladies, Gladys?"

"Not at all." The other woman gave a disdainful sniff and glided away.

"I guess you're here for a dress to wear tomorrow night. Have a seat, and I'll be right back. I'm Marie, by the way." The friendly clerk bustled away.

Fifteen dresses later, Lottie felt like a princess. She stood in the dressing room surrounded by clouds of pink, blue, and lavender, enjoying the rare luxury of having a choice of clothing. With Marie's help, she selected a buttercup yellow frock with puffed sleeves and a full skirt. The smocked bodice and dark blue grosgrain sash gave it just the right touch of elegance for a girl her age.

"You don't want to look too grown-up when you compete," Marie advised. "Your age is your advantage." Turning to Helen she added, "This one has a lot of seam allowance and a big hem. It should last a while."

"I can move my arms in it, too," Lottie said, swinging them back and forth.

Marie wrapped the dress in tissue paper and placed it in a box while Lottie fished six dollars out of her purse. How many hymns had she played to earn six dollars? She pushed the thought aside when Marie placed the dress box in her hands.

"Play your heart out, honey," Marie said in farewell. "You're a shoo-in to win."

"But what about your fiancé?" Lottie asked. "Doesn't he want to win?"

Marie winked. "Oh, don't worry about him. I'm all the prize he needs."

Seven

When Lottie and Helen returned from shopping, Mr. Schultz greeted them smoothly, with no reference to Lottie's mistake, and politely admired her new dress.

Lottie tried once more to apologize. "I really am sorry about the audition, Mr. Schultz. I couldn't remember a note of what I was supposed to play, and I had to do something."

Mr. Schultz patted her shoulder. "Never mind," he said gruffly. "What's done is done."

Cold comfort, but at least he hadn't yelled at her.

Mrs. Forbes came home after the last audition. "I saw some very talented people today," she told them, "and Lottie, you were one. Congratulations! You're going to be in the concert."

"Yahoo!" Helen shouted. "You did it, kiddo."

Lottie gave a dazed smile. "I get to wear my dress after all." She blushed when the grown-ups laughed.

Sleep didn't come easily that night. Lottie gazed into the darkness, replaying her memory lapse over and over again. What if it happened during the concert? She was pretty sure she wouldn't win, because she wasn't playing the right music. But she didn't want to disgrace herself by freezing up again.

After tossing and turning for what seemed like half the night, Lottie got up and went to the window. She looked out at the moonlit garden and prayed, "Dear Lord, don't let me disappoint Pop. Just don't let me disappoint him."

The Shrine Auditorium was packed with spectators for the Dorothy Polk Children's Home Benefit Talent Show. On stage, Marie's square dance group twirled and swayed to the tune of her fiancé's fiddle. Lottie watched from the wings, silently cheering for her new friend. If she couldn't win, she hoped Marie would.

When the dancers left the stage, a curtain opened to reveal the grand piano. Two helpers pushed it to the center, and Lottie walked out to polite applause. She fluffed out her skirt as she sat down, enjoying its ruffled fullness, and took a few deep, steady breaths. Somebody in the audience coughed.

"Flight of the Bumblebee" sprang to life under her hands. Her fingers automatically found the notes they'd played so often. She felt the heat of the spotlights, and the sweat trickling down her dress in back. She sensed 4000 eyes staring at her from the audience, and wondered where Helen was.

When she moved on to the "Battle Hymn of the Republic," she pictured Pop's face. He'd be in his chair by the stove right now, reading the paper and smoking his pipe. She played for him, wishing there were some way he could hear her.

She ended on a grand chord, which was nearly drowned out by applause. She curtseyed, fanning out her skirt with care.

Marie's group surrounded her when she left the stage, slapping her on the back and predicting she'd win. She didn't bother to correct them. Instead she held Marie's hand and told them she thought they were the best, until the stage manager sternly shushed them all so the next performer could begin.

After intermission, Lottie sat with Helen and Mr. Schultz. She wanted to watch all the other acts and judge for herself who should win, but after two or three performances she fell asleep on Helen's shoulder.

Helen shook her gently. "They're announcing the winners now," she whispered loudly. "Come on, Lottie. Wake up."

Lottie struggled to open her eyes as the announcer gave third prize to the opera singer. Lottie clapped politely. She hadn't cared for the lady very much.

The announcer placed a medal on a ribbon around the opera singer's neck, and returned to the microphone. "Second prize ..." He drew out his words to create suspense, "goes to ..." He unfolded the piece of paper in his hand. "Frank Johnson and his square dance guys and gals!"

Lottie clapped and cheered for Marie's group. Second place was better than nothing, though they should have won.

Lottie relaxed in her chair. She was less interested in the first prize winner now that Marie's group was out of the running.

"Ladies and gentlemen, I think you'll all agree that our first place winner is just a little bit talented. Heh, heh." The announcer paused to enjoy his joke. "But seriously folks, it's only fitting that this year's winner of the Dorothy Polk Children's Home Benefit Talent Show is a child. This year, first place goes to ..." Helen clutched Lottie's hand in excitement. "Charlotte Brown."

Helen burst into applause. Lottie stared at the announcer, her eyes round with amazement. Mr. Schultz reached over and prodded her to stand.

On stage, she received her medal and an envelope from Mrs. Forbes. She shook hands politely, and squinted at the audience, feeling shy.

She wanted to go home.

"You can't go home until after the radio show, silly," Helen said the next morning, eyeing Lottie's packed suitcase. "You're going on the *Barn Dance Frolic* tonight, remember?"

Lottie was crestfallen. She'd been up for an hour, neatly folding her clothes and tidying up the sleeping porch so they could catch an early train. "Do I have to go?"

Helen laughed. "Yes, you do. How could you forget about the radio show? That's the most exciting part of your prize."

Lottie sat on the bed with a thud. "I'm ready to go home."

Helen looked at her sister. "You made a bargain, Lottie. When you entered this contest, you agreed to go on the radio if you won. You have to keep up your side of the deal."

"But I want to see Pop."

"Pop would say the same thing. We Brauns keep our word. He'd be pretty disappointed if you ran away."

Lottie raised her stubborn chin. "I'm not running away. I'm just tired of all those people."

Helen thinned her mouth into a straight line. "Tired or not, you're staying."

They stared each other down until Lottie dropped her eyes. "What if I mess up?"

Helen flew across the room to hug her sister. "Oh, honey, you'll be fine. Now let's go call Pop and tell him the news."

At the auditorium, Mrs. Forbes introduced Lottie to the stage manager, a man named Al. "Nice to meet ya, Miss Charlotte Brown," Al said. "Let's go see what's what."

Lottie waved at Helen and allowed Al to lead her backstage. He took her on a tour, explained how she would know when it was time to walk on, and adjusted a microphone to her height.

"You'll sit at the piano, see, and Bob, he's the announcer, will ask you a few questions. Easy stuff, like 'where'd you learn to play the piano, little lady?' Stuff like that. Keep your answer short and say it right into the mic." He put his mouth up to the microphone to demonstrate, and glanced at Lottie, who nodded. She liked his enthusiasm. "Then Bob will say something like, 'take it away, Charlotte,' and you'll go ahead and play. When the audience claps after your second piece, you bow and leave the stage. Got it, Charlotte Brown?"

"Sure. Um, Al?"

"Yeah?" He spoke over his shoulder as he led her offstage.

"Could you stop calling me Charlotte Brown? Because that's not my name."

"Not your name?" Al stopped and looked at her. "Well, what's your name, then?" he asked.

"Lottie Braun." It felt good to get that out in the open. "I'm Lottie, not Charlotte."

"Ah." Al squatted down to Lottie's eye level. "Is your family German, kid?"

"Yes. Why?"

Al nodded. "Look here, Lottie Braun. It's best to have a regular

American name if you're going into show business. You know, Smith or Jones or something like that. If you want my advice, and I know a thing or two, keep the 'Lottie Braun' for home and the 'Charlotte Brown' for the stage."

Lottie tilted her head. "Like a house dress and a church dress?"

Al gave a bark of laughter. "Yeah, like that. Good luck tonight, Charlotte." He winked at her and hurried away.

Lottie sat on a wooden folding chair, chin in hand. Something was fishy about Al's advice. He was right about people in show business. All the ladies in the movies had names like Davis or Garland, and the men were called Gable or Barrymore.

Then it dawned on her. "I'm not in show business," she said.

A nearby stage hand looked at her and laughed. "You could have fooled me."

Eight

For a week, Lottie couldn't go anywhere in Westmont without being congratulated on her performance. People asked all kinds of questions about Des Moines and the talent contest, but most of all they wanted to know about the *Iowa Barn Dance Frolic*.

Lottie answered as best she could. Yes, the Blueridge Mountain Gals were as pretty and sweet in person as they sounded on the radio. No, she didn't get any autographs. She didn't think of it. Yes, she enjoyed being part of the Barn Dance players.

Helen, who'd moved home while Bill was in boot camp, answered her own set of questions. Yes, Lottie sounded wonderful. Nobody else could hold a candle to her. No, of course Lottie wasn't ashamed of her name. Charlotte Brown was a stage name. No, she wasn't going into show business.

Pop enjoyed the hubbub secondhand. Word had spread about the bike he'd overhauled for Lottie, and people had begun asking him to repair all kinds of small vehicles. Glad of the extra income, he spent his spare time in the tool shed, working by the light of a 30-watt bulb.

After a while the uproar subsided. Lottie spent the remaining summer days outside as much as possible, doing chores or riding her bike around town. She stopped in regularly at Aunt Cora's, but didn't have any piano lessons. At Aunt Cora's urging, Mr. Schultz had given her a few weeks off.

She spent very little time at home with Helen. Lottie could not stand to watch her sister travel to and from the mailbox several times before noon.

"Oh, what am I doing?" she exclaimed to Lottie one day, after her third trip down the lane. "Bill will write when he gets time. Meanwhile, there must be something I can do to keep from going crazy."

Helen cleaned the farmhouse from top to bottom, beat the rugs and aired all the bed linens. She talked Aunt Emma into giving up her secret tomato juice recipe, and turned the kitchen into a red-splattered canning factory. She even spent a day with Aunt Eloise, learning her secret recipe for dill pickles.

Pop and Lottie learned to run for cover every time Helen said, "Now, what should we do today?"

One night after supper, Lottie and Helen were picking squash when they heard the telephone ring through the kitchen window. Pop hurried into the house to pick it up.

"I wonder what that's about," Helen said. Local people didn't call each other much, because Miss Aggie at the switchboard was an awful gossip.

"Maybe Cousin Marlene had her baby," Lottie suggested. "Isn't it time?"

"Any day now."

When they brought the squash inside they found Pop at the kitchen table. "What's wrong?" Helen asked.

"That was a man from WHO," he said slowly. "WGN in Chicago wants Lottie to play with its studio orchestra one day next month."

Helen's eyes lit up. "What did you tell him?"

"I said I'd talk it over with the family." He looked at Lottie. "Do you want to be on the radio again?"

Lottie hesitated. She wouldn't really mind, but she didn't want to leave Pop again. "Can you come with me?"

He shook his head regretfully. "September is harvest time, honey. I can't leave the farm. I'll bet you could talk Helen into going along."

Lottie turned to her sister, who practically danced with excitement. She couldn't help but smile. "All right. Let's go."

"Hooray!" Helen grabbed Lottie's hands and swung her in a mad dash around the kitchen. "We're going to Chicago!"

"Not so fast," Pop said mildly. "I'm not sending my girls to the city alone. You need someone older with you. Mr. Schultz would be a good choice, since he knows how to get around in a big city."

The girls looked at each other. "Can someone else go?" Helen asked.

Pop looked at Helen. "Is there some reason I shouldn't ask him?"

"Not that I know of. I have an odd feeling about it, that's all."

Pop turned to Lottie. "Well? Do you have a funny feeling, too?"

Lottie shrugged. "He's okay. He was awful nice to us on the way home from Des Moines."

Pop stood up. "That's settled, then. I'll talk with him on Saturday."

Saturday morning Pop drove into town while Lottie and Helen canned tomatoes.

Helen was full of plans for their trip. "I'll write to Bill's parents and see if we can stay with them. That'll save money, plus I can get to know them better. And we'll go to the lake shore, and see all the tall buildings. Bill says it's spectacular."

"Mm-hmm." Lottie's mind was elsewhere. Would she be able to play the music they sent? Mr. Schultz would help, but what if he didn't know the music, either?

"Old Schultz is chomping at the bit to take you girls to Chicago," Pop said at dinner. "He rubbed his hands together and laughed when I asked him."

Helen looked up curiously. "I've never even seen him smile before. Have you, Lottie?"

"Once or twice, maybe," Lottie said.

Pop buttered a slice of bread. "Perhaps the city air will cheer him up. Cora's not too happy he's going, though."

Lottie looked up. "Will she miss him?"

Pop laughed. "I think she's worried he'll misbehave. Anyhow, Schultz offered to act as your agent, make sure you're paid for your performance, that sort of thing. I think it's a good idea, since he was once a performer."

Lottie didn't care about being paid. She already had a $100 in the bank.

Helen wrote to her in-laws and to Bill, and heard back from Bill a week later. "He says of course his parents will put us up. He's going to call and make sure they know we're coming," she said.

The following Thursday afternoon, Pop drove Helen, Lottie, and Mr. Schultz through pouring rain to the Collison train station. He hugged and kissed the girls, but didn't stay to wave them off. They couldn't have seen him anyway, through the droplets on the window.

Hours later, they stood in the Winnetka train station, wondering where Bill's parents were. Lottie's stomach growled. She wished they had bought dinner on the train.

"They're expecting us?" Mr. Schultz asked Helen for the fourth time.

"I already told you. I wrote and Bill called. They know we're coming."

"Don't bite my head off," he replied mildly. "They're your relatives. Maybe they aren't planning to meet us at the station."

Helen seized on this notion. "I'll bet they expect us to take a cab." She fished a piece of paper out of her handbag. "Here's the address. I wonder what cab fare will cost?"

The cab deposited them at the Turners' home ten minutes later.

"Oh my," Lottie gasped, as she took in the elegant brick house on its manicured lawn.

"Well, come on. Grab your bag." Helen sounded matter-of-fact. She marched up the flagstone walk through the sprinkling rain and rang the bell. A maid opened the door, looked them over, and asked them to wait in the hall.

Lottie sat on a low bench and looked around. The house wasn't any bigger than Aunt Cora's massive Victorian, but it was much smarter. She studied the sparkly chandelier that hung over the curved staircase, and tried to count its crystal drops.

Mrs. Turner glided through the door at the back of the hall, hands outstretched, a smile on her lips. "Helen, dear, we weren't expecting you." she said, wide-eyed.

Helen's smile drooped. "Didn't you get my letter? Or Bill's phone call?"

Mrs. Turner shook her head. "Was he supposed to tell us you were coming? That naughty boy must have forgotten. He never mentioned it at all."

Helen looked flustered. "You must think we're very rude, dropping in on you like this."

"Any other time would be fine." Mrs. Turner oozed graciousness. "But tonight we're having a little party. Just a few friends, you understand. Annie will have to help you put sheets on the guest beds, and get settled. She can find you some supper, too, if you haven't eaten. Annie?"

The maid bustled in from the stairwell and took charge. "Follow me," she said.

Mr. Schultz cleared his throat. "I will wait here until the beds are made."

Mrs. Turner reacted to his cultured voice, just as Mrs. Forbes had. "Of course. And you are?" She favored him with a fascinated smile.

Helen jumped in with introductions, adding, "He's Lottie's agent. She's going to play on the radio tomorrow."

Mrs. Turner raised her eyebrows. "She is? How enterprising. If you'll excuse me, I must get back to my guests." She glided back the way she'd come.

Annie led the girls upstairs and opened a linen cupboard. She handed neatly folded sheets to Lottie and Helen, and directed them to a bedroom at the end of the hall. "You can share that one while His Highness down there takes the one in the attic," she said, indicating Mr. Schultz with a jerk of her head.

"Thank you." Helen gave Annie her first genuine smile since they got off the train.

Annie smiled back. "You gals must be hungry. Take the back stairs to the kitchen when you get settled in. I'll get you something to eat." She stuck her thumb over her shoulder. "I guess you'd better bring Uncle What's-His-Name, too."

After the beds were made, the three unexpected guests found Annie dishing up steaming bowls of corn chowder in the kitchen. "Have a seat." She pointed to a small metal table. Helen and Lottie sat, but Mr. Schultz took his soup to the back porch.

"What's with him?" Annie asked. Helen opened her mouth to answer, but the hired girl charged on. "Are you really going to be on the radio?"

Lottie picked up her spoon. "Yes, ma'am, tomorrow night."

Annie grinned. "Well I'll be darned. She's a radio star and she still calls me ma'am. Which station?"

"WGN."

"No kidding? That's the big time." Annie sounded impressed. "Do you know how to get to the Wrigley Building? What time do you have to be there?"

While Annie and Helen hashed out the best route to the radio station, Lottie went over the music in her head. It hadn't been hard to learn, and she didn't have to play it from memory, so she felt pretty confident. She'd do everything in her power not to mess up while all Chicago tuned in by radio.

In a matter of hours, Helen and Annie were fast friends. She knew all about Annie's steady boyfriend, Frank, and her nosy mother, whom she visited on her days off. Annie in turn listened sympathetically to Helen's worries about Bill, their separation, and what life as a navy wife would bring.

The Turners' party was still going strong when Lottie went to bed.

The next morning at breakfast, Mr. and Mrs. Turner were friendlier. Mrs. Turner told stories about Bill's childhood, and Mr. Turner talked to Mr. Schultz about New York. They wanted to know about their visitors' plans for the day, and seemed impressed at the mention of WGN.

"Will you be staying with us tonight, dear?" Mrs. Turner asked Helen.

"No," Helen said. "Unfortunately, we have to take the train home tonight."

Lottie stared at her sister. This was not the plan. But the set of Helen's mouth and the hurt in her eyes kept Lottie quiet. She didn't mind going home.

"What a shame," Mrs. Turner murmured.

Annie showed them to the door and pulled an envelope out of her pocket for Helen. Helen glanced at it and nodded.

As they settled into the waiting taxi, the envelope slipped out of Helen's gloved fingers and landed face-up on the seat. It was the letter she'd mailed to Bill's parents, and it was open.

Nine

"I'm tired," Lottie said. They'd walked for blocks, dragging their luggage, and still hadn't reached the radio station.

Mr. Schultz leaned more heavily on his cane. "Blame your sister. She's the one who refused to leave her bags with her relatives."

"Yep, and I'd do it again." Helen squared her shoulders. "Stop complaining, you two. We're here."

She led the way through a revolving door into the lobby of Tribune Tower. "Excuse me," she said to a receptionist behind a large desk. "Can you direct us to the WGN offices?"

"Down that hall and to the left." The receptionist sounded like she was doing Helen a favor. "Tours don't start until eleven o'clock."

Helen's brows came together in a frown. "Oh, we aren't tourists." She strode toward the hallway, irritation evident in every line of her body.

Lottie had to trot to keep up. "You mean we don't get to take the elevator?"

Helen looked straight ahead. "Nope."

Mr. Schultz hurried along behind the girls. "I'll bet this building has an observation deck. After you rehearse, we'll go find it."

Lottie looked over her shoulder in surprise. Chicago seemed to bring out the best in her piano teacher, and the worst in her sister.

Helen swept through the radio station doors and up to the front desk. She made a striking picture, her dark eyes snapping and twin spots of pink high on her cheekbones. Lottie could tell she was spoiling for a fight.

"Charlotte Brown is here," Helen said in a fair imitation of Mrs.

Forbes' accent. "She is to play with the studio orchestra tonight."

"Of course." The lady behind the desk smiled warmly. "Please have a seat while I let Mr. Lasecki know. Can I get you anything? Coffee? Tea?"

Some of the stiffness left Helen's voice. "No thank you." She joined her companions, who had collapsed into the padded waiting room chairs. Mr. Schultz's eyes were closed, his hat tipped slightly forward. Lottie sat with her legs curled under her, the yellow dress spread out to avoid wrinkling.

A skinny young man in a baggy pinstripe suit slumped in a chair across from them. His brown hair was slicked into a pompadour, and a dove-gray fedora occupied the seat next to him. A rectangular case lay at his feet. Lottie gazed in fascination at his flowered tie. She'd never seen one so colorful. "You got an appointment?" he asked, a note of envy in his voice.

Helen primmed her mouth into a straight line and looked away.

Lottie glanced at her sister. Since when were they allowed to be rude to strangers? "Yes, we do," she said. "I'm going to play piano with the orchestra."

"Is that so? You're a pianist?" At Lottie's nod he pointed a thumb at his chest. "Johnny Columbus. Trumpeter extraordinaire."

Lottie giggled. "Is that your real name?"

Johnny Columbus looked around furtively. "Maybe. What's it to ya?"

This sent Lottie into a fit of giggles.

Helen glared at the stranger. "We are not interested in your business, real or otherwise," she said in a voice that froze Lottie mid-giggle.

Johnny Columbus was unabashed. "Sure you are, beautiful. Women always want to know my business."

Helen looked so outraged that Lottie feared for the trumpeter's safety.

The receptionist stuck her head around the door. "Mr. Lasecki will see you now, Miss Brown."

Lottie hopped off the chair. Helen and Mr. Schultz rose to their feet, also.

The receptionist looked apologetic. "I'm sorry, but only one of you may accompany Miss Brown."

Helen took a step forward. "I'll go. I'm her sister."

"Not so fast." Mr. Schultz stepped around her. "I'm Miss Brown's agent. It is my job to represent her at a meeting such as this."

"He's right, sister."

Helen rounded on Johnny Columbus, fists clenched. "How dare you? This is none of your …Oh," she cried in frustration, as Mr. Schultz followed Lottie through the door. "Now see what you did?"

Before it clicked shut, Lottie heard Johnny laugh. "I didn't do squat. You brought that on yourself."

The receptionist led them to a windowless office dominated by a large black desk. The plate on the door read "Andrei Lasecki, Director."

Behind the desk sat a small man with a fringe of gray hair and round wire-rim spectacles. A pair of outsized ears dominated his head. He invited them to sit down in an oddly formal accent.

"I would like to confirm the terms of Miss Brown's employment," Mr. Schultz said.

The little man's eyes twinkled. "Very well."

Nothing bored Lottie more than business talk. She looked around. Mr. Lasecki's shelves held stacks of music in no discernible order. Between the stacks were framed photographs of him posing with other musicians. Lottie thought one might be George Gershwin, whose picture she'd seen on a phonograph record.

"One-hundred fifty dollars. That's settled, then." Mr. Lasecki turned to Lottie. "Well, Miss Brown, I've been looking forward to this. Let us take a walk down the hall so you can play for me."

At the little man's insistence, Mr. Schultz returned to the waiting room while he and Lottie moved on to the orchestra studio. Lottie sat at the piano, full of nerves, and placed her music on the rack. She positioned her hands, and noticed that they shook slightly. Her mind went blank as she stumbled into the first measure.

Mr. Lasecki put up his hand. "No, no. There will be time enough for that. I want to hear the *Green Hornet* theme."

Lottie dropped her hands and gaped at the smiling gentleman. "It's called 'Flight of the Bumblebee.'"

"I know, I know." He chuckled. "Of course I know! But I have a son, eight years old. He loves the *Green Hornet*. We listen every week."

Lottie's tense face relaxed into a smile. "Are you in the fan club?"

He leaned in. "Not officially. We are a fan club of our own." He held up two fingers. "Very exclusive."

She laughed.

"Now, play the *Green Hornet* for me."

Lottie placed her hands on the keys. With a last glance at the little conductor, she dove into the waterfall of notes. Several minutes later she emerged to find Mr. Lasecki watching her intently. "How was that?" she asked.

"Very good," he said. "Someone has taught you good technique." He slid onto the bench next to her. "Now, let us look at tonight's selections."

For the next half-hour, Lottie received a master lesson from Andrei Lasecki. Musician to musician, he gave her new fingerings and hand positions, tinkered with her pedaling — "too much playing the organ," he said cheerfully — and generally tweaked her technique.

Lottie absorbed every word like rain on a dry corn field. Each bit of instruction brought her to a new level, superior to anything Mr. Schultz had ever coaxed out of her.

As the orchestra filtered in, Mr. Lasecki patted Lottie's shoulder. "You'll do."

She glowed with pride.

Two hours later, Mr. Lasecki set down his baton. "That will be all. We return at five-thirty." He nodded at Lottie. "You may go too, Miss Brown."

She found Helen and Mr. Schultz in the hall.

"We were upstairs in the gallery," Helen said. "When people started coming through the waiting room with their instruments, we asked if we could watch the rehearsal."

"Where'd Johnny Columbus go?" Lottie asked.

Helen shrugged. "Who cares?"

Mr. Schultz tapped his watch. "Ladies, it's lunch time. I saw a little diner across the street."

Helen raised her eyebrows. "You mean the one next to the bar? I think not. Annie told me about a Woolworth's lunch counter a few blocks down Michigan Avenue."

Helen led the way, with Mr. Schultz glowering at her back and Lottie bringing up the rear. Woolworth's proved easy to find, and Lottie was glad to choose from the familiar menu.

After lunch, they had two hours to kill. Mr. Schultz again suggested the observation deck.

"Oh, yes, please." Lottie bounced on her seat in excitement.

Helen hesitated. "It depends on how much it costs."

Mr. Schultz grunted. "For heaven's sake, she'll make $100 tonight."

Lottie glanced at him. Something didn't sound right about his an-swer, but she couldn't think what it was.

"A hundred dollars that we need to bring home to Pop," Helen said.

"It won't break him if we spend seventy-five cents to look at the skyline," he snapped. "How often will you get to Chicago in your life?"

Helen's eyes filled with sudden tears, which she dashed away with her fingertips. "You're right. Not often. Not to Winnetka, anyway. Let's go."

Lottie made for the door before Helen could change her mind.

○

"I wish I had my sweater," Helen said as they stepped from the ele-vator into the open air of the observation deck. Her carefully arranged hair whipped around her face. "Ooh, Lottie, look at the skyscrapers! I wonder how many there are?"

"Wow …Oh no!" As Lottie moved to follow Helen, the wind lifted her full skirt above her waist. Pushing it back into place was useless, so she bunched the excess cloth in her fists, held her arms stiff at her sides, and took tiny steps toward Helen. Strangers laughed sympathetically as she shuffled by.

Helen made a game of pointing out landmarks. "There's the Water Tower." She pointed to the north. "Grant Park must be down there some-where." She pointed southward. "And way over there is Union Station."

When her knowledge of Chicago ran thin, she glanced sidelong at her little sister and pointed to a red brick outline several blocks away. "That one with the big smokestacks is the Dragon Smog Company. They send smog all over the world, fifty cents a box, any color you want."

Lottie stared at her sister, who was trying not to laugh. "Smog comes in colors?"

"Yes," Helen said. "Gray and black. Red costs extra."

They exploded into giggles, holding onto each other for support, repeating, "red costs extra," as if it were the cleverest thing anyone had ever said. Helen laughed until tears rolled down her face, washing away all the tension of the past twenty-four hours.

"Hey, pipe down over there."

Lottie looked over Helen's shoulder and into the face of Johnny Columbus. "What are you doing here?" she asked.

"It's a free country. I paid my quarter."

Helen turned. "Oh. Hi." Her voice sounded almost friendly as she searched her pocketbook for a handkerchief.

Johnny grinned, showing a dimple in one cheek. "Hiya, sister." He looked at Lottie. "How'd rehearsal go?"

Lottie smiled. "It was great. Mr. Lasecki taught me so much. He made me sound twice as good as I was before."

"The great old man gave you a lesson, huh?" Johnny said. "You must be somethin' special."

"He can't be that old," Lottie said. "He has a little boy."

Johnny laughed. "I only know what I've heard, kid. I haven't actually met him. More's the pity."

Lottie looked around. "Where's your trumpet?"

"Over there." He jerked a thumb over his shoulder.

"Can you really play it?"

Johnny put a hand to his chest. "Cross my heart. Wanna hear?"

Lottie looked around. "You mean right now?"

"Why not?" Johnny took out his trumpet and launched into a languid rendition of "Summertime." His mellow tone brought the song to life.

A small crowd gathered, clapping politely when Johnny finished. As he started into "Blue Skies," several onlookers dropped pennies in his open trumpet case.

"Should we give him a penny?" Lottie whispered loudly.

"No need." Johnny scooped the pennies out of the case and shoved them in his pocket. "The show's free to my friends."

Helen stiffened. "I wouldn't say we're —"

"Relax, beautiful. I ain't talkin' about you. I meant Brown here." He nodded at Lottie. "We musicians have to stick together."

Lottie smiled and nodded back.

"Time to go," Mr. Schultz called.

"Come on, Lottie." Helen took her hand.

Lottie looked apologetically at the trumpeter. "Thanks for playing for us, Mr. Columbus."

"Yeah, sure, kid." He winked. "And it's 'Johnny' to you."

"Okay. Will you listen to me on the radio?"

"Nah, I gotta meet someone."

"Oh. Good-bye." She waved her free hand as Helen led her away.

Lottie performed well under Mr. Lasecki's direction. Years of practice came to her aid as she blended her piano part with the rest of the orchestra. When the program ended, Mr. Schultz and Helen came into the studio.

Helen caught her in a big hug. "You were wonderful, kiddo."

Lottie's eyes lit with elation. "I want to do that again."

Mr. Schultz chuckled. "Never fear. Someday you will."

Mr. Lasecki shook hands all around. "Charlotte is a remarkable musician. May I ask what you plan to do next?"

"We're going home, of course," Helen said.

Mr. Lasecki looked thoughtful. "There's somebody I think Charlotte should meet. He lives in New York City. Could you possibly go to New York? I will personally write and tell him about you."

"And who might this person be?" Mr. Schultz asked.

"Doctor Feodor Karofsky, the great piano instructor. He is known for developing young talent. There is an organization." He paused to think. "Now, what is the name? The MIA? The MIUSA?"

"The AOMI," Mr. Schultz said. "The American Organization of Music Instructors."

"That's it!" Andrei Lasecki turned to Mr. Schultz. "You know it?"

"I was a founding member."

"Ah. It is a small world, as they say," the conductor said. "Then you know about the showcase recital they hold every June. I believe Charlotte would benefit from participating as Dr. Karofsky's student. Now, where is my pen? I will write down his address."

"That won't be necessary," Mr. Schultz said smoothly. "I remember it well."

"That is good. Then you will escort Miss Brown to New York, if he agrees to see her?"

Mr. Schultz nodded stiffly. "I warn you not to mention me in your letter. We did not part on good terms."

Lasecki turned to Helen. "And what about you, Mrs. Turner? Will you accompany your sister to New York?"

Helen frowned. "No. I'm sure my father will not allow Lottie to go so far away. But thank you for your concern."

Mr. Schultz sent Helen a disgusted look. "I look forward to hearing from you," he said to the conductor.

Mr. Lasecki nodded graciously. "You may pick up Charlotte's pay envelope at the front desk. In cash, as you requested. One-hundred fi —"

"That will do nicely." Mr. Schultz interrupted. He swept the girls ahead of him to the front desk and swiftly collected Lottie's pay. "I'll hold onto this for safekeeping," he said. "We can't risk losing it to a pickpocket."

Helen glared at him suspiciously. "Just remember to give Pop the full $100."

He looked smug. "Of course."

Once out on the street, Helen rounded on the old man. "You've got no right to make plans like that for Lottie."

Mr. Schultz blinked. "You have no idea what you're talking about, young lady. A referral to Feodor Karofsky is the highest honor a young artist could receive. If Lottie studies under him, she will develop her skills to the fullest. And if she takes top honors in the showcase, her career will take off. Have you any idea what kind of mark she could make on the world?"

Helen set her stubborn jaw. "She doesn't belong in New York City."

"She belongs wherever she can grow."

"I'm hungry," Lottie said. "How far to the station?"

"I'd better flag down a taxi," Mr. Schultz said, and the subject of New York was dropped.

They had an hour to kill before they could board the Iowa line. Once they found seats in the waiting room, Helen went to find a phone booth and call Pop. While she was gone, Mr. Schultz turned to Lottie. "We're going to New York. By hook or by crook, I will get us there."

Lottie nodded. "And I'm going to play with an orchestra again, too?"

Mr. Schultz gave a satisfied smile. "You'll play Carnegie Hall before you're done."

Helen returned with a chocolate bar, which she broke into thirds. She passed out the pieces, saying, "Make it last. We won't have any more to eat until we get home."

When their train was announced, the three of them made their way to the boarding area, suitcases bumping against their legs. Lottie had one foot on the step when a commotion caught her attention. Two men stumbled down the platform, arms around each other's necks, singing "I've been Working on the Railroad" at the top of their lungs. They halted two cars away and slapped each other's backs with exaggerated affection.

"See you next week, then. I'll pick you up at the station."

"Sure enough. We're gonna set the world on fire."

One man meandered back down the platform, while the other disappeared inside the train.

Lottie tugged Helen's coat. "What's Johnny Columbus doing on this train?"

"Don't look," Helen said. "He's drunk."

Mr. Schultz snorted. "Lucky dog."

Ten

What did he say again?" Pop asked for the third time. It was Sunday, and the adults had convened a pow-wow over slices of Aunt Cora's apple pie.

Mr. Schultz clicked his tongue against his teeth in exasperation. "There is a teacher in New York City, named Feodor Karofsky. He is the best piano instructor in America. His former students fill concert halls across the country. Andrei Lasecki is going to write to Dr. Karofsky and tell him about Lottie. He thinks she should study with him."

"Helen tells me you know this man." Pop stared intently at the old man.

Mr. Schultz smoothed his beard. "We were business associates for a time."

"Can he be trusted?"

"Trusted?" Mr. Schultz shrugged. "Of course. He demands the highest level of propriety from his protégés."

Aunt Cora snorted. "I can just imagine what he thought of you."

"Your lack of faith hurts me deeply," Mr. Schultz said to his daughter. "Ask Helen if I was trustworthy in Chicago."

Helen looked wary. "He did all right. Pop, would you really send Lottie so far away? She's not yet eleven years old."

"I haven't made up my mind." Pop looked at his sister-in-law. "What do you think, Cora? You know more about this stuff than I do."

"She needs a new piano teacher," Cora said. "But she's a child, George. As a mother, I can't imagine sending my daughter half-way across the country. She'd be gone months at a time."

"You did it," Pop said.

"I was fourteen, and old for my age. But I don't recommend it."

Uncle Otto cleared his throat. "I don't like to bring it up, George, but how would you pay for the lessons?"

Pop gave a short nod. "It could be done."

"I have $200 in the bank," Lottie said. Everyone turned to look at her, sitting forgotten at the other end of the table.

Helen asked, "Does that mean you want to go to New York?"

Lottie nodded. "I could pay for the lessons myself, and not burden Pop."

Pop smiled into his daughter's eyes. "That's my good girl. But it's my job to take care of you a while longer."

"Well, one thing is certain," Aunt Cora said. "There is nothing more to be done until we hear from Mr. Lasecki. For all we know, Dr. Karofsky might not be taking new students."

That evening, while Pop worked in the shed, Helen said, "Would you be comfortable in New York with only Mr. Schultz for company?"

Lottie tilted her head to one side. "I'd rather have you there."

Helen gave a half-smile. "Me too, but Bill finishes boot camp in a few weeks."

"I'll miss you so much when you go, Helen." Lottie's heart ached at the thought.

"We'll miss you, too."

But Helen didn't look upset.

○

An invitation from Dr. Karofsky arrived two weeks later. Lottie and Pop celebrated with apple pie. Helen had already joined Bill in California, so she missed the excitement.

The great Karofsky offered an audition only, with no guarantees. He required Lottie to visit for one week and play for him every day, after which he would decide whether or not to take her on. A retainer of $750 would be due at the beginning of her first official lesson.

Pop called another family meeting. While Lottie skulked in the hallway, he questioned all the aunts. "Can any of you take Lottie to New York?"

Aunt Eloise spoke first. "I have never made any secret of my dislike for Cora's father." She paused. "My apologies, Cora. While I applaud your caution, George, I believe we can all agree that I would not be the right woman for the job. Besides, I couldn't leave Diana. She's at such a vulnerable age."

Lottie breathed a little sigh of relief.

"I'd love to go, but I'm afraid I can't be spared right now." Aunt Emma sounded genuinely regretful. "Harry's leg is acting up, you know, so I've been doing a lot of the chores. Marlene needs help with the baby, too. Cora? How about you?"

"I couldn't be gone ten days. The kids just aren't old enough. Besides." She sounded embarrassed. "I'm going to have another one."

"Well, Cora!"

Everyone rushed to congratulate her. When the hubbub died down, Pop said, "Back to the business at hand. Lottie needs a chaperone. Does anyone know a single woman who's suitable for the job?"

"I'm available," said a slightly quavery voice. Lottie cast her eyes up to the ceiling. Aunt Eva had to be kidding.

"Oh, Eva, you don't need to sacrifice yourself. I'm sure George will find somebody suitable for the job." Aunt Emma's voice was gentle.

"Now Emma, you seem to think I'm made of porcelain. I don't break if dropped, you know." Aunt Eva sounded determined. "Ethel was my closest sister. I miss her every day. Until now, all of you have taken care of her daughters while I stood by and watched. This is my chance to contribute."

"I respect your position, Eva," Pop said, "but are you sure? New York's a big place."

"I've always wanted to see the world. This is my opportunity. I can pay my way with the money I've saved."

"There won't be any need for that," Pop said quickly.

"Otto will miss his best bank teller if you go," Aunt Cora said.

"Otto will just have to get along without me." Aunt Eva's voice grew stronger with every word. "Nothing you say will change my mind."

A chair scraped against the wood floor. "Well, Eva, I think you're a fool. But it does solve the problem," Aunt Eloise said. "Now we've got that settled, I'm going home."

Lottie ducked into the piano room as Aunt Eloise waddled past. When she returned to the hall, Aunt Emma was talking.

"….have to be firm. Lottie will need guidance."

"Watch my father, too," Cora added in a low voice. "Don't let him bully you. And don't let him drink."

As Pop drove them home, Lottie looked at him across the front seat of the Ford. "Aunt Eva? Are you crazy, Pop?'

He glanced at her. "What have you got against Eva?"

"She's so old!"

Pop chuckled. "She's not yet forty, honey. Emma's three years older."

"Why is she so frail and quavery, then?"

"I don't know." Pop squinted at the windshield. "She never had much gumption, even as a young girl. I guess the whole family believed she wouldn't amount to much. When you hear something like that about yourself for a long time, you start believing it, even if it isn't true. But she was smart as a whip in school. Your mother admired her for that."

Lottie picked at her fingernail. "Has she traveled anywhere?"

"Sure. She rode up to Ames with us when Frank got married. And one time Emma and Harry took her to the Iowa State Fair. You remember? Her plum cake won Best in Show that year."

Lottie crossed her arms. "Oh, great. She's never left Iowa before."

"No, but she's probably read about more places than you can name. She's worn out two or three library cards with all the books she takes out."

"Well, who wants to go to New York City with a boring old bookworm?"

"Stop that right now, young lady." Pop's tone made her sit up a little straighter. "Maybe Eva's not the ideal person for the job. You might even have to hold her hand a little. But if you want to meet this Karofsky fellow, you're going to have to accept her as part of the deal. Understood?"

Lottie turned her eyes to the window. If Helen were here, she'd know what to do. Why did ol' Bill Turner have to join the navy, anyway?

○

"Would you look at the size of that river, Lottie!" Aunt Eva tugged at Lottie's sleeve. "I don't know how we're going to cross it on that narrow railroad bridge."

Lottie glanced at the brown swirling water. "We'll be all right."

Something about Aunt Eva inspired motherly feelings in other females. Every time the little woman exclaimed over something new outside the train window, Lottie felt like patting her head.

Mr. Schultz seemed to have no such tender thoughts. Early in the day, when Aunt Eva had pointed out the tallest grain elevator she'd ever seen, he'd tipped his hat over his eyes and pretended to sleep. Lottie wished she could do the same.

At noon, Aunt Eva pulled a basket out from under her seat and passed it around. The cheese sandwiches and crunchy apples filled Lottie up, and snickerdoodles baked by Aunt Cora made her less envious of the people who were moving toward the dining car.

"You should take a nap now, dear," Aunt Eva said after lunch. "It's good for children to rest during the day."

Grateful for respite from Aunt Eva's chatter, Lottie folded her coat beneath her head and closed her eyes. When she awoke, the sun had moved around to the back of the train. The scene out the window had changed, too, from golden fields to rows of scrubby houses.

"Where are we?" She rubbed sleep from her eyes.

"Indianapolis," Aunt Eva replied. "The poor side, I believe."

Mr. Schultz opened his eyes a crack, looked out the window, and closed them again.

"Excuse me." Lottie stepped into the aisle. "I need to use the bathroom."

"Wait a moment." Aunt Eva hurried to join her. "You mustn't go anywhere unaccompanied."

Lottie sighed.

Several minutes later settled again in her seat, she felt a deep sense of boredom steal over her. The train was never going to stop. It would continue to streak past fields and towns without stopping until Lottie was an old lady, older than Aunt Eva.

A jog of the elbow broke her mournful train of thought. Aunt Eva held out knitting needles and a ball of yarn. "Would you like to learn to knit?"

Lottie looked cautious. "I'm not very good with needlework."

Aunt Eva stuffed the items back into her bag. "Oh, dear. I hoped to help you pass the time. Did you bring any games?"

"I didn't think of it."

They sat quietly, wondering what to do. Finally Lottie said, "Mr. Schultz might have a deck of cards with him."

It was Aunt Eva's turn to look cautious. "I gave up cards when Reverend Muller was pastor, back before you were born. He said card games were the first step to a life of sin. But I suppose a few rounds of Old Maid wouldn't damage my moral fiber." Her eyes twinkled with unexpected humor. "I ought to be good at a game called Old Maid."

Lottie returned her aunt's smile. For the first time since the family meeting, she thought this trip might turn out all right. "I've never played Old Maid," she said.

"Never?" Aunt Eva sounded shocked. "Well, that settles it. God will have to forgive me for teaching you."

Mr. Schultz handed over a well-worn deck. Aunt Eva removed three of the four queens, and dealt the cards.

The game was simple enough, but Lottie couldn't seem to get the best of Aunt Eva. After losing three games in a row, she threw down her cards. "That does it. I'll never be any good at this."

"How about a different game?" Mr. Schultz said.

Aunt Eva was instantly on her guard. "What kind of game?"

"It's called twenty-one." Mr. Schultz looked bored.

Aunt Eva sniffed. "I've never heard of it."

"It's a counting game."

"Oh." She wavered. "Would it strengthen Lottie's arithmetic?"

He stretched his face into a dry smile. "Undoubtedly."

"All right then. Let's try it."

Mr. Schultz explained the rules of the new game. "The object is to get as close to twenty-one as possible without going over. All face cards count as ten, aces can count as one or eleven, and all the other cards are taken at face value. Understand?"

Aunt Eva nodded. "Got it."

Lottie, struggling to keep the rules straight, looked up in surprise. Mr. Schultz acted like a fox stalking its breakfast, but Aunt Eva smiled confidently.

"I'm the dealer," Mr. Schultz continued. "I will deal each of us two cards, one face up and the other face down. You'll look at your face-down card, but you won't show it to anyone else. Add up the amount on the two cards, and decide if you want another card that might take you closer to twenty-one. Ready?"

Lottie wished she could remember how much a king was worth. Was it ten or thirteen? Oh, why couldn't she have brought a checker board? She knew how to play that. "I think I need another card."

Mr. Schultz dealt one more card, and Lottie turned her cards over. "Am I out?"

"Yes, I'm afraid so. A king, an eight and a seven add up to twenty-five." Aunt Eva sounded apologetic.

Lottie threw herself against the seat and sighed deeply.

"Your turn, Miss Hoffman," Mr. Schultz said.

"I don't need a card."

Mr. Schultz looked expectant. "Turn your cards over."

"I have a jack and an ace." Aunt Eva's eyes twinkled. "That's all right, isn't it?"

"Looks like you've had some beginner's luck," Mr. Schultz said in his most genial voice. "An ace and a jack always win the hand."

Aunt Eva handed the cards to him. "Let's play again."

They whiled away the next few hours with Mr. Schultz's card game. They kept track of their wins and losses in the margin of a newspaper. By suppertime, Mr. Schultz and Aunt Eva were neck and neck, with Lottie trailing far behind.

Lottie threw down her cards. "This is my last hand."

"It's time for supper anyway," Aunt Eva said. "Let's play just one more hand."

Mr. Schultz dealt the cards. "We'll start with Lottie."

Lottie checked her hand. "One card," she said.

He turned to Aunt Eva. "And for you, lovely lady?"

Aunt Eva shook a finger at him. "Stop trying to charm me. It won't work. No cards."

Mr. Schultz dealt himself a card. "I'm bust. Lottie?"

Lottie turned over her hand. "Eight, two and nine. I have nineteen."

Mr. Schultz nodded graciously. "You win against the dealer. Miss Hoffman?"

Aunt Eva flicked her cards over with a finger. "I have fifteen. I believe I beat the dealer too, since you went bust."

Mr. Schultz chuckled. "You do indeed." He looked at her curiously. "With only fifteen points, why didn't you take a card?"

She shrugged. "All the face cards had been played, so I knew we'd get low hands to start with. I figured you'd have to take a card and go bust in the process."

"Have you always had such a remarkable memory?" Mr. Schultz asked with new respect.

"I suppose so." Aunt Eva looked surprised. "I took top prizes in spelling and math in school. Among the girls, of course."

"Ah." Mr. Schultz nodded. "Of course."

Eleven

Monday morning Aunt Eva and Lottie walked the short distance from their comfortable hotel to the home of Dr. Karofsky. A housekeeper ushered them into a cluttered room dominated by a Steinway grand piano. Lottie moved toward the bench, but Aunt Eva steered her away, saying, "Wait until the teacher invites you to play."

Aunt Eva sat on a blue velvet love seat and withdrew her knitting from her bag. Lottie perched next to her, bouncing her knees to let off some steam.

Aunt Eva drew her needles up and through the yarn. "Hold still, please," she said pleasantly.

Lottie held still, but only for a moment. Her knees seemed to bounce of their own accord.

Aunt Eva put down her needles. "Lottie, stop bouncing around. If you must do something, take a walk around the room."

Lottie had never heard such a firm order from gentle Aunt Eva. She vaulted off the love seat and marched to the window. Turning like a soldier on parade, she marched back to Aunt Eva, who sighed and went back to her knitting.

At last the door opened to admit a large man in a shiny black suit. His dignified presence seemed to fill the room. Lottie stared in awe at his bony face and white ruff of hair.

"You are Charlotte Brown, yes?" the man said.

Lottie nodded.

"Present your hands."

She stretched them out.

"Hmm. The nails are clean, but not short enough. Trim them." He looked sharply at her face. "You have long fingers for such a small girl. "You can reach an octave?"

"Yes, sir."

"Well, then." He waved toward the piano bench. "Let us begin."

Aunt Eva tucked her needles into her bag. "When shall I return for Miss Brown?" she asked.

"Eleven o'clock." Karofsky turned his back to Aunt Eva. "We begin with scales and arpeggios."

For the next two hours, Feodor Karofsky tested Lottie on every aspect of technique. He demanded not only scales and arpeggios, but chord theory, dynamic range, and pedal technique. He gave her progressively harder music, looking for correct fingering.

Lottie did her best. The teacher chose composers she'd never heard of. The music sounded dissonant and strange, but eventually she found patterns within.

At the end of two hours, the housekeeper led Aunt Eva into the room. Dr. Karofsky scratched his chin and looked out the window with a distracted stare. "Come back tomorrow at ten," he said. "My housekeeper provides lunch. You stay until two-thirty."

Lottie's face lit up. "Oh, thank you!"

"Do not thank me," he said with a warning look. "I do not yet know about you."

Abashed, Lottie slid from the stool and followed Aunt Eva to the door.

"Bring all your music," Dr. Karofsky called after her. "You must show me what you are accustomed to play."

Lottie paused, her hand on the doorknob. "You mean all my classical music?"

Karofsky frowned. "What else?"

"I play hymns."

"Bah! Leave them."

"Oh, and I know 'Flight of the Bumblebee,'" she added.

He looked offended. "No, no, no. That is not music for piano. Did your last instructor give that to you?"

"No sir."

"From now on, only music for piano." Dr. Karofsky turned his back.

"How was your lesson?" Aunt Eva asked as they walked back to the hotel.

Lottie skipped down the sidewalk. "It was hard. He expected me to know more than I do. But I tried to do everything he asked." She jumped over a crack in the pavement. "I hope it's enough."

"I'll bet you did fine," Aunt Eva said. "He wants to see you tomorrow."

Lottie looked up. "Do I have to eat the housekeeper's cooking? The whole house smells like cabbage."

Aunt Eva frowned. "Any food is good food these days. I'm sure your father taught you that."

Lottie sighed.

Mr. Schultz waited for them in the spacious hotel lobby. "Well? Does the great Karofsky want you?" he asked, a sarcastic note in his voice.

"Yes, tomorrow. That's good, isn't it?" Lottie asked.

He shrugged.

"Dr. Karofsky told me the same thing you did," Lottie said.

"Oh?"

"He said to stick to piano music from now on. No more *Green Hornet*."

Mr. Schultz snorted. "That may be the only thing we've ever agreed on."

"I'm going to the Museum of Natural History this afternoon," Aunt Eva said. "Would you two like to join me?"

Lottie smiled. "Can I have lunch first?"

Aunt Eva nodded. "Let's try the diner down the block. Are you coming, Mr. Schultz?"

"No, thank you." Mr. Schultz made a little bow. "Having lived in New York, I've already seen its museums. I'm going to look up a few friends I haven't seen in a while."

Aunt Eva shook her finger at the old man. "No carousing, now, do you hear? I gave my word to Cora I'd keep you on the straight and narrow."

"I assure you I have no intention of wandering off the path."

Aunt Eva looked uncertain.

"Madam," he said impatiently. "I do not need a nanny."

"Fair enough." Aunt Eva sounded resigned. "Come along, Lottie."

Hand in hand they walked past the hotel entrance to the little diner two doors away. A neon "Open" sign blinked at them as Aunt Eva reached for the glass-plated door. Lottie sniffed the air. "Mmm. Something smells good."

Aunt Eva wrinkled her nose. "It's not at all like home, is it?"

They made their way between the tables and sat down at the counter. Lottie swiveled her round stool back and forth, and regarded her aunt with a newly critical eye. She couldn't reconcile the dithering old maid who worked at the bank with this take-charge woman who intended to keep Old Schultz in line.

She even dressed differently than she had at home. In Westmont, Aunt Eva's wardrobe consisted of dowdy dresses and ink-stained gloves, both necessities for her job. Today she wore a tailored jacket and flowered skirt, and she'd loosened her severe bun to let her hair frame her face. Lottie resolved to write Helen a long letter and include a description of Aunt Eva's new outfit, so Helen would know what New Yorkers were wearing this season.

The following day, Aunt Eva left Lottie on Dr. Karofsky's steps. "You know what to do now," she said. "Remember to eat whatever the housekeeper feeds you."

When Lottie entered the parlor, she saw a pale, thin boy with floppy black hair and pimples sitting on the love seat. He looked her over with a sneer. "You new?"

She nodded. "I'm having a trial week."

"Well, don't get any big ideas. He probably won't take you. Besides, I'm going to win the showcase this year."

Lottie stared at the boy's skinny white hands and said nothing. She tried to imagine him milking a cow. The thought made her smile.

"What are you grinning at?"

She didn't answer.

The door opened, admitting Dr. Karofsky. "Well, Victor," he said to the boy. "I cancelled our lesson for today. Didn't your housekeeper tell you?"

The boy stood. "No sir. Should I come tomorrow?"

"I explained everything on the phone. Three o'clock is your new lesson time." Karofsky sounded impatient.

The boy glared at Lottie on his way to the door.

Lottie worked harder that week than she ever had in her life. She sat at the piano until her back ached, and concentrated so hard her temples throbbed. Lunch tasted wonderful, not because of the cabbage-prone cook, but because Lottie was ravenous. She went back to work after lunch with renewed energy. Karofsky never praised her or looked satisfied with her efforts, preferring to express himself in bursts of clipped instruction or disgusted grunts. His manner kept Lottie on edge and anxious to please.

"You're awfully quiet, Lottie," Aunt Eva said Saturday morning as they walked to Dr. Karofsky's house. Do you like your piano lessons?"

"Yep," Lottie said without hesitation. "They're my big break."

Aunt Eva looked troubled. "That's what you've been told, anyway. I hate to see you so pale and tense. You don't have to do this, you know."

Lottie drew her eyebrows together. "I do if I want to become a concert pianist. Mr. Schultz says someday I'm going to give concerts at Carnegie Hall and perform with orchestras."

"Mr. Schultz says this. Mr. Schultz says that." Aunt Eva sounded exasperated. "If I had a nickel for every sentence you start with 'Mr. Schultz says,' I'd be a millionaire." She knelt on the sidewalk in front of her niece. "Now you listen to me, Lottie. You're only ten years old. These fancy piano lessons will not be the only big break you ever get. You have every right to quit if you don't like the work, or if the teacher is a bully, or for any number of other reasons that I can't think of right now. Don't let that old coot convince you otherwise."

Aunt Eva's words stunned Lottie. "But I like my lessons. I'll die if Dr. Karofsky doesn't take me." She looked at her aunt in bewilderment. "I'm not tense. I promise I'm not."

Aunt Eva searched Lottie's face for a long moment. Then she rose and seemed to collect herself. "Well that's fine then, child. I hope the man does you a world of good." She took Lottie's hand in a businesslike manner and began to walk. "We'd better hurry. You don't want to be late."

Lottie broke into a trot to keep up, her thoughts in a tangle. Of course she wanted to study with Karofsky. Didn't she?

○

"Well? How did it go?" Aunt Eva asked when Lottie emerged from the brownstone at the end of the day.

Lottie gave a little skip. "He's taking me on. I'm to study from eight to two o'clock, Monday through Saturday."

Aunt Eva smiled. "I'm proud of you, dear."

Lottie looked at her prim aunt. There was no sign of the urgency she'd shown that morning. They strolled at a ladylike pace back to the hotel, where Mr. Schultz waited in the lobby.

"Well?" He said gruffly.

Lottie nodded.

Mr. Schultz sat back with a satisfied grin. "So Karofsky's on board, eh? We'll make a star of you yet."

Aunt Eva squeezed Lottie's hand, then let go. "We'll call your father tonight, Lottie. He'll want to know what happened."

When Lottie called Pop with the big news, he gave a shout of excitement on the other end of the phone. "That's great, honey! I knew you could do it. Write and tell me all about it."

"I will," Lottie said. It felt so good to hear Pop's voice. "Boy, I wish you were here."

Pop chuckled. "Don't waste your time missing me. I'll be right here waiting for you when you come home."

A week later on the way to her piano lesson Lottie asked her aunt, "Where will you go this morning?"

"To the bank and the library." Outside of a few errands, she spent the mornings as she pleased.

"And this afternoon?" Every day Aunt Eva planned an educational experience for Lottie when she finished her lesson.

"Central Park, I think. You need to let off steam after sitting still all day."

"That sounds great." Lottie's lessons had intensified since the first week. Karofsky seemed intent on pouring knowledge into her brain as quickly as possible, and she walked away exhausted when a lesson ended. A walk in the park would let her stretch her body instead of her mind, for a change.

The day passed quickly. At two o'clock Lottie put on her coat and said good-bye to her teacher. As usual, she passed Victor the pale boy on her way out of the house. He scowled at her from under his thick brows, and she stared back. She wondered why she made him so mad. Today when she reached the door, he spoke.

"You think you're pretty big stuff, don't you?"

Lottie looked over her shoulder. "Why would you say that?"

He stood at the top of the stairs, his fists clenched. "You knocked me out of the morning lesson time."

"So?"

"So don't mess with Victor Gold, that's all."

She squared her shoulders. "I'm not messing with you, Victor. I can't help it if Dr. Karofsky thinks I'm better than you."

They glared at one another for a full minute before Karofsky called, "Victor. Come in here." The boy swore under his breath and picked up his pace.

Aunt Eva stood on the sidewalk, an umbrella under her arm. She handed Lottie a thick white envelope. "Looks like Helen's handwriting."

"Helen?" Lottie snatched the letter and held it to her chest. "I can't believe it. She finally wrote!"

Her aunt laughed. "Why don't you read it when we get to the park? We'll have to hurry. It's going to rain."

They swung down the street at a smart pace. "What's Mr. Schultz doing today?" Lottie asked.

"Visiting friends again. I saw that Victor boy as I was waiting for you. Do you ever speak to him?"

She made a face. "He's awful."

Aunt Eva chuckled. "I never know if that means he's a chump, or he can't play the piano."

"Well, he can't play worth a darn, either." This wasn't strictly true, but she enjoyed saying it.

When they reached Central Park, Aunt Eva stopped before a sculpture of soldiers wearing bowl-shaped hats and knickers.

Lottie craned her neck to see the inscription. "Seventh Regiment New York," she read. "One Hundred and Seventh United States Infantry. In Memoriam. Were they soldiers in the Great War?"

"Yes." Her aunt's voice shook. "Several of my classmates marched off to war in similar uniforms. They didn't all come home."

Lottie glanced up. "What's wrong?"

Tears ran down Aunt Eva's cheeks as she stared at the bronze soldiers. "That one looks just like him," she murmured.

Lottie took her aunt's elbow and steered her to a park bench. "Let's sit down."

Aunt Eva sank onto the bench, then fumbled for her handkerchief and wiped her nose. "This is so silly. Sometimes I miss him — them — those boys so very much."

"Aunt Eva, did you have a sweetheart?" Lottie asked in amazement.

Eva began to weep in earnest. Lottie stroked her arm and waited.

When her tears finally subsided into hiccoughs, she said, "God bless you, Lottie, nobody ever asked me that before. At home they think I'm incapable of romance."

"Oh, not really," Lottie said, but it was true. Poor Eva Hoffman, they said. Couldn't find a man. She was lucky her brother owned the bank. At least she'd never lack for a job.

"I've never told anyone about Fred Walker. Papa wouldn't let us girls have sweethearts until we were sixteen. He'd have tanned my hide if he knew Fred and I were sweet on each other. He was three years older than I, and studying to go to the university. We were friends, real friends." Her eyes glowed with the memory. "He talked to me like an equal, and that's a rare quality in a man."

Lottie fished a hankie out of her pocket and handed it to Aunt Eva.

"Thank you, dear." She blew her nose. "I was only fifteen when Fred joined up. He asked me to wait for him, but he didn't have the money for a ring. I don't have so much as a cigar band to remember him by." She sighed. "He made it to France, then died of the Spanish flu. Mr. and Mrs. Walker were devastated, and so was I. But they had the luxury of mourning publicly. I suffered alone."

"Why didn't you tell anyone?"

"I was afraid I'd be laughed at. Nobody expects a fifteen-year-old to know her own heart, especially if she's skinny and awkward and has to wear spectacles. Fred was handsome, you know," she said proudly.

Lottie stared at her. "What about your sisters? Couldn't you tell them?"

Eva wrinkled her nose. "Especially not them. Emma was married, and Eloise couldn't keep a secret. Your mama was all wrapped up in your pop by then, so I kept it to myself."

Lottie nodded sympathetically. She knew how it was when a sister fell in love.

"Besides, they'd never believe Fred Walker loved me," Eva continued on a wistful note. "They considered me the dumb Dora of the family. All book smarts. No common sense. They still do."

"Why didn't you ever marry?"

"Nobody measured up to Fred, I suppose. Not to mention the fact that nobody asked me. I guess that part of my life is over now. I've gotten used to being alone." She gave a watery chuckle. "Spinsterhood has its advantages, too. I couldn't have come to New York with you if I had a husband."

Lottie smiled. "I'm glad you're here."

"Oh, pshaw." Aunt Eva looked abashed and changed the subject. "Go ahead and read your sister's letter."

"I nearly forgot." Lottie drew the letter out of her bag.

Helen's short letter was full of praise for sunny San Diego. She'd quickly made friends among the other officers' wives, and had attended several parties at their quarters. Bill's name came up only briefly, as he'd been at sea for a week and a half.

Lottie folded the letter and slid it back into its envelope. Helen hadn't mentioned home or Pop at all. She'd closed her note with a breezy, "I miss you!" but it didn't sound like she did.

That evening after dinner, Lottie, Aunt Eva, and Mr. Schultz gathered in the sitting room of their hotel suite, as usual. Lottie answered Helen's letter while Mr. Schultz and Aunt Eva played cards. She was glad to be excluded from the game. Mr. Schultz had introduced her aunt to the idea of betting toothpicks, and their competition was intense. They could last for hours without either side winning, a fact that seemed to delight them both.

Once in a while Lottie caught Mr. Schultz looking at Aunt Eva with a speculative gleam in his eye. Strangely enough, sometimes she caught Aunt Eva staring back the same way.

"Can I ask you a question?" Lottie asked at bedtime.

"Anything," her aunt replied.

"Do you still think gambling is a sin?"

Aunt Eva smiled at her niece. "Yes, I do."

"Then why…" she hesitated.

Aunt Eva did not seem offended. "Why do I play cards with Mr. Schultz?"

Lottie waited.

"Have you ever heard the old saying, 'It takes a thief to catch a thief'?"

Lottie shook her head.

Aunt Eva squeezed her hand. "Then you're going to have to trust me."

Twelve

Lottie wondered where Mr. Schultz spent his days. When asked, he always said, "I'm visiting old friends." She had trouble imagining grumpy Mr. Schultz with that many friends.

When Aunt Eva dared to question him, he said, "Writing home to Mama, are we?" She turned red and fell silent.

"I can see his point," Aunt Eva told Lottie. "He's a grown man, albeit a dependent one. If he were drinking, I'd pack his bag and send him home on the first available train. But he's not."

"Then what is he doing?" Lottie asked.

Aunt Eva looked thoughtful. "I intend to find out."

One evening, Mr. Schultz invited Aunt Eva to a party at the home of one of his friends. "We can leave Lottie here with the door locked. She'll be safe."

"Go ahead," Lottie said when the good lady seemed to waver. "I'll be fine by myself for a while." She was a little tired of constant companionship.

"Well, I don't know," Aunt Eva began. "Who are these friends of yours, Mr. Schultz? Are they respectable?"

"Yes, yes." He sounded impatient. "They're from my days in the orchestra. It'll be a quiet little evening, I promise."

"Oh, dear. Well, in that case, I suppose I could." As a rule, Aunt Eva didn't flutter anymore, but she fluttered about now in a great show of confusion.

"Good." The old man rubbed his hands in satisfaction. "You won't mind if we play some cards, will you?" He made it sound like an afterthought.

Aunt Eva's eyes brightened. "That sounds fun. Just give me a minute to freshen up."

Mr. Schultz prowled around the tiny sitting room. He paused at the window, drumming his fingers on the sill and humming quietly to himself. He turned as Aunt Eva emerged from the bedroom, and his eyes flashed approval. "You look very nice."

Lottie turned to look, and nearly fell out of her chair. Aunt Eva had bypassed her new wardrobe in favor of a faded gray dress from the Collison Emporium. She looked like she'd just locked up the bank after a hard day's work. Even her shoes were run down at the heel.

Aunt Eva smiled at her shocked niece. As she followed the old man out the door, she turned around and gave a theatrical wink. Mystified, Lottie moved to the window to watch them leave the building. She hoped Aunt Eva knew what she was doing.

Lottie wrote letters to Helen and Pop, and finished a book of Sunday school stories to please Aunt Eva. At nine o'clock she went to bed, only to be startled awake sometime later by the turn of the key in the lock.

"How was your evening?" she asked sleepily when Aunt Eva came to bed.

"It went exactly as planned."

Lottie didn't stay awake long enough to wonder what that meant.

The next morning at breakfast, Mr. Schultz looked like a bear with a sore paw. He snapped at Lottie for burning the toast, and told her she'd be a lousy housewife some day. He wouldn't even look in Aunt Eva's direction.

Lottie did her best to tiptoe around him. When they walked to Karofsky's, she asked if Mr. Schultz was sick.

Aunt Eva smiled grimly. "His health is fine. It's his vanity that hurts. And his billfold. Yes, his billfold is quite a bit thinner."

And with that riddle, Lottie had to be content.

○

Victor Gold lay in wait when Lottie finished her lesson. He stuck out his foot and tripped her as they passed on the stairs. She pitched forward, catching herself on the railing in time to avoid a nasty fall. His mocking laughter followed her out the door.

Aunt Eva wasn't waiting on the sidewalk as she usually did. Lottie stood on the steps of the brownstone for fifteen minutes, looking anxiously down the street. She could hear Victor's fortissimo pounding through the open parlor window. He had no dynamic range.

Lottie walked home after half an hour's wait. She watched for Aunt Eva, who always traveled the same route, but she did not appear. Lottie's fears grew with every step. When the hotel came into sight, she broke into a run. She sprinted through the lobby and took the stairs two at a time.

She heard loud voices as she reached the third floor hallway, and recognized one as Mr. Schultz. The other voice belonged to a stranger. The door to their room stood ajar, leaving a triangle of light on the faded hall carpet. She stopped where she was.

"I tell you it's an airtight scheme," Mr. Schultz bellowed. "I just need another day."

"That is what you told Mr. Bellusi yesterday," the stranger said, "and yet there is no money today. The boss thinks you want him to look like a fool."

"I would never do that. My partner is new at the game. She needs a little coaching." The old man's voice shook. "All I ask is one more day."

"Mr. Bellusi does not care about your partner," the other man said. "He only cares you owe him money. You gotta pay up, hear?"

"Give me until tomorrow. I beg you."

Lottie heard a metallic click. "Tomorrow, then," the stranger said, and his shadow blocked the light in the doorway.

She turned and galloped back down the stairs.

Aunt Eva came through the hotel doors as Lottie reached the lobby. Lottie ran into her arms, sobbing. "There's a man upstairs with Mr. Schultz. I think he has a gun."

"Hush, child. I know." She wrapped her niece in a protective hug. Over her head she said, "Now do you believe me?"

"Hmm. Were shots fired?" a male voice asked.

Startled, Lottie looked up from her aunt's arms. A silver-haired man in a gray suit and black neck tie stood in front of them. "No. Who are you?"

The man touched the brim of his hat. "Detective Reed of the New York Police Department."

Lottie swiveled her head toward Aunt Eva. "Are we going to get arrested?"

"No, dear. The police officer is here to help us."

"Can you tell me what happened, little girl?"

Lottie looked at him. "Aunt Eva didn't pick me up from my piano lesson this afternoon. She's always on time, so I thought it was strange. After a while, I decided to walk home. I thought I'd meet her on the way there.

"But I never did see her. And then I remembered Mr. Schultz was angry with Aunt Eva this morning at breakfast, and I thought, what if he did something to hurt her? So I ran the rest of the way."

"That's my brave girl," Aunt Eva said.

"I see. Has he ever struck your aunt before?" he asked.

"No, of course not." Lottie was shocked at the idea. "He mostly just grumbles at us. But today he seemed so different. He scared me. And Aunt Eva ..." She sent her aunt an apologetic glance. "Aunt Eva seemed different, too. Like she knew a really good secret. Mr. Schultz hates it when someone gets the best of him."

The detective pulled out a notebook and pen. "So then you went upstairs?" he prompted.

Lottie nodded. "I heard yelling when I left the stairway. Mr. Schultz said he'd have the money tomorrow, and the other guy said he'd better. Then I heard the click of the gun, or whatever it was, and I turned around and ran."

Detective Reed finished scribbling in his notebook and stuck it in his breast pocket. "Perhaps we should check on Mr. Schultz. Lead the way, Miss Hoffman."

Aunt Eva took Lottie's hand and guided her to the stairwell. As they led the detective upstairs she said in a low voice, "Don't worry, Lottie. I'll keep you safe, no matter what."

Lottie squeezed her aunt's hand, her eyes wide with fear and excitement.

"Detective?" Aunt Eva said.

"Hmm?"

"Please let me do the talking first."

The door was shut and locked when they reached their room. Aunt Eva used her key to open it. "Mr. Schultz?" she called.

He answered from behind his bedroom door. "Where've you been?"

Aunt Eva glanced at Detective Reed, who put a finger to his lips. "I went to pick up Lottie, but she wasn't finished with her lesson. Karofsky is keeping her longer today."

The detective pushed Lottie gently into the hallway and motioned for her to stand against the wall, out of sight. He stood next to her, listening intently.

Lottie heard the door open and shut, and Mr. Schultz said, "Good. Then you and I have time for a little talk. Your dirty little trick last night put me in a tight spot." His voice came closer. "And don't try to pretend you don't know what I mean, you card-counting old maid."

"I knew what you were up to." Aunt Eva's voice was casual. "You were taking side bets on my games. You figured no one would believe I'm good at twenty-one because I look like a frumpy old maid."

Mr. Schultz laughed. "It should have worked, too. You don't even know enough to call it blackjack."

"Well, I'm smart enough to know a crook when I see one. I wasn't about to help you."

"You made a fool of me, is what you did." The old man's voice took on a whiny note. "Why'd you do it? We could have made a lot of money running that con."

"We?" Aunt Eva sounded incredulous. "You weren't going to share the profits with me."

"Oh, is that what's bothering you?" He sounded relieved. "I'll cut you in. Look, we'll go eighty-twenty. I know another place we can play tonight, if you'll play along this time."

"Why do you want this so badly?" Aunt Eva asked.

There was a pause. "I borrowed a little money, and the guy wants to get paid. If you'd just cooperate, I could be free and clear in one night."

"I have a better idea." Aunt Eva swung open the door. "Detective Reed?"

Mr. Schultz swore. The detective shot a warning glance at Lottie and stepped into the room. "Relax, buddy," he said. "You're not under arrest. Not yet, anyway. Have a seat."

"I'll stand. What do you want?" Mr. Schultz asked.

"This young lady tells me you were present at a floating casino last night."

"Yeah? What other lies did she tell you?"

"Oh, I don't think Miss Hoffman is lying." The detective's voice grew friendly. "From her description, you've been playing with the O'Reilly gang. They'll kill you if they catch you counting cards, you know."

Lottie heard a quiet gasp from Aunt Eva.

Detective Reed continued. "You owe it to the lady to provide your-selves with some kind of protection."

"What do you have in mind?" Mr. Schultz sounded deeply suspicious.

"Give me the location and password of tonight's game, and I'll let you play for an hour before I shut it down."

Mr. Schultz barked out a laugh. "An hour! What am I, a miracle worker?"

"How much do you owe?"

"Three thousand."

Lottie stifled a gasp.

"Two hours, and I'll have an officer waiting to escort you and your winnings to safety." The detective's voice was persuasive.

"How do I know the lady will do her part?" A whine crept into Mr. Schultz's voice.

"I'll do it," Aunt Eva said.

Detective Reed's voice turned persuasive. "By the sound of things, Miss Hoffman hid her light under a bushel last night. In my book, that means you're set to make a killing tonight. Am I right?"

"I see your point."

There was a short, tense silence, broken by the detective. "I could leave you to the tender mercy of your loan shark."

Mr. Schultz grunted. "There must be lots of ways to bring down this gang. Why do you need us?"

"One of O'Reilly's men shot a cop two weeks ago. The whole gang's in hiding. Miss Hoffman here is the first break we've had on the case."

"You're welcome," Aunt Eva murmured.

The detective continued. "The gang doesn't suspect you, so we've got surprise on our side."

"All right. I'll do it." Mr. Schultz heaved a sigh. "Not that I have a choice."

"Good." Detective Reed sounded satisfied. "O'Reilly's got a lookout named Charlie Flatnose. Looks like a prize fighter. You seen him?"

"Sure," Aunt Eva said.

"Can you stay out of his way, Miss Hoffman?" He sounded concerned.

Lottie scrunched her eyes shut and waited for Aunt Eva to start twittering, but she said, "I think so," in a composed tone.

They talked a little longer, filling in the details of the plan. Finally Detective Reed started for the door. "That'll be all, then. We'll see you tonight."

"I have one request." Mr. Schultz's voice was gruff. "Don't involve the child in this mess. I'm an old sinner, I know, but I've always meant well by her."

"I'll leave that decision up to Miss Hoffman, here," the detective said.

"I want to protect Lottie, too." Aunt Eva's voice was soft. "Detective, I'll see you out." She followed him into the hall and closed the door behind her.

"Thanks for your help in there." Detective Reed regarded Aunt Eva with frank interest. "Lady, you are not at all what I expected when you walked up to my desk this morning."

A blush crept into Aunt Eva's cheeks. "Yes. Well."

To Lottie's relief, the detective didn't wait for a reply.

Lottie stared at her aunt, full of suppressed excitement. Aunt Eva smiled back and raised her voice for Mr. Schultz's benefit. "Well, would you look who's here. It's Lottie! Did you walk home?"

"Yes, I did," Lottie replied just as loudly. "You forgot to pick me up."

Thirteen

Lottie glanced at Mr. Schultz for the forty-fifth time. He sat as always, his head low over his plate, eating his corned beef hash, purchased from the deli across the street. This afternoon he'd sounded like he gave a darn whether she lived or died, but now she couldn't tell by looking at him.

She sighed. Maybe she'd imagined it. She looked at Aunt Eva, calmly taking tiny bites of limp cooked cabbage. She might have been going to a Saturday movie matinee for all the excitement she showed.

Lottie pushed a forkful of cabbage around her plate. Playing dumb was the hardest job of all. She wanted to yell, "The O'Reilly gang gets it tonight," like Jimmy Cagney in a gangster movie. Instead, she bit her lip and kicked her feet against the rung of her chair.

If she'd learned those silly card games, Detective Reed would have asked her to help tonight. But she was only ten, going on eleven. Why, oh why, couldn't she be older?

At eight o'clock, Aunt Eva and Mr. Schultz announced they were going out again, and made a great show of instructing Lottie not to let anyone in. Lottie did her best to sound surprised, and assured them she'd be fine.

As soon as they left, a knock sounded on the door. Lottie stared at it, wondering what to do, until the knock sounded again. "Yes?" she called, mimicking Aunt Eva's confident voice.

"It's Detective Reed. I'm leaving an officer to guard your door tonight."

"Thank you," Lottie called, but he was gone. For an hour, she listened to the policeman pace up and down the hall while she tried to read. At last curiosity got the better of her. She unlocked the door and stuck her head out. "I'm Lottie. What's your name?"

The policeman tipped his hat. "Officer Fitzpatrick. Everything okay in there?"

Lottie nodded. "Would you like some hot chocolate?"

A smile lit the young officer's ruddy face. "I sure would."

Lottie held the door wider. "You can sit at the table while I heat the milk on our hot plate."

Fitzpatrick shook his head. "I'm not supposed to enter your room."

Lottie shrugged. "All right. I'll bring it out to you."

A few minutes later she slipped into the hall, two cups balanced in her hands. Officer Fitzpatrick took one from her, and they sipped their chocolate in uncomfortable silence.

When the mugs were empty, Lottie asked, "What's it like being a cop, Officer Fitzpatrick?"

"Call me Fitz. Sometimes it's exciting, sometimes dull," he answered. "This is one of the dull times."

She nodded. "I wanted to go tonight, too. Instead, I can't even go down to the lobby and play the piano. I'd much rather do that than read the books my aunt gives me."

"I know something you'd like." Fitz reached into his front pocket. "I carry this everywhere." He held out a harmonica.

She took it. "My cousin Peter has one of these, but he can't really play it. Do you know how?"

He laughed. "Do I know how?" He raised the harmonica to his mouth, and soon a sweet, nameless tune drifted through the hall.

A few doors away, a woman stuck her head into the hall. "Quiet out there. Some people are trying to sleep."

"Sorry, ma'am." Fitz looked at Lottie. "I guess I could go inside with you. I could teach you to play, if you want."

"Oh, yes!"

Fitz stepped into the hotel suite and gave a low whistle. "Nice place you got here."

Lottie looked around indifferently. "It's pretty nice, I guess. Now, how do you play that thing?"

She spent an hour learning the mouth organ. She spent another hour making up tunes for the policeman's entertainment. At eleven o'clock, Fitz said she could keep it with her for the night, on the condition she went straight to bed. He returned to sentry duty in the hall.

Lottie lay wide awake in the darkness and wondered when Aunt Eva would get home. When the luminous dial of the alarm clock read two-fifteen, she wondered if Aunt Eva would come home.

At three, she got up and put her clothes back on. It was no use pretending everything was all right. Aunt Eva and Mr. Schultz were probably dead. She opened the door and found Fitz sound asleep in the hall.

At least she had the harmonica for comfort. Closing the door, she went to sit at the table, where she played soft and mournful melodies and waited for the sun to rise over Manhattan.

The rattle of a key in the lock startled her awake. She lifted her head and felt the imprint of the harmonica on her cheek. It took a moment to remember where she was.

"Lottie!"

Aunt Eva rushed into the room, her face alight with excitement. Detective Reed and Officer Fitzpatrick followed, in heated conversation.

"I wasn't asleep, sir. I'm sure I wasn't." Fitzpatrick sounded desperate.

"You were snoring," Reed snarled. "If anything happened to the little girl, you'll lose your badge."

Lottie slid from her chair and padded over to the policemen. "Hi, Fitz. Here's your harmonica. Too bad I only got to keep it for half an hour." She scrunched up her eye in a stagey wink.

Fitz's eyes crinkled at the corners. "Thanks, kid."

"He wasn't asleep, Detective Reed. He was teaching me how to play."

Detective Reed's mouth opened, but no sound came out.

Aunt Eva chuckled.

"That's right. Nobody waits for the wounded man." Mr. Schultz hobbled in, leaning heavily on his cane. His left arm hung from a sling, his face etched with gray lines of fatigue.

"You can be very proud of Mr. Schultz," Aunt Eva told Lottie. "He was wounded in the line of duty."

Lottie's mouth formed an O of admiration. "Did you get shot, Mr. Schultz?"

"Why on earth would I get shot at a party?" he said testily. "I fell off a curb and cut my arm." He stumped off toward his bedroom. "Later you'll have to explain why there's a cop in our sitting room. I'm going to sleep."

Aunt Eva smiled. "He's determined to protect you, Lottie. The least you can do is pretend you don't know what happened."

"Well did he get shot?" Lottie whispered.

"A bullet grazed his skin." Officer Reed said. "Things got a little out of hand when we raided the place. If it wasn't for your aunt here, things could have been a lot worse. She had the good sense to pull the old man out of the way when Flatnose Charlie aimed his gun."

Aunt Eva flushed, but looked steadily at the detective. "Thanks for everything."

"I'll be in touch, Miss Hoffman," the detective replied.

Lottie wanted to giggle at the look in his eyes. It reminded her of Bill when he looked at Helen, only Detective Reed was old.

At the door, Officer Fitzpatrick tossed the harmonica to Lottie. "Here, kid. Remember me when you're famous."

The afternoon papers were full of news about the raid on the O'Reilly gang. The front page of the *Times* featured the headline, "O'Reillys Caught by Tourist Bait," with a big photo of Aunt Eva next to a police car, supporting Mr. Schultz, who had blood dripping down his arm.

Lottie read every word of the highly embellished article while Mr. Schultz blustered on about unsuitable reading material. When she finished, she put her arms around his neck and hugged him wordlessly. He hugged her back for the briefest moment, then turned away and loudly blew his nose.

When Lottie opened Karofsky's door the next day, the housekeeper barred her way. "No more lessons," she said. "The Master doesn't associate with criminals."

"I'm not a criminal," Lottie said in confusion.

The housekeeper held out a copy of the *New York Post*. "That is your aunt, no?" She pointed from the picture to Aunt Eva, waiting on the sidewalk.

Lottie finally understood. "Oh, but she's not a criminal either. She was helping the police." She ducked under the housekeeper's arm and made for the stairs. "I'll tell Dr. Karofsky about it. He'll understand."

"Come back here, you!" the housekeeper called, and hustled up the stairs behind her.

Lottie heard familiar music coming from the studio. Victor Gold sat at the piano, a triumphant sneer on his lips. Karofsky stood beside him, looking slightly pained. His face darkened at the sight of Lottie. "How dare you come up here?"

"Dr. Karofsky, there's been a misunderstanding." Lottie rushed into an explanation about Aunt Eva and Detective Reed, and the O'Reilly gang.

Dr. Karofsky motioned for silence. "I do not care what your aunt was doing." He grabbed the newspaper from his housekeeper and pointed at Mr. Schultz. "She was with that crook, Carl Schultz. He's related to you, isn't he?"

Lottie nodded.

"I knew it! He sent you here to spy on me. Well, I'll have nothing to do with that no-good Kraut or his hangers-on. Now, get out, or I call the police!"

"Then give us back our money." Aunt Eva pushed past the bristling housekeeper.

Karofsky's eyes narrowed. "Consider it a down payment on what Carl Schultz owes me." He advanced on Lottie, who backed away. "Now, get out of my house." He snatched at her and she fled into Aunt Eva's arms.

Aunt Eva backed from the room, her arms around Lottie. "I'll be in touch with my lawyer." Taking her niece's hand, Aunt Eva marched down the stairs, head high. Behind them, Victor Gold cackled gleefully.

Lottie wanted to run back to the hotel, but Aunt Eva forced her to a sedate walk until they lost sight of the brownstone. "Never run away with your tail between your legs," Aunt Eva murmured, "no matter how badly you've lost."

Lottie grabbed her aunt's hand. "How did you know I needed you?"

Aunt Eva frowned. "I heard what that woman said to you at the door. No niece of mine will be treated that way."

Mr. Schultz shook with anger when they told him the news. "That low-down Polack," he blustered. "Just wait till I get my hands on him.

I'll shake him till his eyes bleed."

"Get hold of yourself, Mr. Schultz," Aunt Eva said sharply.

He sat down with a thud. "This is my fault. The child is going to suffer for my sins, just like Cora did."

Aunt Eva put her hands on her hips. "What exactly did you do to Dr. Karofsky?"

Mr. Schultz's shoulders sagged. "I robbed him blind."

Aunt Eva gasped.

He rested his head in his hands. "We were business partners. He taught piano while I taught cello. We started the AOMI, and built it into a prestigious organization. The June showcase was my idea." He raised his head. "We were the most respected men in our profession."

"Go on," she prompted.

He shrugged. "The respect stopped when it came to my personal life. Everyone knew I spent my weekends at the racetrack. There was nothing to keep me at home, with Cora living so far away. Karofsky was so straitlaced, with his society wife and perfect children. I knew I wasn't welcome in his home." He laughed bitterly. "It's funny that he's the one who ended up alone."

"Maybe he wasn't as perfect as he seemed," Aunt Eva said. "What happened at the racetrack, Mr. Schultz?"

"Whenever I came up short with my bookie, I borrowed from the AOMI account. I figured I'd put the money back when I started winning again, but I never did. Karofsky suspected there was something wrong and started sniffing around the account books. I got scared and arranged to send the piano to Cora." He looked at Lottie. "Remember?"

She nodded.

"But before I could ship it, he found out the truth and brought charges against me." He sighed. "That was the same day the men came to pack up the piano, so I stuck all my gin bottles in a suitcase and begged a ride to Iowa."

"What happened to the rest of your belongings?" Aunt Eva asked. "You arrived in Westmont with next to nothing."

"They took it all to pay my debts." He gave a harsh laugh. "They even took my cello, my livelihood. And it still wasn't enough."

Aunt Eva put her hands on her hips. "What on earth were you thinking to allow Lottie to take lessons from that man? Didn't you know he'd make trouble for you again?"

"He's the best," Mr. Schultz said simply. "Lottie needs the best."

"But you must have known what would happen if you went with her. You couldn't keep your presence a secret forever."

Lottie had to strain to hear the old man's answer. "I couldn't help myself. I had to come." He gave a mirthless chuckle. "All this time Cora thought it was the drink I couldn't resist, and I'll admit I was in pretty bad shape when I first arrived in Iowa. But betting is my downfall. I came back to New York to gamble." His mouth twisted bitterly. "One more chance to redeem myself, I thought. One more shot at winning my life back. And now look what's happened."

"Yes, now look," Aunt Eva said softly. "You're right back where you started."

The old man kept his gaze on the carpet. "I don't mind so much for myself," he said. "But I've hurt the child so."

"It's all right," Lottie slipped her hand into his. "I'll have other chances."

He squeezed her hand. "You will if I have anything to do with it," he said fiercely. "New York is full of opportunities. We'll find you a different teacher and win the June Showcase anyway. We'll beat that old rascal at his own game."

"Oh, I don't want to stay here," Lottie said earnestly. "I want to go home."

Mr. Schultz looked shocked. "Not stay! But you have to. You're on the edge of a big breakthrough."

Lottie shook her head. "I need to see Pop again, and play the church organ, and eat Aunt Cora's mashed potatoes." She looked at her aunt. "Tell him, Aunt Eva. You know what I mean."

"She's right, you know," the lady said. "Lottie needs home more than anything."

The old man brought his cane crashing to floor. "New York is her home now."

"No." Aunt Eva spoke gently. "New York is your home, Mr. Schultz. Isn't that it? And if you could make a living here, you'd stay." She put a protective arm around Lottie's shoulders. "But Lottie can't be your source of income. She's just a little girl."

He glared at her. "How dare you imply I'm using the child for financial gain, madam? Why, for all these years I've given her lessons for free. Where would she be without my help?"

"She'd be home, where she wants to be." Her even voice cut through the old man's bluster. "Not in a city where she doesn't have a single playmate, putting in work days that would tire a grown man."

They stared each other down, Aunt Eva calm and steady-eyed, Mr. Schultz red-faced and scowling. He looked away first. "You may have a point."

Aunt Eva smiled. "I do."

He looked up. "Well? What are you waiting for? Better start packing before I change my mind."

Aunt Eva's smile turned rueful. "Oh, I'm not going with you. I've taken a job as a bank teller. I'm staying in New York."

Fourteen

"Are you sure we did the right thing, not telling Pop first?" Lottie asked as the train pulled out of Penn Station.

"I think so," Mr. Schultz replied. "It will be easier to explain the situation face to face."

Lottie sighed. "I just wish it wasn't Thanksgiving."

"They'll serve turkey and mashed potatoes in the dining car, so you won't miss out entirely."

"It won't taste like Aunt Cora's."

"No, but it will have to do." Mr. Schultz changed the subject. "What shall we do to pass the time? Your aunt made me leave all my cards with her."

Lottie giggled. "She gave me a book to read." She held it up. *Moral Stories for the Young*. But all the kids are such goody two-shoes, I don't want to finish it."

"She's an old maid to the core," Mr. Schultz said. "A few years in New York should do wonders for her, especially with the good detective as her friend."

"I can't wait to tell the folks at home about Detective Reed." Lottie's eyes were bright. "They'll never believe it."

"Make sure I'm there when you tell your Aunt Eloise." Mr. Schultz leaned back and tipped his hat over his eyes. He soon began to snore.

Lottie opened her book and tried to read, only to throw it aside fifteen minutes later. "I can't do it," she muttered. With a glance at her sleeping guardian, she scooted into the aisle.

She passed through the vestibule to the next car, which was full of businessmen with newspapers propped in front of their faces. In the car after that, a small child wandered up and down the aisle. Lottie knelt to speak to him, but he toddled back to his mama on fat legs, so she moved on.

She had nearly reached the observation car at the end of the train when she encountered a large group of men dressed alike in black suits and red ties. Most of them were in shirtsleeves, their ties loose around their necks. Some held musical instruments which they polished with soft cloths. They talked loudly among themselves, shouting jokes and insults back and forth. Once in a while someone blew a loud note on his horn. Lottie shrank into herself as she moved through their midst.

She'd almost made it through the car when an arm shot out to stop her. "Hey, don't I know you?" said a voice.

"Johnny?" Lottie turned, astonished. "What are you doing here?"

Johnny Columbus looked as surprised as Lottie, and pleased to see her. "I'm with Walter Harms and the Neverland Orchestra. Part owner, as a matter of fact. We're headed for Indianapolis. Here," he shoved his seat mate's feet off the facing bench. "Take a load off."

Lottie glanced over her shoulder. "I'm going to the observation car, but I'll stay for a minute." She slid onto the seat.

"Ain't ya gonna introduce us?" Johnny's pudgy seatmate nudged him.

"Hold your horses, Carlyle." Johnny looked annoyed. "Brown, this is Carlyle. Carlyle, meet Brown, the best little piano player I ever heard."

Lottie smiled. So he'd heard her on the radio.

"Chahmed, I'm sure," Carlyle said, waving his arms in a comic half-bow.

Johnny ignored his seatmate. "What are you doing here?"

"I went to New York with my Aunt Eva and Mr. Schultz, who you saw in Chicago, and auditioned with a teacher named Feodor Karofsky," Lottie began. "We're on our way home to Iowa."

"Iowa?" Carlyle poked Johnny in the ribs. "How come everyone's from Iowa? "

"Shut up." Johnny threw an elbow at his friend. "Is your gorgeous sister with you?"

"No. She lives with her husband in California now."

He didn't miss a beat. "Too bad. How'd it work out with this Karofsky guy?"

She licked her lips. "Well, I started my lessons, and they were going pretty good. But then Mr. Schultz got in trouble with a loan shark, Aunt Eva went to the cops, and they ended up bringing down the whole O'Reilly gang. Karofsky fired me because he hates Mr. Schultz, so we're going home."

Johnny stared at her. "You mean you didn't visit the Statue of Liberty?"

She grinned. "We meant to, but we didn't have time. Oh, and the police detective fell in love with my aunt. At least, I think he did. She decided to stay in New York and be a bank teller."

He stared at her, his mouth hanging open.

Carlyle leaned forward. "So you're a real high-class piano player, huh?"

"Not high-class, maybe, but I can play. I'm the church organist back home. And I've been on the radio twice," Lottie said proudly.

Carlyle looked thoughtful. "The radio, eh? Can you sight read?"

"Of course."

"Ever play swing?"

"No, but I bet I could."

Carlyle whistled. "I bet you could, too. You interested in a job, by any chance?"

The idea intrigued her. She wouldn't mind earning her own keep again. "I'd have to ask Mr. Schultz."

Carlyle stood up. "Hey, Harms," he called.

Two seats away a tall, black-haired man unfolded his long legs and ambled toward them. "Yeah?"

"I think we found a replacement for Smitty."

Harms looked around. "Where?"

"Right there." Carlyle pointed at Lottie.

Johnny nodded. "She'd be great, Walt. I heard her play in Chicago." He turned to Lottie. "We lost our piano player in Philly."

Lottie recognized Walter Harms as the man who had been with Johnny at the train station in Chicago. He was easily the best-looking man she'd ever seen. "I could see if Mr. Schultz will let me do it," she said softly.

Harms looked down his long, straight nose. "No offense, kid, but we're a professional outfit. I don't know what kind of stories these jokers have been telling you, but we only hire adults." He went back to his seat.

"You're making a mistake," Carlyle called.

Lottie could feel the eyes of the other band members on her. "How do you know?" she whispered. "You don't know me."

"No, but I know who Karofsky is," Carlyle said. "I used to read about him in the paper, back home in the Bronx. If he took you on, you gotta be good."

"She is good." Johnny stood up, his eyes on the bandleader. "I'm going to talk some sense into Walt."

Lottie turned to Carlyle. "I'm sorry Mr. Harms said no. It would be fun to play with a dance band."

"We'll just have to wait until you're eighteen," Carlyle said. "How old are you now?"

"Ten. I'll be eleven in February."

Carlyle slapped his forehead. "Never mind."

Lottie was beginning to enjoy herself. "What instrument do you play, Carlyle?"

"Trombone. Want to hear it?"

"Yes, please."

Carlyle reached up to the luggage rack and pulled out his trombone case. Lottie watched in fascination as he played the opening bars of a swing tune.

"How do you know where to stop the slide to make each note?" she asked.

"It's easy, kid. Here, I'll show you."

An hour later, Mr. Schultz found Lottie surrounded by the band, playing scales on Carlyle's trombone. "Where have you been, young lady?" he said in his most forbidding tone.

Lottie looked around. "Oh, there you are," she said. "Don't you remember Johnny Columbus?" She indicated Johnny with a nod of her head.

Johnny stuck out his hand, but Mr. Schultz was in no mood for social niceties. He pointed at Lottie. "Put that thing down."

Lottie handed the trombone back to Carlyle with an apologetic look. "Thanks," she murmured. "It was a lot of fun."

She scooted past Johnny, who said, "Nice seeing you, Brown. Remember me to your sister."

She made a face at him. "Bye."

Mr. Schultz dragged her down the aisle behind him. From the quiver of his moustache, she knew she was in for a scold.

For the rest of the afternoon, Lottie glared through red-rimmed eyes at the despised book, which lay open in her lap. Mr. Schultz sat across from her, wide awake, staring out the window. He'd read her the riot act about talking to young rowdies who called themselves musicians.

At dinner time, they sat next to one another in the dining car, silently chewing their sliced turkey, eyes trained on their plates. Lottie barely tasted her Thanksgiving feast.

"Ahem."

Walter Harms stood before their table, waiting for Mr. Schultz to look up. He blocked the aisle, earning dirty looks from the waiters as they hurried up and down with their trays.

Mr. Schultz set down his fork and stared at the young man's necktie through ice-cold eyes.

Mr. Harms took a deep breath. "I hear Miss Brown plays the piano." He smiled at Lottie, who stared back without blinking. "I admire the way she picked up the trombone so quickly. It's clear she knows quite a bit about music. I need a piano player for a one-night engagement in Indianapolis. I'd like to hire her."

"What's the engagement?" Mr. Schultz asked.

"The Palace Ballroom. We play tomorrow night. It's a public hall, no liquor license. Just good, clean dancing."

Mr. Schultz looked skeptical. "You'd put us up in a hotel?"

The bandleader nodded. "We sleep decent."

"And payment?"

The bandmaster named a figure. "If it works out, I could hire her permanently."

Lottie crossed her fingers under the table, but Mr. Schultz shook his head. "It won't do. She doesn't play your kind of music." He returned his attention to his food.

Walter Harms hesitated, then turned on his heel and made his way back down the dining car.

Lottie watched him leave, flattered that he'd noticed her. She'd enjoyed herself with Johnny and Carlyle and the rest until Mr. Schultz broke up the party. She'd have liked to show them what she could do on piano.

After dinner, she rested her head against her folded cardigan and stared out the window until her vision blurred and her eyelids sagged.

She awoke to the sound of Johnny's voice. "Are you a musician, sir?"

"Yes," Mr. Schultz replied.

"Then I hope you'll understand. We've been trying to make a go of this band for a couple of months now, and it's been one bad break after another. The Palace in Indianapolis is the best job we've ever had, but if we show up without a piano player, we might as well pack it in. Now, I think Lottie here can do the job, or at least fake it pretty good, and we're a safe outfit. We even have a parson with us. At least," he amended, "he wants to be a preacher. I'm begging you to help us out."

Silence followed this speech, though Lottie sensed Johnny's presence next to her. She cracked one eye open just in time to see Mr. Schultz slip a fifty dollar bill into his breast pocket. Johnny had offered the form of persuasion the old man liked best.

Lottie opened her eyes and gave an exaggerated yawn. "Did I sleep long?"

"Charlotte," Mr. Schultz said, "I've changed my mind. I'm going to let you stop in Indianapolis and play with the orchestra. Now what do you think of that?"

"All right." Lottie grinned at Johnny.

He winked back. "You're gonna do great, kid."

○

At three a.m. the Neverland Orchestra rushed through Union Station in Indianapolis, stowing equipment in the trunks of waiting taxis. The man they called Parson hailed a cab for Lottie and Mr. Schultz. It took them to a downtown hotel, where Lottie trudged upstairs to her tiny room, flopped onto the bed and promptly fell asleep.

"Charlotte." Mr. Schultz banged on her door the next morning. "It's time to rehearse. They're waiting for you downstairs."

"Why do I still have to be Charlotte Brown?" she asked on the way downstairs.

"It's a kind of protection against the future."

Lottie frowned. He might as well be speaking Turkish.

"Here's Brown," Johnny called as she entered the lobby.

Walter Harms turned with an expectant look, which was quickly replaced by one of uncertainty. "You're sure about this, right?" he said to Johnny.

Lottie's heart sank. She looked critically at her brown wool coat and tan oxfords. They'd seemed so grown-up when Aunt Eva picked them out at Macy's. But she saw the truth in the bandleader's eyes. She was just a little girl.

Mr. Schultz nudged her shoulder. "Move along," he whispered. The band was disappearing through the hotel doors. They had to hurry to catch up.

Bright sunshine dazzled her eyes, but failed to revive her spirits. She trained her gaze on her shoes, shoulders hunched, dejection in every step.

Johnny Columbus dropped back to walk beside her. "You're not nervous, are you, Brown?"

"Nope." She kept her head down and hoped he'd go away.

"Yeah, I knew you weren't." Johnny laughed. "It's just second-rate horn players like me that get nervous."

She looked up. "You do?"

"Sure. I mean, I did before I made the big-time." Johnny waggled his eyebrows to show he was joking.

Lottie couldn't help laughing. "Is it really the big time?"

"No." He grinned at her. "But it's not a bad outfit. Walt Harms is a man who's going places, and him and I are partners, fair and square. I figure I'm golden as long as I don't slow him down."

"Hey, Columbus," Carlyle yelled. "Come settle a bet."

"Bye, kid. You'll be great."

"Thanks. I feel better."

When she took her place at the piano, her doubts returned. She looked over her music while the band tuned up. "Stardust." "In the Mood." "Beer Barrel Polka." She'd heard them all before, but hadn't played them. What had Johnny said? Just don't slow him down. This was going to be a disaster.

Walter Harms tapped the music stand with his baton, and the hubbub stopped. "'Stardust' from the top, gentlemen." He raised his arms. Let's get this over with, Lottie thought, and plunged in.

The bandmaster tapped his baton wildly on his music stand. Lottie looked up, startled.

"What're you doing, kid? You don't come in for eight measures. Where's Columbus?" He pointed an accusing finger at Johnny. "You said she could play. She can barely reach the pedals."

"Give me a minute, Walt." Johnny picked his way across the brass section and sat next to her on the piano bench. Lowering his head, he murmured, "I know you can do this, Brown. I heard you on the radio. You're the best musician in this room, bar none."

Lottie looked up through humiliated tears. "You think so?"

"I know so. Remember to watch Walt. Wait for the down beat." He demonstrated with his index fingers, up, down, up, down. "Like that. And count your rests. You want me to stay and turn pages?"

Lottie gave a watery smile. "No, I'll be okay. I lost my head for a minute, that's all."

"Right." Johnny slid off the bench. "Don't take Walt personally," he added. "He's got a short fuse."

Lottie closed her eyes and pictured Helen and Bill waltzing to the tinny sound of Aunt Cora's phonograph. They loved "Stardust." This arrangement would put them in seventh heaven.

"Is the piano player ready?" Walter Harms' voice dripped with sarcasm.

She opened her eyes and nodded. "Ready when you are."

This time she made her entrance on time, and played without obvious mistakes. When the song ended, they moved on to the next piece without pause. Lottie took this as a sign of acceptance. She hadn't been singled out, either for criticism or praise.

When rehearsal ended, Carlyle ambled over to the piano. "Gee, Brown, you really are a high-class piano player. Can you give me lessons?" Several of the others shouted their approval, and Lottie felt a surge of happiness.

Out of the corner of her eye, Lottie noticed Walter Harms talking intently with the first sax, a man named Hobart. Mr. Schultz stood nearby, a blank expression on his face. It didn't surprise her when he approached the bandleader a few minutes later. Leaning close, he blandly delivered his message while the younger man's face darkened with anger. The two stared one another down until Walt nodded shortly and Mr. Schultz stumped away, leaning on his cane. Walt caught Hobart's eye and shook his head.

"What was that all about?" Lottie asked as they walked back to the hotel. "And don't tell me you don't know what I mean."

A smile played around Mr. Schultz's mouth. "I overheard the good conductor directing his publicist to print new posters featuring a ten-year-old pianist for tonight's show. I merely pointed out that if he used you as a publicity draw, he'd owe us bonus pay. He decided against the idea, more's the pity."

Lottie looked at him. "But if he'd done it, you would have given all the money to Pop when we got home. Just like you're going to give him Johnny's bribe from the train, right?"

"Johnny's bri— well, you are growing up." Mr. Schultz chuckled. "I thought I'd snuck that one by you."

She would not be deterred. "So you'll give it to Pop."

"No." Mr. Schultz shook his head regretfully. "I'm keeping Johnny's money. Consider it my fee for acting as your agent." He looked steadily at the little girl who'd become his meal ticket. "Your performance fee is yours to do with as you like. If you give it to your father, however, you'll want to think twice about telling him where it came from."

Lottie frowned. "You mean I should lie to him?"

The old man shrugged. "He won't be happy about his little girl running around with an all-male dance band."

"But they're a good outfit."

"How are you going to convince your father of that? He could make things pretty uncomfortable for your Aunt Eva. He'll say she neglected your safety when she stayed in New York."

"Isn't it your fault we stopped in Indianapolis?"

Mr. Schultz inclined his head. "I assume he'd be angry with me, too."

She huddled into her coat and wondered what to do.

◗

It was hot and dark in the ballroom. Sweat gathered on Lottie's forehead and dripped down her nose. She sensed the movement of the dancing couples, though she couldn't see over the top of the piano. To her right, tiny lamps lit each music stand.

Walter Harms looked dashing in his tuxedo. When he turned to the audience and sang "You Made Me Love You," she understood why he was the bandleader. He was dreamy.

She hadn't expected the orchestra to perform so well. In rehearsal, they'd been a relaxed and genial group, even slightly lazy. Tonight every man played as if his life depended on it.

At midnight, the band played "Goodnight, Irene," and the dance was over. Lottie watched the men put away their instruments and marveled at how wide awake she felt. Several of them shouted compliments to her on their way out the door.

"Nice job, short stuff."

"Knew you could do it."

"Thanks for helping us out."

Walter stepped past with a blonde in a low-cut dress. "Thanks again," he said over his shoulder.

Lottie blushed. "Can we stop for a piece of pie?" she asked on the walk home. "I saw a place near the hotel."

"Little girls belong in bed this time of night," Mr. Schultz said.

A whine crept into her voice. "Nobody else has to go to bed. I heard Johnny and Carlyle say they were going out somewhere."

"They're not going for pie." Mr. Schultz sounded amused.

"I don't get why everyone gets to have fun, and I have to go to bed." She kicked at a pebble on the sidewalk.

"We're catching a seven o'clock train to Chicago. They're going on to Evansville at noon. Another town, another piano player. That's how it goes, child." Mr. Schultz placed a hand on Lottie's shoulder. "This is over. All that's left is to get some sleep and go home."

She kicked the pebble into the street. Tomorrow she'd be home. She'd see Pop and sleep in her own bed. What had she said in New York? She wanted to go home, and never leave Iowa again. Well, that's what she was going to do.

Too bad there weren't any big bands in Westmont.

Fifteen

"*Blessings all mine, with ten thousand beside.*
A-men."

Lottie put her hymnal away with relief. Two weeks wasn't enough time to get used to the new church organist.

Two weeks wasn't enough time to get used to anything. Not the monotonous school day. Not her standoffish classmates. Not Aunt Cora's perpetual exhaustion.

The change in Pop was the hardest adjustment. He'd acted more shocked than happy when she showed up unannounced. The loss of Karofsky's sponsorship seemed to hit like a physical blow. When she'd given him the money from the Neverland Orchestra, explaining that it was a refund from Karofsky, he'd stared at her in disbelief.

"I paid the man $750, and this is what I get for a refund?"

Lottie glanced at the ten dollar bill in her hand. "Please take it, Pop. Please."

He'd driven into town to talk to Mr. Schultz, and come home angry. Lottie could hear him banging around in the shed, but at supper time he didn't say a word about it. He'd kept his distance since then, too distracted to talk at meals, too busy to play checkers after dinner. Lottie could find no explanation for the wall he'd built between them, except that he was disappointed in her.

"Amen." Reverend Walker completed the benediction.

Aunt Cora crossed the aisle. "I hope you two are coming to dinner."

Pop nodded. "Thank you, Cora."

Lottie reached for her coat. Dinner at Aunt Cora's was better than cold ham and silence at home.

After dinner, Lottie followed Harvey, Mona, and little Anne to the barn to hunt kittens. "Bet you can't jump down from the loft and land in that pile of hay," Harvey said.

"Why would I do that?" Lottie asked as she peered into the old feed trough. "The kittens aren't here. Let's go inside."

Harvey would not be sidetracked. "Because you're a chicken if you don't."

"No I'm not." Lottie didn't understand boy logic.

He turned to easier pickings. "Mona's not a chicken. Are you, sis?"

"Nope." Mona swiped at her nose and left a dirty streak. Bits of straw stuck to her braids. "I can do anything you can do."

Harvey looked smug. "Bet you can't jump down from the loft."

"Can too. I just don't want to."

"If you could, you would." Harvey crossed his arms and looked superior.

Mona stamped her foot. "You go first, Harvey Hoffman."

"All right." Harvey licked his lips and started up the tall ladder. "I'll show you how it's done. Then it's your turn."

"Hey, Anne, come here. I found them." Lottie scooped a kitten out of the tool box, and handed it to her youngest cousin. She picked up an orange striped one and rubbed its softness against her cheek.

"Harvey!" Mona's shriek pierced Lottie's thoughts.

Lottie turned to find Harvey sitting on the dirt floor a foot away from the hay pile, nursing his swelling wrist. Mona stood over him, wringing her hands. "You missed the hay, Harvey!"

"Did not. I landed wrong," Harvey said in a wavering voice. "Go get Ma."

Lottie ran for the house. "Aunt Cora," she yelled, banging the kitchen door behind her. She dashed through the empty kitchen. "Aunt Cora? Harvey broke his arm."

She found all the adults, even Mr. Schultz, in the gun room, staring at the radio. They looked toward Lottie, but didn't seem to see her.

She stood in the doorway, gasping for breath. "Harvey fell out of the hay loft and hurt his arm."

Aunt Cora came back to earth. "I'd better get the bandages." She bustled out of the room.

Lottie looked at the men. "What's wrong?"

Mr. Schultz cleared his throat. "The Japanese attacked the United States today. They bombed our ships in Hawaii. We're at war."

Lottie swallowed hard. "Is Bill all right?"

"I don't know." Pop turned to Otto. "I think it's time for us to go home. Thank Cora for dinner."

Lottie peeked in on Harvey as she left. Aunt Cora had wrapped his arm in a bandage and settled him on the sofa in the front room. Mona sat next to him, full of concern for her big brother.

"What's going to happen?" Lottie asked on the way home.

"Bill's likely to be sent to sea right away. I'm pretty sure Helen will need to come home."

Lottie squashed a spark of joy at the thought of seeing Helen. The war had come. She had no right to be happy.

Helen arrived Thursday evening, her suitcase by her side. "Don't get too used to me," she said. "Bill says this war won't take too long." But her eyes slid away, like she didn't believe her own words.

Pop left for the barn after the greetings were over.

"Where's he going?" Helen asked.

"Out to the shed." Lottie changed the subject. "The whole town is talking about the war. Peter wants to join up when he turns eighteen in January. Aunt Emma's beside herself. She wants him to take over the farm. She says it's because Uncle Harry's laid up, but everyone knows she wants to keep him safe."

"I can't blame her for that." Helen's eyes looked sad.

"Is Bill okay?" Lottie asked.

Helen forced a cheery tone. "I guess so. He shipped out on Monday, and I haven't heard from him since. Sorry about Dr. Karofsky, by the way."

"Oh, it's all right. Pop took it pretty hard, but Mr. Schultz says I'd have come home anyway after Pearl Harbor." Lottie stepped to the ice box. "You must be starved. Do you want something to eat?"

Helen smiled. "You sound so grown up. I'll take some tea. What do you mean, Pop's disappointed?"

"He's been different since I came home. He doesn't talk at dinner, and he goes out to the shed right after. It's like he doesn't want to be around me." Lottie set the teakettle to boil.

"Oh, I don't believe that."

"Wait and see." She made the tea and sat across from her sister at the kitchen table.

Helen blew the steam off her cup. "You've changed a lot, kiddo."

Lottie grinned. "I'm the same as ever."

"No-o-o, you're not." Helen looked her over. "Your hair is darker, for starters. It's got some gold in it. You're a bit taller, but just as skinny as ever. And what are you wearing?"

Lottie glanced at her sailor dress. "Aunt Eva bought it for me. Do you like it?"

"I love it." Helen fingered the navy blue twill. "But I don't just mean you look different. You're different on the inside. More grown-up."

Lottie felt lighter than she had for a long time.

Sixteen

Helen spent the next week in a whirlwind of activity. She cleaned and baked and aired out the house, without regard for the December temperatures. She made dinner every evening, a chore Lottie was glad to give up, and sat in the warm kitchen afterward, mending or knitting socks for Bill.

Lottie was glad of the company as she studied at the kitchen table. Once in a while she looked up and caught Helen with her knitting in her lap, her mind a thousand miles away.

A week before Christmas, Lottie walked home from school with Harvey and Mona. Aunt Cora and Helen sat at the kitchen table, poring over a page in the *Des Moines Register*. Helen's eyes were red-rimmed.

Aunt Cora looked up from the paper. "Help yourselves to the ginger snaps and go play."

Lottie grabbed a cookie and waited as Harvey and Mona trooped out of the room. Then she slipped into a chair across from Helen. "What are you reading?"

The two women exchanged glances. "We came across an article about blackout curtains," Aunt Cora said. "It says we need them in case of air raids."

Lottie coughed on a crumb. "You mean the Japs might bomb Iowa?"

"It's possible. Helen and I are figuring out how much black fabric it would take to make curtains."

Helen folded the newspaper and handed it to Aunt Cora. "We'd better hurry and get it done. It says here they're running out of material at the fabric stores."

"I'll go with you to the fabric store." Lottie took another bite of cookie, feeling reassured. Helen was at her best with a big project.

Uncle Otto poked his head into the kitchen. "Hi, girls. Any idea what your Pop was doing in Fort Madison today?"

Helen shook her head. "Are you sure it was him? He does all his business in Collison."

"It was George, all right." Uncle Otto frowned. "I tried to catch up to him, but he turned the other way when he saw me coming."

○

On Saturday, they found the Woolworth's fabric department stripped clean of blackout cloth. It was the same story at Kerry's Department Store. Sighing, they joined a long line of housewives waiting to order more fabric.

Lottie unbuttoned her coat and loosened her scarf. If she had to wait long, she'd overheat.

A young woman stepped up to the line and did a double take. "Helen! I didn't know you were home."

Helen turned to the newcomer. "Oh, hi, Alice. Seems like forever since we graduated. You remember my little sister, Lottie."

Alice waved at Lottie and promptly forgot she was there. As the older girls caught up on the news, Lottie's attention was caught by another conversation.

"My Johnny's coming home for Christmas this year," said the first voice.

"So he finally quit trying to be a trumpeter?" The second, a nasal soprano, replied. "That must make his father happy."

"No. We're not that lucky. His band plays in Collison right after Christmas, so he's taking a few days at home. We take what we can get, I guess."

The other woman clicked her tongue against her teeth. "I'm sure glad my Sam's a mechanic. It's steady work."

"Isn't he joining the army?"

"Next." The sales clerk waved at Johnny's mother. "Hello, Mrs. Higginbottom. How are things in Columbus Junction?"

Lottie gasped as she pictured Johnny Columbus boarding their train in Chicago. Had he gotten off in Collison? She couldn't be sure.

Lottie tugged Helen's sleeve. "Can we stop at the library?"

Helen looked surprised. "I guess so. Why?"

"I need a book."

"Since when do you read?"

"Aunt Eva showed me how fun it was," Lottie said on a burst of inspiration. "She got me going on a bunch of good books."

Lottie found the notice on the library bulletin board: "The Collison Elks' Club will host a public dance Saturday, December 27, featuring Walter Harms and the Neverland Orchestra. Admission 50 cents. Come one and all."

For the next few days, Lottie took every opportunity to go to Collison. When Pop went to the feed store, she tagged along. When Aunt Cora needed yarn for a baby blanket, Lottie showed an interest in learning to knit. But the day Lottie asked permission to go with Peter to the army recruiter, Helen said, "What on earth is so interesting about Collison?"

Lottie stared at the floor. "Nothing."

Helen narrowed her eyes. "It's not like you to hide things, Lottie. I want to know what's going on right now."

Lottie thought fast. "You caught me. I've been looking for the perfect Christmas gift for you, and I finally found it."

Helen put up one hand. "Stop it. I know what you're giving me for Christmas. It's a felt needle keeper."

"How do you know?"

"You give me the same thing every year." Helen waved her hand impatiently. "Now, stop trying to change the subject and tell me what's going on."

Lottie's shoulders drooped. Helen was not going to give up. "All right. I'll tell you. But you have to promise not to tell Pop."

"I promise."

It was a relief to talk about Indianapolis. Lottie told her about the band, how nice they all were, and how well they played. She explained about the lie she'd told when she gave Pop the money. "Mr. Schultz said Pop would be angry if he knew we did a show with an all-male band."

"You're right. He would be angry," Helen said. "Mr. Schultz should have taken better care of you."

"He did take care of me." Lottie told her about the incident with the publicity posters.

Helen was not impressed. "It doesn't sound like that band leader can be trusted. And I don't like Mr. Schultz asking you to lie like that. I'd like to tell him what I think of him for such a trick."

"But don't you see? He knew what to do. And he wouldn't let me go out for pie after the dance. He made me go to sleep instead."

Helen looked doubtful.

"If you'd really like to tell off Walter Harms, they play in Collison on the twenty-seventh." Lottie ducked her head. "That's why I've been going into town all week. I thought I might run into Johnny. Silly, I know."

Helen's face softened. "Oh, honey, I know you think you made friends, but believe me, those men don't have time for a little girl."

"I wasn't a little girl to them. I was the pianist."

Helen smiled. "It doesn't change the fact that you're still a kid. Besides, most of them will be drafted soon, and there won't be a Neverland Orchestra."

"No!" Lottie thought she might explode. "Now I have to see them. I have to, don't you see?"

Helen ruffled Lottie's hair. "Sorry, kiddo. It just won't work."

One night after dinner, Helen followed Pop to the shed. She returned to the house, shaking her head. "I asked him what's bothering him. He says it's none of my business." She frowned. "I've never seen the shed so full of broken tools and bikes and things. This side business of his is taking over his life."

"What about the day he went to Fort Madison?" Lottie asked. "Did you ask about that?"

Helen frowned. "He got mad at me. Told me to quit worrying."

It was a dreary Christmas. The family gathered at Aunt Cora's as always, but nobody felt like celebrating. The uncles sat in the gun room and discussed the war, while the aunts worked in preoccupied silence in the kitchen.

Lottie spent the morning alone. She didn't want to play with the younger kids, who were whooping it up in the attic. The twins and Peter had gone hunting, and Diana was nowhere to be found. Lottie lay on a blanket in the back hall closet and tried to decide which aunt was the gloomiest. Aunt Emma bore the greatest burden, between Uncle Harry's poor health and Peter's war fever. Aunt Cora moved slowly because her feet hurt, and her belly now preceded her into every room. Aunt Eloise, whose twin boys were only fifteen and thus safe from the war, felt fine, but she didn't have the first idea how to lighten the mood for everyone else.

Lottie closed her eyes and thought about the band. After a week of arguing over the Elks' Club dance, she and Helen were barely on speaking terms. Now, instead of two silent people coexisting at the farm, there were three. And Lottie was no closer to her goal.

The aroma of roast turkey finally drove her from her hiding place. She had just stepped into the hall when the doorbell rang. Aunt Emma hurried to open it, calling, "Frank's here!"

"Merry Christmas, Emma!" Uncle Frank enveloped his older sister in a hug as his pretty wife Karen stepped into the hall behind him.

The years dropped away from Aunt Emma's careworn face as she hugged Frank, but she couldn't help scolding. "You should have warned us you were coming. How do you know we'll have enough food?"

"I told you we should have called," Karen said.

Frank's laugh filled the hall. "Not enough food? In this family? I think we'll be all right."

Karen held out a basket. "I brought rolls and a sweet potato casserole."

"Oh, how thoughtful." Aunt Emma handed the basket to Lottie and hugged her newest sister-in-law. "Come on back to the kitchen and see everybody."

The day turned brighter with Uncle Frank in their midst. The conversation moved from war to family, and they sat around the table long after dessert, talking of old times.

"Say, do you remember the concerts you kids used to get up on Christmas?" Uncle Frank asked. "Did you plan anything like that for today, Helen?"

Helen laughed self-consciously. "It's not my job anymore, Uncle Frank. I'm a grown-up now."

"You? A grown-up?" Uncle Frank sounded shocked. "Just because you're married doesn't mean you can't be a kid at heart. What do you say we roll back the rugs in the front room and do a little dancing? I'll bet Lottie knows some dance tunes."

"Do I ever!" Lottie would have said more, but she caught Mr. Schultz's warning eye.

"All right. Let's dance," Helen said quickly.

"That's our cue, boys." Peter pushed out his chair, and the twins followed suit. "If there's dancing involved, we've got somewhere else to be."

Helen grabbed Peter's arm. "You mean you're brave enough to join the army, but you're afraid of a little dancing? There won't be enough partners if you guys disappear."

"Not our problem." Peter shook off her hand.

"Dance with the girls, Peter. I'd do it myself if it weren't for this danged leg." Uncle Harry's gravelly voice stopped his son in his tracks.

Peter looked at his father's crutches for a long moment. Then he turned his troops toward the front room. "Come on, boys. Let's get those rugs put away."

Under Uncle Frank's direction, the boys moved the furniture and slid back the pocket doors until there was enough space for everyone.

Lottie crawled over an easy chair to reach the piano bench. Aunt Cora had a sheet music arrangement of "String of Pearls" that she tried to follow, but she drifted into Walter Harms's arrangement instead.

"Nice work, Lottie," Uncle Frank called when the song ended. "Those fancy New York piano lessons really paid off."

She laughed. If he only knew!

At first the dance floor belonged to the young people, but as the evening wore on, the aunts and uncles joined the fun. Mr. Schultz squired his daughter through a foxtrot and danced a solemn waltz with his granddaughter.

The boys danced with hangdog expressions on their faces until Aunt Karen taught them to jitterbug. The energetic leaps and hops were a vast improvement over their parents' stately moves.

One by one the dancers tired and dropped out. Lottie played gamely on until only Uncle Frank and Aunt Karen remained. She ended with "Goodnight, Irene," and shut the lid over the piano keys.

Uncle Frank sprawled in an armchair. Linking fingers with his wife he said, "We should go dancing sometime, Helen. You're not half-bad."

Lottie sat next to her sister. "You should see her with Bill. They're terrific."

"It must be terrible with him gone," Aunt Karen said.

"He'll be home soon," Helen said in the falsely cheerful voice Lottie hated. "I try not to think about where he is and what he's doing. I just concentrate on seeing him again."

Uncle Frank sat up. "Let's go dancing this weekend. It'll take your mind off your troubles. What do you say?"

"Is that appropriate right now?" Aunt Karen asked her husband.

Uncle Frank grew serious. "I think so. We have to carry on as usual or go crazy. Don't you think so, Helen?"

Helen made an effort to smile. "You're right. Bill doesn't want me to go around with a sad face all the time. I'll go dancing, if you wish."

"Great! Where should we go?"

Helen glanced at Lottie. "The Neverland Orchestra is playing in Collison on Saturday."

"I've heard of those guys," Karen said. "Oh, Frank, we've got to go."

"You can't go with us, and that's all there is to it," Helen said on the way home.

"Please, Helen? I promise I won't be any trouble."

Helen turned to Pop. "Tell her she can't go to a grown-up dance."

Pop glanced at Lottie. "She's right, honey. You've got no business at a public dance. I don't even know why you want to go. Wait until you're older."

Lottie threw herself against the seat and glared at the back of Helen's head. She had to see the band.

Seventeen

Lottie made a show of going to bed early Saturday night. When she reached her room, she changed back into her clothes and shoved her pillow under the covers. With a last pat, she pulled open the window and reached for the tree outside. The window slammed behind her and she froze, but nobody came. She swung off a branch, sprinted across the yard and jumped into the Ford, where she burrowed under the blankets on the floor in back.

She lay in the darkness for a long time, until she heard the front door slam and footsteps crunch in the gravel. Helen was humming as she slid behind the wheel. Oblivious to Lottie's presence, she sang along with the radio all the way into town.

She parked in Aunt Cora's driveway and got out. "Isn't this a coincidence," Lottie heard her say. "We all got here at the same time."

"How convenient," Aunt Karen replied.

Lottie crawled out from under the blankets and poked her head above the window. The three adults stood between her and Uncle Frank's car, talking and laughing. Lottie hadn't bargained for this. In all her plans, the adults met each other inside the house.

"Go inside," Lottie whispered. "Aunt Cora wants you." But no amount of wishful thinking moved them off the driveway. At last they piled into the front seat of Uncle Frank's car and drove away.

Lottie sat up. They'd left her. She flung herself into the front seat in time to watch the car disappear around the street corner. "No!"

Lottie squeezed her eyes shut and wondered what to do. She had no ride home, and no ride to Collison. She couldn't stay out here in the freezing cold, but to go inside would raise all kinds of unwelcome questions.

When she opened her eyes, her gaze fell on a bump under the floor mat. Helen had left the key. Lottie climbed over the seat and grabbed it. It was a good thing Pop had shown her how to start the car.

She pushed the clutch as far as she could and turned the key. The engine roared to life. Lottie perched on the edge of the seat and hit the gas, but the car died when she let up the clutch. This was going to be harder than she thought.

Lottie's second attempt was more successful, though the engine made an unfamiliar scraping noise as she turned the key. She had the car in first gear when Uncle Otto suddenly yanked open the door and wrenched the key out of the ignition. "What do you think you're doing?" He dragged her onto the driveway and held her at arms' length, panting hard.

Lottie kept her gaze on the gravel. "I… I wanted to go to Collison, but Helen wouldn't let me."

"So you thought you'd drive there yourself? All the way to Collison on a below zero night, and you don't even know how to drive. You'd have been killed for sure."

"I'm sorry. I didn't think it through." She risked a glance at Uncle Otto's face. He looked more frightened than angry, but his grip on her arms was uncomfortably tight. "How did you know I was here?"

"I heard you rev the engine." He sighed. "You'd better come inside."

Aunt Cora heated some milk for Lottie while Uncle Otto called Pop. "You're a wild one right now, child," she said. "What will your father say when he hears you snuck out of the house?"

Lottie pressed her lips together and looked away. "Probably nothing. He doesn't notice anything I do."

"I've never heard you speak so disrespectfully." Aunt Cora carried the milk to the table. "Where on earth is this coming from?"

"What's all the fuss? I heard yelling." Mr. Schultz glowered at Lottie from the doorway.

"Nothing to worry about, Papa. Lottie came into town with Helen. Otto is going to take her home. Everything's fine."

Aunt Cora's calm protection proved Lottie's undoing. Tears flowed silently down her cheeks, causing Mr. Schultz to back out of the kitchen. "I'll be going then."

Uncle Otto stepped past his father-in-law. "I can't reach George. Lottie, where's your Pop tonight?"

"He's in the shed, fixing machinery, just like every night." Lottie sniffed. "That's where he goes after supper."

Aunt Cora frowned. "It must be ten o'clock. Surely he's not still out there."

"Sometimes I wake in the night and the light's still on." Lottie shrugged. "He's been different since I got home from New York."

Uncle Otto exchanged a look with Aunt Cora. "Get your coat on, Lottie. I'm taking you home."

Lottie could imagine what Pop would say about her adventure. "Can't I stay here for the night?"

"The sooner we get you home the better," Aunt Cora said. "Your father will be worried sick when he finds out you're gone. He might be out looking for you already. Did you think of that?"

Uncle Otto pulled onto the main road in silence. Lottie shivered on the cold back seat. She thought about Helen, no doubt having the time of her life in Collison. Had she even given Lottie a passing thought?

Pop wouldn't be looking for her. He'd probably gone to bed without realizing she was gone. He didn't seem to care what she did these days. She hunched further into her coat and gave in to self-pity.

"Hey!" Uncle Otto's startled tone forced her to look up. An orange glow lit the horizon, and she smelled smoke.

"What's that?" Lottie asked.

"There's a fire at your place." The car leaped forward. Uncle Otto raced up the lane, spitting gravel off the back wheels. When he reached the house, he threw the car in park and ran, with Lottie at his heels.

Fire engulfed the shed, and had spread to the barn. Uncle Otto ran to the barn door.

Lottie raced to the house. She tore through the kitchen and up the stairs. "Pop! Pop, wake up! The barn's on fire."

Pop wasn't in his bedroom. She flew to the bathroom, then her room, turning on every light she passed, but Pop was nowhere. Weeping hysterically, Lottie flung herself out the kitchen door, screaming Pop's name.

By now more neighbors had gathered. One man helped Uncle Otto rescue the milk cow and the team of horses, while several others formed a bucket brigade from the pump to the barn.

Aunt Emma found Lottie as Peter joined the men. "Are you all right, child?"

Tears froze on Lottie's cheeks. "I can't find Pop. Have you seen him?"

"Dear God." Aunt Emma glanced at the burning shed.

Lottie raised her hands to her face. "No. He wasn't in there. He couldn't be."

"Oh, honey." Aunt Emma placed an arm around her niece and propelled her toward the house. "You've got to go inside where it's safe. Let the men find your father."

Lottie tried to break away, but Aunt Emma proved surprisingly strong. She half-carried her into the kitchen and pushed her gently into a chair. "Now, why don't you tell me about it?"

Lottie hid her face in her hands, dry-eyed. Aunt Emma rubbed her back gently and waited, but Lottie could not bring herself to say what she was thinking.

Hours passed, filled with the shouts of the neighbors and the sounds of frightened animals. The horses were hitched to chains to pull down the barn, and the fire died back, but the animals' winter feed would burn for a long time.

It was two o'clock when Uncle Otto stepped into the kitchen, his face and clothing black with soot. "There's nothing more we can do. The folks are going home."

"Did you find him?" Lottie asked, but she read the answer on her uncle's defeated face. Then the tears and words burst out of her. "It's my fault. It's all my fault," she repeated over and over, incoherent with grief and shame.

Uncle Otto fell to his knees and took Lottie's face in his blackened hands. "I want you to listen to me. This is not your fault. Even if you'd been home, you couldn't have done anything about this fire. The shed went up all at once, from the looks of things. By the time you got out of bed and across the yard, it would have been too late to stop it."

Lottie threw her arms around Uncle Otto's neck and sobbed, her tears making tracks in the soot on his coat. She wanted to believe him so badly.

Helen came in at dawn, out of place in her dress and dancing shoes.

Uncle Otto, Aunt Emma and Peter sat with Lottie at the table, exhausted but unwilling to leave. Helen went straight to her sister. "Where's Pop?"

Lottie shook her head.

Helen glanced toward the doorway in helpless confusion.

There, with stricken faces, stood half of the Neverland Orchestra.

Eighteen

"Let's go, boys," Johnny said. "This isn't the time for pancakes."

Lottie watched them with dull eyes. Yesterday, she'd have given everything to have Johnny and his friends in her living room. This morning, they weren't important at all.

The last man out the door was Parson, the sax player. "Hold on," he said to the other men, and made his way back to the kitchen. "Can I pray for you folks before I leave?"

At a nod from Uncle Otto, they bowed their heads and Parson began. "Our God and heavenly Father, strengthen the members of this family to meet the days ahead. Teach them to rely on one another and on You in their suffering, and bring glory to Your name. Through Jesus Christ our Lord we pray. Amen."

The family left on the heels of the band, with promises to return later in the day. Helen made Lottie go to bed, where she immediately fell asleep.

She awoke hours later, disoriented by the afternoon sunshine, until the acrid smell of smoke opened a floodgate of painful memories. She dragged herself down to the kitchen, where Helen sat with her hair uncombed, staring dully out the window.

Unable to speak of Pop, Lottie said, "What was the band doing here?"

Helen glanced at her. "I recognized David Parker — the band calls him Parson — on saxophone. He's one of Bill's friends from the college. Most of the boys are from around here, did you know that?"

"No." Lottie tried and failed to muster some interest in the band members.

"Johnny recruited a bunch of them. Walter Harms only had himself, his brother Sammy, and one other guy."

"Hobart?"

"Yes. Anyway, I went to say hello to David, and everyone acted glad to meet me. They're still short a piano player. Johnny asked if you wanted your job back, but I said no. He took it into his head to come ask you himself, and the rest of Johnny's friends invited themselves along. It was almost morning by then, so I said I'd make breakfast. We piled into Uncle Frank's car and sang all the way back to Westmont." She turned her face to the window again, remembering. "It feels like a sin to sing like that when Pop was dying. I never should have gone to that dance."

Lottie went to her then, and slipped her arm around her neck. Helen put her head on Lottie's shoulder, and they stayed that way for a long time.

With no fire department in Westmont, it fell to the sheriff to investigate. He poked around the shed the next afternoon and declared Pop dead on the basis of his findings.

They held the funeral on New Year's. The church overflowed with mourners, including Aunt Eva, who came from New York with her new husband, Detective Reed. They'd been married by a justice of the peace on Christmas Eve. The aunts were scandalized.

Parson and Johnny slipped into the sanctuary and stood at the back. Johnny caught Lottie's eye and nodded sympathetically. They left before she could speak to them.

One white-haired gentleman, a stranger, took Helen aside after the service. He talked to her at length in a low voice. Lottie started across the room to ask Helen who he was, but was stopped by Diana.

"Where will you live now?" Diana asked.

Lottie crossed her arms. "Same place as always."

"That's not what my mom says. She says the farm will go to Aunt Emma. It's to stay in the Hoffman family."

Lottie put her hands on her hips. "We're still in the Hoffman family, Diana. We're staying put."

Diana pursed her lips in a maddening smile. "We'll see."

Aunt Eva spent a few minutes with Lottie later in the afternoon. "I brought you a present," she said, handing Lottie a gift-wrapped rectangle. "I know how you love to read. Try Chapter Seven."

"Thanks." Lottie smiled weakly.

Aunt Cora did her best to make Helen and Lottie stay in town that evening. "We've got room. Mona and Anne can move in with Harvey for the night."

"No thanks, Aunt Cora. We need to go home," Helen said firmly.

Lottie breathed a sigh of relief.

"Do we really have to move?" she asked in the car.

"Not necessarily," Helen said. "It's up to Uncle Harry. The farm is his now."

"Where would we go?"

Helen glanced at her sister. "Let's cross that bridge when we come to it."

"All right." Lottie yawned. "Who was that man you talked to at the funeral?"

"He's a doctor from Fort Madison. Pop started seeing him for chest pains a few months ago." Helen frowned. "He thinks Pop might have had a heart attack in the shed. Maybe the fire started while he was unconscious."

"Do you think that's what happened?" Lottie suddenly felt wide awake.

Helen lifted one shoulder. "Could be."

"Then I couldn't have saved him."

"Nobody could have saved him," Helen said. "Nobody."

They spent New Year's Day in solemn quiet. Helen wrote a long letter to Bill, while Lottie played her harmonica upstairs in her bedroom. The effort to invent new tunes kept her thoughts at bay.

Both girls avoided the kitchen window, with its view of the ruined outbuildings. Peter had moved the animals to his dad's place, so they had no outside chores.

Uncle Otto called the next morning and asked to see the girls right away. When they arrived at the bank, Uncle Otto ushered them into his private office. "What do you know about your father's finances?" he asked.

Helen folded her hands in her lap. "Nothing. He never talked about money, except to give us a household allowance. Why?"

"As you know, I'm the executor of his will." Uncle Otto rearranged some papers on his desk. "I received a call from a bank in Fort Madison. It seems he took out a second mortgage on the farm."

Lottie felt Helen stiffen. "When?"

Uncle Otto glanced at Lottie. "November."

"So that's how he did it." Her voice was flat.

Uncle Otto gave a short nod. "Trips to New York don't come cheap. The terms of the loan were shoddy, to say the least. The bank is foreclosing on the farm."

The color drained from Helen's cheeks. "There must be some way to save it. Uncle Harry wants it, doesn't he?"

Uncle Otto sighed. "Harry can't run his own place now, as sick as he is, much less buy your father's. Peter's not going to stick around to do it for him, either. Besides, your father's debt was large. None of us can afford to cover it."

"You're a banker, Uncle Otto. Can't you see a way around this?" Helen sounded desperate.

"If your father had come to me, I could do something," Uncle Otto said. "He was too proud to tell me he needed help, I guess. As it stands the loan is legal."

"I've been wondering about the repair business," Helen said. "The fire destroyed all those bikes and mowers and things. What do we do about that?"

Uncle Otto's expression softened. "I've heard from several of his customers. Nobody wants to make a claim against the estate. They don't want to make things any harder on you than they already are."

Helen's chin went up. "But we owe them."

Uncle Otto waved one hand impatiently. "You girls belong to Westmont. This is the way we treat our own. Now, I suggest you go home and decide who the two of you want to live with until Bill comes back."

Nineteen

A few days later they packed their belongings and moved to the big house on Jefferson Street. They had no other choice. Aunt Emma and Uncle Harry had become measurably cooler since they learned of the foreclosure.

Lottie found her present from Aunt Eva when she cleaned out her room. It lay in her dresser, still gift-wrapped, no doubt another dreary story about perfect children. Maybe she should leave it for the auction. Helen had stressed that they could not afford to waste space. But she loved Aunt Eva, so she chucked it into the trunk.

Aunt Cora welcomed her nieces with open arms. Mona, Anne, and Harvey, who now shared a bedroom, weren't as warm. As an adult, Helen was out of their power. But Lottie was their age. She was fair game for squabbles and teasing. Lottie did her best to defend herself, but the constant fussing wore her down.

One afternoon she hid from the others in the closet under the stairs. The aunts were visiting in the kitchen, and their conversation projected through the heat vent that ran through the closet floor.

"What will you do when the baby comes?" Aunt Emma asked.

"Mrs. Anderson will come in to help as always," Aunt Cora said in her gentle voice, "and the baby will sleep with Otto and me."

Aunt Eloise snorted. "For a month or two, maybe, but it'll soon outgrow the cradle. What then?"

"I think I'll convert the attic to bedrooms."

"That's still a lot of feet under your dinner table." Aunt Emma said.

Aunt Cora's voice was tight. "We'll manage."

"I hope you all remember," Aunt Eloise said, "I said that trip to New York was a crazy idea. And look what came of it. Two orphan girls, their father dead from overwork, and the farm lost to us. That's what comes of running after fame and fortune."

"That's enough, Eloise," Aunt Cora said. "George died in a fire. And it isn't the girls' fault he borrowed money from those crooks in Fort Madison. Of all the banks to do business with!"

Aunt Eloise sniffed. "He still caused an unfair burden for the rest of us. Lottie won't be an adult for seven or eight more years, and she has no means of support. She's a charity case, plain and simple."

"I assume she'll live with Helen and Bill once the war ends," Aunt Emma said mildly.

"What a way to start a marriage," Aunt Cora murmured, then gasped. "Oh, I didn't mean that. Everybody lives with complications. Helen and Bill will figure it out."

Lottie sat upright in the dark, her eyes stretched wide with new grief. She was a complication.

○

Lottie didn't see much of Helen that week, though they shared a room. Helen rose early and went to bed late, and filled the hours in between with activity. She cleaned house for Aunt Cora, contributed to the war effort by rolling bandages, and wrote long letters to Bill. She never spoke of Pop.

One night Lottie awoke to the sound of Helen's sobs. She slipped out of bed and crossed the room to lie next to her big sister. Helen put her arms around Lottie, and soon her weeping quieted. They didn't speak of it in the morning.

On the tenth of January, Aunt Cora didn't come downstairs. Uncle Otto sat in the gun room, an unlit pipe clamped between his teeth. Helen made breakfast, then bundled up the children and sent them off in the cold. They passed Nurse Anderson on their way down the sidewalk.

The thin sound of a baby's cry greeted them after school.

"The baby's here!" Mona and Anne said in unison, and ran for the stairs.

Lottie and Harvey followed at a slower pace. As they reached the front hall, a second wail chimed in with the first. The cousins looked at each other. "Twins?" Lottie whispered.

Harvey turned his eyes to the staircase. "Oh boy, I hope not."

Aunt Cora sat in the middle of her bed, a baby cradled in the crook of each elbow. "Their names are Frank and George," she said proudly, "after their uncles."

Harvey wore a stupefied grin. "They're boys. I never thought of that."

The children crowded around, touching the babies' tiny hands and exclaiming over the downy hair on their heads. Lottie stood at the edge of the group and wondered what to do.

After supper, the Hoffmans gathered in Aunt Cora's bedroom while Lottie and Helen washed the supper dishes. "It's going to be busy around here," Lottie said. "I guess Aunt Cora will need you more than ever."

"I guess so." Helen glanced at her. "Aren't you excited about the babies?"

Lottie rubbed a platter dry. "There'll be a lot of feet under the dinner table, that's all."

Mr. Schultz stumped into the kitchen, leaning heavily on his cane. "This came in the mail today," he said, handing an envelope to Lottie. She looked at the return address: Loretta Higginbottom, Columbus Junction, Iowa.

Lottie pulled two unmatched sheets of stationery out of the envelope. On the first, Loretta Higginbottom explained that her son Johnny had asked her to forward a letter. The other was from Walter Harms.

Dear sir:

I want to hire Charlotte Brown permanently to be our piano player. I am willing to pay double wages for a year, and provide for a chaperone for Miss Brown, as she is a minor. Several of my musicians have joined the army, and I am shorthanded.

Here is a copy of our schedule for the next month. Send a telegram care of my hotel.

Walter Harms

Lottie held the letter to her chest and looked at Mr. Schultz. "Oh yes, please, let's do it! You'll go, won't you?"

Mr. Schultz sat heavily on a kitchen chair. "I'm wrong for the job. If you spend your life on the road, you'll need a female companion who can share your hotel room."

Lottie's heart sank. "So it wouldn't work." She gave the letter back.

Helen wiped her hands on her apron. "Let me see that." She studied the words with a frown. "This was written three weeks ago. The only date left is this Friday in Omaha."

"What does it matter? I can't go anyway." Lottie hung up her dish towel.

Helen lifted one hand. "Not so fast, kiddo. I need to think."

Lottie watched her sister in the quiet kitchen. Upstairs, contented voices rose and fell, as the Hoffman children got ready for bed. Nurse Anderson brought a baby into the hall, crooning to him in her soothing voice. Uncle Otto tripped over something and let out a yelp of pain.

Helen made up her mind. "Let's go."

The news that Helen and Lottie were leaving caused very little uproar. Only Aunt Cora was genuinely upset, and she was too tired to argue. "The door is open," she told them. "This house is your home, no matter what."

Uncle Otto couldn't quite meet their eyes as he urged them to stay.

Mr. Schultz watched them pack without saying much. There was something wistful in his constant presence. The night before their departure, he stopped in their bedroom doorway. "I'm going with you tomorrow."

Helen looked up, a little defensive. "I'm a seasoned traveler, you know. There's no need to worry about us."

He ignored her. "Harms hired me to play string bass."

Helen raised her eyebrows. "You can do that? I thought the cello was your instrument."

"I'll pick it up."

Helen gave him a measuring stare. "Have you told Aunt Cora?"

He shrugged. "She's knee-deep in children. If anything she'll be relieved. One less mouth to feed."

Helen bent her head over her suitcase. "We leave at seven tomorrow morning."

Twenty

"Boy are we glad to see you," Johnny said when they stepped off the train in Omaha. "We're losing guys right and left. Carlyle's entire section joined up at the first of the year, along with our tenor sax. We lost the piano player to a recruiting station in Sioux City."

"It's been thin, all right." Parson strode along behind them, carrying the girls' suitcases. "Last night we looked more like a quartet than an orchestra."

"Say, why haven't you boys joined up?" Helen asked.

"I tried," Johnny said. "They said I had a bad ticker."

Helen looked doubtful. "Heart trouble? You?"

"I swear on a stack of Bibles." Johnny put his hand over the deficient organ. "Parson here is color blind."

"Shut up, Columbus." Parson picked up his pace.

"He's sensitive," Johnny said with a grin. "Say, beautiful, you wouldn't be willing to sing a few numbers with Walt, would you? We know you've got the voice for it."

Helen snorted. "I'm not part of the bargain, boys. My husband barely approves of this plan as it is." This last bit was pure speculation, since Helen hadn't yet written to Bill.

"Aw, tell her we need her, Parson." Johnny appealed to his friend.

"I'm with Helen." Parson flashed a smile in her direction. "Bill wouldn't take kindly to his wife putting on a slinky dress and singing for a crowd."

Walter Harms met them in the hotel lobby, his bow tie hanging loosely from his shirt collar. "We're on in two hours, so leave your luggage with the desk clerk. We're catching a train for Saint Joe after the show."

"You mean we have to sleep on the train?" Helen asked.

He looked her over. "This is what you signed up for. Would you rather turn around and go home?"

Helen said nothing.

It was snowing when they reached the dance hall. Lottie's shoes were soaked, but she didn't mind. She found her music on the piano and began to warm up.

Helen sat on a folding chair and watched the orchestra rehearse. When they finished, she stepped over to the piano. "You'll need a couple more dresses if you perform every night," she said, pointing to the yellow dress they'd bought months ago in Des Moines. "I'll make them for you, if that tyrant will give me enough time to find a store when we reach Saint Joe."

"But you don't have a sewing machine," Lottie said.

Helen's eyes narrowed. "I'll think of something."

There was plenty of room on the dance floor. Walt did his best to keep things lively, but the response was tepid until he introduced the band. Lottie stepped away from the piano as he called her name, and a murmur went through the crowd. The mood picked up after that.

When the dancing ended, several people stood around Lottie's piano and pelted her with questions.

"Where'd you get that talent, little girl?"

"Does your mother know you're out this late?"

"Weren't you on the *Barn Dance Frolic*?"

"Can I have your autograph?"

On the train two hours later, Lottie poked Helen through the top of her bunk. "What're you doing up there?"

"I'm sewing a loose button back on your dress. Go to sleep, Lottie."

"It was good tonight, wasn't it?"

"Yep."

"Don't you think Walter's handsome?"

Helen's face appeared, upside down, from the top bunk. "First off, handsome is as handsome does. And second, lower your voice. People can hear you."

They had a two-night job in St. Joseph, so they got off the train and checked into a hotel. It was a seedy old building with stains on the ceilings of the rooms, but Helen examined the sheets and pronounced them clean.

"What do we do now?" Lottie asked. "It's hours before lunch."

Helen flopped back onto her bed. "Are you sleepy? We could take a nap."

Lottie laughed. "That's silly. Let's go look for a five-and-dime so you can buy material for my dress."

"Not yet." Helen's eyes were closed. "Give me five minutes."

Five minutes later, Helen was sound asleep.

"All right then," Lottie said loudly, "I'll go shopping by myself."

Helen didn't move.

Lottie grabbed her coat, shut the door softly and started down the hall. A few doors down, she stopped at the sound of voices.

"I'm telling you the Cubs have a shot this year." It was Bobby Richards, the second trombone player.

"You're out of your mind. The Dodgers will win the World Series, and I can prove it." Carlyle sounded excited.

Ugh. Baseball talk. She moved on down the hall and stopped again when she recognized Walter's voice, raised in anger. "I'm the face of this band. People expect to do business with me. They don't want some slicked-back kid in a zoot suit signing their contracts."

"Maybe if I did sign the contracts, we'd get paid our fair share." Johnny sounded furious. "We went into partnership, Walt. That means everything's 50-50. The money, the business. Everything. If you're not gonna play fair, I'll take my boys and go."

"You do that. See how far you get."

Lottie rushed from the shouting, past the front desk, and out the door.

The street was full of traffic as she ran down the sidewalk and turned the corner. Seeing no stores, she kept going. Maybe there would be something in the next block.

It felt good to run. She'd sat too long on trains in the past few days. She crossed another street and kept going, shaking off the anxiety brought on by angry voices.

It was a warm day for January, and she began to heat up beneath her coat, so she stopped to unbutton it and look around. She still hadn't passed a five-and-dime, and it was time to go back to the hotel.

Lottie turned around to retrace her steps. When she reached the first corner, she paused. Nothing looked familiar. Had she gone straight? Had she turned? She couldn't remember.

She walked across the street and up the sidewalk, searching for clues. Had she passed that yellow building? That advertisement for paint? She didn't know. She retraced her steps to the corner, and turned down the cross street.

This time she passed a bakery, and the smell of fresh bread clicked in her brain. She was on the right track. At the next corner, she repeated the process, going up the street, turning right and circling back before she figured out where she'd come from.

By the time she reached the hotel, she felt rather proud of herself. She'd gotten lost and found her way home without any help. Pop would have been proud.

Parson stood at the front desk, talking with Bobby Richards. "Hiya, kid. What were you doing out there?" Behind the round wire-rim glasses his blue eyes were concerned. "Were you by yourself?"

"Yes, I was," Lottie said. "I went for a walk, and got a little lost, but I made it home all right. It's a beautiful day."

Parson looked thoughtful. "Well, good for you. Next time, though, let somebody know when you want to leave a hotel. All right?"

"All right." Lottie turned and skipped away.

Helen awoke when she stepped into the room. "Sorry about that, kiddo. I guess I fell asleep. Is it lunch time yet?"

Lottie nodded. "I'm starved."

They found the rest of the band eating lunch in a diner across from the hotel. Lottie plowed through her meatloaf as if she hadn't eaten in weeks.

"Use your manners," Helen admonished between tiny bites of her own meal. "Just because we're not home doesn't mean you can forget everything Aunt Cora tried to teach you."

Parson ambled over to their table. "Mind if I join you ladies?"

Helen smiled at him. "Not at all, David."

He turned an empty chair around and sat down, resting his arms on its metal back. "Your sister had a little adventure this morning," he said to Helen. "Did she tell you about it?"

Helen's eyes widened. "No, she didn't. What happened?"

"Go ahead." Parson turned to Lottie.

Lottie looked away, feeling cornered. "I went for a walk and came back, that's all."

"By yourself?" Helen sounded troubled.

Lottie nodded.

"I can see we'll have to talk about some ground rules for traveling to new places. We'll do that when we go back to our room." Helen glanced at Parson. "Thanks, David. I'll take care of it."

Though Helen had dismissed him, Parson stayed where he was. "Have you thought about Lottie's schooling?"

Lottie glared at him. "I don't have to go to school. I have a job."

"I hadn't thought about school," Helen said. "We came away so quickly, I guess that detail escaped me. I suppose I'll have to be her teacher."

Lottie stared at her in disbelief. Helen would make a good army general, but she'd be a terrible teacher.

Parson cleared his throat. "I'll tutor her if you'd like. It'll give me something to do when we have time on our hands. Besides, I'm going back to college once I save enough money, and I need to keep my brain active."

Lottie turned her baleful gaze on Parson. "I don't want to go to school. I'll die of boredom."

Parson's smile transformed his round face. "I'll try to make it interesting."

"It's a deal," Helen said in relief.

Unfortunately, Parson was a man of his word. The next day after lunch, he presented Lottie with a page of assorted math problems. "I need to find out what you know so I know where to start," he said.

She took the paper in two fingers. "Can't we start with something else, like geography? I know the forty-eight states."

He grinned. "Do the problems, Lottie."

The worksheet took much longer than she expected. She knew how to do everything except long division, but her skills were rusty. She'd spent most of the last school term in New York, and Aunt Eva, bless her heart, hadn't been a very consistent teacher.

"Here you go, Parson," she said as she handed it to him that evening before the show.

"Great." He tucked it into his saxophone case. "I'll take a look at it tomorrow." He turned away to talk with another band member.

She headed for the piano with a sense of accomplishment.

"What did you do this afternoon?" Lottie asked that night when Helen kissed her good night.

"Oh, I took a little nap and mended the sleeve of Carlyle's coat." Helen sounded sleepy. "Those boys need looking after."

Lottie smiled. Helen had a project.

Twenty-one

News spread about the child piano player. Each night when Lottie took her bow, the audience applauded, and people waited to meet her after the show. She talked with them, and signed autographs, but it didn't keep her from noticing the habits of the rest of the band. If the dance hall served beer, most of the men drank a cold one before they packed their equipment. Walt's little brother Sammy usually tried to slip in on that action, but they turned him away with a good-natured push.

Parson put away more than his share of equipment, and sat down with Mr. Schultz to talk about music. He took a good deal of ribbing for this habit, but it gratified the old man.

Walt's flashy looks and golden voice generally attracted women in slinky dresses and thick lipstick. He often disappeared with one of them for a while before the band moved on. One woman in particular, a platinum blonde in a fur coat, showed up at least once a week.

Helen snorted with disgust when Lottie pointed this out. "He's a tom cat," she said with deep disapproval.

"What about the rest of them?" Lottie asked. "Are they tom cats too?"

"No, but they all have their faults. Johnny has a quick temper." Helen counted them off on her fingers. "Bobby never let the truth get in the way of a good story, and Carlyle studies the racing form religiously."

"And Sammy's always complaining," Lottie said.

Helen looked thoughtful. "It must be hard to be Walter's brother. Here's Sammy, only fourteen years old, with no choice about playing for his brother's band. He's a pretty good drummer, and I've never heard Walt say a kind word to the poor kid."

"Well, I wish he would, so Sammy would be nicer to me."

Helen tugged one of Lottie's braids. "Don't let him get to you, kiddo."

On Saturday, a week after she joined the band, Lottie stood in line to receive her wages. When she reached the front, Walt held out $6.

Lottie looked at it. "I thought you said you'd pay me double, because of Helen."

"It was an off week." Walt shrugged. "We didn't make enough. You understand. It'd be different if your sister was willing to sing for us. As it is, she's dead weight."

"That's not it at all. Our deal included Helen as your chaperone." Johnny stood next to his partner, looking acutely uncomfortable. "Now, I don't like to go back on a promise, but it's like Walt says. We barely made payroll. If it makes you feel better, Walt and I didn't get paid at all."

"O-okay." She looked from one to the other uncertainly. Something didn't smell right.

"Let's go, Charlotte." Mr. Schultz watched the proceedings with a practiced eye. "One of those men is playing the other for a fool," he murmured as they walked away.

Lottie glanced over her shoulder. "Which one?"

He did not reply.

Lottie turned eleven on the first day of February, a few miles west of St. Louis. Helen gave her a purple sateen dress with a layer of crinoline under the skirt, and the boys threw her a party. Carlyle tracked down a day-old bakery cake, and Lottie served it as they waited for the next train. It was a little dry, but the boys didn't care. They could eat nearly anything.

Not so with Helen. She took one bite and hurried out of the room. Lottie followed her to the public bathroom, but Helen locked the door.

While she waited, a woman with a baby approached. "Are you in line?" she asked, tipping her head toward the bathroom door.

Lottie shook her head. "I'm waiting for my sister."

They avoided one another's eyes as Helen retched on the other side of the door.

"Does she have the flu?" The woman shifted the baby to her other hip.

"I don't know, ma'am."

A minute later, Helen emerged. The woman took in her pale face and slender body. She dropped her eyes to Helen's wedding ring, then back up to her face. A message seemed to pass between them, leaving Lottie mystified. Helen turned to her. "Go back to the party, kiddo. I'm all right."

As Lottie turned to go the woman said, "How far along are you?"

Johnny was dancing a frenzied jitterbug for laughs when Helen returned to the party. "Sit down, Johnny. I've got something to say," she said. Johnny opened his mouth to make a joke, but something in Helen's face stopped him. He sat.

Helen looked around nervously. "I have good news and bad news," she began.

"Give us the good news," Bobby Richards said.

She looked at him with a half-smile. "I'm going to have a baby."

Lottie stared at her sister in shock.

Some of the men shifted uncomfortably in their chairs, while others offered half-hearted congratulations.

"What's the bad news?" Walt said abruptly.

"Lottie and I will have to go home."

Hobart nodded. "That's true, Walt. We can't keep a pregnant woman with us. She'll slow us down."

Walter frowned. "When is it due?"

"Late August, I think."

"Are you well enough to travel?"

"I think so."

"Then we'll keep going. We've got shows to do, and Lottie's a good draw." He brushed the crumbs from his lap and stood up.

"Now, look here, Walt." Johnny stood up. "The lady should have the last word in the matter."

Walt gave him a long, measuring look. "All right," he said softly. "Why don't you ask her?"

A dull flush crept up Johnny's cheeks. He looked at Helen. "What do you want to do?"

"We'll stay," she said crisply, "until I hear from my husband."

"It's settled." Walter looked smug. "We go on as usual."

Twenty-two

I'm so tired of spelling words I could just spit." Lottie flopped back in her seat and glared at Parson. "Can't you see it's spring outside? Nobody should study when the weather gets warm."

Parson laughed. "You can't quit school on the first warm day of the year. I only gave you twenty words. Spell them right, and we're done for the day."

"You're heartless." She bent her head over the word list. "When I'm a famous piano player, nobody will ever ask me to spell 'thoroughfare.'"

His smile disappeared. "Music is a hard way to make a living, especially for a woman. It doesn't hurt to develop some other skills."

She looked up. "If it's so hard, why are you here? Johnny says you want to be a minister."

"Johnny thinks anyone who's not ashamed of God must want to be a minister." He shrugged. "I want to be a professor, but I ran out of money to finish college. I figured the easiest way to earn more was to play my saxophone, but now I'm not so sure. I guess I expected the band to do better than it has. Our friend Johnny was a pretty convincing recruiter."

"You're not leaving are you?"

He grinned. "I can't. I'm responsible for your education. Now, memorize those words, and I'll take you to a bookstore when we get to Rockford tomorrow."

Lottie made a face. "No thanks. I don't like to read."

Parson looked surprised. "What do you have against reading?"

"My Aunt Eva used to give me books. They were awful dull."

He laughed. "I'll help you pick something exciting. Ever hear of

163

Treasure Island?"

They pulled into Rockford in an April snowstorm. Wet flakes the size of quarters clung to their coats as they moved equipment into the dance hall.

Aunt Cora had forwarded a packet of Bill's letters to the hotel. Helen spent the afternoon in their room, reading and re-reading them. When it was time to go to the ballroom, she placed the letters in her purse. "I want them near me, Lottie. Is that silly?"

The boys wouldn't allow Helen to carry any equipment, so she and Lottie arranged chairs and set up music stands instead.

"Do you think we'll have a big crowd tonight?" Lottie asked.

"Yes, if the snow stops," Helen said. "We usually do all right on Saturdays. How are your lessons coming?"

Lottie shrugged. "Parson says we need more books. He wants to take me to a bookstore tomorrow before we leave Rockford."

"He can't keep using his own money on your schooling." Helen frowned. "Have you read the book Aunt Eva gave you at the funeral? You brought it with you, right?"

Lottie nodded. "It's still wrapped."

"Then you can show it to him tomorrow. Who knows? Maybe it will be useful." Helen put her hands on her hips and looked around. "There. We're finished, so you can go practice."

Lottie sat at the piano and thumbed through her folder, looking for the new music Walt had bought in St. Louis. She could hear Walt and Johnny arguing with each other outside the doors, and the companionable warming-up sounds of the wind instruments. Behind her, Sammy fiddled with his drum kit.

Lottie turned to look at him. "Do you ever get tired of hearing your brother yell?"

"Do you ever get tired of being a twit?"

Lottie faced the piano again, disgusted. It didn't pay to talk to Sammy.

The snow stopped in time for a good-sized crowd to fill the ballroom. Johnny and the boys played the new tunes with fresh enthusiasm, and their energy transferred to the dance floor.

From behind a tall upright, Lottie could hear the thump of wooden floorboards as the couples swung around the room. Out of the corner of her eye, she spied Walt's regular girl lounging against the wall, looking bored. One man after another asked her to dance, but her gaze never wavered from the bandleader as she refused them. When he sang to the audience, the girl's face sharpened into fierce possessiveness.

The dance ended, and Lottie talked with a few curious couples before packing her things. She noticed without surprise that the blonde girl was gone, and so was Walt. Johnny and the boys argued happily about sports as they put away their instruments, and even Sammy hummed a few bars of "In the Mood." A good night indeed.

Lottie had stuck one arm into her coat when a commotion sounded outside. A large man burst through the doors and stormed across the ballroom. "Where is she? Where's my wife, the worthless hussy?"

Every head turned toward the newcomer. For a moment, all was quiet.

Johnny licked his lips and stepped forward. "Who are you looking for?"

"You know who I mean," the man said furiously. "My Zelda, the wench. She's been following youse guys around from place to place. I hired a private detective, so don't try to deny it. Which one of you is makin' a fool out of me? I'm gonna kill you."

The slight vibration of a cymbal caught Lottie's attention. She turned her head in time to see Sammy disappear through the nearest exit.

"Hey! Where's he going?" The man charged into the orchestra, knocking over chairs in his haste.

Parson stepped into his path. Pointing a finger into the man's chest he said, "Well, now, why don't we talk about this calmly? You wouldn't want to do anything rash."

As peaceful as he was, it was easy to forget that Parson was a big man.

"Don't get in my way." The angry husband tried to pass him.

Parson didn't budge. "I understand your feelings, sir, but I can't allow you to kill anyone. It won't help, you know. You'll just end up in jail."

The man's temper cooled a fraction as he looked into Parson's steady eyes. "All right. I won't kill him, but I still plan to teach them both a lesson. Now let me go."

Parson held his gaze for another moment before he stepped aside. The man thundered past him and out the door, only to return a few minutes later. "They're gone, and so is my car." He grabbed Parson by the collar and drew back his fist. "If it wasn't for you, I'd have had 'em."

Bobby Richards grabbed the man's forearm and yanked back hard before he could swing. The man turned on his assailant and Parson dealt him a right to the jaw. He went down in a clatter of folding chairs. The boys stood over him, fists raised, but he didn't try to rise.

"I got it, don't worry." He rubbed his jaw. "Any of youse ever gets tired of this gig, I might have an opening for a bodyguard."

Parson put out a hand and helped the man to his feet. "Sorry about your wife, sir. I don't hold with that stuff myself."

"I can see that." The man got to his feet. "Aw, I'm better off without her, I guess."

Johnny clapped him on the shoulder. "Can we give you a ride anywhere?"

By the time they reached the hotel, the boys were on good terms with their unexpected guest. Al Parisi was a businessman from Joliet whose much younger wife had caused him no end of trouble. "Makes me almost sorry I married her," he said.

When they pulled up to the hotel, Al said, "Damnation, my car's not here. Now where have they gone?"

Johnny patted his shoulder. "Come on inside while I go look for Walt."

The entire Neverland Orchestra stood around the front desk while Johnny headed off down the hall. No one made a move to go to their room.

Helen nudged Lottie. "Come on, kiddo. Time for bed."

"Not yet." Lottie turned pleading eyes on her sister.

"Now." Helen tugged her into the hall. Mr. Schultz followed.

When they passed Johnny and Walt's room, the door stood open. Johnny was in the middle of the room, a dazed look in his eyes. When he saw Mr. Schultz he said, "Sir? Could you come in here a minute?"

"What's going on?" Lottie asked Helen as they climbed the stairs.

"Nothing we can help with."

"How do you know?"

"Because we're girls. Come now, let's get you to bed."

○

She awoke to the click of a suitcase latch. "Why are you packing?"

166

she asked Helen. "We play again tonight, don't we?"

Helen pushed the suitcase aside and sat down on the bed. "Sammy came back last night with Mr. Parisi's car. He helped Walt and that woman run away to California."

"Goodness!" Lottie's eyes widened. "They didn't take Sammy along?"

"No. Walt left him here to face the music." Helen looked disgusted. "What a jerk!"

Lottie pointed at the suitcase. "But why are we leaving? We can play without Walt, can't we? Mr. Schultz would be a good conductor. Of course, we won't have a singer."

Helen shook her head. "Walt stopped at the hotel on his way out of town and took all the band's money. Johnny's flat broke now. He doesn't have enough to pay our hotel bill, or buy train tickets, or anything."

"Won't we get paid tonight?"

"Not enough. Walt took half the fee in advance, so that's gone too." She sighed. "That's it, Lottie. We'll have to go home."

"But we're doing so well." Lottie's eyes filled with tears. "Mr. Schultz is happy, I'm happy. You like the boys, don't you, Helen?"

Helen nodded. "Sure, but it can't be helped. Without that money, the Neverland Orchestra is history. Now, it's time to get up and start packing. We have to get out of here before the hotel finds out we can't pay our bill."

Lottie swung her legs over the edge of the bed. They felt like lead.

Fifteen minutes later she was dressed and nearly packed, and holding Aunt Eva's gift-wrapped book in her hands. "Helen?"

"Yes?" Helen turned from the mirror where she'd been fixing her hair.

"Can I give this to Parson before we go home?"

Helen tilted her head to one side. "Are you sure you want to give it away?"

Lottie nodded. "He'll enjoy it more than I would."

"Go ahead then, if you can find him."

Lottie walked to the lobby, and found her tutor talking to Johnny.

"Hey, Brown." Johnny's greeting lacked its usual cheer.

"Hey, Johnny. Sorry about Walt and everything."

"Yeah, well, you lose some, you lose some."

"Uh-huh." She turned to Parson. "I have a good-bye present for you."

He looked at it. "What's this?"

"It's a book my Aunt Eva gave me, but I want you to have it because you like to read." She pushed it toward him. "Here."

He smiled. "She probably picked a book for a girl, not a man."

"Oh." Lottie dropped her arm to her side, deflated.

"That doesn't mean I don't want it," Parson said with a quick look at Johnny. "Of course I want a present from my best student." He took the book from her, and put out a hand as she turned to go. "Now, you have to stay and watch me open it." He untied the string and slid his finger beneath the yellowing tape. The paper gave way to reveal *Treasure Island*, leather-bound with gilt-edged pages.

"Wow!" Lottie and Parson spoke at once. He looked up. "This is really nice, Lottie. You can have it back if you want."

She shook her head. "No, it's yours."

"Well, take your letter at least." Parson drew a sheet of scented paper from between the pages and handed it to her.

Dear Lottie,
Here's a little gift from the great Karofsky.
Remember to start with Chapter Seven.
Love,
Aunt Eva

Without a word, she took the book from Parson. It fell open to Chapter Seven.

Seven one-hundred dollar bills and a fifty fanned across the page.

Twenty-three

I won't take it." Johnny said for the fourth time.

Lottie watched him pace around the tiny hotel room from her seat in the middle of the bed. Helen and Parson stood next to the window, while Mr. Schultz leaned on his cane near the door.

"You have to," Helen said. "There's no other way to square up with the hotel."

"I don't care. I won't take advantage of you like that."

Mr. Schultz snorted. "Don't be a fool, boy. If we skip out on that bill, we'll go to jail. Better to pay the hotel than the bail bondsman."

"I don't take handouts from women."

Helen rolled her eyes. "Oh, for the love of —"

"May I make a suggestion?" Parson's calm voice cut through the argument.

Johnny stopped pacing. "Let's hear it."

"Stop talking about favors and handouts, and start thinking like a businessman." Parson pointed at his friend. "You need capital. Helen and Lottie are the bank. Settle on an amount, draw up some loan papers, and pay them back at interest over a period of time."

"What about collateral?" Mr. Schultz sounded amused.

Johnny clutched at this straw. "I've got nothing of value."

Parson was undeterred. "If you default on the loan, Lottie and Helen get the Neverland Orchestra, its equipment, and all of its music."

"And a list of your contacts in the music business," Mr. Schultz said.

Parson glanced at Mr. Schultz. "That too."

"Sounds good to me," Helen said.

"And me," Lottie added.

Johnny looked around at the faces of his friends. "All right. You've talked me into it. Lottie." He turned to her. "Go spread the word that we still have a band, and there's a meeting in my room in an hour."

"Yes, sir!" She saluted on her way out the door. When she returned, a business meeting was in full swing.

"How much is he borrowing?" she whispered to Helen.

"Two hundred dollars," Helen whispered back. "Sh. He's on a roll."

"Parson, my friend, you'll be the bookkeeper." Johnny wrote on the back of Aunt Eva's note as he talked.

"But he's already my teacher," Lottie protested.

"He's a big man. He can handle a lot of work."

Mr. Schultz cleared his throat. "Since you're handing out jobs…"

"Yes?"

"Harms was a terrible booking agent. Couldn't negotiate a fair deal to save his life. Not to mention he was skimming off the top. I could do a better job."

Johnny considered the proposal. "I'll take you on trial, and see how it goes after a month. Sound all right?"

"So I have to prove myself?"

"Yep."

The old man's lips stretched into a smile. "You're starting to sound like a businessman."

An hour later, all nine members of the Neverland Orchestra stood or sat around Johnny's room. Some drew nervously on cigarettes. Parson puffed contentedly on a pipe, while Mr. Schultz fiddled with the silver handle of his cane.

Hobart stubbed out his cigarette. "Get on with it, Columbus. My train leaves in an hour."

"Well, I hope you won't be on it." Johnny's smile lit the room. "I hope none of you will. You see, the Neverland Orchestra is under new management."

The guys looked at each other uncertainly. Carlyle spoke up. "Look, Johnny, I love you like a brother, but I can't stay where there's no money."

"I'm not asking you to. Boys," he glanced at Parson. "I've had an influx of capital."

Parson nodded. "We can pay your wages for another month. That's what Lunkhead here is trying to say."

Lottie felt the men relax. "Oh, well why didn't you say so?" Carlyle slapped Johnny on the back. "I'll go warm up for tonight's show."

"Not so fast." Sammy's eyes narrowed. "Are you managing the band now, Johnny? Because personally, I don't think you're up to the job."

Johnny took this calmly. "I'm the leader, but I'm not alone. As the only honest man among us, Parson will keep the books. And Mr. Schultz here has offered to be our booking agent. But when you look up at the conductor's stand this evening, I'll be standing there. I want you to stay, Sammy, but if you can't, I wish you well."

Sammy shrugged his thin shoulders. "I guess I'll stay."

"Say, boss? Who's going to sing?" Hobart glanced at Helen.

"Nobody." Johnny's voice was firm. "From now on, we're an instrumental group. That means we've got to hold our performance to a higher standard, since we won't have some flashy crooner to hide behind."

"Where'd the money come from?" Bobby Richards asked suddenly.

Johnny looked from Parson to Mr. Schultz and back. By previous agreement, none of them brought the girls into the conversation.

"Let's say it's an unexpected windfall," Mr. Schultz said.

The men accepted this.

Lottie looked around at her band mates, now talking and joking with each other. It wasn't a bad group. Johnny played trumpet, Carlyle trombone and Hobart clarinet. Parson and Bobby rounded out the wind instruments on saxophone, and Lottie, Sammy, and Mr. Schultz made up the rhythm section. They could use a singer and a few more brass players, but it would do for now.

The Neverland boys had the time of their lives that night. The combination of Walt's absence and guaranteed wages put all the men in a good mood, and Johnny's ebullient directing style made for a night of good fun. His effervescence infected the crowd, which showed its appreciation with a long round of applause at the end.

As the crowd drifted away, the guys headed for the bar at the back of the room, only to be stopped by Parson.

"Not so fast, boys."

"Aw, c'mon, Parson. Don't be a spoil sport." Carlyle tried to pass him.

Parson held his ground. "I can't stop you from drinking, boys, but you'll do it on your own dime. I fixed it with the manager. He won't charge any more drinks to the band."

"Walt didn't mind buying us a round or two," Hobart said.

Johnny stepped up beside his friend. "You want us to buy your drinks or pay your wages?"

Richards was the first to give in. "C'mon, boys, the first round's on me."

Johnny watched his former drinking buddies proceed across the room without him.

Parson put a hand on his shoulder. "They respect you for taking a stand, you know."

Johnny looked at him. "You think so?"

He smiled. "I know it."

Twenty-four

Mr. Schultz was very good at drumming up business for the band. Ballroom owners welcomed the courtly old man as a nice contrast from the brash young men they usually encountered, and he knew how to negotiate. By early June, Parson's ledger showed a solid profit, and Johnny hired three more musicians.

At Mr. Schultz's urging, Johnny finally drummed up the courage to leave the circuit of Midwestern dance halls and ballrooms where the band had found success, and follow an eastward path. They worked their way around the outskirts of Chicago and up through southern Michigan before moving on to Ohio.

Lottie and Helen stepped off the train in Dayton one morning after a short night. "I'm exhausted," Lottie said through a yawn.

"Me, too." Helen put her arm around Lottie. "Maybe we can catch a quick nap when we reach the ballroom."

"No hotel this time?"

"Nope. We're due in Cincinnati tomorrow."

They sighed in unison as Mr. Schultz caught up to them.

"Why so glum on such a beautiful day?" he asked.

"We're tired." Helen eyed him suspiciously. "What's got you in such a good mood?"

He favored them with a rare smile. "This afternoon I'm taking the two of you on a field trip to meet one of my favorite people."

Lottie exchanged a puzzled glance with Helen. "And who might that be?" Helen asked.

"That's for me to know and you to find out." And with that the old man stumped off toward the taxi stand.

"A field trip?" Lottie felt her energy revive. "I've never been on a field trip."

Helen chuckled. "Your whole life is a field trip, kiddo."

○

The small wooden sign read, "Dayton Academy of Music." Lottie and Helen stared at the three-story brick mansion.

"Quit lollygagging, you two." Mr. Schultz was half-way up the tree-lined walk. "The inside is even prettier than the outside."

They ran to catch up and reached him as he rang the doorbell. "I'm Carl Schultz. I have an appointment with Madame D'Abri," he told the maid who answered.

The maid led them to an office at the back of the house. Mr. Schultz waved the girls into the only two chairs, and stood gazing expectantly at the door.

It was opened a few minutes later by a tiny woman in a loose fitting smock, black stockings, and shoes that had been all the rage during the Great War. Her curly gray hair was confined in a barrette at the nape of her neck. She advanced into the room with arms outstretched. "Carl!"

"Jacinthe." Mr. Schultz took her tiny hands and they regarded each other with deep affection. "How have you been?"

Lottie had never heard the old man sound so foreign, or so warm.

"I am well." Madame D'Abri withdrew her hands from his grasp. "And who have we here?"

"This is Cora's niece, the child I told you about in my letter. Charlotte Brown, meet Madame D'Abri, the headmistress of the Dayton School of Music."

Lottie stood up and put out her hand to shake, but instead Madame pulled her into a loose hug and kissed both her cheeks. "Oh my dear, Cora has told me so much about you! It is Lottie, is it not?"

Lottie nodded, too stunned to speak.

"And this is your sister Hélène, yes?" She made Helen's name sound

174

exotic. "No, no, do not get up. You must rest."

Helen smiled at the lively little woman. "So very nice to meet you."

"My condolences on the loss of your papa." Madame turned her bright gaze on Mr. Schultz, whose ears turned pink with pleasure. "So. I am to hear the young lady play."

He inclined his head.

"Bon. You and Hélène may wait for us in the yellow sitting room. I will ring for refreshments." She turned to Lottie. "Come with me, child."

Lottie followed Madame D'Abri up a flight of stairs, past an airy room full of pianos. At each piano sat a child playing finger exercises in unison. At the end of the hall, Madame ushered Lottie into a small room furnished only with a piano, a bookcase, and a wooden chair. She closed the door and blocked out the noise of the other children.

Madame gently pushed Lottie toward the bench. "Have a seat, child. Did you not bring music?"

Lottie shook her head. "Mr. Schultz didn't tell me what we were doing this afternoon, or I would have."

"Ah. He must have his little surprises." Madame took a book from the bookcase next to her and opened it in the middle. "Try this."

Lottie looked the unfamiliar piece over curiously. She could not read its title, which was written in a foreign language, but she was quite familiar with Mozart. Placing it on the music rack, she began, and soon "Twinkle, Twinkle Little Star" took shape beneath her fingers. Startled, she glanced at Madame, who laughed.

"Monsieur Mozart has played a fine joke on us, no? Stop at measure sixteen."

Lottie complied, saying, "I could play on. I've played Mozart before."

Madame held up her hand. "To sight read is not our intention today. Music is more than playing notes correctly. Play the piece again, only this time, fill it with joy."

Lottie stared at the notes, suddenly off-balance.

"Ah, you are confused," Madame said. "Perhaps it would help if you told me a happy memory."

Lottie closed her eyes to think. It took a long time, but finally a picture formed in her head. "I had a bicycle when I was at home," she said.

"I could ride it anywhere I wanted all by myself. It made me happy to pump my legs up and down and feel the wind on my face."

"Very good! Now, make me feel the way you felt on your bicycle."

Lottie frowned. "But the notes are not bike riding notes."

"They can be." Madame shrugged. "Monsieur Mozart supplied the raw materials. You give it the meaning."

Closing her eyes once more, Lottie pictured her bike. It was blue, with a brown wicker basket attached to the front. She saw her bare feet on the pedals, and felt the handlebar grips under her palms. She opened her eyes and began, and each note became part of the scene: the whir of tires on blacktop, the flap of her shirt in the breeze.

She played to the end of the theme and without thinking moved on to Variation One, which suited her mood exactly with its exuberant runs and trills.

"All right, all right." Madame held up her hand for Lottie to stop. "Very good for a first try. Now we shall go back to the beginning. I want you to play with reverence."

"Reverence?" Lottie frowned.

"Yes." Madame gave a decisive nod. "The feeling you have in church, you know. Awe."

"Ah." Lottie turned back to the keyboard, thinking fast. She didn't remember feeling awed by the little church in Westmont, but she knew what Madame wanted. All at once she remembered Mr. Schultz at the church organ, flooding the room with that Bach fugue, and the awe she had felt at hearing proper organ music for the first time. Taking a deep breath, she pushed that reverence into her finger tips.

When she finished the first movement she stopped and looked at Madame, who sat quite still. "How was that?"

Madame tilted her head, birdlike. "Not bad, not bad. Reverence is difficult for a child. You've had so little time to learn how big the world truly is. We will try a different emotion. Give me sadness."

This time Lottie didn't need time to think. With Pop's face before her mind's eye, she began again.

The song that emerged bore little resemblance to her previous effort. Every note carried the weight of sorrow, each phrase expressed her longing to see her father, to touch his scratchy face once more. Mozart's intellectual exercise became a vessel for her pain. She played to the end of the piece and turned a tear-stained face to her instructor.

Without a word Madame pulled the little girl to her chest. Lottie burst into tears, and laying her hot cheek against Madame's cool shoulder, she wept.

"Cora was my dearest friend, if not my most musical pupil," Madame said an hour later as she poured coffee for her guests. "She came to me at age fourteen, and stayed four years, returning to New York every summer to care for her papa. It was on one of her last trips home that she met your Uncle Otto on the train, and I lost her to true love in the wilds of Iowa."

Lottie chuckled at this description of her home state.

Helen took a sip of the dark liquid, and set down her cup. "But why did Aunt Cora study with you if she was not a musician?"

Madame D'Abri looked sharply at Mr. Schultz. "I will allow her father to answer that."

Mr. Schultz reddened. "Her mother and I were both musicians. How was I to know our daughter would not have the gift?"

Madame shook her finger at the old man. "By listening to her. But that is neither here nor there. I am grateful that you sent her to me, for she became a lifelong friend and faithful correspondent. She has told me a great deal about you girls." She smiled at her youngest guest. "How do you like your macaroon, my dear?"

Lottie nodded enthusiastically, her mouth full of light pastry.

"Bon." Turning to Mr. Schultz she said, "I would be delighted for Lottie to join the Academy for the fall term."

Mr. Schultz glanced sidelong at Helen's startled face. "I am glad to hear it."

Madame stood up. "We can discuss the details in my office."

"Just a moment." Helen raised one hand. "This is not Mr. Schultz's decision to make. It's mine. Mine and Lottie's. We're going to need some time to think about it."

"You don't have time," Mr. Schultz snapped. "The train leaves at midnight."

Helen put up her chin. "I will not be railroaded, Mr. Schultz."

"We're wasting this busy woman's time. She needs a decision."

"Stop. Stop!" Madame clapped her hands for attention. "We shall leave the young ladies alone to discuss my offer. Come along, Carl."

Mr. Schultz rose reluctantly and followed her out of the room.

"We can't afford to keep you here," Helen said as soon as the door closed. "I like Madame, and I know this is a good, safe place, and maybe you'll hate me for saying so, but we can't."

Relief flooded Lottie's chest. "I know. It's all right."

Helen rushed on. "Maybe the Neverland Orchestra isn't the best atmosphere for a little girl, and I don't know what we'll do when the baby comes, but I can't leave you here. I can't let you go."

"Helen." Lottie shook her sister's arm. "I don't want to stay."

"You don't?" Helen looked startled.

Lottie slipped her hand into Helen's. "It isn't home."

Helen looked anxiously into her sister's eyes. "Do you miss Westmont very much?"

"No." Lottie shook her head. "I miss Pop. With him gone, you're all the home I have."

"I know how you feel." Helen reached for Lottie's other hand. "Lottie, I promise you here and now that you'll never lose me. No matter what."

Madame smiled warmly when she heard the girls' decision. "The offer stands. Lottie may join the academy at her pleasure. I do not care when." She frowned at Mr. Schultz. "Do your best not to pout, Carl. It is not becoming."

She ushered her visitors to the door and waved them down the sidewalk. "Au revoir! Do not forget!"

○

Lottie was still thinking about Madam D'Abri that evening as the concert began. The familiar procession of dance tunes took on new meaning as she tried to play with emotion. She half-expected Madame to come to the dance and watch her perform, but no tiny woman in a black smock ever appeared.

They boarded the train after midnight and settled into their seats. It was only two hours to their destination, so they sat upright, knowing a hotel room awaited in the next town. Mr. Schultz settled into the seat across the aisle and leaned toward Helen.

"You should have taken Madame's offer."

Helen bristled. "Maybe we would have considered it if you'd given us fair warning."

He raised his eyebrows. "You should have trusted me to know what's best for your sister. The Dayton Academy is an excellent place for a child of her abilities."

"It's time you trusted me for a change," Helen said quietly. "My sister and I can take care of ourselves without your everlasting interference."

"Yes, I can see that." The old man looked pointedly at her swelling midsection. "Have you decided what you'll do when the baby comes?"

Helen reddened. "It won't be here for another three months."

"In other words: No." He shrugged. "Babies have been known to come early."

Helen bit her lip. "I'm sure you have a solution."

"You rejected my solution this afternoon. What does Bill say?"

"His last letter said he wanted me to go to his parents."

Mr. Schultz snorted.

Helen looked away. "It's out of the question."

"What about your Aunt Eva?" Mr. Schultz asked.

She looked surprised. "In New York?"

"We're headed in that direction, in case you hadn't noticed." He gave a tiny smile. "She's a very capable woman, your aunt. I'm sure she would rise to the occasion."

"What will the band do while I'm taking care of a newborn?" Helen asked.

"Columbus would jump at a job on Fifty-Second Street. He'd think he hit the big time."

Helen relaxed in her seat. "I wouldn't mind staying in one place for a while. It would sure make it easier to get letters from Bill." She glanced at the old man. "If you're sure you can work it out?"

He gave a satisfied nod. "I can."

Twenty-five

My dears, you are a sight for sore eyes!" Aunt Eva beamed at Helen and Lottie. "Welcome to our humble home. And hello to you too, Mr. Schultz."

He inclined his head. "Lovely to see you again, Mrs. Reed."

"I'm sorry to make you room with the rest of the band," Aunt Eva said. "We only have the one guest room, and I'm sure you wouldn't be comfortable on the sofa."

Lottie gazed around the bright sitting room filled with fragile bric-a-brac. She smiled at the thought of Mr. Schultz trying to sleep amid the lacy cushions that filled Aunt Eva's sofa.

Helen hugged her aunt. "It's so kind of you to take us in."

"What's family for?" Aunt Eva said simply. "Of course you're welcome here. Are you quite comfortable, dear? I could put a pillow at your back."

Helen shook her head. "No thank you. It is a bit warm in here, though."

"It's this beastly August weather. I hate to open the window because of the traffic noise." Aunt Eva turned to Lottie. "I have a little surprise for you, young lady. I stocked up on books I know you'll just love."

"Thanks, Aunt Eva." Lottie smiled weakly. "I did like *Treasure Island*. Especially Chapter Seven."

Helen chimed in. "Oh yes, thank you for that."

Aunt Eva's face lit up. "It was all Mr. Reed's doing. That old Karofsky struck a nerve with him. He can't abide a cheat." Glancing at Mr. Schultz she added, "Present company excepted."

He looked away.

"Now tell me where the band is going to play."

Mr. Schultz cleared his throat. "We have a temporary arrangement with the Stoplight Room on Fifty-Second Street."

"The Stoplight Room?"Aunt Eva thought a moment. "I don't think I've heard of it."

"It's new. That's why the manager was willing to take us on. We won't get rich, but the boys will gain experience, and we might catch an agent's attention. In return, the club has cheap entertainment for the whole month of August," he glanced at his hostess, "when all the sane people have left for the shore."

Lottie turned to Sammy the next afternoon as they set up for rehearsal. "How's your hotel?"

Sammy had unbent quite a bit since his brother left the band. "It's all right. I drew Old Schultz as a roommate, though. Did you know he snores?"

She rolled her eyes. "I've shared enough train rides with him to figure that out."

He laughed. "Your aunt, is she nice?"

"She's great. Detective Reed is a little gruff, but I like him. Why?"

Sammy fiddled with the height of his stool. "Seems like you have all the luck with relatives."

"You could come to dinner sometime, if you want."

He gave her a tentative smile. "All right."

Sammy came to dinner a week later in a coat and tie, his hair reeking of Brylcreem. Mr. Reed greeted him with a formal handshake. Aunt Eva led him to the softest chair in the house and plied him with questions.

"Where are you from, Samuel?"

"Chicago, ma'am."

"Oh." Aunt Eva pursed her lips. "Cubs or White Sox?"

Sammy grinned. "White Sox."

Eva's eyes twinkled. "What a shame. Do you still have family there?"

He looked away. "No, ma'am. My parents are dead, and the last I knew, my brother was in California."

"I see." Her eyes were sympathetic. "Sounds like you could do with a home cooked meal."

At dinner Sammy kept the questions at bay by filling his mouth full of fried chicken. But after dessert, when Mr. Reed left the table to read the evening paper, Aunt Eva took up the thread again. "Tell me, Samuel. Are you a good student?"

Sammy wiped his mouth with his napkin. "I don't know. I haven't been to school since I was ten."

She looked shocked. "No school! A bright boy like you? Why don't you take your lessons with Lottie?"

He half-smiled. "I wouldn't be good at that stuff."

She frowned. "If you can keep the beat and count out measures, surely you can do arithmetic, Samuel. You must give it a try."

His smile widened. "Yes, ma'am. If you say so."

"I do." She cut him another piece of cake. "Do you like being in a band?"

This threw Lottie into agonies of embarrassment. "Aunt Eva!"

Sammy set his napkin on the table and looked up at his hostess. "No, I can't say that I do."

Lottie swung her head around to look at him. "What?"

He shot her a defiant look. "When I was little I drummed on everything. Tables, floors, even my bed at night. After my parents died, Walt wanted to join a band real bad, but he didn't know what to do with me. So he got a drummer friend of his to give me a few lessons, and hired us both out to a local band, for practice. He said if I didn't go along with him, he'd put me in a boys' home." He cleaned the crumbs off his plate with his fork. "He sucked all the fun right out of it, Walt did."

"But even after he left, you stayed with the band." Her voice was gentle.

"What else could I do?" he said angrily. "I'm not old enough to join the army."

"You're a smart young man," Eva said. "We'll think of something."

The next afternoon at rehearsal, Lottie tried to apologize for her aunt, but Sammy cut her off. "She asked all those questions because she cared about the answers. You can't fault someone for that."

"She likes you. I had to hear about you all through lunch today." Lottie raised her voice an octave. "That Samuel is so smart. Too bad he's a White Sox fan."

"Ah, cut it out." Sammy slugged her shoulder, but he didn't look mad.

Aunt Eva had a talk with Parson, who in turn talked Sammy into joining Lottie's classes. He soon pulled even with her in English and history, and moved ahead in math by leaps and bounds.

○

The Stoplight Club was a small, dimly lit nightclub with no dance floor, a place where people gathered at small tables to talk and listen to music. Overnight Johnny transformed the Neverland dance band into a swing combo. The new music came as a relief to Lottie, who had grown tired of playing the same Big Band hits. She spent hours practicing the unfamiliar syncopation with Sammy and Parson. The rest of the guys preferred to do their learning after the Stoplight closed, at other clubs on Fifty-Second Street. Since most of those lessons involved liquor and women, the Neverland Swing Combo was second-rate at best.

Mr. Schultz followed his own path, neither rehearsing nor making the rounds after hours. Every night he accompanied Lottie home, not to be seen again until the next evening at show time.

"Hey, what does Old Schultz do all day?" Sammy asked one day when he arrived for rehearsal.

Lottie looked up from a new piece she was marking. "What do you mean?"

"He goes out alone every morning around the same time, with a big briefcase under his arm, and doesn't come back. Where does he go?"

She shrugged. "Why don't you ask him?"

"Why don't you? You know him better."

She narrowed her eyes. "All right. I will."

Lottie broached the subject that night when Mr. Schultz escorted her home. "We weren't very good tonight, were we?"

"Correction," he said. "You were good, and I was. But no, for the most part the band was terrible."

"We could improve if more people came to rehearsal." She raised innocent eyes to his face. "You, for instance. Why don't you come to our rehearsals?"

"I'm busy during the day," he replied.

"Oh? Doing what?"

He chuckled. "That's none of your beeswax, little girl."

They walked on in silence as Lottie cast about in her mind for another way to approach the question. Before she could think of something, Mr. Schultz said, "Would you like to study with Karofsky again?"

The question caught her off guard. "No," she said. "Just because I complained about the band doesn't mean I want to leave it."

"You're not even a little tempted? He could do wonders for your career."

"It wouldn't be possible, would it?"

"What if it were?" He sounded impatient.

"I still wouldn't want to. Not after what he did to you," she said. "Besides, his house smells like cooked cabbage."

Mr. Schultz gave a rumbling laugh. "I remember. And I appreciate your loyalty. Still, I'd like to see you back in the classical world, where you belong."

Lottie smiled. "I'm happy with the band."

They reached the apartment building and Mr. Schultz opened the door. "After you, child."

Lottie walked upstairs, lost in thought. Why didn't she want to take piano lessons? She loved Bach and Mozart so much more than Glenn Miller. But she'd never see the boys again if she quit the band. She couldn't stand the thought of it.

Lottie usually arrived home to a dark apartment and tiptoed off to bed, but tonight Aunt Eva greeted them at the door with a tired smile. "It's a boy," she said simply. "He arrived about an hour ago."

Lottie's stomach plummeted into her toes. Until this moment, the baby had been imaginary. Now that he was here, she wondered if he was such a good idea.

Aunt Eva mistook Lottie's speechlessness for excitement. "Come along and meet your nephew, dear. Mr. Schultz? Won't you come, too?"

But he had already retreated to the stairs.

Lottie tiptoed into the bedroom, where Helen rested against a mound of pillows, crooning to the tightly swaddled bundle in her arms. "This is Billy," she said with a glowing smile.

Lottie peeked over the blanket's edge and into the wrinkled red face of her nephew. As she leaned in for a closer look, one tiny fist escaped its bounds and shot straight toward her. She jumped back in surprise.

Helen laughed softly. "He says hello to you, too."

Lottie looked at her sister, whose face shone with love for the little bundle in her arms, and felt a tiny pinprick of jealousy. But when she glanced back at the baby, her heart melted, for his blue eyes were looking straight into hers.

Helen reached for Lottie's hand. "I'm going to need your help, kiddo. Do you think you're up to it?"

Lottie, overwhelmed with her first case of baby-worship, nodded. "I'll do anything you ask."

In the six weeks that followed, Aunt Eva made Lottie's promise rather difficult to keep. She too had fallen in love with Billy, and appointed herself second-in-command on the baby care front. She became adept at changing tiny diapers and heating bottles to the correct temperature, and she was a one-woman dynamo of feeding, burping, and rocking. As a result, there was very little for Lottie to do at home, and she continued her routine of school, rehearsals, and performing.

Sammy fell into the habit of dropping by every day for lunch. He was the only person who could distract Aunt Eva from the baby. She fussed over Sammy, and he lapped up the attention, though he tried to brush it off when he and Lottie were alone. "I'm just there to talk to the detective. He tells interesting stories."

One afternoon Eva said, "Samuel, if you could do anything in the world, what would it be?"

He took a bite of meat loaf. "I'd join the army."

Mr. Reed grunted. "Wouldn't we all."

Eva took a sharp breath and let it out slowly. "All right. What would you do if the war was over?"

Sammy looked surprised. "Build something, I guess. I'd like to build houses like the kind my folks lived in."

Mr. Reed paused, his fork half-way to his mouth, and looked at the boy with new interest. "Construction?"

His wife gave a satisfied smile. "I like that."

"What was that all about?" Lottie asked on the way to the Stoplight Club. She put on her Aunt Eva voice. "What do you want to be when you grow up, Samuel?"

He gave her a playful shove. "Lay off your aunt, twerp. She's a nice lady."

She shoved back. "I'll say whatever I want. She's my aunt. Oh, drat!" She stopped in her tracks, all teasing forgotten.

Victor Gold waited by the back door of the club.

Twenty-six

Lottie grabbed Sammy's coat sleeve. "Don't leave me," she said urgently.

Victor sauntered toward them. "So this is where washed up prodigies go to die."

"What are you doing here, Victor?"

He raised his eyebrows, the picture of innocence. "Can't a guy look up an old friend? The reviews are in the all papers. The Neverland Band stinks, but their pianist plays like a dream. A little blonde girl from Idaho." He sneered. "It had to be you."

"It's Iowa." Lottie folded her arms across her chest.

"That's what I said."

She tapped her foot impatiently. "What do you want, Victor?"

His eyes narrowed. "I know you're trying to get Karofsky's attention. I've seen that old gangster watching his house. He's not going to take you on again, you know."

She stared at him, confused. "Old gangster?" Suddenly the mists cleared. She gave him a lofty smile. "You mean Mr. Schultz. Well, I think he'll win the day. You'll see. Karofsky will take me back, and you'll be out on your you-know-what."

"We'll see about that." Victor took a menacing step toward Lottie, only to run into Sammy, who moved to protect her. "Sure. Hide behind your pal," Victor sneered. "But I'm warning you. You've messed with Victor Gold for the last time."

And with that parting shot, he stalked away.

Sammy watched until he disappeared around the corner. Turning to Lottie he said, "You all right?"

She nodded. "Victor Gold is a creep, but I don't see how he can hurt me."

"Me neither." Sammy frowned. "Did you mean what you said about that Karofsky guy? Are you leaving the band?"

"What? No!" Lottie put her hands up. "I said that to make Victor mad."

"Oh." He hesitated. "I'd understand if you did leave. Everyone knows you're better than the rest of us."

Lottie stamped her foot. "Stop talking like that. I'm not leaving." She reached for the door. "Look at it this way. At least we have some idea where Mr. Schultz goes all day."

That night Lottie arrived home to find Helen sitting up with Billy in the kitchen. "Hey, little boy," she crooned, dropping to her knees beside the baby.

"Want to hold him?" Helen said. "He's going back to sleep."

She looked up, her face eager. "Sure. I never get to touch him."

Helen stood and indicated the rocking chair. "Sit down. I'll hand him to you."

He felt like a soft piece of heaven in Lottie's arms. She looked at Helen with starry eyes. "I could go on like this for ever."

Her sister smiled ruefully. "That's funny. I'm ready to do anything but sit in this apartment rocking a baby."

"Why don't you come to the club and see the show?" Lottie asked.

"A baby at a nightclub?" Helen said. "It wouldn't be right."

"You could leave him with Aunt Eva. She'd love to take care of him and give you a night out."

Helen glanced toward the bedrooms. "Aunt Eva takes care of him far too much as it is," she said, her voice low. "If you must know, I'm ready for a little less help from her."

Right on cue, Aunt Eva shuffled into the kitchen in her robe and slippers. "What are you girls doing up?" she said. "I should rock the baby and let you sleep."

Helen stood and put an arm around her aunt, turning her gently toward the hallway. "Nonsense, Auntie. Go back to bed. We're fine."

Eva pulled away. "Now, Helen, you're a new mother. You need your rest."

"So do you," Helen said, a hint of steel in her voice, "and I'm not tired."

Aunt Eva faltered before Helen's show of strength. "Very well. I'll see you in the morning. But don't blame me if you're exhausted."

Helen waited for the bedroom door to close and turned to Lottie. "Maybe I will bring Billy to the Stoplight Club. It will do us both some good."

An idea occurred to Lottie. "Why don't you come an hour ahead of time, when we're warming up? You can visit everyone, hear some music, and have Billy home before bedtime."

Call time for the band was seven o'clock, an hour before the show started.

"Look who I found," Lottie called, leading her sister up to the stage. The clashing sounds of instruments tuning up slowly petered out as the men noticed their visitor. Carlyle stepped off the platform for a good look at the baby.

"So this is the little guy." He pushed a meaty finger into Billy's fist. "What's up, little fella? My, you're a fat one!"

Helen beamed with pride. "He's growing by leaps and bounds. How do you know so much about babies, Carlyle?"

He chuckled. "I've got five sisters, so I guess I should know something."

With the ice broken, everyone had something to say.

"Good to see you, Helen."

"That's a nice looking baby you've got there."

"We've missed you around here."

Johnny hurried in from the stage door. "Sorry I'm late, guys." He stopped in his tracks. "Well hello there, beautiful!"

Helen flushed. "I've come to show off the baby."

He glanced into the carriage and back at Helen. "He's a pip, isn't he?"

She glowed with motherly pride. "Yes, he is."

He might have gone on looking at Helen indefinitely, but a slight "ahem" brought him back to the job at hand. "It's time to start," he said apologetically.

"Go ahead. Billy and I will go find a seat." Helen smiled. "Lottie wanted me to hear the new numbers."

Johnny put out a detaining hand. "Stay up close. I've got an announcement that affects you too." Turning to the band he said, "Pipe down, everybody. There's something I need to tell you." When he had their attention he continued. "The Stoplight Club won't be renewing our contract. We're out a week from today. I haven't had any luck booking shows with the other clubs around here, but don't worry. I'm sure Mr. Schultz will come up with something to take us into the winter. Isn't that right, Mr. Schultz?"

Lottie looked at the old man, whose face was guarded. "I'll do my best," he said in a flat, unconvincing tone. "But your best bet might be a regional tour."

Her eyes slid to Sammy, hunched over his drum set. She'd never seen him so glum.

Helen, on the other hand, looked as bright as a new penny, a rare occurrence since they'd arrived at Aunt Eva's house. "Do you think we'll go back on the road?" she asked the next morning.

"Maybe." Lottie looked at her sister's satisfied face. "I hope so, for your sake."

Aunt Eva's reaction was less positive. "You're all leaving?"

Lottie nodded.

Her voice trembled. "But we've gotten on so well. Are you sure you want to go?"

"You and Mr. Reed will enjoy the peace and quiet again," Helen said.

Eva shook her head in disbelief. "I don't see how you can take a six-week-old baby on the road like that. It isn't right."

That night, when Lottie tiptoed to bed after the show, a light was on in the Reeds' room, and she could hear the murmur of voices.

○

Johnny called a meeting for the following Sunday afternoon, and arranged to hold it in Aunt Eva's living room since the club was closed on Sundays. All week Lottie felt the tension among the band members as they discussed their options. Carlyle had met a girl, and wanted to stay in New York. Bobby, who had tried and failed at betting on the horses, couldn't wait to get out of town. Several people wanted to play smaller crowds again, where the criticism wasn't so fierce.

Lottie walked around in a state of constant turmoil. One minute she couldn't wait to get back on the road. The next, she couldn't imagine traveling with a tiny baby. She dreaded going back to the same small number of dance standards, yet she missed the sight of brightly dressed couples whirling around a ballroom.

One thing was certain. Helen needed a break from Aunt Eva. The good lady's constant efforts to help with Billy provoked an irritation that would turn into a raging fire if something didn't happen soon.

Mr. Schultz and Johnny carried on intense conversations at the club, their heads bowed over a tablet of paper covered in the old man's crooked penmanship. Parson joined them on Saturday night after the show, listening as each man talked and nodding in understanding. Once, he turned and looked directly at Lottie.

"What did you say about me?" she asked Mr. Schultz that night as he walked her home.

He glanced at her with wry humor. "Nothing gets past you, does it, Miss Nosy Parker? Well, I was going to tell you anyway." He sounded smug. "Karofsky has offered to take you back as a student."

Lottie stared in disbelief. "How did you get him to change his mind?"

"That is a story for another day. Here we are." He opened the front door of the apartment building and ushered her inside. "Now, what do you think? Are you ready to return to the life you deserve?"

"That's how you see it?" Her voice rose. "I'm wasting my time with a swing band?"

He made an impatient sound. "Spare me the dramatics. We both know you outclass this outfit by a mile. Your gifts could place you among the elite of the performing world, but only if you develop them properly. Will you take the offer or not?"

"Do I have a choice?"

"Of course. It would be a waste of time and money if you didn't want to take the lessons."

A thought occurred to her. "And how would I pay this time? We both know he won't teach for free."

"He and I have come to an understanding about payment, which you don't need to worry about."

Lottie wanted to push for more details. What on earth had the old man cooked up this time? But when they reached the apartment, he opened the door and gently pushed her inside. "Give me your answer at the meeting tomorrow," he said. "Sweet dreams."

She made a face at his retreating back. She doubted she'd sleep tonight, much less dream.

She didn't fall asleep for hours, and slept in Sunday morning. Still tired, she dragged herself into the kitchen to find Sammy sitting at the breakfast table with Mr. Reed. "What are you doing here?" she asked in surprise.

Aunt Eva, standing at the stove, answered for him. "Mr. Reed and I thought he might as well eat breakfast here, since the meeting starts in an hour." She peered at Lottie in concern. "Are you feeling well, sweetie?"

"I didn't get much sleep." Lottie yawned to illustrate her point. "Where's Helen?"

"She took Billy for a walk. Can I do something for you?"

Lottie brightened. Aunt Eva was very good with Mr. Schultz. "Maybe." She glanced at Mr. Reed and Sammy, plowing through their breakfast. "Could you spare a minute?"

Aunt Eva led her into the empty sitting room and sat with her on the love seat. "What's this all about?"

Lottie explained Mr. Schultz's offer, including the fact that the lessons would be free.

Aunt Eva narrowed her eyes. "Well, I'll say this for Mr. Schultz. He's always looking out for your career. I hope he's found an honest means of getting his way this time." She looked at Lottie. "Do you want to take lessons again?"

"Yes. And no." Lottie closed her eyes. "Let me try to explain. I learned more from Dr. Karofsky in two months than in the rest of my life put together. But I hated the way he treated me that last day. He was nasty and rude."

"I remember."

She raised troubled eyes to her aunt. "How do I know he wouldn't do that again sometime? Also, I'm pretty sure the Neverland is going on the road. If I stay here, it means I'll never see Parson and Johnny and the rest. I love those guys, even if they're not first-rate musicians."

Eva smiled. "They're not?"

Lottie shook her head. "No, they're not. But it doesn't matter because they're good people. They've treated us right every time."

Aunt Eva put an arm around her. "Sounds like you're making up your mind without my help. I'd love it if you stayed and took lessons. I'll miss you like crazy if you go. But I'm pretty sure you and Helen will both be happier on the road."

"Do you think so?" Lottie said, surprised at her aunt's insight.

Eva sighed. "I planned to be such a blessing to your sister in her time of need, but somehow I've done it all wrong." She held up a hand to stop Lottie's protest. "I've seen the frustration in her eyes when she thinks I'm not looking."

Lottie threw her arms around her aunt. "No, Aunt Eva. We're grateful. We are."

"Don't." Eva drew herself upright. "I don't pretend to know how Helen will cope, but I know she's leaving. With or without you, I might add."

Lottie drew back, frightened at the thought. "She wouldn't leave me."

"She will if you're safely established here. She needs to do what's right for herself and the baby, and I'm getting in her way." Aunt Eva stood up. "We all want what's best for the ones we love, dear. Why don't you stay in here and think things over? I need to clean up breakfast."

Lottie sat on the love seat, elbows on knees, chin in hands, and thought until her head ached. When the Neverland boys arrived for the meeting she was still there, and no closer to a decision.

The sitting room filled up quickly, with instrumentalists on every chair, table, and window sill. They were eerily quiet, eyeing each other suspiciously as they wondered what would happen next. Johnny arrived last, along with Mr. Schultz and a man Lottie had never seen before.

Before the meeting could begin, Aunt Eva stepped into the room and pointed at the old man. "Mr. Schultz? I need a word."

He followed her through the doorway, like a child anticipating a trip to the woodshed.

Johnny delayed the meeting for several minutes, waiting for Mr. Schultz to return. Finally, as his band mates grew restless, he began. "All right, boys. I think we'd all agree it's been a pretty tough week. But with the help of Mr. Schultz, I've come up with a plan that should carry the band through until spring at least. If it works out, we'll be set for a good long time after that. Ah! Here he is now."

The old man stumped into the room, leaning heavily on his cane. Aunt Eva followed him in, gave Lottie a bright smile and nod, and left.

Johnny put a hand on Mr. Schultz's arm. "Would you take it from here, sir?"

"Very well." The old man turned to survey the crowd. "Some of you are wondering how I've occupied myself since returning to New York." He glanced at Lottie, who had the grace to look guilty. "While you boys were sleeping off your hangovers, I've gone about reviving my former business as a teacher of music. I went to see an acquaintance, who entrusted me with the musical education of his daughter. My work pleased him, so he passed my name along to a few friends, and pretty soon I had a good little list of students." He cleared his throat, his eyes on Lottie. "I used my earnings to clear up some mistakes from my past."

She gave a little sigh of relief.

"As a result of my diligence, I've made a new life for myself here. I will not continue to play for the Neverland Orchestra. I will, however, remain in the capacity of agent."

This impressive statement brought no reaction from his audience, so Mr. Schultz continued. "I would like to introduce you to the father of one of my students." He indicated the stranger. "This is Mr. Paul Philbert, lately of Atlanta, Georgia. Mr. Philbert owns eighteen dance ballrooms scattered throughout the southern United States. At my invitation, he has visited the Stoplight Club on several occasions and he liked what he heard. He wants to hire the Neverland to play his dance halls. Naturally, the compensation will be generous."

The guys looked at each other uncertainly.

Johnny spoke up. "Think about it, boys. A guaranteed paycheck and year-round warm weather."

"Sounds good to me," Parson said. "How 'bout the rest of you fellows?"

Carlyle grinned. "Sorry boys, but I'm staying here. I got down on one knee to Marie last night. Wedding bells are gonna ring."

There was a general uproar as everyone tried to pound Carlyle on the back at once. When they calmed down again, Johnny said, "Well?

What do the rest of you have to say?"

Sammy spoke up. "Uh, I've been offered a job on a construction crew." He glowered at the surprise on everyone's faces. "What are you looking at? Not everybody wants to count measures for the rest of his life."

Lottie was dying of curiosity. "When did you find time to get a job?"

He grinned. "It found me. Mr. Reed has a friend in the business. He and the missus want me to stay with them, too."

One by one, the other band members spoke. Most of them were willing to go south, but Bobby Richards had a question. "What's Lottie going to do? We ain't much good without our ace piano player."

Everyone turned to look at her, and the force of their combined attention was almost too much for her composure. She looked to her sister for guidance, but Helen shook her head. "This is your decision, kiddo."

Mr. Schultz cleared his throat to get her attention, and glared so fiercely that she wanted to burst into hysterical laughter. Johnny shot her a brilliant smile, but his eyes were anxious. At last Parson threw her a lifeline. "You know what you want, Lottie," he said in his steady voice. "You're a smart kid."

She smiled back, and looking only at him, said what was in her heart. "I'm going with the band."

One week later the Neverland Orchestra boarded a train for Atlanta. Aunt Eva and Sammy went to the station to see them off. While Helen and Eva debated the best way to warm a bottle on a train, Lottie stood awkwardly with Sammy.

"Don't forget to write," she said, though she didn't believe he would.

He stuck his hands in his pants pockets. "You either. I'll want to know how the band is getting along."

"Sure," she said, and darted a look over his shoulder for the tenth time.

Sammy grinned. "I don't think he's coming."

She feigned confusion. "Who?"

"Mr. Schultz, that's who."

She dipped her head. "He didn't say good bye."

"He doesn't think you'll be gone very long. He's betting you'll get tired of dance music and come running back to ol' Karofsky.

Lottie's eyes flashed. "Well, I won't."

"You know that and I know that," Sammy said. "But you can't tell nothin' to the old man."

She nodded, and glanced past him once more.

Helen touched her arm. "We have to board now."

Lottie turned away slowly. "Bye, Sam."

He raised a hand. "Bye."

A great wave of sadness washed over Lottie as she found her seat. When the train began to move, she looked back at Aunt Eva and Sammy, wondering if she'd ever see them again. Then she caught her breath. Behind them stood the old man, leaning on his cane, one arm raised in a dignified salute.

Twenty-seven

"Hey, Brown." Johnny made his way down the compartment, swaying with the motion of the train. "Want me to watch that little guy for a while?"

"Gladly." Thirteen-year-old Lottie nudged the toddler on her lap. "Billy, go with Johnny."

"Johnny?" Twenty-month-old Billy turned to look at his tall friend. "Go Johnny." He slid off Lottie's lap and grabbed Johnny's hand.

Johnny chuckled. "I guess he knows where the fun is."

"Tell the boys no candy this time." Helen looked up from hemming a small pair of trousers. "It's bad for Billy's teeth."

"All right, Mother." Johnny made a face as he followed Billy down the aisle. "We'll be good."

Lottie slumped in her seat with a sigh.

Helen glanced at her sister. "Tired?"

"Yes." She closed her eyes against the Tennessee sunshine streaming in the windows. "I think I'll take a nap."

"Go ahead. We'll be in Chattanooga in an hour."

"I know." For a year and a half, they'd made the same big circle through the southern states. Lottie could recite the entire train schedule without a mistake.

"Why are you so tired lately, kiddo?" Helen put a cool hand to Lottie's forehead. "Are you getting sick?"

Lottie pulled away. "I'm not sick. I'm tired. Tired of trains. Tired of dance music. Tired of the same towns, over and over."

"I like knowing where we're going. It's good to see a friendly face behind every hotel desk."

"Sure you like it, because you know they'll save Bill's letters for you. But I'm bored out of my mind."

"Oh, stop complaining." Helen sounded cross. "You could have stayed in New York if you'd only said the word."

She was tired of Helen's quick temper, too, but she thought she understood it. Bill's letters, which had never been plentiful, had stopped altogether, and Lottie knew she was worried.

Lottie feigned sleep, but opened her eyes when Johnny returned, a crying Billy in his arms.

"This is what happens when you take candy from a baby." He handed the weeping child to Helen, who rocked him back and forth, humming softly until he grew quiet. Johnny dropped into his usual place across from her. "I'd like to know how you do that. It's like magic."

Helen kissed her son's yellow curls. "It's mother magic."

"Magic." Johnny gazed with unguarded tenderness at Helen's bowed head. "That sounds right."

Lottie stood abruptly. "I think I'll stretch my legs. Johnny, could you move?"

"Sure." Johnny stuck his long legs into the aisle to let her by, his eyes still on Helen.

Lottie walked away quickly, her insides in a knot. Johnny's feelings were plain to everyone but Helen. It was only a matter of time before she noticed, and then nothing would be the same.

Lottie slipped through to the next car, and on to the next, where she found the rest of the band. Little remained of the group that played the Stoplight Club a year and a half earlier. Richards hadn't made it out of New York before his number came up with the army. Last Lottie had heard, he was serving in the Pacific. Hobart had called it quits after a year or so, and found a job in a munitions factory. Lottie didn't miss either of them as much as she missed Sammy and Carlyle, but their departure meant more new faces replaced the old familiar ones. She couldn't see the point in getting to know any of the new guys. Most of them only stayed a few months before joining up, so she'd taken to thinking of them as instruments instead of people.

She looked over the group, searching for her one remaining friend. "Anyone know where Parson is?"

"I think he's in the next car down." A sandy-haired trumpet looked up from oiling his valves. "He said he wanted some peace and quiet."

"Thanks."

She found him sitting alone, reading a newspaper. "How's the war going, Parson?"

He looked up. "Not so good. We still haven't invaded Europe." He folded the paper and set it aside. "Have a seat, kiddo. Have you finished your homework?"

This was the drawback to Parson. She pulled a face. "You really know how to ruin a girl's day, you know that?"

He laughed. "So I've been told. Go get your books. I'll help you."

She heaved a deep, adolescent sigh. "Do I have to?"

"Do you hate it that much?" He looked surprised. "I thought you were getting along pretty well."

She bit her lip. "I don't mind algebra. I just don't want to go back to my seat."

Parson frowned. "Is Johnny up there again?" For some reason, Johnny's lovesick ways always made Parson mad.

Lottie nodded. "Would you come back with me? Please?"

He glanced out the window and sighed. "All right. If you need me to."

"I do." Johnny behaved himself better around Parson.

Her precautions proved unnecessary. When they got back to her seat, Johnny looked more thoughtful than lovesick. He looked up as they approached. "Parson, you're just the man I wanted to see. I've thought of a brilliant plan to put new life into the band."

Parson looked cautious. "Oh? What's that?"

"Hire a singer." Johnny's face split into a blinding smile. "We need a new face, someone who can reach the audience. With so many boys in uniform these days, a pretty girl would be just the ticket."

Parson leaned against the back of Helen's seat and looked at his business partner. "We've talked about this before, Johnny. We've got enough personnel problems on our hands without adding a single girl to the mix."

Lottie pushed past Johnny's knees and dropped into her seat. This was a familiar argument. It would not end quickly.

Johnny leaned forward. "Think about the private birthday party we're doing in Chattanooga. Wouldn't Mrs. Coultrey love it if we had somebody to sing 'Happy Birthday' and 'For He's a Jolly Good Fellow' to her husband? That's how all the other bands do it. Think about it. That's all I ask."

"You know how I feel about this," Parson said. "People like us well enough without a singer. We don't need some floozy around."

"What if we hired a nice local girl just for the night of the party? The new drummer — what's his name?"

"Marshall," Helen said.

"Yeah, Marshall's from Chattanooga. I'll ask if he knows somebody."

"Just for one night?" Parson said slowly. "We could give it a try, I guess, if we can get someone decent. Helen?"

Helen shrugged. "Nobody can corrupt a child's morals in one night."

Lottie scowled. "I'm thirteen."

"Exactly." Helen and Parson spoke at once.

Johnny stood and clapped Parson on the back. "I'm glad you see the light, old man. Now I'll just toddle along and look in on the rest of the band." He made his way down the aisle and disappeared through the vestibule doors.

○

"Any letters for me, Tom?" Helen asked at the front desk when they checked into the Hotel Chattanooga. She'd befriended every clerk on their circuit in her effort to catch Bill's letters.

"No ma'am." He looked sympathetic. "You haven't had any for a while, huh?"

"No." Helen turned to Lottie, who led Billy by the hand. "We'd better get moving if we're going to eat lunch before rehearsal."

Lottie slipped her free hand into Helen's. "Do you think that's the singer?" A young woman sat on the edge of a chair in the lobby, fiddling with the clasp of her pocket book. She'd caught her ash-blonde hair up in tortoiseshell combs, and wore a pearly shade of pink on her lips.

"Maybe," Helen said quietly. "Don't stare, Lottie. She's probably nervous enough as it is."

"I think she might pass Parson's floozy test," Lottie said in a stage whisper. "I hope she can sing."

"Lottie!" Helen was scandalized. "Don't be rude."

"Sorry." She glanced over her shoulder, but the girl didn't seem to have heard.

She felt a little thrill an hour later at rehearsal, when Johnny introduced the ash blonde to the band. "Folks, this is Monica Hunter. She'll be singing for us tonight."

A murmur of appreciation went through the boys as Monica gave a pert wave. "Glad to meet y'all," she said in a soft Tennessee drawl. "I hope I do all right."

Monica possessed a pleasant singing voice and a natural talent for working a crowd, and it brought out the best in the band. For the first time in months, Lottie expected an interesting evening.

Mrs. Coultrey's party was a white tie affair, her mansion decked with elaborate floral arrangements for the occasion. The band set up in a receiving room with French doors open to the magnolia-scented lawn. It made a startling change from the bare public ballrooms they usually played.

Monica was the hit of the evening with both the guests and the band. The guests took pride in their hometown girl, and the boys took turns trying to drum up a conversation. Her manners were faultless. She neither encouraged the boys nor disappointed the guests.

Lottie enjoyed watching the action from the sidelines for once. She was tired of the curiosity seekers who wanted to talk to the child prodigy. She didn't feel like a child, and wished fervently that her body would grow to match her age.

"My, it's hot in here!"

Lottie looked up to find Monica leaning on the piano. "It's Charlotte, isn't it?"

"Yes." Lottie smiled. "Lottie, actually. Looks like you're a hit tonight."

"Oh, I'm not half as talented as you. I've never performed for such a big crowd. Do you mind?" Monica indicated the bench.

Lottie slid over to let the older girl sit. "Do you play?"

"Sure." Monica arched her pretty eyebrows. "I know 'Chopsticks' like the back of my hand."

"Chopsticks?"

The singer stared in disbelief. "Do you mean you've never played 'Chopsticks'?"

"No." Lottie's cheeks turned warm.

"All right. Hold up your fingers like this." Monica held her pointer fingers side by side, and waited for Lottie to do the same. "Now put them on F and G, like me, and copy what I play."

Lottie caught on quickly to the simple piece. There was nothing to it, really, and she wondered why she'd never heard it before. Not up to Mr. Schultz's standards, she supposed.

After sixteen measures, Monica instructed her to repeat her part, and began the accompaniment. "Now improvise," she said after the first time through, and then, "Double time!" after the second.

They ended in a flurry of breathless laughter and light applause, surrounded by several of the newer boys. Lottie felt shy until she realized she wasn't the center of attention. The boys were all looking at Monica, who cast her eyes down at her lap and peeped up through her lashes in an engaging manner.

Lottie slipped off the bench in search of a glass of water, but couldn't help looking back at her new friend. She made a mental note to practice that trick with her eyelashes later, when she was alone.

"Nice work, Lottie." Parson stood at her shoulder. "I've never heard you play 'Chopsticks' before."

"I just learned it." She didn't look around. "What do you think of Monica?"

"I think she's a pretty girl who can sing. Past that, I couldn't say."

"Well, I think she's nice."

"Me, too." Johnny walked up in time to hear her defend her new friend. "What's more, she can really swing."

Parson looked cautious. "What are you thinking, Columbus?"

Johnny reached for a water glass. "She could be a good addition to the band."

Parson snorted. "You've known her a couple hours. Besides, she may not want a permanent job."

"There's no harm in asking," Johnny said. "Let's try her out at our show tomorrow night, just to make sure, then offer her a permanent job. She's free to turn us down."

Parson looked dubious. "She's pretty young to join a band."

"Young seems to work all right for us." Johnny said with a nod at Lottie.

"Lottie has Helen to look out for her." Parson sounded frustrated.

"Helen's not much older than Monica," Johnny pointed out. "And don't tell me Helen's a married woman. Believe me, I remember."

"Speaking of Helen," Parson said, "don't you want her opinion? She'd have to spend a lot of time with this girl, so I think she ought to have a say."

"I don't see anything wrong with the idea," Helen told Parson the next morning. "Lottie introduced her to Billy and me last night, and she seemed like a fine girl. A bit too heavy on the lipstick, maybe, but she likes children, so she'd fit in all right. It'd be nice to have someone new to talk to around here. Don't you think, Lottie?"

"Yes." Lottie clasped her hands under her chin and tried to look winsome. "Say yes, Parson."

He threw up his hands. "All right. If she sings well tonight, we'll offer her a job."

Monica snapped at the job offer. Johnny suggested she take a later train so she could go home and pack, but she'd brought her suitcase along, "Just in case y'all offered."

"Don't you want to say goodbye to your folks?" Parson asked.

"Oh, they won't miss me," she said with a little toss of her head.

Twenty-eight

Monica was a shot in the arm to the road-weary Neverland Orchestra. Old hands brushed up on their technique to impress the lovely singer. The younger boys competed for her attention off-stage. And, as Johnny predicted, she was good for attendance. One night in Birmingham, Monica came down with the flu and couldn't perform. The next night they had the smallest crowd ever. After that, Johnny raised her pay.

Lottie thought her new friend deserved all the attention. In her limited experience, Monica was the most wonderful girl she'd ever met. She was sweet and beautiful, and brimming with easy laughter, a relief from Helen's sober presence.

Monica knew a dozen different ways to do hair. Within a week, Lottie gave up her braids for a more grown-up style. The singer also owned several shades of lipstick, which she let Lottie try. "Pinch your cheeks to put some color into them," she said. "It will keep you from being so pale all the time."

Lottie took her advice, looking anxiously in the mirror before every show for signs she looked more adult.

When Helen noticed these changes, she clicked her tongue in a fair imitation of Aunt Eloise. "It's fine to play at being grown up, Lottie, but don't forget you're only thirteen. What looks all right on a grown woman is still a little old for you."

She walked away before Lottie could answer, so she settled for making a face at Helen's back. What did Helen know? Not everyone was blessed with natural beauty.

It was Parson who put an end to Lottie's cheek-pinching. "What's wrong with you?" he said one night before a show. "You look like you've got scarlet fever. Go ask Helen to feel your forehead."

Lottie took a long look at her pale face in the mirror that night, and vowed to accept her lack of beauty. It would be her cross to bear.

Monica knew everything about boys. She whiled away long train trips with stories about the boys who asked her on dates back in Chattanooga, the places they took her, and what they tried to do with her on their way home.

Lottie didn't let on how interested she was in this subject, for fear of being teased. But lately she felt an odd fluttering sensation when she thought about the good-looking new trumpet they'd hired in Birmingham. Boys were a mystery, and Monica seemed to have the key.

One afternoon as they chugged across Alabama, Lottie said, "Which boy did you like the best, Monica?"

The older girl laughed. "What makes you think I had a favorite?"

Lottie shrugged. "I don't know."

Monica threw a friendly arm around her shoulders. "Well, as it happens, I do have a favorite. You can keep a secret, can't you, Lottie?"

"Sure."

Monica lowered her voice. "I'm secretly engaged."

Lottie's eyes opened wide. "Wow."

"Shh!" She pulled Lottie down into the seat until their heads were barely visible.

"What's his name?" Lottie whispered.

"Hank." Monica checked the seats around her to see if anyone was listening. "Henry Smith. I met him at the railroad station."

"How romantic," Lottie sighed. "My aunt and uncle met on a train."

"Oh, he wasn't on the train." Monica giggled. "He was sweeping the floor and emptying the trash bins. But it was love at first sight. When Daddy wasn't looking, I told him when I'd return, and he was there waiting for me when I got off the train."

Lottie gasped. "He swept you off your feet right there at the train station?"

"No, silly." Monica looked appalled. "Daddy would never approve of me seeing a janitor. We had to sneak around behind my family's back. That's why the engagement is secret."

"Oh, of course." Lottie felt vaguely stupid.

Monica twirled an ash-blonde curl around her index finger, a far-away look in her eyes. "Hank is such a darling. If Daddy would only give him a chance, I know they'd get along."

"If you don't mind me asking, how could you stand to leave Hank in Chattanooga and take the job with us?"

Monica laughed. "Hank's not in Chattanooga any more, honey. He's in the military now. Gee, you're a good listener."

Lottie savored the compliment. If she couldn't be beautiful, she'd settle for being a good friend.

With the war in its third year, Lottie placed their audiences in two categories. The small-town crowds were sparse and made up of more women than men. But when they played near a military base, the numbers reversed. Young men in uniform filled the ballrooms, far outnumbering the local girls they were there to meet. Lottie thought they looked dashing, and liked to pick one out of the crowd, imagining the deeds of valor he would accomplish on the battlefield.

She knew better than to talk this way around Helen, though. Where Lottie saw heroes, Helen saw defenseless boys heading into dangers unknown, and she scolded her little sister sharply for glamorizing the war.

"Don't take it personally," Monica advised one afternoon as they waited for the rest of the band in a shabby hotel lobby. "I'll bet it eats her up, not knowing whether her husband is alive or dead. She's such a tragically beautiful person, don't you think? No wonder Johnny's in love with her."

"Sh." Lottie placed a finger to her mouth, scandalized at Monica's frankness. "Don't say that."

"Why not? Everyone knows it's true." She leaned closer. "And I'd bet any money Parson's crazy about her, too."

Lottie jumped from her seat to defend her friends. "I'm warning you, Monica. You can't talk about the boys that way."

"Talk about which boys?"

They turned to find Helen standing behind her. Lottie felt her cheeks begin to burn. "Oh, some boys Monica knew back home." Her words tumbled over one another. "Nobody you know."

Monica came to her rescue. "Lottie's right," she said with a straight face. "I was just tellin' stories again."

One hot Saturday in June, they unpacked for a show in Shreveport, Louisiana. "This is a good one," Lottie told Monica. "With Barksdale Field nearby, we usually have a full house."

"Ooh." Monica's eyes shone. "Men in uniform always make me think of Hank. Which dress should I wear, Lottie?"

"The red one." It was her favorite, with its daring halter neck.

"I wore that old thing last night." Monica smothered a yawn. "What about the blue one, honey?"

Lottie shrugged. "All right." Monica's dresses were all pretty.

"Doesn't she look smashing in blue?" Lottie said to Helen that evening.

Helen smiled. "Monica is a pretty girl. I'm glad you have a friend."

The ballroom was packed with couples dancing cheek to cheek even through the fast numbers, and the crowd seemed to grow by the hour. They closed out the first set with "I'll Be Seeing You," but as Monica crooned the familiar words, a ruckus broke out near the entrance to the hall.

"Monica! That's my Monica!"

The shout came from a dark-haired soldier who was pushing his way through the crowd. "Monica Leigh, is that really you?"

The singer watched the soldier approach, a stunned look on her face. "Hank!" And with that she jumped off the stage, into the G.I.'s arms.

The ballroom erupted in spontaneous applause. Sensing a big moment, Johnny led the band into "It Had to be You."

After a long and very thorough kiss, Monica raised her head and pointed at the piano. "Lottie, honey," she called, "this is Hank!"

Lottie laughed so hard she nearly fell off the piano bench.

Twenty-nine

What do you mean she's not coming back?" Lottie asked the next morning when Helen broke the news. "She can't stay with Hank, can she?"

Helen's mouth tightened at the corners. "The point is that she did stay with Hank. Last night. They intend to walk over to the courthouse and get married today, and look for a room she can rent in town."

"But who's going to sing for us?" Lottie was on the verge of tears.

"Nobody, I guess. The band will go back the way it was before she came. Now, get dressed. Johnny's called a meeting."

Half an hour later, Lottie, Helen, and Billy headed for Johnny's room by way of the front desk.

"Any letters?" Helen asked the clerk. The hope in her eyes tugged at Lottie's heart.

"Not today, Mrs. Turner." The clerk shook his head sympathetically. "The U.S. Mail just isn't what it used to be."

"Thanks." Helen's smile didn't waver. "Come on, you two. We don't want to be late."

When they reached Johnny's room, Helen stopped. "Lottie, you take Billy and go on in, all right? I'll be back in a few minutes."

Lottie watched Helen walk away, her posture rigid. "Come on, Billy," she said. "This won't take long."

Billy ran into the room ahead of her and climbed up next to Parson. "Cookie?" he said.

Parson reached into his pocket and pulled out a package of broken saltines. "This is the best I can do, buddy." He pulled the little boy onto his knee. "Now, let's keep quiet so everyone can hear."

"I guess you've all heard that Monica left us high and dry," Johnny said. "We'll go back to the old instrumental arrangements for tonight."

"Uh, boss?" The lead clarinet raised his hand. "Are you going to replace her?"

Johnny hesitated. "We're thinking about it."

"What?" Parson shot him an incredulous glance. "I thought we agreed we wouldn't."

Billy chose that moment to crumble his saltine all over Parson's trousers. "More cookie?"

"No." Parson set him on the floor. "Go find Lottie."

One of the trumpets stood up. "Some of us have been talking, and we're going to look around for something else if you go back to the old format."

"Oh, you are?" Johnny's neck turned red. "Why would you do that? Don't we pay you on time?"

The trumpet looked uncomfortable. "Sure you do. That's kind of the problem. We're used to the money we're making with a singer out front. Our paychecks weren't as big when we were just an instrumental group."

"Yeah," the clarinet chimed in. "If we don't have a singer tonight, the crowd'll be pretty disappointed, especially after last night's show stopper."

Johnny held up his hand. "Well, that can't be helped. We don't have a spare singer lying around."

Somebody snickered, but Lottie couldn't tell who. A couple of the boys exchanged knowing glances, but nobody said anything.

"Right, then." Parson stood up. "Meeting's over. Lottie? What's that crazy kid doing?"

Billy sat on top of the chest of drawers, looking around proudly.

Lottie reached for him. "Your feet go on the ground, silly."

Billy stuck his thumb in his mouth and gave her a solemn stare.

"Oh, I give up." Lottie pulled him in for a hug. "Let's go find Mama."

She balanced Billy on her hip and turned to leave. The room was empty except for Parson and Johnny. "Bye, you two." They were too busy glaring at each other to respond.

"The boys are right about tonight," she heard Johnny say as she left.

Parson raised his voice. "I know what you're going to say, and it wouldn't be right."

Lottie held her nephew close and strained to hear.

"She wouldn't have to wear one of Monica's dresses, you know." Johnny spoke reasonably. "The crowd would respond to her just as she is, especially because her husband's in the South Pacific."

Parson snorted. "Sure, and it'd only be for one night, too. I've heard that one before."

"Don't you think she should make her own decision?" Johnny's voice rose.

"I don't even think we should ask her." Parson was shouting.

Lottie's heart sped up, as it always did when people started yelling. "Time to find Mama," she whispered to Billy.

Helen lay face-down on the bed in their hotel room, with only one damp red cheek visible. She stretched her arm out to pull Billy close, but he wiggled out of her grasp and slid to the floor.

Lottie sat on the end of the bed. "He doesn't sit still very well," she said with a tentative laugh.

"No." Helen looked at her through tear-wet lashes. "What did they say in the meeting?"

"Parson doesn't want to hire a new singer, but Johnny does. They almost had a fight about it. Some of the guys say the band will lose a lot of money without a singer." Lottie paused. "Especially tonight, because of all the men from the base. Helen, why were you crying?"

Helen swung her legs over the side of the bed and sat up, looking dazed.

"Is it because of Bill?" Lottie asked.

Helen nodded, her eyes fixed on her lap. "I haven't had a letter in a couple of months. I keep hoping there will be a packet of them waiting at our next stop, but the truth is, Bill just hasn't written. I don't know if he's missing or dead, or alive on some tropical beach somewhere, dancing with the island girls." She attempted a laugh which ended on a sob. "I don't know which would be worse."

"Billy, get down from there." Lottie plucked the little boy off the wide window sill and set him down.

Helen continued. "I feel like I'm eighty years old. Just once I'd like to stop being a war wife and feel young again. Oh, I sound so pitiful! So many women have it worse than me."

Lottie threw her arms around her sister. "I wish there was something I could do."

Helen hugged her tightly. "Give me a minute. I'll be okay."

"Helen?" Lottie pulled back so she could see her sister's face. "Johnny wants to ask you to sing tonight."

"Me?" Helen looked surprised. "What makes him think I could pull that off?"

"Everyone knows you can do it. They've all heard you sing Billy to sleep."

"But that's different. Nobody watches when I sing to Billy."

Except Johnny. Lottie held the words back. "Remember the old Christmas concerts? You sang for those."

Helen shook her head. "That was family. Nobody's scared of family."

"And the glee club in high school. The director gave you solos."

"I'm not going to do it, Lottie." Helen jumped to her feet. "I'm a plain, ordinary wife and mother. It wouldn't be right to put on a low-cut dress and get up in front of a crowd of men. What would Bill say?"

Lottie was saved from finding an answer by a knock on the door. Monica stuck her head inside. "Am I interrupting anything? I've come for my suitcase."

"Come on in." Lottie felt suddenly shy in front of her friend. "Congratulations."

"Thank you!" Monica put out her left hand. "This is my wedding band. Isn't it sweet? Hank says he'll buy me a diamond when he gets out of the service, but this'll do for now."

"It's lovely."

Helen stood by, watching Monica. "Are you sure you won't come back tonight and sing? I'll bet Hank's buddies would love it."

Monica shook her blonde head. "No, I sure can't. Hank's commanding officer gave him one night's leave, and we're going to spend a quiet night alone. Besides, Hank has strong feelings about his wife being a singer. He doesn't want all those G.I.s ogling me." She giggled. "Did you ever hear anything so straitlaced?"

Helen shot Lottie a triumphant glance. "I think he's right. I was just saying that Bill would feel the same way if I were to get up there and sing."

"Oh, I don't agree." Monica's eyes widened in surprise. "You've got all kinds of class, Helen. Nobody could do anything but respect you, especially if you wore your Sunday best dress, and treated the boys like brothers. Or you could look out in that audience and pretend every one of those boys was your husband. It'd be like a... What's that word, Lottie?"

"A tribute?"

"Yeah, a tribute to Bill." Monica gave a nod of satisfaction.

Helen wavered a moment, then turned away with a wry smile. "Thanks for the advice, Monica. Your suitcase is over there."

"Right." Monica shrugged, picked up her belongings, and left.

Lottie stared blankly at the door, wondering what to do next.

"Is that really how people see me? As a respectable lady?" Helen's voice was shaky.

Lottie nodded eagerly. "The boys in the band wouldn't dare talk to you like they talked to Monica."

Helen stared at herself in the mirror over the bureau. "Would anyone believe I'm only twenty-one?"

Lottie had no idea how to respond to Helen's mood. She'd never seen her sister upset in just this way. "Why don't I take Billy out for a walk?" she said, and held out her hand to the little boy.

"Walk." Billy scrambled up from the floor.

Helen didn't turn or say goodbye.

Lottie took her nephew outside to enjoy the warm sunshine. They walked up and down in front of the hotel, climbing on a decorative stone wall and smelling the flowers that grew by the door. She drew out the fun until lunch time, when most of the band passed her on their way to a nearby restaurant.

"Aren't you coming?" Parson asked her.

Lottie slid off the stone wall. "We'll be right there, as soon as I get Helen."

"I'll save you a seat."

To Lottie's relief, no trace of tears remained on Helen's face. She looked fresh and pretty in a clean blouse, her hair smoothed back in a style she'd copied from a ladies' magazine. "Sorry about my moodiness," she said. "I'm feeling better now."

When they reached the lunch counter, Parson waved them over to a booth and helped slide the wooden tray onto Billy's high chair. "What are you hungry for?" he asked cheerfully.

"I'll have a patty melt," Lottie said. "I'm so hungry I could eat a horse."

"Mind if I join you?" Johnny stood before them.

Parson frowned. "Get lost, Columbus. There's no room."

"Sure there is. Move over, Brown." Johnny slid in on Lottie's side. "How's tricks, Helen?"

"I'm fine, Johnny." Helen smiled around the table. "In fact, I'm glad you're all here, because I've got something to say."

Both men gave her their full attention.

"Johnny, I hear you'd like me to sing with the band tonight."

Johnny nudged Lottie. "Tattle tale."

"And Parson." Helen turned to her seatmate. "I understand you don't."

Parson looked at his hands. "Well, I don't want to put you in a bad spot."

"I'm not in a bad spot." Helen's eyes sparkled dangerously. "I'm in a good spot. Among friends, am I right?"

Parson and Johnny nodded in unison.

"Well, listen up, friends. I am going to sing tonight."

Johnny shot Parson a triumphant look.

Helen glared at him. "But not because you want me to, Johnny. I'll sing for Bill, and for all the boys in uniform." She looked at Parson. "I don't care if you're ashamed of me for doing it. For just one night I want to feel young again. Tomorrow you can start looking for another singer."

Parson dropped his gaze. "I'm not ashamed of you," he said. "Do you mind if I ask what you'll do with Billy?"

"Billy will be fine. I'll put him to bed in the back room before the show starts. He'll sleep through anything. Isn't that right, Lottie?"

"Uh-huh." Lottie felt a little stunned. Was this her sister?

"Right," Helen said. "Oh, look. Here's our food. I haven't felt this hungry in months." She picked up a sandwich and bit into it with gusto, oblivious to the stares she was getting from everyone else.

"That's settled, then," Johnny said carefully.

Parson nodded. "Looks that way."

"When do we rehearse?" Helen asked with her mouth full.

An hour later, Lottie watched the band as her sister warmed up. Doubt showed on most of their faces. She couldn't blame them.

"We'll begin with 'Dream a Little Dream.'" Johnny tapped on his music stand. "From the top."

Helen got through the song without a hitch. She looked calm and sang confidently, though her hands shook a bit. True, she didn't have Monica's stage presence, but her pretty voice held a sincerity that brought the sentimental ballads to life.

"All right." Johnny looked like he was trying not to grin. "We'll move on to 'Don't Sit Under the Apple Tree.'"

He set the tempo half as fast as usual, a move that tripped up a clarinet who wasn't watching. Johnny cut off the music impatiently. "Watch me now, boys. We're taking it a little slower than usual."

"Are you doing that on my account?" Helen asked.

Johnny nodded. "It's your first day."

Helen's eyes flashed impatiently. "Why don't you try me at full tempo before you go making special allowances? Nobody wants to hear 'Don't Sit Under the Apple Tree' sung as a ballad."

Johnny looked like a little boy who'd been caught in mischief. With a shrug he turned back to the band. "From the top. Full tempo."

"How did you know all those words?" Lottie asked after rehearsal.

Helen raised her eyebrows. "They seeped into my bones night after night while I sat backstage with Billy. Sometimes I thought I'd go crazy if I had to listen to the show one more time. It's different being in it, though. I get to interpret the songs my way, instead of listening to Monica do it exactly the same every time."

Lottie thought about this. "What are you going to wear?"

"My good black shirtwaist," Helen said. "I don't have anything else."

It was Lottie's turn to raise her eyebrows. "Couldn't we go shopping?"

They smiled at each other as the idea took root. "I'm sure there's a dress shop open somewhere in Shreveport this afternoon," Lottie said.

Helen lost her smile. "We can't waste money that way."

Lottie stopped on the sidewalk, her hands on her hips. "Helen Turner, you should buy a new dress once in a while. The way y'all go around looking like a starved crow just makes me want to cry," she said in a fair imitation of Monica's southern drawl.

Helen's face relaxed. "It has been a while since I bought anything new."

○

"Where's Helen?" Johnny paced the stage. "We go on in ten minutes. Lottie, where'd you leave your sister?"

"She's in the back room, putting Billy to sleep," Lottie said. "Give her a minute. She's a little nervous."

Parson frowned. "I told you this wasn't a good idea. Not everyone can carry off a live performance. We shouldn't have asked her." He turned to Lottie. "Go tell her she doesn't have to do this. No, never mind. I'll tell her myself." He took a step, but pulled up short.

Helen stood at the edge of the stage, a vision in emerald green satin. "Honestly, Parson. Sometimes you sound like a fussy old woman." She stepped forward, the simply cut fabric shimmering in the light. She smiled at him, an odd light in her eye. "Do I look all right?"

From behind the piano, Lottie could only see Parson's rigid back and clenched fists. For a moment he didn't move, but at last he took a step back, saying, "You always look nice, Helen," in a tight voice.

Johnny looked like his eyeballs were about to fall out of his head as Helen moved to the microphone. It took a wolf whistle from the trumpet section to bring him back to himself. Clearing his throat loudly, he said. "Enough of that, boys. Nice dress, Helen."

"Thanks." Helen's smug little smile made Lottie want to laugh.

The Neverland Orchestra had its best night in a long time. While not perfect, Helen was a crowd pleaser, singing her heart out to the men in uniform. She won their sympathy as she talked about Bill serving in the Pacific, and little Billy waiting for his daddy to come home.

Once Johnny recovered his equilibrium, he became the perfect foil for Helen's patter. His admiring, "Hey, gal, how 'bout a date?" was met with Helen's, "Just wait till my sailor gets home, mister." The crowd roared with approval.

Lottie was having the time of her life. Here was the old Helen, with her energy and sparkle, the Helen from her childhood. War, loss, and motherhood had submerged her in a bog of work and worry, but tonight she'd cast it all off for a taste of youth. Every man in the room looked at her and thought of his sweetheart back home. The looks on their faces told the story of countless carefree young women who'd promised to wait, as Helen waited for her Bill.

Even the boys in the band looked happy. Every one of them liked Helen, who mended their clothes and listened to their troubles. She could be counted on for sound advice, or a verbal kick in the pants, depending on the situation. They all seemed glad to let her stand in the spotlight for a change.

All but Parson. He remained his sober self as he bent to his baritone saxophone, his eyes on his music, looking around as little as possible. Lottie noticed the absence of low notes in the music, and knew he must be faking tonight. She'd caught others at that game, but never Parson.

Sometime after the break, the patter between Helen and Johnny took on a more personal tone. Lottie felt a thrill of alarm as Johnny voiced the thoughts that glowed in his eyes every time he looked at Helen. He said it all in a joking tone that hid his intentions from the audience, but he fooled nobody in the band. Parson stopped pretending to play and simply glared at Johnny, his saxophone leaning from its neck strap, his big hands lying slack on his knees. The newer boys exchanged knowing leers, pointing at one another with secret, pay-up-on-the-bet gestures.

Helen was the real surprise. For three years she'd acted oblivious to Johnny's feelings, laughed at his compliments and studiously ignored his sincerity. Tonight, she gave as good as she got, leading him on in a comic style, but with desperately serious undertones.

Fascinated, Lottie watched the flirtation unfold before her eyes and tried to think of Bill, to muster some sympathy for the absent husband. But he was only a face in the mist, and Johnny — dear, patient, earnest Johnny — stood five feet away, making her sister young again.

The show ended with "I'll Be Seeing You," and not a dry eye in the place, including Helen's. For a moment, she slipped back into the role of waiting wife, and caught the audience's mood to perfection. In great good humor, the audience walked into the night, singing snatches of melodies, and left the band to itself.

Johnny exchanged a long look with Helen before turning to the band. "That's it, everyone. Pack it all up and leave it here. We'll collect it tomorrow afternoon before we board the train for Memphis."

Lottie filed away her music amid the familiar clatter of instruments going into cases and chairs being folded and stacked. Out of the corner of her eye she watched Parson step toward Helen, only to be called away to settle an argument. Before he could return, Johnny took Helen's hand and led her off the stage and out a side door. A sudden memory of Walter Harms and his harem of floozies flashed into Lottie's mind, but she dismissed it. Monica had given her a pretty good idea of what Walter had been up to, and she couldn't imagine Johnny or Helen acting that way.

Helen and Johnny hadn't returned by the time all the equipment was put away, but Lottie wasn't worried. She'd probably find them in the hotel lobby, and wouldn't she give Johnny a hard time then for leaving everyone to do his work!

She walked into the back room to put on her coat and found Billy sound asleep on a mound of blankets, curly eyelashes resting on his round cheeks. She raised her eyebrows. "Now, how am I going to get you back to the hotel, I wonder? You're dead weight when you're asleep."

"Need some help, Lottie?" Parson came to stand beside her.

Lottie pointed at her nephew. "Would you mind?"

"Not at all." He scooped the baby into his arms, blankets and all, and headed for the door. "At least one of you girls wants my help tonight," he said in an undertone.

Lottie blinked. "What did you say?"

"Never mind." He turned to look at her. "People can be their own worst enemy sometimes, that's all."

Parson held Billy in his arms all the way back to the hotel and through the empty lobby. He accompanied Lottie to her room, where he lowered the baby to Helen's bed and turned to go. "Lock your door tonight, Lottie. You'll be safe enough that way."

"But what about Helen?"

He gave her a long, hard look. "She has a key." And he left, closing the door softly behind himself.

Lottie stared at the door with a puzzled frown, the evening's excitement tainted by Parson's cold anger. She wished for some way to soothe his temper, but seeing none, she shrugged and put herself to bed.

She awoke to the sound of murmured voices outside the door, silence, and more murmuring, and opened her eyes to find weak rays of sunlight filtering through the blinds. The clock on the bed stand read five-thirty.

Helen tiptoed into the room with her shoes in one hand, her hair hanging loosely down her back.

"Hi," Lottie whispered.

Helen jumped. "Oh. You're awake?"

Lottie gave a sleepy nod. "You're just coming to bed?"

"Yes." Helen turned her face away. "Um, would you see to Billy when he wakes up? I'm about ready to drop."

And drop she did, onto her bedspread without taking off her dress. Lottie stared at the ceiling, listening to Helen's regular breathing and wondering what on earth one did when one stayed out all night.

When Billy began to stir, Lottie got them both dressed and slipped downstairs to find something to do. She found Parson in the lobby, his nose buried in the Sunday paper.

"Can I have the comics?" Lottie rattled the page in his hands.

He didn't move. "Go away, Lottie."

"Well, I like that! What did I do?" She made a face at Billy, who tugged on her hand. "All right, buddy. We'll go outside and leave Parson to his paper."

She led the little boy into the warm sunshine, where they collected pebbles until he said, "Billy want cookie."

"Time to go in, then," Lottie said. "We'll fetch some crackers from the room, and bring them outside to eat."

Billy and Lottie played a makeshift game of follow-the-leader into the lobby, where they met a saxophone and two trumpets on their way to breakfast. "You kids want to join us?" they asked.

"Sure, but I have to get money."

"Ah, don't worry. We know you're good for it."

Lottie gave in with a sense of relief. Now they could eat without waking Helen.

An hour later the group rolled back through the lobby, their bellies full of pancakes. "Thanks, guys. We'll see you later," Lottie called on her way past the reception desk.

"Oh, Miss." The clerk leaned across the desk to get her attention.

Lottie stopped with a friendly smile. "Hi, Marty. Any mail for us?"

"As a matter of fact, there is." He held out an envelope. "I moved the mailboxes this morning to set a mousetrap, and found this on the floor underneath. I hope our carelessness hasn't caused you any trouble."

"I'm sure it's all right." Lottie's voice trailed away as she examined the letter. With a half-smile at Marty, she picked up Billy and hurried down the hall.

"Helen," she said breathlessly. "You've got —"

She stopped short. Helen stood by the window, still in her green dress, her eyes shooting sparks at Parson, who stood a few feet away. Looking at Lottie she said, "What is it, honey? Parson's just going."

"I'll stay," Parson crossed his arms.

Lottie looked from one to the other, aware of a strange electricity in the air. She held out the letter. "It's from Aunt Cora."

"Give it here." Helen snatched the envelope from Lottie's fingers. "Why did it come on a Sunday?"

"Marty said it got lost under the mailboxes."

"Why, this is a month old." Helen tore open Aunt Cora's thick stationery envelope and pulled out a Western Union telegram. Her face went white. "Oh, dear God."

Parson leaped across the room and caught Helen just before she hit the floor. Lifting her to the bed he said over his shoulder, "Pick up that letter, Lottie."

Lottie scanned the telegram and passed it to Parson. Missing in Action, it said. Bill had been MIA for a month. She collapsed into a chair and pulled Billy onto her lap.

"Helen." Parson held her hand gently in his. "Come on, open your eyes."

Helen looked up, her brown eyes full of misery. "What have I done?"

"Nothing that God can't forgive." Parson's face held only tenderness now. "Go home, Helen. For once in your life, let someone else be strong, and go home."

"But Johnny…"

His face darkened. "I'll take care of Johnny."

Helen's gaze fell on Lottie. "What about Lottie? It wouldn't be fair to her to leave the band."

A delighted grin spread over Lottie's face. "I'd love to go home."

Helen looked at Parson like a bewildered child. "Tell me what to do, David."

He knelt beside the bed. "There's a train leaving at noon. You have to be on it. For your sake, for Bill, — even for Johnny — get out of here."

"All right." She fixed trusting eyes on his concerned face. "We'll go."

He stood up, relieved. "It's for the best. Get yourselves packed, and I'll take you to the station in an hour."

Given a deadline, Helen pulled herself together. "Lottie, get the suitcases. Make sure to pack everything, because we're not coming back."

Lottie slid Billy off her lap and automatically reached under the bed for her luggage. Her heart was roiling with mixed emotions she refused to name. Later, she'd have time to count her losses. Just now, she knew Parson was right. They had to get Helen away.

Deep down she knew this was the end of the Neverland Orchestra. It had been dying a little at a time as each member left, and this would finish it off. There might be a band after this, but it would never be the Neverland.

An hour later Parson accompanied the three travelers to the station and put them on a northbound train. They hung out the window to say goodbye to him, standing alone on the deserted platform. "Tell Johnny I'm sorry," Helen said softly.

"You leave Johnny to me," Parson said. "You girls take care of each other, now."

Helen nodded, a tear slipping down her cheek. "Parson, will you miss us?"

"Sure." His voice jerked. "Sure I will."

The train was moving now. Helen settled onto the cracked leather seat, but Lottie stuck her head out the window to watch Shreveport disappear into the past.

Thirty

"Look after Billy for me, won't you, Lottie?" Helen said when the city streets gave way to cotton fields. "I can't keep my eyes open anymore."

Lottie glanced at the dark smudges under her sister's eyes and held out a hand to Billy. "Come on, champ. Let's get out of Mama's way."

Billy slid down from the green bench seat and took Lottie's hand. "Caboose?" he said with a winsome smile.

Lottie chuckled and let him tug her down the aisle. She, too, liked to sit in the caboose and watch the rest of the train snake ahead of her, around curves and over bridges.

They found a seat near the back, and pressed their noses to the window, side-by-side. Lottie pointed out all the depots they passed, and tried to teach him to say 'river.' Billy was more interested in the telegraph poles that passed with mesmerizing regularity. He watched them until his eyes began to droop, and before long he fell asleep.

Lottie shifted the sleeping toddler sideways on her lap, his head tucked under her chin, and looked around the compartment. Most of the other passengers were locals, she guessed, traveling as families on Sunday outings. Some looked uncomfortable in their best clothing, while others were more casually dressed and carried picnic baskets. Lottie envied the larger groups of brothers and sisters, but took comfort in the dear weight of Billy, sleeping against her body. "You're as good as a brother," she whispered into his downy hair.

Lottie was almost asleep herself when she felt a tiny sting on her forehead and heard an explosion of smothered laughter. She opened her eyes a fraction and spied a rubber band on the seat next to her. Across the aisle and up a row, she saw two white-blond crew cuts bobbing together at seat-level. Careful not to wake Billy, she picked up the rubber band and fired back.

The missile hit the nearest boy square on the ear as he lifted his head above the seat. "Ow!" he said in surprise. "Who did that?"

Lottie grinned. "Who do you think?"

The other boy, younger than the first, raised his head. "But you're a girl."

Lottie looked at the first boy. "That's a smart brother you've got there."

He laughed and looked at her with frank interest. "Where'd you get such good aim?"

"I have a lot of brothers." This explained the Neverland Orchestra nicely. "I've learned to sleep light."

The boy, who looked about Lottie's age, swung across the aisle and plopped down next to her. "I'm Neil and that's my brother Mike. We're going to California to live with my grandmother. Where are you going?"

"Iowa." Lottie looked around. "You mean nobody's traveling with you?"

"Nope," Neil said, "and boy are we bored." He produced a deck of cards from his pocket. "Want to play gin rummy?"

"No, I'm not very good at cards. Besides, I have to watch my nephew."

Neil looked at Billy. "You could lay him on an empty seat."

Lottie looked doubtful. "I don't know if I should. I promised my sister…"

"Oh, come on." Neil fixed his blue eyes on her with a pleading expression. "Any girl who can shoot a rubber band like that has to be good at cards, and we need a third player for the good games."

It was nice to be needed, especially by this boy. "Oh, all right," Lottie said finally, "but I don't gamble with money."

Lottie rolled Billy onto the seat by the window, and sat with her legs in the aisle. Neil and Mike each took an aisle seat across from her and did the same. Their laps formed the playing surface for a game of crazy eights, which lasted until Billy awoke a half-hour later. He found a dozen different ways to disrupt the game, forcing Neil to shove the deck back into his jacket pocket. "It was fun while it lasted," he said with a shrug. "Have you ever been to California?"

Lottie shook her head, glad to keep the conversation going. "What's it like?"

Mike piped up. "It's warm and sunny, and you can see the Pacific Ocean."

"Sounds nice," Lottie said. "But doesn't it get awfully hot?"

Neil shook his head. "My mother says it's not humid like Louisiana. And there are orange trees and avocado trees right in people's back yards."

Lottie tilted her head. "What's an avocado?"

Neil shrugged. "I guess I'll find out when I get there."

She liked his frank manner. "California sounds nice. My sister lived there with her husband for a few months before the war."

"Yeah?" Neil brightened. "Maybe she knows what an avocado is."

"I can ask her." She reached for Billy, hanging over the back of Neil's seat like a limp wash rag. "Come along, champ. Let's go find your mama."

"Come back," Neil called as she made her way up the aisle. "We'll play cards again."

Helen was awake and hemming a skirt when Lottie boosted Billy onto the seat and asked, "What's an avocado?"

Helen seemed not to hear the question. "Where have you been?" she said without looking up. "I was beginning to worry."

Helen's sharp tone took some of the shine off Lottie's morning. "We went to the back of the train, and Billy fell asleep."

Helen bit off a thread. "You should have brought him back to me."

"We were perfectly safe. I met two boys who are traveling by themselves, and we played a couple of games of cards."

"You have to be careful of strangers, Lottie."

"I know that. I've been on a train before."

Helen's expression didn't change. "It's different now. We don't have the band looking after us anymore. We have to stick together."

Lottie crossed her arms. "These boys are nice. I want to go back and play cards again."

"No." Helen nodded at the seat across from her. "Sit down. We need to have a talk."

Lottie sighed and slumped into her seat.

Helen reached for Billy, who climbed across her lap and pressed his nose against the window. "I'm not going to Iowa."

Lottie sat up straight. "Where are you going?"

Helen glanced at her, and away again. "I'm taking Billy to California to wait for the war to end. I want to get as close as I can to Bill. It's the least I can do."

Lottie frowned. "What about me?"

"You should go home to Aunt Cora." Helen looked up then, and the shame in her face nearly broke Lottie's heart. "She'll do right by you, Lottie. Lord knows, I haven't."

"That's not true!" Lottie flew across the seat and wrapped her arms around Helen's neck. "You've done a great job raising me."

Helen burst into tears on Lottie's shoulder. "No I haven't. Oh, Lottie, I've made such a mess of everything!"

"Don't cry, Helen." Lottie felt years older as she held her weeping sister. She didn't understand the depth of Helen's unhappiness, but she somehow knew she could make it better. "I'll go to California with you. We're family, remember? Family sticks together."

Helen lifted her tear-stained eyes to Lottie's face. "Are you sure? Wouldn't you rather go home to Westmont?"

"No." Lottie made her voice firm. "I hear California is a great place to live."

Helen gave a tremulous smile. "It really is. You're going to love it."

Lottie sat back with a little sigh. Ever since Parson had set them on a course for home, she'd been filled with anticipation. She wanted to see Aunt Cora and Uncle Otto again, and ride her bike, and play with her cousins. But Helen clearly needed her to go to California, and she wouldn't let her sister down.

At least she would already have friends in California. After all, Neil and Mike were going there too. The thought made her stomach feel fizzy with excitement.

Her excitement lasted until they reached Kansas City, where she and Helen boarded a train for Los Angeles while Neil and his brother took a different one to San Francisco. California, as it turned out, was a much larger place than Lottie expected. She could practically hear Parson scolding her for her poor geography.

She was going to miss him.

Thirty-one

They rented a room in Santa Monica, ten minutes from the beach. This suited Helen, who wanted to stare wistfully out to sea while she waited for Bill to come home. Lottie liked their big bedroom at the back of the old house, with its bank of windows that opened to let in the ocean breeze. An orange tree stood outside, close enough that Lottie could pick a piece of fruit for breakfast. The room had been a sleeping porch, so there was plenty of space for two beds with a dresser between, a crib, and a rocking chair — luxury after the procession of hotel rooms they'd slept in for so long.

The first time Billy saw the beach, his eyes grew big and he pointed at the waves and said, "Big water." Lottie took his hand and ran into the waves, where they laughed and screamed as the salt water lapped over their feet.

Helen arranged the beach towels out of reach of the tide and sat with her arms loosely clasped around her long legs as she gazed out to sea. She seemed unaware of the attention she drew from passersby, but Lottie noticed. "Come on," she said to Billy. "Let's go build a sandcastle next to Mama."

"No." He plopped on his bottom in the shallow waves. "Big water."

She knelt beside him. "We can swim again later. Mama needs us now."

Billy tipped onto his back and dug in his heels, prepared to resist with all his might, but the effect was ruined when a wave rolled over him, filling his mouth and nose with water. He sat up, spluttering.

Lottie chuckled. "Let's go build that sandcastle now."

229

Mrs. Quinn, the landlady, was a widow who worked in an airplane factory while she waited for her sons to return home from war. In return for room and board, she hired Helen to clean house and cook the evening meal, which they all ate together. "I'm glad you've come," she said one night. "It's been awfully lonely around here with my boys gone."

She and Helen became friends after that, and often sat in the cool of the evening, talking of what they'd do when the war was over. When Mrs. Quinn invited her to an evening meeting of her church sewing circle, Helen was delighted. "You won't mind watching Billy, will you?" she asked, and didn't wait to hear the answer. She knew Lottie didn't have anything else to do.

Mrs. Quinn didn't own a piano. "I never thought of such a thing," she said when Lottie broached the subject. "Music's all right for church and such, but I don't much care for it otherwise."

Lottie tried not to show her disgust.

Billy ran a temperature one hot August morning, so Helen put him down for a nap. "Lottie, go out and get some fresh air," she said. "He's going to sleep all afternoon."

Lottie hurried out of the house, banging the screen door behind her. "Be back by supper time, and don't talk to strangers," Helen called anxiously.

"All right." She ran down the front walk, glad for once to be on her own. She was tired of the beach, and had some change burning a hole in her pocket, so she turned inland and made for the street of shops where Helen did the marketing.

She bought candy at the drug store, and a new barrette at the five-and-dime. Then, to prolong the fun, she wandered on down the street, farther than she'd ever gone before.

Three blocks later, she stopped to stare into the wide windows of Miss Crenshaw's Parisian Dance Studio. Twelve little girls stood before a mirror, bending and straightening their knees in rhythm. A tall woman directed them, her back to the street. Her gray-streaked twist of black hair bobbed to the same rhythm as the girls' knees.

An upright piano stood to one side of the dancers, with a young man hunched over the keys. As Lottie watched, the children's knees moved faster and faster, until the lady called an abrupt halt and said a few words to the pianist. He nodded and began again, but it was no good. He couldn't keep the tempo steady.

This time, the lady moved to his side and placed a hand on his bowed shoulders. She shook her head slowly as she spoke, and when she was finished, he rose and left the room. The lady picked up a rectangular white placard and placed it in the window. "Pianist Wanted. Inquire within."

Lottie passed the young man on her way inside.

The tall lady looked up as she stepped into the room. "I'm not taking students," she said in a low, pleasing voice.

"I'm Charlotte Brown. I've come about the position." Lottie pointed to the sign in the window.

The lady's eyebrows rose. "Well, Miss Brown, you work fast. You're a little young for the job."

"Yes, ma'am. But it won't cost you anything to give me a try-out."

Twelve little girls giggled behind their hands at Lottie's boldness.

The lady laughed. "All right. Have a whack at our practice music."

Lottie sat on the bench and flexed her fingers. Adrenaline flowed as she began the simple exercise. Steadily she worked her way to the end, then dropped her hands and looked up.

"That was flawless." The lady stared at her. "I'm sorry to say I can't pay you what you're worth."

Lottie grinned. "Does that mean I've got the job?"

"It's yours if you really want it."

"Oh yes, I do!"

The lady looked doubtful. "Don't you have to ask your mama?"

"I-I probably should," Lottie said. "You won't hire anyone else while I'm gone, will you?"

The lady's face softened. "I don't see any other candidates lining up for the job. It's yours until tomorrow. Can I have your answer by then?"

"You sure can." Lottie jumped off the piano bench and ran for the door, then stopped short. "My sister's going to be curious. Who should I say I talked to?"

The lady gave a funny little curtsey. "Miss Evelyn Crenshaw."

Lottie led Helen back to the dance studio the next day, and waited anxiously while the two women discussed terms.

"A dollar a week is slave wages," Helen said, "but if you throw in piano practice time after hours, I'll agree to it."

Miss Crenshaw raised her eyebrows. "You don't have a piano at home?"

Helen looked regretful. "Not at this time."

Miss Crenshaw opened her mouth, but Helen cut her off. "It's a long story," she said quickly. "Perhaps one day Lottie will have time to tell it."

Miss Crenshaw accepted this in silence.

On the way home, Helen said, "You'll have to be home by six o'clock on Tuesdays and Thursdays, so I can go to the sewing circle with Mrs. Quinn."

"I will," Lottie said earnestly. "I'll watch Billy any time you like. Oh, I'm so glad I get to play piano again!"

Lottie started the next afternoon with a class of bouncy five-year-olds, followed by a group of girls her own age. She smiled at them as they walked past, in case they wanted to be friends, but they ignored her.

Miss Crenshaw retired to her apartment above the studio when classes ended, and Lottie rolled the piano around so it hid her from the window, and opened her music. She lost herself in the precision of a Mozart sonata, glad for once to choose her own music. Pop had once said he liked the first movement, so she played it through twice, along with the repeats, prolonging the memory of Pop.

A metallic crash interrupted her the third time through. Lottie jumped. "Who's there?" she called out.

"Tony DiFranco." A black-haired boy near her age entered the studio, pushing a mop in a galvanized bucket. "I wondered who was making all that noise." He flashed a lazy grin.

"Noise?" Lottie glared at the boy. "Fat lot you know."

"I know plenty about stuff that matters," Tony said. "Take baseball, for instance. I'll bet you don't know who holds the record for the most strikeouts in a single season."

She folded her arms across her chest. "I don't care, either. Baseball is the worst game ever invented."

He raised his black eyebrows. "To each his own, I guess." He pulled the mop out of the bucket and swiped it across the floor. "Go ahead.

Play some more. I can take it."

She stared at him in silent outrage, but he didn't seem to notice, so she turned her attention back to the music. The sonata had lost its thrill somehow, so she let her fingers find the opening chords for "In the Mood."

"Hey, that's more like it. What's your name, kid?" He shoved his mop around the front of the room.

"Lottie." She played on. "And I'm not doing it for you."

He kept the mop moving. "That's okay. The only tune I really like is 'Take Me Out to the Ballgame.' I'm going to play for the big leagues some day."

She narrowed her eyes. "Sure, and I'm going to play Carnegie Hall."

"Why not?" He sounded surprised. "A lot of people like your kind of music."

She switched to "Danny Boy." "Life doesn't always happen the way you want it to."

"Life will never happen at all if you don't go after it."

He stood behind her now, swishing the mop to and fro. Lottie steeled herself not to look around. She wouldn't want him to think this conversation interested her. She brought the Irish air to a close and glanced at the clock. "Oh rats! I'm going to be late." Looking up, she could have cried.

The boy was gone, and she was surrounded by clean, wet floor.

Thirty-two

Lottie had trouble keeping her attention on Miss Crenshaw's classes the next afternoon. Her mind kept wandering to Tony, wondering if she would see him that evening. She'd thought of plenty of retorts to his insults, and she was eager to try them out.

She'd chosen her after-hours music carefully. The detached ornamentation of Mozart didn't please this boy, so she exchanged it for the lush themes of Mendelssohn's *Songs without Words*. She'd been playing for about twenty minutes when Tony entered, pushing the mop and bucket. Lottie glanced up when she heard him, and her fingers crashed to a halt. Tufts of white cotton stuck out of his ears.

"You can't possibly hate my playing this much," she shouted.

"Eh?" He pulled one cotton ball out and looked at her. "Oh, don't let me stop you. I'll pull these out when you get to the 1940s section of the concert."

The bench fell over with a crash as Lottie jumped to her feet. "You wouldn't hate this music if you understood it."

Tony leaned on his mop handle. "That's what I think about baseball." His gaze fell to her clenched fists. "Look, kid. Even I can see you've got talent. You can't get all worked up every time some yahoo like me says he don't like Beethoven. It ain't good for your health."

Lottie consciously relaxed her shoulders. "Shouldn't you take your own advice? Just because I don't like baseball ..."

"Yeah, now, that I just don't get." He turned away, putting the mop in motion again. "Not liking baseball is un-American."

"Why, you …" Lottie stared at his back in outrage. She had no idea how to deal with this aggravating boy. Her fingers found the piano keyboard of their own accord and launched into a loud, mistake-filled rendition of "Casey Jones."

Tony adjusted his earplugs and started to whistle.

The next evening when he finished mopping to Beethoven's *Moonlight Sonata*, Tony said, "I'll make a deal with you."

Lottie's guard went up. "What kind of deal?"

"You come to a baseball game and look at it through my eyes. I promise I'll explain everything so you'll understand. If you're not a fan by the end of the day, I'll buy you a box of Cracker Jack."

Lottie narrowed her eyes. "I think your deal's a little lopsided. I'll only go to your baseball game if you promise to come to a concert with me, and give it a fair shake."

Tony broke into a grin. "What'll I get if I hate it?"

"An ice cream soda, my treat."

"We're on, then." He stuck out a hand. "Put 'er there, sis."

"I can't," she said reluctantly. "I don't have the money to buy tickets to a baseball game or a concert."

Tony laughed. "Me neither, but that never stopped me. I'm going to the Stars game on Sunday afternoon. You up for it?"

"That depends." She pretended to think. "I've heard the stands are full of swanky movie stars at those games. I wouldn't know what to wear."

He looked disgusted. "If there are any movie stars, they won't be sitting with us, I can tell you that. So are you coming are not?"

She smiled. "Sure."

But on the way home from the studio, Lottie realized she had a problem. Helen was not going to let her go to a baseball game across town with a boy she barely knew. Not since the incident on the train. And especially not since this boy had dark hair and dark skin, and talked like a New York tough.

Lottie went home and told Helen she had to work an extra rehearsal on Sunday afternoon. Helen looked up from the letter she was writing. "Don't let Miss Crenshaw take advantage of you," she said with a frown. "I ought to go down there and tell her you're entitled to a day off, just like the rest of us."

"Oh, I don't mind," Lottie said. "I won't get to work as much once school starts, so I might as well put in the time now."

Helen pinched the bridge of her nose. "We do need the money. Billy, get down from there."

Lottie reached for Billy, who had climbed onto the back of a chair and plastered his face against the window behind it. "I'll walk to the studio by myself, so you and Billy can stay home."

"All right." Helen sounded tired. "Seems like all I do is stay home these days. Stay home and think."

○

Sunday afternoon on the way to the bus stop, Lottie pulled out the directions Tony had given her the day before. She counted six stops and got off at the corner of Fairfax and Beverly, where he waited on the sidewalk.

"Hurry up," he said. "The game starts in ten minutes." He grabbed Lottie's hand and they ran two blocks to the ball park.

She'd just gotten used to the feel of her hand in his when he dropped it to point to a group of people rushing toward the gates. "That right there is our ticket inside. Come on."

Lottie followed Tony into the middle of the crowd, and they passed through the gates unnoticed. He led her up the steps to the top of the stands, where they collapsed into two empty seats.

"What a kick," Lottie said when she got her breath back. "Are you sure we're safe?"

"Sure. They won't ask for our tickets or nothing." Tony squinted at the ball field. "Here comes the first pitch."

She looked at the men on the field far below. "Which one's the pitcher?"

He stared at her in disbelief. "Are you telling me you don't even know who the pitcher is?"

She would not make this easy. "Should I?"

Tony stuck his elbows on his knees and hunched forward, his face gloomy. "This is going to be harder than I thought. Okay. The pitcher's the one standing on the mound."

Lottie hid a smile. "You mean that little hill out there?"

A look of pain crossed his face. "Yeah, that little hill. He's throwing the ball to the guy with the bat."

She relented a little. "And the guy with the bat is going to try to hit it."

He looked relieved. "You've got that part, at least. C'mon, batter! Swing!"

She cupped her hands around her mouth. "Swing, batter!"

He rewarded her effort with an approving smile. "You catch on quick."

She returned his grin. "It's all coming back to me now." Seeing his puzzled look she added, "I was raised with a bunch of — boy cousins, you might say."

It was a glorious afternoon for baseball. True to his word, Tony explained every aspect of the game with the enthusiasm of a true fan. By the bottom of the ninth, with the Stars down by one run, Lottie understood fastballs and curve balls, singles, doubles, triples, and homers. When she yelled, "Can of corn!" at a pop fly, Tony declared victory. "You sound like you've been watching baseball all your life. I made you love it."

"You made me understand it," Lottie corrected. "I still wouldn't spend every Sunday at the ballpark."

"Do you like it better than you did when we came in?"

"Sure."

He grinned. "Then I don't have to buy you any Cracker Jack."

She smacked his arm. "Yes you do. You said I'd love baseball. Anything short of 'love' and I win. Oh!" She broke off to watch a hit from the Stars' second baseman. "It's out of here! A home run! Stars win! Stars win!"

Tony gave her a smug grin. "Sounds like love to me."

They split the cost of the Cracker Jack box.

Lottie was a half-hour late getting home. She expected an interrogation from Helen, but Mrs. Quinn met her at the door with Billy by her side.

"You're late." Her voice was sour. "Your sister went to a sewing circle meeting and left Billy with me."

Guilt flooded her chest. "Didn't you want to go, too?"

Mrs. Quinn raised her eyebrows. "Somebody had to stay behind with the baby."

"Yes, ma'am." She took Billy's hand and led him toward the stairs. "Have a nice evening, Mrs. Quinn."

The landlady's voice softened. "Dinner's on the stove. I'll be in my bedroom if you need me."

Lottie changed course and headed for the kitchen, questions buzzing in her brain. It was odd for the sewing circle to meet on a Sunday, and stranger still for Mrs. Quinn to stay home with Billy.

She took a bowl of beef stew to the back porch and ate while the little boy did lopsided somersaults on the lawn.

"Watch me, Wottie," he called before each roll.

"I see you," she called back.

After the umpteenth repetition, she called, "Time to go in," and Billy ran to her on wobbly legs. Scooping him up, she said, "I'll bet you're dizzy. Let's go upstairs."

He burrowed into her shoulder, thumb in mouth, as she took her dish to the kitchen and set it to soak. By the time she climbed the stairs to their room he'd fallen asleep, but she didn't put him to bed right away. Instead she sat in the chair by the window and enjoyed the dear weight of him on her lap.

Helen woke her hours later with a touch on the shoulder. "Lottie. Time for bed."

Lottie opened groggy eyes to see Helen's freshly scrubbed face hovering above her. "Did I fall asleep?"

"Yes, dear." Helen helped her out of the chair. "Billy's in bed already, and I've got your nightie right here. Now put up your arms. That's the way."

"What time is it?"

Helen paused in the act of buttoning Lottie's night gown. "Never mind. We'll talk in the morning."

Thirty-three

A deal's a deal," Tony said a week later. "When are you dragging me to this concert?"

Lottie shrugged. "I really don't know how to find a concert in this town, so you're probably off the hook."

"Why don't you talk to Miss Crenshaw about it? She likes stuff like that."

Lottie broke into a grin. "It almost sounds like you want to go."

Tony mopped away from her. "I'm trying to hold up my end of the bargain, that's all." He pulled a piece of paper out of his back pocket. "I saw this on a bulletin board."

Lottie took the flyer. "The Smithson Chamber Orchestra."

"It's your kind of music, see."

She glanced at him. "Where's St. Bartholomew's Church?"

"It's over on First Street. Not far at all."

"This sounds good, then." Lottie gave a decisive nod. "I'll see you Saturday night."

"I'm going out Saturday night," Helen told Lottie at dinner. "A group of us sewing circle girls are going to the movies. Doesn't that sound like fun?" She spoke in anxious little bursts, not quite meeting Lottie's eyes.

Lottie stared at her. The sewing circle met all the time now. "You spend every blessed evening with those women. Do you really need to see them on Saturday night, too?"

"We work hard," Helen said in a shaky voice. "We deserve a little fun, too."

Lottie sighed, thinking of the concert. "Can you take Billy with you?"

"No-o-o." Helen hesitated. "This is a grown-up night. Sorry, kiddo."

241

"All right." She pushed the disappointment away. "Billy and I will stay home, then."

"I can't make it on Saturday," she told Tony the next day. "My sister needs me to babysit."

He leaned on the mop handle. "Seems like all you do is babysit. How old is the kid?"

"Nearly two."

Tony nodded. "I've got a sister who's three. Boy, can she ever sleep." He shook his head in wonder. "Nothing wakes that kid up. I'll bet it's because we live near the train tracks. She's been hearing the trains come through since she was born, so they don't bother her anymore."

Lottie giggled. "Billy's like that too. He started riding trains when he was six weeks old, so nothing wakes him up."

"No kidding." He raised his eyebrows. "Why'd you move around so much?"

She dropped her eyes. "It's a long story."

She thought about their conversation as she walked home later that night. She thought about Tony every night as she walked home, but this time an idea occurred to her. Billy really was a sound sleeper. Would it hurt to go to Saturday's concert after he went to bed?

She gasped. How could she even think of such a thing? Imagine what would happen if Helen came home before her. She'd never trust Lottie again.

But it would be easy to get home before Helen, who came in later and later from her sewing circle meetings. And she was tired of babysitting while her sister went out and had fun.

She reached the house and ran upstairs to their room, where Helen, dressed to go out, sat in the rocker with Billy. "You can't practice so long after work," she said with a snap to her voice. "I told you I need you home by seven."

Lottie's inner turmoil bubbled to the surface. "Why? So you can go running off with your friends every night?"

Two white dents appeared around Helen's mouth. "I'm helping supply our troops with socks and blankets and bandages."

"Do you have to make them all yourself?"

Helen gasped. "That was un-called-for, Lottie. I think all this independence has gone to your head. You get more defiant every day."

Billy, half-asleep on his mama's lap, began to wail.

"Give him to me," Lottie reached for the baby. "I'll put him to sleep."

Helen's arms tightened around her son. "No. I guess I won't go tonight. The ladies will have to do without me."

Lottie dropped her arms. "All right then." She sat on her bed and wondered what to do next.

Helen rocked Billy to sleep and tucked him into his crib without speaking or looking at Lottie. She gave the baby a final pat, and went to stand by the open window, her back to the room.

Even her back looked angry, Lottie thought. She wished she'd relent, and come across the room so they could hug and make up. It would be heaven to have a sister she could confide in again. She'd love to tell her about Tony and their arguments over music and baseball. She might even find the courage to confess about the Stars game. Surely Helen would forgive her if she knew they'd been safe the whole time.

Helen drummed her fingers on the sill, an impatient little gesture that began to drive Lottie crazy. At last she turned and looked at the crib. "He's asleep," she said.

Lottie followed her gaze. "Yes." She glanced at her sister and sighed. "Helen, I'm not mad anymore. You can go if you want."

A smile flitted across Helen's tense face. "Thanks, kiddo." She reached for her pocket book and sewing bag. "I really do work hard, you know."

Lottie's eyes filled with tears. "I know. I'm sorry I said those things."

"That's all right." Helen gave her a brief hug. "I'll be home in a few hours."

Lottie went to bed shortly after Helen left, but she was too restless to sleep. She was glad they'd made up, but she wished Helen had stayed. Lottie imagined her saying, "No, honey, I'm staying with you tonight. Now, what shall we do?"

But Helen wasn't that kind of sister. She hadn't been for a long time. Lottie should be used to that fact by now.

○

The next night she told Tony, "I can go on Saturday after all. I'll meet you outside St. Bartholomew's a little before eight."

Tony grinned. "Let the torture begin."

Saturday night, Helen kissed Billy good night and left for the movies, trailing the scent of dime-store perfume. After she left, Lottie rocked the sleepy baby and tucked him into bed. She stood looking at him for several minutes, measuring the rise and fall of his breathing. When she was positive he was asleep, she turned out the light and left, locking the door behind her. Noiselessly she glided downstairs, past Mrs. Quinn's room, and into the night.

The orchestra concert wasn't crowded, so Lottie and Tony couldn't sneak in for free. She bought his ticket instead, though he protested loudly about a girl having to pay his way.

"It's my turn to make you love music," she said. "Making you pay would be a poor way to start, don't you think?"

He conceded her point, but insisted, "I'll buy you a soda afterward, then."

Lottie glanced anxiously at her watch. "If we have time."

He shook his head in disbelief. "Man, she keeps you on a short string."

"Not really." She handed him a program. "Let's find our seats."

Lottie explained the different instruments to Tony, and told him what she knew about Mozart. When the music began she left him alone, closing her eyes to listen, delighting in Mozart once again.

The concert lasted only an hour. When the lights went up, Lottie came back to herself slowly, reluctant to leave the warmth of the music. "Wasn't that amazing?" she said on a sigh.

Tony didn't reply. He was sound asleep.

○

"Hey, I'm sorry," he said again.

Lottie quickened her pace down the sidewalk so he had to jog to keep up.

"Come on, now. I'm still buying you that soda, right?"

She glared at him. "Don't I have to buy? I lost the bet."

"No you didn't. I liked your music. The stuff I heard was good. It really was." He grasped her arm. "Stop a minute."

She waited.

Tony slipped his hand into hers. "I'm glad you let me come with you. Now, how about that soda?"

His apologetic smile got to her at last. "It's all right, Tony." She glanced at her watch, and her eyes widened. "But I'll have to take a rain check. I've got to get home."

She walked away, ignoring Tony's exclamation. When she rounded the corner she broke into a jog. She was taking no chances on beating Helen home.

Ten minutes later she let herself in the front door and tiptoed upstairs, her heart in her throat. She closed her eyes before she turned the doorknob, desperately afraid that Helen would be there.

The room was dark. Lottie breathed a sigh of relief and crossed to the crib, where Billy slept in blissful peace, ignorant of his aunt's neglect.

"So that's that," she said, and softly kissed his sweet face, "and I'll never do it again."

Thirty-four

"I have an idea," Tony said when he saw Lottie on Monday. "My brother works the door at a swing club off Wilshire Boulevard. He says they've got some really hot bands. He'll let us in if you want to go. I can pay your ticket this time."

Lottie thought this over as she practiced her scales. It would be fun to see a swing band from the audience for once, but she couldn't imagine explaining it to Helen. "I don't think so," she said with regret.

"Why not? You'd be safe. My brother won't let us near the liquor." He stopped working to look at her. "Or are you just a music snob? Swing clubs aren't good enough. Is that it?"

Lottie hit a sour note and dropped her hands to her lap. She'd never told Tony about the Neverland. "I'm not a snob," she said. "I just don't think Helen will let me go."

"So don't ask her."

She looked up warily. "I don't want to do that."

He swiped a few square feet and said, "Well, I want to go. Let me know if you change your mind."

Lottie walked home slowly, her mind in turmoil. Tony could be excused for thinking she might be allowed to go. She'd let him think Helen knew about their other exploits. She wanted his good opinion more than anything in the world. What would he think of her if she didn't go with him? Was there a way to please Tony and Helen both?

Supper was ready when she reached home. Billy greeted her from his high chair. "Hi, Wottie. I hungry."

"I hungry too, champ," she replied, and went to wash her hands.

"I've had a couple of letters today," Helen said over chicken and dumplings. "Mr. Schultz wrote to say the Neverland broke up the day we left."

"Oh." Lottie set her spoon down. "That's so sad. Where did the guys go?"

Helen pulled the letter out of her pocket and spread it out on the table. "He's not sure. Parson called to tell him they were through. He said he was going back to college, and he didn't give a rip what the rest of the guys did."

"Good for Parson. He belongs in college." Lottie drew her eyebrows together. "Do you think Johnny's all right?"

Helen smoothed a bent corner of the page with her fingernail. "Oh, I'm sure he is," she said with an odd little laugh. "Johnny's one of those people who always lands on his feet."

Lottie nodded, her eyes on her plate. It hurt to think about Parson and Johnny. She pushed her chair away from the table. "I'm not hungry. Do you mind if I go upstairs?"

Helen put out a hand to stop her. "Wait, I haven't told you about Aunt Eva's letter. She's coming to see us."

Lottie's eyes flew to Helen's face. "Really? When?"

"She doesn't say, only that she plans to visit Westmont and then continue on to California." Helen looked up. "She needs to see for herself that we're all right."

"Hooray!" Lottie cried. "That's the best news I've heard in a year."

"Hooway." Billy chuckled.

Lottie swooped to kiss his cheek. "That's right, Billy. You're going to love Aunt Eva."

Aunt Eva's letter made up for the news about the band. Lottie sat at the table once more and polished off her dumplings. As she sopped up the last bit of gravy with her bread she said, "I can't wait to show her the Pacific."

Helen smiled. "You can't live in a state of excitement over this, Lottie. Aunt Eva will probably stay in Iowa a couple of weeks. It could be next month before she sends word she's coming."

Lottie's smile drooped. "That long?"

"I'm afraid so."

Tony was stuck on the idea of going to his brother's swing club. He found a way to mention it every time he saw Lottie, until she finally said, "When are you going?"

"Saturday." His eyes lit up. "You mean you'll come?"

She sighed. "I guess I'll find a way. But only to get you off my back."

Tony's grin lit his whole face. "Atta girl!"

Lottie worked on her escape plan on the way home. She would tell Helen she was needed at the studio. It had worked in the past.

But Helen proved difficult to convince. "Absolutely not," she said when Lottie broached the subject. "That woman takes advantage of you shamefully. And do we see a penny more in wages? No."

"But it's a steady job," Lottie pointed out. "I don't want to risk losing it. You said yourself we could use the money."

Helen thinned her mouth into a flat line. "She's lucky to have you, and she knows it. You have to draw the line with people, Lottie. Tell her no."

"I can't go, Tony," she said the next evening. "My sister said no."

"I told you not to ask her," he said, disgusted. "When are you going to stop acting like a little kid, always running to Mama for permission?"

Lottie bowed her head above the keys and wished desperately for a way out of this problem. She was tired of this endless tug-of-war between Tony and Helen. Why couldn't she please them both?

"Oh, Lottie," Helen said Thursday night as she walked out the door. "I'm going out Saturday night. One of the girls asked me to serve punch at a USO dance. Bye now."

Lottie stared at the closed door. "Well, how do you like them apples?"

Billy paused from climbing onto the bed. "Apple?"

She reached for him. "None for you, champ. Time to get down." He arched his back against her restraining arms, and nearly slid out of her grasp. "How'd you get to be such a squirrel?" She hoisted him to her shoulder and flew him off to put his pajamas on.

Lottie sat by the window a long time after Billy fell asleep, staring through the branches of the orange tree at the sky beyond. The lights of the neighborhood dimmed the stars, but the moon shone, round and white, and the leaves whispered their fragrant invitation to come outside and enjoy the night.

She released the latch on the window screen and pulled it up, then stuck her head and shoulders out the window. A stout tree branch hung at eye level, perfect for holding her while she swung her legs free.

Before she knew it, Lottie was safely on the ground. She wanted to laugh at how easy it was. Why hadn't she known this before? Stepping into the crook of the tree, she clambered back up and soon stood in the middle of the bedroom once again.

"I did it," Lottie said to the empty room, "and now I'm going to bed."

Friday evening Lottie found Mrs. Quinn standing on the front porch steps with a suitcase in her hand, looking worried.

"Hi, Mrs. Quinn. Is anything wrong?" Lottie asked.

"My mother fell and broke her hip," Mrs. Quinn said, a tremor in her voice. "I have to go to Bakersfield to nurse her. Oh, where is that cab?"

"I hope she gets better soon."

Mrs. Quinn took her attention off the street for a brief moment. "Thank you, Lottie. You're always so polite." She hesitated as if she wanted to say something more.

Lottie waited expectantly until Helen called from the kitchen. "Lottie? Is that you?"

She opened the screen door. "Well, I've got to go."

Mrs. Quinn seemed relieved. "Yes, dear. Be a good girl, now."

"Did the taxi come yet?" Helen asked when Lottie reached the kitchen. "It was just pulling up. How long will she be gone?"

"Who knows? Will you be all right by yourself tomorrow night?"

Lottie turned away to hide her irritation. "What choice do I have?"

Helen looked relieved. "You're growing into such a sensible girl."

Saturday afternoon, Lottie stopped to buy candy on the way home from work, sugar buttons for Billy and sourballs for herself. She decided against a bag of licorice whips for Helen. Let her drink the punch at the USO party if she wanted something sweet.

Billy greeted the candy with a delighted squeal. Lottie gave him six brightly colored buttons, and put the rest in the top drawer of the dresser for later.

"Will you dance with the soldiers?" Lottie asked as she watched Helen get ready to go.

Helen smiled and daubed a little perfume on each wrist. "I don't know. I've never done this before. The girls tell me it will run pretty late, though. Don't wait up."

"I never do." Lottie popped a sourball into her mouth, preventing further conversation.

After Helen left, Lottie put the sourballs away and dragged Billy's wooden block set out from under the bed. They filled the hour before bedtime with building and demolition. Lottie thought about her old friend Sammy, and wondered what he was building these days. She'd have to ask Aunt Eva.

At bedtime Billy refused to be rocked until he had more button candy. Lottie gave him a pink one and a green one, and rocked him until his head grew heavy against her chest. As she tucked him into bed, the breeze in the orange tree caught her attention. Another beautiful night beckoned.

Lottie sat by the window and enjoyed the breeze until Billy's breathing grew deep and regular. Then, before she could stop herself, she left, locking the door behind her.

She stopped at the street corner and looked back, frightened of what she'd done, but the house looked like a fortress, rising against the city night sky. Nothing will happen, it seemed to say. Go in peace.

She turned and ran.

Tony had given careful directions earlier in the week, and the club proved easy to find. It was small, set back from the street, but the crowd in front of the door pointed her right to it.

For a minute the scene frightened her. She looked around in hopes of finding Tony, but saw only strangers. A big man stood at the door, taking money and waving people inside. There was something familiar about his face, so she walked up to him and said, "Excuse me. I'm looking for Tony DiFranco?"

The man looked down at her with a tolerant smile. "You know my brother, huh?"

She nodded.

He jerked his head toward the door. "Go ahead inside. He should be at a table near the stage. And he better not be touching no beer."

Lottie slipped past Tony's brother and into the twilight beyond.

Loud, familiar music led her into the crowded ballroom, where she found Tony at a table near the band. "Well, look who cut the apron strings," he said in a voice tinged with admiration.

Lottie looked beyond him, a little irritated. "Is the band any good?"

He shrugged. "How should I know? That's your department." He patted the seat next to him. "Take a load off and listen a while."

She angled her chair toward the band and sat down to listen. The band had better rhythm than the Neverland, though the singer didn't hold a candle to Monica. The piano sounded tinny, but that was hardly the pianist's fault. Pianos varied from place to place.

"So?" Tony said. "Should I like the band or not?"

She shot him a curious look. "You really can't tell for yourself?"

"Can you tell which pitch a pitcher will use before he lets go of the ball?"

She laughed. "Fair enough. The band is better than some I've heard."

Lottie tapped her foot to the rhythm of "Begin the Beguine" as Tony left to order two ginger ales from the bar. She stared idly at the brass section with an odd sense of déjà vu. It was funny how one trombonist could move so exactly like another. Suddenly she sat bolt upright. She hadn't seen Bobby Richards in almost two years. Could it really be him?

She made her way to the other side of the stage for a better look. There sat Richards, natty in his gray suit and striped tie, sweat from the hot lights beading on his forehead. He moved the same way she remembered, swaying with the rhythm, holding his head at a slight angle. She watched him for a full minute, her heart swelling with good memories.

"Oh, miss?"

Lottie looked around. Behind her, a man with a movie camera said, "I'm trying to get a clear shot of the stage. Could you step to one side?"

"Sorry." She moved, and soon was lost in thought. She jumped when Tony spoke into her ear. "Hey, where'd you go? I put the drinks on our table."

She turned. "I wanted to see the band up close." She pointed to Richards. "I know that guy."

Tony didn't believe her. "No you don't. You just think you do."

She raised her eyebrows. "I'll prove it."

After the first set, Lottie stepped onto the stage and tapped the trombonist's shoulder. "Richards?"

His face broke into a delighted smile. "Well if it isn't Brown!" His delight turned to concern. "Hey, what're you doing here? I know it's been a few years, but you can't be old enough for this place already."

Lottie flushed. "It's all right. I'm here with a friend." She jerked a thumb at Tony, watching from the floor. "The question is, what are you doing here? I thought you were in the army."

Richards held up his right arm, which ended in a stub below the wrist. "Couldn't hold a gun anymore," he said cheerfully.

Lottie's mouth fell open. "Oh, I'm sorry."

He waved away her pity. "Don't worry about it, kid. It was my ticket out of the fighting. Hey, are you still handy with the ivories?"

"Sure." She raised a restraining hand. "But I'm not looking for a job, so don't even ask."

He laughed. "I wasn't going to. There's someone I think you should meet, though."

Richards stepped off the stage and motioned for Lottie to follow him. She reached for Tony's hand and tugged him with her through the crowd.

Richards guided her toward a portly middle-aged man who looked out of place in the party crowd. "Mr. Thompson is from Movietone News," he said. "You know, the newsreels in the movie houses."

Lottie nodded. Of course she knew about Movietone News.

Richards threw her a self-effacing grin. "He's doing a story on me, the one-handed trombonist who fought at Guadalcanal. You probably saw the cameraman filming me as I played. But he'll be a lot more interested in you, Brown. I guarantee it."

But when he told the reporter about Lottie, the man looked bored. "Kids in Hollywood are a dime a dozen," he said, lighting a cigarette.

Richards shook his head. "Look, this kid's better than Vladimir Horowitz himself. It won't cost you anything to listen to her."

Mr. Thompson blew out a cloud of smoke. "Get her up there, then. But I make no promises."

Richards looked at Lottie. "You up for this, Brown?"

Lottie glanced at Tony, who looked impressed. "Movietone News!

That'd really be something."

That did it. Turning to Richards, she said. "Can you get me up there? I don't want to mess things up for anyone in the band."

Richards grinned. "Yeah, it'll be okay." With a hand at her back, he guided her to the stage for a word with the bandleader. Lottie couldn't hear what was said, but before long Richards waved her over to the piano.

The rest was as easy as wearing an old shoe. She knew the music, the arrangement coming easily to her mind. Her fingers danced across the keys, and she felt the old sense of camaraderie with the rest of the band, though they were strangers to her tonight. After the first number, she rose from the bench, but the piano player made her sit again. "Go ahead," he said. "I'm still getting paid."

Two songs later, the Movietone reporter stopped her. "Miss Brown, would you mind coming down from there? I'd like to discuss terms."

She jumped off the stage to solid applause.

"Do you have an agent?" Mr. Thompson asked as he handed her a glass of water.

She took a sip, grateful for the cool liquid on her throat. "No, sir."

The reporter smiled. "Then who do I talk to about featuring you on a news reel? Your story fascinates me."

The question landed like a bucket of cold water over Lottie's head. How would she explain this to Helen? She gave the reporter a searching look. "You'll need to talk to my sister. But I'm going to ask a favor first."

His eyes narrowed. "Shoot."

"Could you possibly discover me somewhere other than this dance club?" She twisted the glass in her hand. "My sister doesn't know I'm here."

He crossed his arms and leaned back in his chair. "Where do you suggest I find you, then?"

"I know," Tony said suddenly. "Maybe you hear about her from me tonight, and show up at the dance studio to check her out. She works every day from noon to five."

Mr. Thomas looked from one pleading face to another, and threw up his hands. "Oh, all right. It's not a big deal. But I've got a deadline to meet, kids. Let's say I discovered you last week, and I'll show up tomorrow afternoon to talk to your sister."

Lottie looked at Tony, who gave a little nod. She turned to the reporter. "Thanks a lot, Mr. Thompson. I'll see you tomorrow." She told him the address and turned to Tony. "I've got to get home," she said. "I can't be late."

He took her hand. "I'll walk with you."

They threaded their way through the crowd to the door, and kept going down the sidewalk, away from the swing club. When the noise had faded to a distant roar, Tony said, "Where'd you learn to play like that?"

She looked up. "Like what?"

"I never saw you swing like that before. If it makes any difference, you made me love music tonight."

"Thanks, Tony." She lowered her eyes to their intertwined hands. "I had a good time, too. Do you think that reporter will really follow through?"

"Just see if he doesn't! Hey, Lottie…" He pulled her to a halt on the dark sidewalk. She turned to answer him and stopped at the look in his eyes. He leaned in and kissed her, his lips firm and tentative at the same time. One of her hands stole to his neck as she kissed him back.

The kiss ended, and Tony placed his forehead against hers. "You're my girl. You know that, right?"

She nodded, suddenly shy. "Sure, Tony. I've felt that way from the first time I saw you." A church bell rang in the distance, and a dim fear intruded on Lottie's happiness. Pulling back she said, "What time is it?"

He checked his wrist watch. "Twelve thirty. Why?"

Lottie began to walk. "I've got to go."

He kept up easily. "I'll go with you. Make sure you're safe."

She gave a shaky laugh. "The only way I'm in danger is if I don't get home before Helen." She turned a pleading look on Tony. "Don't follow me. I can go faster if I'm by myself."

He pulled up short and watched her flee. "If that's the way you feel."

"I'm sorry. I'd stay if I could." Lottie ran back and kissed him quickly. "I'll see you Monday."

He squeezed her hand. "Can't wait."

Lottie ran until she was two houses from home, then stopped, gasping for breath, and formed a plan. She'd walk past the house on the other side of the street, just in case Helen was waiting on the porch. She could check for a light in the window of their room, and determine whether Helen was home or not.

She crossed the street and walked in deep shade, her eyes on the house in the distance. When she was directly across from it, she noticed two figures on the porch. She paused behind a parked car, her heart beating double time, but neither form was slender enough to be Helen. Then one spoke loudly enough for her to hear.

"I told you we shouldn't surprise them, Eva. Everyone is asleep."

"Well, why doesn't the doorbell wake them?" The other voice sounded frustrated.

Lottie dropped behind the car. Aunt Eva and Aunt Cora were standing on her front porch.

As the aunts squabbled gently, Lottie crawled from shadow to shadow until she was past the house. Then she crossed the street, doubled back and ran through the side yard to the orange tree. She had both hands on the bottom branch and one foot in its crook when she heard a third voice float around the corner of the house. Helen was home.

Lottie scrambled up the tree, heedless of the damage to her dress and socks, praying each branch she grabbed would hold. She reached the window and struggled to lift the screen, wondering why she hadn't thought to leave it open just in case. It lifted at last, and she thrust her body through, landing on the floor at the end of the bed just as the key turned in the lock. She stood, twigs in her hair, her dress torn at the waist, and gasped.

Billy was not in his crib.

The door opened. Helen and the aunts entered, chatting happily, but seeing Lottie they stopped in surprise. "Why Lottie," Helen said. "What are you doing up?" Her eyes went to the crib. "Where's Billy?"

Lottie's mouth was too dry to form an answer. Her eyes were fixed on the bed by the window, where Billy lay, eyes closed, mouth slightly open, both hands lying slack on his chest. A black bruise on his forehead stood out in stark contrast to his pale, blue-tinged face.

"Billy!" Helen leaped across the room to pick up her baby, but Lottie was there first.

"Wake up, Billy. Wake up, little guy." She shook him gently. "C'mon, champ. Wake up for Lottie."

"Get away from him." Helen pushed her to the floor and picked up her son. Bending her ear to his tiny mouth, she listened intently, her face twisted in anguish. "He's not breathing."

Equal to any emergency, Aunt Cora took charge. "Eva, shut those windows," she said. "There's no sense waking the neighbors." Turning to Helen she said, "Give him to me, dear. Perhaps there's something we can do."

She placed the baby on the bed and undressed him as she talked to Helen in a low, soothing voice. "Was he well when you left tonight? Any unusual cough or stuffy nose?"

"No." Helen's answer was muffled.

"What about fever? Did he feel warm?" As the examination continued, Lottie crouched by the dresser shaking with fear. She set a hand down to steady herself and picked up something round. A sourball. Looking up, she noticed the top dresser drawer hung open. Billy had spilled all the candy on the floor. "He's choking." Her voice came out as a whisper. Trying again she said, "Aunt Cora? He's choking."

Aunt Cora looked down at the candy in Lottie's hand. "Oh, my Lord." She tipped Billy's head back and plunged a finger into his slack mouth, ignoring Helen's incoherent protest, and fished around. "Got it." She turned the boy sideways to let a sticky green ball slide onto the coverlet.

"Thank God!" Helen cried, but Billy didn't move. Everyone held their breath, their eyes on the lifeless child. Aunt Cora's lips moved in prayer as she took Helen's hand.

After a long minute, Cora shook her head. "He's gone."

"No!" Helen's scream rattled the windows and she collapsed, sobbing, beside her child, clutching him to her breast.

Cora reached across Helen's legs to Lottie, still cowering on the floor, and hauled her up by the armpits. "Get out of the way, Eva. Lottie needs the bathroom."

Yes she did, Lottie thought with vague surprise, and barely made it to the bathroom down the hall before the retching began. She knelt on the hard tile floor, gripping the toilet bowl, and heaved until nothing came up but bile, while Aunt Cora placed a wet washcloth on her neck and murmured, "There, child. Get it all out." When at last her stomach calmed, she slid to the floor, head throbbing, and tasted death in her mouth.

She should be dead. The phrase repeated in her brain. She should be the one on that bed. She deserved to die. Squeezing her eyes shut, she concentrated on the cool porcelain beneath her cheek and the chant that pounded in her head, and lay still.

She awoke to searing pain across her right cheek and Helen's livid face hovering above her own. "Get out," she hissed. "Get your ugly face out of my sight, you worthless excuse for a human —"

"That's enough, Helen." Cora's sharp voice cut through the stream of invective. "Nothing can come of that kind of talk. Lottie, come with me."

Lottie reached for the towel rack to pull herself up, and edged past her sister, who fairly glowed with rage. She followed Aunt Cora out of the bathroom on shaking legs. "Where are we going?"

In reply, Cora took her elbow in a vise-like grip and propelled her downstairs. In the naked light of the kitchen bulb, she placed her hands on her niece's shoulders. "Now. Tell me what happened here tonight."

Lottie clasped her hands so tightly her knuckles turned white. "I was supposed to watch Billy tonight while Helen went to a USO dance with her sewing circle. Only I wanted to go out tonight too, with a friend who asked me to see a band. I was so mad at Helen for leaving me all the time, and Billy's such a good sleeper..." She stopped.

"So when he went to sleep you snuck out to see your friend." Aunt Cora's voice was grim. "What harm could it do?"

Lottie nodded, tears running down her cheeks. "I swore to myself I'd never do it again, but I really didn't think it would hurt just this once. We went to a dance club where a big band was playing. I saw a trombone player from the Neverland..." She raised her head, a new horror in her eyes. "The Movietone News!"

Aunt Cora looked blank. "The news reel?"

"I met a reporter tonight. He wants to do a story on me for the Movietone News. He's stopping by tomorrow afternoon to talk to Helen."

Aunt Cora nodded toward the window, where early morning lit the sky. "You mean today. It's a good thing we've got you on the morning train."

Lottie raised shocked eyes to her aunt's face. "Where are you sending me?"

Aunt Cora's mouth tightened at the corners. "You're going to Madame D'Abri. You remember her?"

Lottie nodded.

"Eva will escort you to Dayton where Madame will meet your train."

Lottie gasped. "What about Helen?"

"I'm taking her home."

"And Billy?" Lottie whispered his name.

Cora swallowed. "Billy will be buried in a cemetery in Los Angeles. Eva called her husband, who knew a man who could help us."

"Can't I stay for the funeral?" Lottie asked, knowing the answer.

Cora shook her head. "Your train leaves in an hour." When Lottie began to weep anew she added, "Be grateful. If it were up to Helen, you'd be in police custody right now."

There was a rustling at the top of the stairs. "Cora?" Eva called. "I'm ready."

Cora hurried away and returned, Lottie's hat in her hand. "Put this on. It's time to go."

Lottie jammed it on her head and followed Aunt Cora to the door, where Eva waited. "Take my hand, Lottie. We have to hurry."

Lottie climbed into the waiting taxi and turned to look out the window. Mrs. Quinn's house stood, calm and regal in the early morning light.

Thirty-five

April 1984

*L*ottie settled into her first-class airplane seat and watched the rest of the passengers file past. Closing the tiny window shade, she settled in for a nap. In spite of the Plaza Hotel's excellent bedding, she hadn't slept a wink. Helen's presence at a concert always had that effect.

Miranda Charles, her new assistant, met the plane in Kansas City. "Good to have you back, Miss Braun," she said as she took Lottie's bag.

Lottie smiled. Miranda's professional distance pleased her. She couldn't abide people who presumed a chumminess that didn't exist. "I'm glad to be back. Perhaps we could go over my schedule on the drive home."

"Certainly." Miranda held out the keys to the Mercedes. "I'll grab your suitcase and show you where I parked."

Lottie refused the keys with a shake of her head. "Just this once, would you mind driving?" She smiled at her assistant. "Don't look so flabbergasted. I didn't sleep well last night."

Miranda frowned. "You weren't near the ice machine, were you? I insisted when I booked your room that they keep you away from the ice and the elevator."

"And they followed your instructions." Lottie waved a slender hand. "I'm not even sure the Plaza has ice machines. They're certainly not noisy. I simply couldn't sleep. Now, shall we get on with it?"

Miranda wove smoothly through the afternoon traffic, talking all the while. "You'll notice the music department moved the senior recital back a week to April 28. Note the reception afterward. As this year's visiting professor you're expected to attend."

Lottie consulted the calendar on her lap. "It's odd that they hold it in the afternoon. Are classes over, then, after the recital?"

Miranda nodded. "Your contract ends on the thirtieth."

"And I move on to Cincinnati August first." She glanced at her assistant. "How do you feel about going with me? It isn't easy, changing cities every year or two."

"So far I like the life. The salary is generous, and so is the vacation time." Miranda changed lanes and exited the highway. "Oh, before I forget, Children's Mercy Hospital wants you to participate in the ribbon-cutting ceremony on their new wing. Nothing too time-consuming. You'll smile at some children, shake hands with the board of directors. A few pictures, a couple of autographs and you'll be done."

Lottie's mouth hardened into a thin line. "Absolutely not. I told them at the beginning that my name was not to be associated with the project."

"But they're so grateful for your donation. It's understandable —"

"I won't hear of it." Lottie turned her face to the window. "Tell them no."

Miranda gave a tiny sigh. "Very well."

Three weeks later, Lottie sat near the front of the auditorium and listened as her latest group of protégés showed off their skills. The smile on her face felt stiff, not because of the performances, but because she still wasn't sleeping well. The memories stirred up by Helen's note still plagued her in the night.

The concert ended, and the audience moved across campus in the late afternoon sunshine to a reception at the president's mansion. Lottie stood at the tea table, adding sugar to a steaming cup when Miranda Charles tapped her shoulder. "May I have a word with you, Miss Braun?"

She left her teacup and followed her assistant out of the room. "What is it?"

"This came for you an hour ago." Miranda handed her an official-looking envelope. "It's registered mail. I signed for it."

Lottie examined the return address. "Williams and Williams, Attorneys at Law. Collison, Iowa." She looked up. "What makes you think it's important?"

Miranda looked uncertain. "As far as I know, you have no professional ties to Iowa."

"But your research found that I was born there, so you figured this must be personal." Lottie's eyes narrowed. "You did your homework."

A weaker person would have wilted under her hard stare, but Miranda straightened her shoulders. "It's my job to look after your best interests, Miss Braun."

Lottie glanced at the envelope once more. "So it is." A smile flickered across her face. "Do you have a letter opener?"

Miranda's shoulders relaxed. "Will a nail file do?"

"Thank you." She slit the envelope. "Oh, and will you go find my cup of tea?"

Lottie took the letter to a nearby window seat and spread it out on her lap.

Dear Miss Braun,

I am sorry to inform you that your sister, Helen Parker, died of cancer on the 22nd of April. As she left you a substantial legacy, we urgently request that you be present for the reading of her will. We would like to set a date as soon as possible for said reading. Please contact our office upon receipt of this letter and ask for me.

Respectfully yours,

Edgar Williams Senior

"Here's your tea, Miss Braun." Miranda's voice startled Lottie out of her thoughts.

"Thank you." She raised the cup to her lips, oblivious of the tremor in her hands. Indicating the letter with a tilt of her head she said, "I'll need your help with this matter. Call the lawyer on Monday and tell him I refuse. He can proceed without me."

Miranda reached for the letter, glanced at its contents and slipped it into her purse. "I'm sorry for your loss, Miss Braun," she said politely, then plunged forward as Lottie's teacup fell from a hand gone suddenly slack. "I need a doctor!" she shouted, her arm around her employer's shoulders. "Miss Braun has fainted."

○

"That lawyer in Collison won't take no for an answer, Miss Braun," Miranda said Monday afternoon. "He said you could call him yourself if you're so bent on refusing, and he'd see what could be done." Her lips twitched at the thought of all the other things Edgar Williams had chosen to say. She'd liked his blunt insistence on talking to the great lady herself.

Lottie's brows drew together. "Oh I'll call him all right. Where's the phone number?"

Miranda handed her the lawyer's letter. "It's on the letterhead, there at the top."

"Give that to me." Lottie snatched the paper and marched into her study.

Miranda smiled to herself when the door banged shut. After a year of employment, this letter was the first indication that the great Lottie Braun had been born into a family like ordinary people. Something told her this matter was not going to go away.

Ten minutes later Miss Braun emerged, muttering to herself. She seemed surprised to find Miranda waiting in her sitting room. "Oh, it's you," she said with an unusual lack of courtesy. "Cancel all my appointments for Thursday. I'm driving to Iowa."

"Yes, Miss Braun." Miranda reached for her schedule. Just to be safe, she'd rearrange Friday, too.

Thirty-six

The closer Lottie got to Collison, the sicker she felt. She could hardly believe she'd let that old coot talk her into this crazy trip. What on earth could Helen have left her? Some trinket of their mother's? That could have been boxed up and mailed. A memento of their days with the Neverland Orchestra? She hoped not.

She reviewed what she knew about Helen's life. It wasn't much. While Lottie was still at the academy, she'd read an article in the newspaper about the liberation of a Japanese prison camp, and Bill had been listed among the dead. She'd tried and failed at the time to feel sad for the brash young man she barely remembered. Instead she felt only relief that he never would know about Billy.

"Billy." She said the name aloud, testing her voice for steadiness. She assumed his death would have passed into family lore. Stories like that didn't stay secret. She needed to be prepared for the things her relatives might say.

Her thoughts returned to Helen. Somewhere along the way she must have remarried, since her last name was now Parker. Naturally she would have children, too. Lottie mentally girded herself to meet Helen's offspring. "How do you do?" she said to the bugs on the windscreen. "I'm so sorry about killing your brother."

Hysteria took over then, laughter and tears bubbling out at the same time. She pulled into a rest stop, her vision too blurred to see the road, and let her feelings off the leash. When she felt better, she mopped her cheeks with a tissue, fixed her makeup, and got back on the highway.

She parked in front of the law office with a few minutes to spare, and gathered her courage. "I can do this." She faced her reflection in the vanity mirror. "I am Lottie Braun, world-renowned concert pianist. Nobody can take that away from me."

She stepped into the offices of Williams and Williams and announced herself to a plump woman with a regrettable permanent wave.

"We've been expecting you." The woman opened the door marked Edgar Williams Sr. "Won't you please go in?"

Ed Williams greeted her with a warm handshake and no reference to the battle they had waged on the phone. "I'm happy to meet you at last," he said. Turning to a dark-haired woman sitting in one of the client chairs he said, "Patti Parker, this is your Aunt, Lottie Braun."

"It's Patricia." The young woman remained seated, her eyes wary. "So you do exist," she said. "I've heard about you for years, but never believed you were real. It was like being related to George Washington."

Lottie inclined her head. "You have the best of me, then. I didn't know about you at all."

The girl looked away without answering, so Lottie found a chair and arranged herself in it, composing her features into a calm she didn't feel.

Ed Williams selected a paper from the pile on his desk. "Suppose we get started."

Lottie looked startled. "Is this everybody?" she asked, and earned a disgusted glare from her niece.

Mr. Williams looked like he wanted to smile. "Yes," he said gravely, "you and Patti are Helen's only heirs, I'm afraid."

"Oh." Lottie felt bewildered. She'd always imagined Helen with a big family. "Go on, then."

"I will now read the last will and testament of Helen Braun Turner Parker, widow of David Parker, late of the City of Collison, County of Des Moines, Iowa."

Lottie raised a hand, and the lawyer paused. "I'm sorry. Did you say David Parker? Helen was married to David Parker?"

Patti clicked her tongue impatiently, and Mr. Williams looked stern. "Perhaps you could hold your questions until I'm finished reading, Miss Braun. I assure you, Mrs. Parker's will is the soul of brevity."

Lottie sat back in her chair, her thoughts jumbled. Helen had married Parson.

She glanced at her niece, now biting a thumbnail. She looked to be in her late twenties, with Helen's flawless complexion and — now she thought of it — Parson's eyes. An attractive girl, though faint lines around the mouth betrayed unhappiness. Who could blame her after losing both parents so young?

She returned her wandering attention to the lawyer as he listed Helen's bequests. "To my daughter, Cora Patricia Parker Moore, I bequeath all of my personal effects, household goods and furnishings, excepting my home at 2856 Harmony Lane. That home, and the property on which it stands, I bequeath to my sister Lottie Braun in compensation for the years of homelessness she has endured at my hands, and in forgiveness of all her debts to me, both real and imagined."

Ed Williams looked up from the paper in his hands. "Would you like a glass of water, Miss Braun? You look a little pale."

Lottie barely heard him over the roar in her ears. Mr. Williams left the room and returned, bearing two glasses of ice water. Handing one to each woman, he said, "Let's take a little break now."

After a few refreshing sips, Lottie became aware of Patti's steady stare. Turning slightly in her chair, she faced her niece, and read the jealousy in her eyes.

"Homeless? I don't understand," Patricia said. "You're a world-famous piano player. You probably own houses all over the world."

Lottie couldn't help smiling at this assessment of her wealth. "As a matter of fact, I don't own any property." She wondered how Helen knew. "But I'm far from homeless."

"Then why do you get the house?" It came out as a wail. "I'm the one who grew up there. Mother had no right to give it to somebody else."

"Ah, but she did, Patti," the lawyer said calmly. "She had a perfect right to give it to anyone she pleased."

Patti folded her arms across her body. "If Daddy was alive, he wouldn't have let her do it."

Lottie stared at her in fascination. Had this been their family dynamic?

Ed Williams rolled his office chair sideways to a lateral file against the wall, and opened a drawer. After a quick search, he pulled out a document and spread it out on his desk. "On the contrary, Patti. Your father planned to do exactly the same thing."

Lottie and Patricia nearly bumped heads in their eagerness to see the document he held. Mr. Williams pointed one long finger at a paragraph which read:

"In the event that my wife, Helen Braun Turner Parker, does not survive me by at least thirty (30) days, I bequeath all of my personal effects, household goods and furnishings, excepting my home at 2856 Harmony Lane, to my daughter, Cora Patricia Parker Moore. That home, and the property on which it stands, I bequeath to my sister-in-law, Lottie Braun, in complete agreement with the wishes of my wife."

Complete agreement. Lottie sat back with a sigh. Parson approved of this harebrained idea.

"This can't be happening." Patti jumped to her feet. "Mr. Williams, tell me you can do something about this will. You know how much I love that house. You've lived next door since before I can remember."

"Indeed I have." A smile played around Ed Williams' lips. "My hands are tied, however. I can do nothing to alter your parents' wishes."

Patti turned to her new-found aunt. "You can refuse to go along with it, though. Please say you will, Miss Braun. Surely you can see how unfair this is."

Lottie sized up Patricia Parker as she would a new piano student, and didn't like what she saw. She couldn't abide self-pity, and right now it flowed out of her niece's very pores. "Where do you live?" she asked suddenly.

The younger woman looked surprised. "I have an apartment in Chicago."

"Chicago proper, or one of the suburbs?"

"I'm right downtown. Why?"

"Do you like it there?"

Patti Parker's brows drew together. "What are you getting at?"

Lottie turned to the lawyer. "What happens next, Mr. Williams?"

Ed Williams looked amused. "I'd like to discuss your next steps over dinner. My wife is cooking up a feast just in case I can persuade you to be our guest. Patti, won't you come, too?"

The girl picked up her purse. "I'm finished here. I have to pick up my little girl from the babysitter by bedtime." She tossed her head, and her bangs bounced out of her eyes. Turning to her aunt she said, "You're crazy if you think you can waltz into Collison after all these years and pick up where you left off. People around here are suspicious of newcomers, even if they're famous, and they'll make your life miserable. Let me know when you're ready to give up. I'll be happy to take that house off your hands."

Patti slammed the door behind her, and Lottie raised her eyebrows. "Is she always such a ray of sunshine?"

He chuckled. "She's a piece of work, all right."

Lottie leaned forward. "I can't possibly accept the house, Mr. Williams. I'm touched by Helen's thoughtfulness, but my career requires me to travel extensively. I'm not cut out to be a homeowner. Besides, what would the neighbors think of Helen's sister moving into her home? It seems awfully presumptuous."

The lawyer leaned back in his chair and waited until Lottie blew herself out. When she fell silent, he said, "Why don't you take some time to think about the matter? If you truly don't want the house, you'll have to put it on the market, and that will take time."

"What about Patricia? Won't it pass directly to her?"

"It doesn't work that way." Mr. Williams' brows came together in a frown. "Patti Parker spent eighteen years trying to escape this backwards Iowa town. Whatever she said today, she does not want to be tied to a house in Collison. Please don't let her little guilt trip sway your decision."

Lottie looked around helplessly. "I confess I'm all at sea here."

Ed Williams leaned forward. "Why don't you come for dinner, then? We'll eat Martha's excellent cooking, and I'll give you a tour of Helen's place afterward."

Thirty-seven

*L*ottie followed Ed Williams' directions to a shady street on the north end of town. Pulling up to the curb, she admired his house, a rambling Victorian set back from the street, with a wide front door and friendly wrap-around porch. By the looks of the neighboring bungalows, the Williams owned the original farmhouse, around which a subdivision had been built. She sighed. Something about the house reminded her of Aunt Cora.

With an effort, she turned her attention to Helen's cheery bungalow, and did a double take. Mr. Williams stood on the bungalow's porch with his arm around a sweet-faced woman in an apron. They waved for her to join them.

"Welcome to our home, Miss Braun," Mrs. Williams said when she reached the porch.

"Please call me Lottie. And these are for you." Lottie held out a bouquet of flowers she'd found at the florist's shop near campus. Pointing at the Victorian, she said, "You'll think I'm silly, but I could have sworn you lived over there. Isn't that the address you gave me?"

Ed smiled. "You must be thinking of the address in the will. That's your house, Lottie."

She turned her eyes to the farmhouse, its windows now a pink reflection of the sunset, and felt her resolve slip.

Ed and Martha Williams proved excellent dinner companions, entertaining Lottie with stories both personal and general about the town they loved. She reciprocated with tales of her life abroad and at home, the places she'd seen and the people she'd met.

Ed sat on the board of directors at Collison College, and listened with great attention to Lottie's experiences as a visiting professor. "Did you ever consider becoming regular faculty at any one school?" he asked.

"No," Lottie answered, her eyes on her plate. "I never wanted to stay anywhere long enough."

She missed the glance that passed between husband and wife, but couldn't mistake the hope in his voice when he said, "I know some people at the college who are dying to talk to you, should you decide to keep the house."

Lottie smiled politely. "I'll keep that in mind."

After dinner she pleased her hostess by helping to clear and wash dishes. "You remind me of Helen in many ways," Martha said with sigh.

Lottie washed a plate and set it carefully in the drainer. "Did she ever tell you about our life together?"

Martha glanced at her guest. "A little."

"Did you know she was married before?"

"Yes." Martha looked sad. "Helen and I were close in age. We both went through terrible things because of the war."

Lottie's hands went still. "What did she tell you?"

Martha frowned. "That she and her husband were married before the war broke out, and he was stationed in the Pacific, and died in a prison camp." She glanced at her guest. "It's a shame, of course, but not an uncommon story."

Lottie made herself reach for another plate. "Is that all?"

Martha placed the dry plate on the shelf and turned to her guest. "I'm not sure what you're driving at, Miss Braun. I assume it has something to do with the reason you two didn't speak."

Lottie bowed her head, tears stinging her eyes.

Martha continued. "I can assure you I know nothing that would make you uncomfortable. Helen spoke of you with unwavering pride and affection. I've wondered over the years why, if she loved you so much, she didn't go to you and make things right, but I never asked." She placed her hands on Lottie's shoulders. "And she never told me."

Lottie raised wet eyes to meet Martha's gaze, and nodded. "Thank you for saying that. I'm so glad my sister had a friend like you."

Tears welled in Martha's eyes. "The street ran both ways, my dear. There was no better friend in the world than Helen Parker."

Lottie gave a watery smile. "I'm beginning to see that."

Martha laughed and turned away, wiping her cheeks. "Look at us. Poor Ed won't know what to make of two weeping women." She handed Lottie a tissue. "Here. Dry your eyes and go make him give you a house tour. You won't be sorry."

Helen's home was beautiful inside and out. Lottie stood in the wide entry hall and breathed the scent of fresh floor wax. Every surface gleamed.

Ed and Lottie climbed the stairs to the third floor and worked their way down. She examined every detail as they moved from room to room, exclaiming over antiques she remembered from one or another aunt's home. Helen had crafted a home filled with mementos of family life: Patti's bedroom, with its white eyelet canopy; the living room, dominated by a shabby flowered sofa; the dining room, where a family portrait smiled down from the wall. It spoke of personal history, a life well-lived.

"What's this?" Lottie asked, opening a door in the first floor hallway.

"A sewing room, I believe." Ed brushed past on his way to the kitchen. "You'll want to make some updates in here." He stopped. "Miss Braun?"

Lottie stood in the tiny sewing room, drinking in every detail. The sewing table was piled high with neatly folded fabric. Next to it stood a cabinet filled with thread and notions. She instinctively knew the low file cabinet in the corner would be filled with used patterns. The room practically called Helen's name.

She turned, and gave a start. Helen had covered one wall with pictures of her creations, most of them very likely worn by Patti in various stages of childhood. But the center of the collection, framed and behind glass, was the purple dress she'd made for Lottie's eleventh birthday. The dress made her feel like a child again, with yellow braids and hands that barely stretched to an octave. If she closed her eyes she could taste stale birthday cake.

A touch on the arm brought her back to the present. Giving herself a little shake, she followed Ed Williams to the tiny kitchen, an old-fashioned room with a green tile floor and linoleum counter tops. She surveyed the ancient stove with a dismayed laugh. "It's a good thing I don't really cook. I wouldn't know how to work that contraption."

He smiled. "Does that mean you're staying?"

"Maybe." She raised doubt-filled eyes to his face. "The truth is, I don't deserve a home as beautiful as this. If you only knew —"

"No, no, no." He waved a dismissive hand. "I'm a lawyer, not a priest, Miss Braun." Reaching into his coat pocket, he drew out a fat envelope. "After Helen got sick, she made an appointment with me to discuss her estate. She made short work of Patti's inheritance, but spent a great deal of time on yours. Part of her plan went forth today in my office. But this letter," he placed it in Lottie's hands, "was only to go to you if you showed an interest in keeping the house." He put up his hands to ward off her questions. "It was sealed when she gave it to me. I don't know what she wrote, but by the looks of things, you'll be a while reading it." He walked across the kitchen to the back door. "Why don't you make yourself comfortable? Take as long as you need. Stay the night, if you want. After all, it's your house."

Lottie stretched out on the old flowered couch in the living room, and opened Helen's letter. Placing her reading glasses on the end of her nose, she spread out the pages and began to read.

Dear Lottie,

Welcome to my home. Oh, how I've wanted to say those words to you! And since you would not let me say them in life, I say them now. Look around. Stay a while. You could do worse than Collison, Iowa.

David and I were happy here. We were married thirty years, Lottie. Thirty years of love and companionship, and the shared joy of raising a child. He died four years ago of a heart attack. It was a terrible blow, but I knew I'd live through it. I'd survived much worse. I worried for Patti, but never for myself.

I've wished a thousand times I could share the story of our courtship with you. Folks around here think we met in 1948 at a farm auction east of town. They said it was the darnedest case of love at first sight they'd ever seen. We acted like we'd known each other forever. Neither of us ever set the record straight, but I'd have liked to share the joke with you, kiddo.

After the Neverland broke up, David finished his mathematics degree at Northwestern, and landed a job as an assistant professor at good old Collison College. He moved back to the area the spring before we met, and was surprised to learn I lived nearby. He'd turned his back on the band, closed the book on it the day he left Shreveport on a northbound train.

I was glad to see him again. I'd spent years going through the motions of life, living in Aunt Cora's spare room and working at the bank, and I was finally ready to take an interest in my surroundings. I no longer woke every morning to the memory of Billy's sweet voice, nor dreamed of his tiny, shrouded form. I still blamed you for his death, hated you for it, but I'd blocked myself from thinking of you at all. I believed this meant I was healed.

David asked about you right away, as we sat in his car, admiring the view of the Mississippi from the overlook, on our first date. "Where's Lottie now?" he said.

I opened my mouth to tell the lie I'd perfected. "She's in school in Ohio. We expect great things from her some day. The family is so proud." I'd said it a hundred times to a hundred well-meaning acquaintances. But David was different. I looked into his honest blue eyes and knew I couldn't tell him a barefaced lie.

So I settled for my version of the truth. "We no longer speak," I began. I told him about our life in Santa Monica, how we'd both found jobs, but mine kept me homebound, and yours seemed to take up more and more of your time. I told him how lonely I was, cleaning all day with only Billy for company, and how important the sewing circle became to me. I said the circle started meeting every night, and I needed you to watch Billy so I could go. I needed you to do your part, and you let me down, sneaking out when I needed you most. Billy's death was your fault, I said.

Lottie pinched the bridge of her nose, a headache throbbing behind her eyes, unable to read another word. Helen hadn't told her anything she didn't know. She lived every day with the burden of her guilt. This was what she'd always feared, why she would never meet her sister after a concert. She couldn't have faced Helen's recriminations in person.

She swung her legs off the couch and went to the kitchen to look for something to drink. A search of the cupboards turned up a kettle and tea bags, and the stove proved easier to work than she'd thought. She boiled water and let the tea steep too long, to put some distance between herself and Helen's accusations.

She returned to the sofa, cup in hand, and sloshed a little tea over the next line in the letter.

You have so much to forgive me for, Lottie. I was wrong, so wrong about you, but I was full of bitterness in those days.

David listened intently, nodding in all the right places. When I finished my story he sat for a long time, looking out at the river, deep in thought. Finally, "My mother was in a Red Cross sewing circle during the war," he said. "They were called gray ladies."

I blinked. I'd poured my heart out to him and he wanted to talk about gray ladies.

"They met once a week. The rest of the time they sewed at home." He turned to look at me. "I find it strange that you met so often."

It was my turn to stare out the windshield, a painful flush growing on my cheeks. I wanted sympathy, not an inquisition. I opened my mouth to protest his doubts, and closed it again.

"Where were you the rest of the time?" he asked softly.

I lowered my eyes, unable to answer.

The minutes stretched out. At last he said, "Helen?"

I shook my head. "You'll hate me."

"Try me."

I squeezed my eyes shut. "I was with Johnny."

Lottie lowered the page to her lap and gazed unseeing at her surroundings. "Now, why didn't I think of that?" she said to the air.

I felt the tension leave David's body, as if somehow he'd expected my answer. In for a penny, in for a pound, I poured out the ugly truth. How I'd dragged the three of us to California to make up for that last night in Shreveport. How I planned to be a perfect wife while I waited for Bill, but the boredom wore on me, working at home with the baby all day, with nobody to talk to. I couldn't muster an interest in the beach, or in my son, if it came right down to it. I'd lived too long with constant change. Mrs. Quinn's house felt like a little domestic hell.

There really was a sewing circle, Lottie. It met at Mrs. Quinn's church, a worthy group of Christian ladies who gossiped comfortably as they knitted socks for soldiers. I went for a while. But one Sunday afternoon, while you worked extra hours at the dance studio, Johnny showed up at Mrs. Quinn's front door. He looked desperate, and I thought I'd never seen anyone so welcome in my entire life.

He'd gone to Westmont looking for me, and found one of Aunt Cora's brood who was willing to talk for the price of a quarter. Armed with a return address torn from one of my letters, he hopped a train to California.

How could I resist such devotion? Johnny's dreams had fallen apart, and he'd come looking for me. Me! I walked with him down the beach that day and listened to his troubles, and he bought me dinner at a little restaurant where we lingered for hours.

So began the myth of the sewing circle that met every evening.

Do you hear that, Lottie? That's the sound of my heart breaking all over again at the memory of David's face when I told him. His disappointment pierced me right to the center of my hardened heart. "What about Bill?" he said at last. "Did you ever think about him?"

Angry tears clogged my throat. "Lottie was lying, too, you know." Yes, I stooped that low. "The day after Billy died, a boy came to the door looking for her. Tall, slender, good-looking. He was the reason she snuck out and left my son alone."

David rubbed a hand over his face. "Where is she, Helen?"

I didn't like the look in his eyes. "Aunt Eva took her to Ohio. *She's studying music in Dayton, just like nothing ever happened.*"

"So she's what — seventeen now?"

I had to do addition in my head. I'd frozen you in time as a thirteen-year-old delinquent, never to grow older, or wiser for that matter. David's question shattered that image. For the first time in four years I felt a spark of curiosity about you. "I guess so."

"Does she come home much?"

I shook my head. "Never."

No visits, no letters, no Christmas cards. As if you didn't exist. Exactly the way I wanted it.

Without further comment, he turned the key in the ignition and nosed his car toward Westmont. He let me out with a brief "Good night" *after miles and miles of silence, and I thought, that's it. I'll never see Parson again.*

That night I dreamed of you as a little girl. We were walking up the lane to the farmhouse, where Pop waited on the porch. You pulled your hand out of mine and ran to him, but when he stretched out his arms, you both disappeared. I awoke to moonlight streaming through the window, and the heartbreaking knowledge that I'd lost not one but two children in Santa Monica.

David called the following Sunday and asked me to go for a drive. I let out a breath I'd been holding for a week and said yes. He was kindness itself on that second date. We talked about everything under the sun, except the past. I waited for him to bring it up, and when he didn't I said, "I've done a lot of thinking since the last time I saw you."

"Oh?" *He kept his eyes on the road.*

I twisted my hands in my lap. "I'm going to say this, and then you can take me home." *I gulped.* "Way back in Shreveport, you were right about me. I never should have bought that green dress, or sung with the band, or gone out with Johnny afterward. I was drowning in self-pity, and too far gone to see sense, though that's not an excuse." *I took a shaky breath.* "I-I cheated on Bill, and lied to Lottie, and if I hadn't done those things, Billy would be alive today. I'm responsible for his death, every bit as much as Lottie. More, really, since I was the adult."

I waited, my eyes on my clasped hands, for David to turn the car around and head for Aunt Cora's. The sooner he separated his goodness from my dirt, the better. Instead, he pulled into a gravel lane and stopped the car. I glanced up from under my lashes, to find him looking at me, his face full of compassion. "Do you remember what I told you the day you left Shreveport?" he said.

I gave a shaky laugh. "You said a lot that day."

"I said there's nothing God can't forgive."

That brought my head up. "Do you really believe that?"

"Yes."

I shook my head. "Not this stuff, David. God would never forgive the things I've done."

"He already has. It says so in the Bible." He reached out to cover my hands, but seemed to change his mind. Instead, he started the car. "I'd love to tell you more, but not here. Not this way."

I looked around the deserted lane, hidden from the road by late July corn fields. "What's wrong with here?"

His mouth hardened into a firm line. "I'm not Johnny, Helen. Unlike him, I care about appearances. I won't meet you on the sly and then leave you to face the music alone."

I nodded, remembering the way Johnny had turned tail and run when Aunt Cora met him at the door that last day in Santa Monica. David would have stayed.

He went on. "If you'll let me, next Sunday I'll visit you at your aunt and uncle's house. We'll sit on your front porch and drink iced tea, and I'll tell you what I know about forgiveness." He glanced at me, a smile in his eyes. "Would that be okay?"

I smiled back through hopeful tears. "Yes."

We were married two years later.

David taught me everything I know about God's grace and mercy. Because of his patient love, I finally believed that God could forgive me for Billy's death. David pointed out early on that I needed to find you and offer you the same forgiveness, but it took me a while *to work up the courage. I first tried to find you in 1952. I wrote to the Dayton Academy of Music, but Madame D'Abri had died, and the new director did not know your whereabouts. Later that year I found a news item in the Sunday* Des Moines Register *about a concerto competition in Paris. You were listed as the winner. It didn't help me find you, but at least I knew you were alive.*

A few years later, you started making records. I own them all. David encouraged me to write to the publisher for your address, but you'd put that privacy clause in your contract. They could not tell me anything. For many years, that's how it went. Every time I tried to contact you, I ran into a brick wall. Only once was it breached, by an assistant I assume you fired soon after. She chatted with me on the phone one afternoon when Patti was about thirteen. Yes, Miss Braun lived in Ann Arbor, but not for much longer. She was a funny one, so austere, and always alone. No, I shouldn't write. Miss Braun was going on tour, and wouldn't return to the University of Michigan. Did she have a permanent home? Lord, no.

Lottie remembered that assistant. She hadn't lasted long. Her mouth hinged in the middle, as the saying went.

That Christmas, David gave me a ticket to your concert with the Chicago Philharmonic Orchestra. One ticket. We struggled to make ends meet, just like everybody we knew. It was February 1969, and I found an usher to deliver my note backstage. Meet me afterward, I said. Do you remember? Your answer came cold and quick. "No."

Lottie nodded, remembering. It was the last note she'd opened and read, until a month ago.

I went home, deflated. It was hopeless, I told David. She'll never forgive me for hurting her so badly.

He took my hand and reminded me that we serve a mighty God. "She needs us," he said. "Keep trying."

Lottie closed her eyes on a sudden wave of pain. Until yesterday, she had believed that Helen wanted justice, not forgiveness. Every time she sent a note backstage, Lottie imagined an avenging angel bent on public humiliation. She had no idea why she hadn't been punished long ago for Billy's death, but her sense of self-preservation was too strong to let Helen mete out that punishment in public.

How could she have been so wrong? Helen offered forgiveness, not condemnation. The perpetual weight on Lottie's soul grew lighter with the knowledge.

> *On this last trip I sat at Lombardi's until it closed, determined to give you every opportunity to change your mind. I knew I was dying, that it would be my last chance to make things right, but still a small part of me felt relief when you didn't show. Cancer wreaks havoc with the human body. I look a fright these days.*
>
> *And so we come to the house. It was David's brilliant idea. "She's never had a home," he said. "We can give her ours." But he didn't just mean four walls and a roof. He meant everything Collison has to offer. Neighbors, family, meaningful work. It's all here for you.*
>
> *Please take it, Lottie. You can build a life here. Start with the house, and the Williams next door. Talk to the dean of the college. You'd be a coup for any music department.*
>
> *Nobody knows how Billy died. Not Patti, not our Hoffman relatives. Nobody.*
>
> *Take the house.*
>
> *Take it, Lottie.*
>
> *Take it.*
>
> *Love,*
> *Helen*

In the gray light of dawn, Lottie rubbed her sore neck with hands grown stiff from holding the letter. She'd been awake all night for the second time in a month, only this time she felt wonderful. She looked around the stately old front room, with its marble-tiled fireplace and faded wallpaper. So this was what home looked like.

Letter in hand, she wandered through the kitchen to the back deck, where streaks of orange sunrise showed above her neighbors' rooftops. An apple tree, heavy with bloom, glowed softly in the morning light. Lottie plucked a blossom from an overhanging branch and brought it to her nose, inhaling deeply.

Across the wide lawn, Ed Williams stood on his back porch, a mug of coffee in his hand. Seeing her, he waved.

Lottie waved back. "Good morning, neighbor," she murmured. "What a beautiful day."

Book Club
Discussion Questions

1. How did Lottie's Iowa roots affect her life? Would the story have been different if she had grown up in California or New York City, for example?

2. If Mr. Schultz had not moved to Iowa, do you think Lottie would have become a performer? If not, how might her musical gifts affected her life?

3. Did you learn to play a musical instrument as a child? How has that experience affected your life?

4. Compare the Des Moines talent show with talent shows of today, such as American Idol. How have the showcased talents changed? How do the changes in talent shows reflect changes in our society?

5. With the effect of social media today, do you think it would be easier or harder for Lottie to keep Helen at arm's length? How might our society's openness about emotional issues change Lottie's situation?

6. Can you escape your upbringing? Discuss your experience with returning home as an adult.

7. Is it harder to forgive another person or to forgive yourself? Is it harder to forgive or to accept forgiveness?

8. Parson tells Helen, "There's nothing God can't forgive." Do you agree? Are some sins bigger than others in God's eyes?

CROSSRIVER

If you enjoyed this book, will you
consider sharing it with others?

- Please mention the book on Facebook, Twitter, Pinterest, or your blog.

- Recommend this book to your small group, book club, and workplace.

- Head over to Facebook.com/CrossRiverMedia, 'Like' the page and post a comment as to what you enjoyed the most.

- Pick up a copy for someone you know who would be challenged or encouraged by this message.

- Write a review on Amazon.com, BN.com, or Goodreads.com.

- To learn about our latest releases subscribe to our newsletter at www.CrossRiverMedia.com.

JANE M. TUCKER

Jane M. Tucker is a lifelong reader and writer who has a deep love for the art of storytelling. In fact, her favorite job at church is telling Bible stories to children. She's been a dedicated follower of Jesus since she was nine years old, and you can find strong Christian principles throughout her stories. Jane proudly hails from the great state of Kansas and her weekly blog, "Postcards from the Heartland," is about her life in the Midwest. Having lived in Wisconsin, Iowa and on the Kansas/Missouri line, she has a deep love for the region. Her blog is filled with stories about her micro-travel adventures as she introduces her readers to places even she didn't know existed. Jane lives with her husband and three children in Overland Park, Kansas.

www.JaneMTucker.com
Facebook.com/JaneMTuckerAuthor
www.Twitter.com/JaneMTuckerAuth

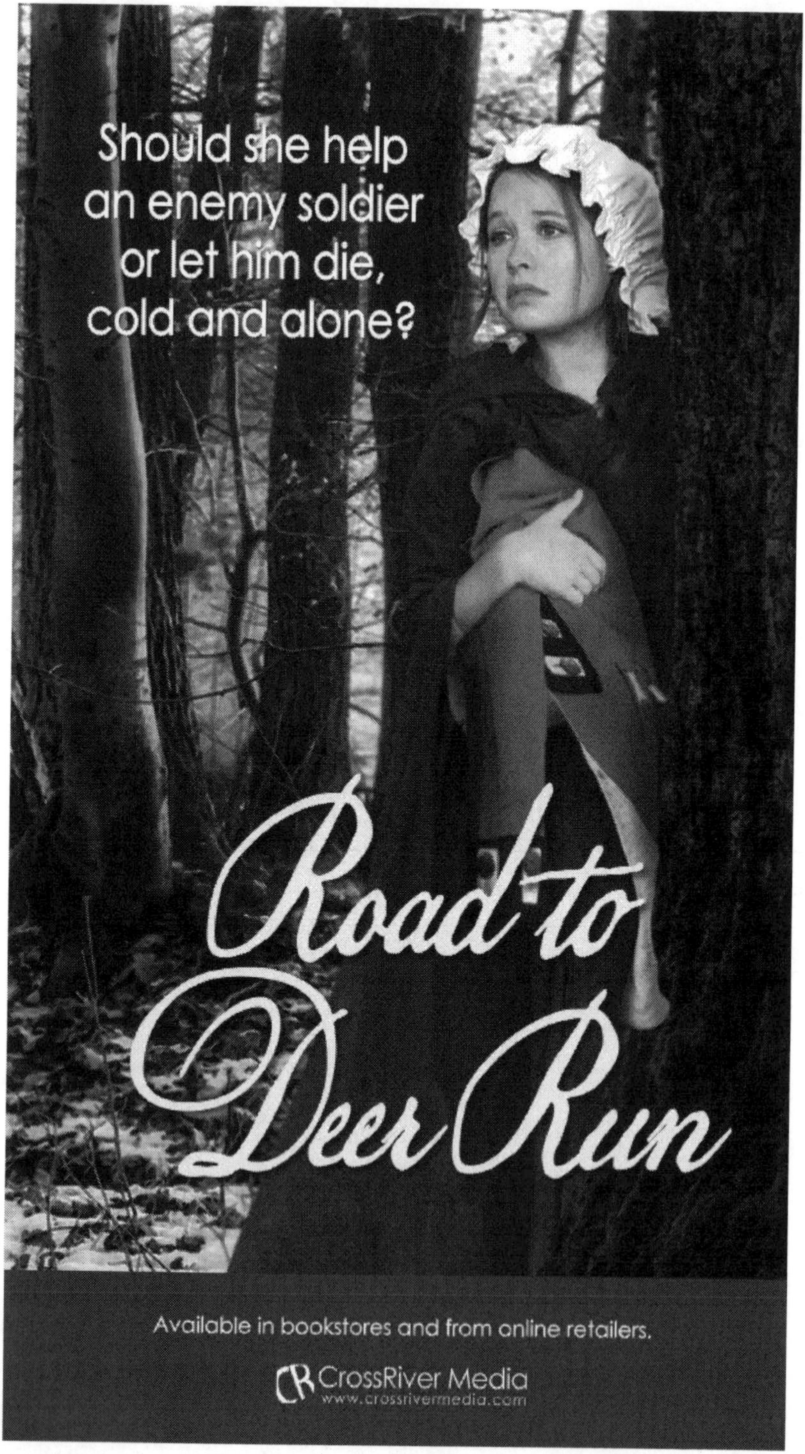
Should she help
an enemy soldier
or let him die,
cold and alone?
Road to
Deer Run
Available in bookstores and from online retailers.
CrossRiver Media
www.crossrivermedia.com

MORE GREAT BOOKS FROM CROSSRIVERMEDIA.COM

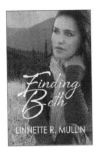

FINDING BETH

Linnette R. Mullin

Three years ago, Beth Gallagher lost her brother, Josh, in a tragic accident. Grief-stricken and estranged from her father, she turned to the one man her brother warned her about – Kyle Heinrich. Now she's discovered his dark side. She flees to the Smoky Mountians to clear her mind and find the answers she needs. Will she have the resolve to follow through? And, if so, what will it cost her?

POSTMARK FROM THE PAST

Vickie Phelps

In November 1989, Emily Patterson is enjoying a quiet life in west Texas, but emptiness nips at her heart. Then a red envelope appears in her mailbox with no return address and a postmark from 1968. It's a letter from Mark who declares his love for her, but who is Mark? Is someone playing a cruel joke? As Emily seeks to solve the mystery, can she risk her heart to find a miracle in the *Postmark from the Past*?

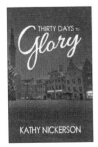

THIRTY DAYS TO GLORY

Kathy Nickerson

Catherine Benson longs to do one great thing before she dies while Elmer Grigsby hopes to stay drunk until he slips out of the world unnoticed. Against a Christmas backdrop, Catherine searches for purpose while fighting the best intentions of her children. She gains the support of her faithful housekeeper and quirky friends. Elmer isn't supported by anyone, except maybe his cat. When their destinies intersect one Tuesday in December, they both discover it is only *Thirty Days to Glory*.

GENERATIONS

Sharon Garlock Spiegel

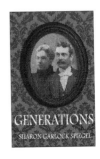

When Edward Garlock was sober, he was a kind, generous, hard-working farmer, providing for his wife and growing family. But when he drank, he transformed into a unpredictable bully, capable of absolute cruelty. When he stepped into a revival tent in the early 1900s the Holy Spirit got ahold of him, changing not only his life, but the future of thousands of others through Edward.

52813091R00159

Made in the USA
Middletown, DE
21 November 2017